MW01174464

Sylvia Mulholland

Sylvia Mulholland lives in Hamilton, Ontario and works as a lawyer, specialising in intellectual property. She has written occasional columns on working women for the Toronto *Globe & Mail* and is currently working on her second novel, LINGERIE TEA, which will be published by Sceptre. Her husband is a plastic surgeon and they have two children.

SCEPTRE

Woman's Work

SYLVIA MULHOLLAND

SCEPTRE

Copyright © 1997 Sylvia Mulholland

First published in 1997 by Hodder and Stoughton
A division of Hodder Headline PLC
A Sceptre Paperback

The right of Sylvia Mulholland to be identified as the Author of the
Work has been asserted by her in accordance with the Copyright,
Designs and Patents Act 1988.

10 9 8 7 6 5 4 3 2 1

All rights reserved. No part of this publication may be
reproduced, stored in a retrieval system or transmitted
in any form or by any means without the prior written
permission of the publisher, nor be otherwise circulated
in any form of binding or cover other than that in which
it is published and without a similar condition being
imposed on the subsequent purchaser.

All characters in this publication are fictitious and any
resemblance to real persons, living or dead, is purely coincidental.

A CIP catalogue record for this book is
available from the British Library

ISBN 0 340 67483 0

Printed and bound in Great Britain by
Caledonian International Book Manufacturers, Glasgow

Hodder and Stoughton
A division of Hodder Headline PLC
338 Euston Road
London NW1 3BH

For Mully

Acknowledgements ∫

I wish to thank the following women for their assistance with *Woman's Work*. Margaret Atwood, for inspiration at an early stage; my agent Bev Slopen, for her continuing encouragement, tenacity and optimism; my editor and publisher Sue Fletcher, for her good humour and clarity of vision; and Gunilla Sondell and Ingrid Ericsson for their great help with the rude Swedish bits.

The two-income family became an established majority in the 1980s, from a statistical abnormality in earlier decades.

Globe & Mail

SUMMER

At the top of the bluffs, the water-filtration plant shimmered in the heat: remote, silent and mysterious. What was inside it, Claire had no idea. She'd heard rumours, of course, that those majestic, Classical Revival buildings housed only a dank network of open sewers, with rows of air-filled condoms bobbing along on top of the water. Now that she was off work, she would have a chance to find out; to take one of the free 'discovery' tours that were offered to the public, weekdays. But did she really want to know what was in there, she wondered. Wasn't it more fun to fantasize? In recent weeks, she'd been imagining that she owned one of those austere, copper-roofed buildings, that it was her house and she could fill its vast spaces any way she liked – throw a gala ball for a thousand people, import a dining-room table as long as Windsor Castle's, or plan out a hundred rooms, all for her own personal use. It had to be her size that was making her crave unlimited space, and their house in the Beach seem poky and cramped. Though it was a small one – she and Ben could sit against opposite walls of the living-room and share the same footstool – she'd always found it adequate before.

She stepped down off the retaining wall at the foot of their property, landing with a sort of plopping grunt, like the fat cat she'd once owned who made the same sound when he jumped from the windowsill where he liked to take the sun. How huge she had become! It gave her pause, as they say – and probably gave a few others pause as well: her husband, Ben, for example, and everyone at Bragg, Banks and Biltmore, the law firm where Claire worked. The women, of course, were outwardly sympathetic, though morbidly fascinated by her appearance; the men were appalled, or, in the case of Alexander Spears who'd always let Claire know how attractive he found her, somewhat shaken.

Her arms and legs were smooth, plump and firm, like the kielbasa sausage she'd been raised on; the rest of her pale and spongy as well-cooked pyrohy. Such similes had popped easily into Claire's head, offered by her father's side of the family. It was the Old Country, she felt, reclaiming her, recognizing a woman now capable of pulling a plough and swinging a sickle. Gone (but not, please God, forever!) was the scrawny, smartly dressed Bay Street lawyer of only a few months ago.

Claire tried to view her changing dimensions with an abstract scientific curiosity. She was, after all, an intelligent, highly trained professional. And, more to the point, it was either that or panic.

A few stones from the retaining wall, loosened by her shifting weight, suddenly tumbled on to the beach and, for the first time, Claire noticed that the wall was falling apart in places. It was supposed to have been put in just months before she and Ben bought the house, and should have been good for a decade at least.

As with most homes in the Beach – the eastern edge of Toronto that hugged the shore of the lake – the Cunninghams' sat on a tilt and appeared to be sagging into the sand. There was no part of it that was square or flat or level, and the front porch was likely home to a billion termites, though the agent had jabbed a pen-knife into the top step to demonstrate that it wasn't. The Cunninghams had been swept up by the real estate roller-coaster (Claire's knuckles were still white, her hair blown back from the experience), frightened by predictions of infinitely rising prices into buying any home they could afford just to 'break into' the market. At the time, one couldn't even buy a garage in the city for less than a hundred thousand, so the slumping, detached, single family dwelling (with a garage!) that they'd found at the end of the Beach seemed a fantastically good deal. The street was actually quite attractive: lots of ancient black oaks, quirky but rather grand beach-front homes with gracious sweeping porches. The Cunninghams had been almost deliriously optimistic as they cruised down Pine Beach Road in their agent's Mercedes. Until they reached number 67. It was the butt end, the fag end, as if the street had suddenly given up on its pretences and dribbled away to a splat. The house had certainly seen better days – better decades for that matter – but it *was* right on the lake. Prime Beach, the agent called it.

The previous owner, a man by the name of Proctor, had done a quick-and-dirty renovation to number 67. Though they'd never met him, Claire and Ben nicknamed him 'Hookman-Nailman-Screwman' because of the multitude of hooks, nails and screws he'd left behind, peppering the walls with so many holes it looked as though the mob had fought a gun battle in there. And they were forever discovering bits of Mr Proctor's slip-shod, penny-pinching handiwork: the wrong type of solder in the upstairs plumbing that eventually let the tub water drain down into the front hall, the missing sub-floor in the kitchen which led to the buckling and crackling of the cheap press-on tiles. Ben and Claire used to laugh about these things, chanting, in unison, as if doing a fifties' radio ad: *'It's a Proctor! It's got to be bad!'* But they didn't laugh much any more. Mr Proctor's legacy was getting expensive.

Less than six months after they bought the house, the market had bottomed out, and since they would never recover close to what they'd paid for it, the Cunninghams were gradually coming around to the idea that they would probably grow old and die in 67 Pine Beach Road. Claire's first husband, Simon, would have thought it 'typical' of her to rush into buying the house without properly investigating its condition and re-sale potential. (And Claire could hardly blame Ben for buying it, since he was happy living anywhere, he often said.)

When she married Ben, Claire believed him the antithesis of Simon; his short dark feistiness a sharp contrast to Simon's tall blond reserve. But as time went on, she began to realize how much alike the two men were. They were both driven perfectionists, obsessed with their careers. Only their focus was different. Simon crunched numbers; Ben rearranged human flesh. And their mothers were clones of each other too: plucky, diminutive women who'd raised their families, then gone back to get the university degrees they'd sacrificed before, and who enthused endlessly about all the marvellous eye-opening stuff to which they were continually being exposed.

Turning away from the lake and the worry of the retaining wall (not a real problem, Claire assured herself – what were a few loose stones but normal wear and tear?) she lumbered back through her shabby garden. Now that she was on maternity leave, it was only her shadow she had to avoid; there were no shop windows or mirrored walls to confront her with her enormity. She didn't even want to know her weight when her obstetrician tsk-tsked over it at the start of each monthly visit, and was grateful that his scale measured only kilograms and she was too metrically retarded to convert the number to pounds. But, though pregnant, she wasn't yet barefoot as well: there was still one pair of Ben's old sneakers that fitted her swollen feet. The last pair of shoes she'd bought herself a year ago – green lizard Amalfis – looked Cinderella-small; into them, like an ugly step-sister, she could now wedge only a couple of immense toes.

Baby Harry (already named thanks to amniocentesis) rolled over inside Claire and gave her a poke. They'd decided on the name Harry for its directness, its simple honesty, its suggestion of royalty.

As she made her way back to the house, Claire took a cookie from her overall pocket and stuffed it into her mouth, hoping Ben wouldn't choose that moment to gaze out from his study window. She knew what he was thinking as he looked at her lately, that it wasn't all baby layered over her hips, bulging around her bra straps. Heartburn radiated spiny fingers of fire up through her diaphragm as the cookie eased its way into her stomach. She'd discovered that if one uncomfortable symptom of pregnancy subsided, it was only to be replaced by another that was worse. First had been suddenly enlarged breasts – achy and hard as unripe melons – followed by a persistent nausea that sent her scurrying past the hotdog vendors, with their putrid-smelling goods, who seemed to be on every street corner of the city that summer. Escalating blood pressure came next, followed by swollen legs, backache and haemorrhoids.

Then there was the emotional mess of pregnancy. She'd sewn a Noah's Ark wall hanging for Harry's room, blubbering over a popular song on the radio about a boy who grew up to be a sports hero only to be wiped out in a car crash. She'd choked along with the lyrics, hot tears and blood, from her often-pricked fingers, plonking on to the grey felt that was destined to become a pair of elephants. At night she lay on her bed, watching the stars glimmer between the slats of the venetian blinds as Harry rolled and drifted inside her. What a tragically short time she and this little being would have together, she thought. In her mind, he was already eighteen, independent or off at school. And she was the mother whose phone calls he barely tolerated – rolling his eyes at her concerns about his socks and eating habits – or else avoided altogether. She'd cried over that too, missing him even before he was born. Then she'd wept some more, about the lousy cruel world she was bringing him into, her massive chest heaving as she washed his tiny sleepers with their bright, anguishingly innocent colours.

By Claire's last trimester, fears about Ben and their marriage had wrapped themselves around her brain, digging in, clinging tight. Had she made the right decision to marry him? There were omens that their marriage would not work out, right from the start. The charming restaurant where they'd eaten lunch before the ceremony was destroyed by fire soon after; the café where they'd gone for cake and champagne went bankrupt. Their only witnesses and guests – a couple chosen for the apparent solidity of their marriage – split up a month after the wedding, the husband running off with a younger woman he'd met at a poetry workshop.

'It's just your hormones talking,' Ben had assured Claire when she hinted, darkly, about her fears. 'You're not yourself. You've been taken over by an alien named Harry. But don't worry – you'll lose all that extra weight in no time.'

And what if I don't, Claire wondered. Ben was certainly leaving no doubt about his expectations. Was he giving her an ultimatum? A time limit? Was this a threat of some kind? She began to think about the nurses to whom he was exposed every day. There was a nurse practically everywhere he turned: scrub, circulating, OR, recovery-room. They would all be slender young women in crisp white or pink uniforms who understood the stresses of a surgeon's life the way a mere wife never could.

Blue eyes would bat empathetically over the top of a surgical mask as Ben's forehand was wiped, his gloves (tight and rubbery as condoms) fitted on to his hands, the scalpel passed to him.

'But look at you in your profession,' Ben had argued, 'silver-tongued devils in expensive suits sitting in every other office. I bet they've all got their eyes on you.'

So why aren't you jealous, Claire wondered gloomily, but she replied, 'The situations are totally different. The men around me aren't there waiting to fulfil my every whim. They don't think I'm some kind of – of god!'

'God-*dess*. And I bet your old pal Alex Spears does.'

'You are severely deluded.' Claire had waved him away, thinking that really, some conversations were just too silly to continue.

'Well, maybe our situations are different, as you say,' Ben had said. 'You see, I *trust* you.'

What's not to trust? Who's going to chase after a beluga whale, unless it's someone with a harpoon, Claire had thought sourly as her husband turned away from her to look over some slides he'd just got back from the photo-finishers, their discussion already history.

And, if all of that wasn't enough, the post-natal hormonal roller-coaster was still to come. Ben thought she was joking when she'd suggested they hire a surrogate to bear their child, and of course she had been. But only up to a point. It was quite common for women to be having first babies in their late thirties or early forties but no one talked much about the cost. It had to be easier for a younger woman, even one Ben's age. Women marrying younger men was another 'increasingly popular trend' according to magazine articles and talk-shows. But nobody talked about the cost of that either.

Magazine articles had been getting under her skin lately, Claire realized, bending over and struggling for breath as she collected some buggy lettuce to use in a salad for dinner. 'Grow a Salad Garden!' the centre-page spread had chirped. The results of Claire's efforts were about as successful as last year's 'Sew a Field of Wild Flowers!' which had been accompanied by a pattern for a 'Make-in-a-Day Wild Flower Quilt', now a rag-bag of frayed and crumpled patches, entangled with threads, stuffed in the bottom of her closet.

'Wild flowers? In the city? You mean like ragweed?' Her mother's face had creased and puckered in all directions as she struggled to process an idea which clearly offended the natural order of things. Elfriede was a patient and careful gardener, a nurturing woman who could grow anything and was always full of helpful hints about pruning roses and stain removals and using the perfumed strips from magazine ads to scent lingerie drawers. Claire had never known her mother's mother, but her father's mother – her baba – had been of a more practical bent, favouring plastic over living flora for her front garden, liking its predictability of bloom and ease of maintenance. Her backyard had been all trellises and stakes and twine, dedicated to the growing of cucumbers for making fat, garlicky dill pickles that ripened for years in dust-covered jars on gloomy cellar shelves, next to the makeshift water closet with the light that was pulled on by a series of strings networked across the ceiling.

As for Claire's own gardening, she should have stuck to weeds, as her mother supposed, since that was all, it seemed, she could successfully grow. She was an arbitrary gardener, accidentally crushing delicate shoots and sprigs as she clomped around in Ben's shoes. It was a good thing she hadn't been born a century earlier. As a pioneer she would have been weeded out herself by the first Thanksgiving, if the shock of discovering what the Canadian climate was really like hadn't killed her first. They had to have come over in summer, those pioneers, naively thinking they'd stumbled upon a Promised Land with its sparkling lakes, leaping fish, bountiful croplands. But then the leaves would have started to change colour and drop, the cold and damp creeping in, until, before they knew what had hit them, they were stuck knee-deep in a full-blown Canadian winter, waiting miserably for spring to be dug out and thawed. If they lived that long.

She shook the soil from the pallid green leaves in her hand and examined them closely. Who would have thought that gardening could be such hellishly hard work, so unrewarding, and that things that grew out of the ground could be so *filthy*? But she was the one who'd wanted a garden and she couldn't expect much help from Ben. He was too busy trying to get his research paper done – a study of the use of prosthetic noses in the treatment of cancer patients. Until he finished his paper, those slides of his would litter every surface in the house – ghastly photos of body parts (or cavernous places where parts used to be) stapled, clipped, clamped and splayed out on laboratory tables, the morgue lighting tinting each with the lurid hues of cheap pornography. Claire refused to touch them, afraid it would hex the baby, that Harry would be born with a cleft palate, a huge port-wine stain, or something worse.

Shielding her eyes with a grubby gloved hand, she squinted up at the second-floor window of the spare room Ben used as a study. He had only a week off to complete the paper which he hoped to present at an international conference in San Francisco, after which he would start the push to complete his last year of plastic surgery training. Why couldn't he have taken his week off *after* Harry arrived, Claire had grumbled. But there were complex reasons why he could not, having to do with co-ordinating the staffman's vacation, the coverage of the emergency room, the clinical fellows and interns. One lowly resident's wife doing something as mundane as reproducing was not a matter to be given any consideration at all, it seemed, in the grand scheme of the teaching hospital.

Twirling the limp lettuce leaves in her hand, Claire Cunningham, out-to-pasture lawyer, turned as the telephone began to ring inside the house. Ben, who wore industrial-strength headphones when he worked at home, wouldn't hear it, or wouldn't answer it if he did.

Claire's pace quickened. For a large woman, she was remarkably light on her feet, she reflected, not without some pride. Nearing the house, she strained to count the rings. If they stopped in the middle of the fourth, it meant her secretary, Davina, was sending a fax. A ringing phone – a call, a fax – often meant new work. Unless it meant Prue (Ben's mother) or Elfriede. Or Claire's sister Christine. She hesitated for a second, debating which of the three she would least like to hear from at that moment, then took a deep breath and lumbered on to meet her fate. Responding promptly to a telephone's twitter, even in shabby sneakers and mud-caked gardening gloves, and even though it might be her mother-in-law on the line, was a part of Claire's being – as much a part as tiny baby Harry who had now begun kicking urgently inside her.

2 ♪

Davina gave the telephone receiver a reproving look before clunking it back into its cradle. If Claire didn't pick up the phone by the fifth ring, it was unlikely that she would. She hadn't called in to get her voice-mail messages either. From Davina's desk, surrounded on three sides by an upholstered divider of an indeterminate beige brocade, she could see Claire's desk, Claire's wilting office plant, her telephone and the red message light winking anxiously on the side of it. Claire hadn't given Davina her password to access her phone-mail, so there was no way of discovering what intriguing messages might have been left on it, what new business, what urgent matters. And after only nine days, the messages would be systematically deleted from 'archives', without notice.

What if Claire were having the baby already, Davina suddenly thought – that might possibly excuse her thoughtless behaviour. She checked her desk calendar but concluded that it was still too soon. Much as she disliked the idea of Claire being taken over totally by the processes of birthing, breast-feeding and diaper-changing, having the baby – finally getting it *over with* – had a decided appeal.

Davina readjusted her neck-scarf – she'd tied it in a Hacking Knot, as shown on page two of the booklet called *Living with Scarves* that she kept in her desk drawer. She'd considerately photocopied the booklet for Claire who'd confessed to not having much of a knack with scarves. *'Living with Scarves*?' she had laughed (rather ungratefully, Davina thought). 'Makes it sound like an affliction, doesn't it?'

Having nothing much else to do, and annoyed afresh by the

13 •

fact that Claire was not answering her phone, Davina began stuffing the large manilla envelope she meant to send to Claire that afternoon. A similar package had gone out earlier in the day, but Davina'd heard nothing back in terms of instructions or follow-up. And it wasn't as though Claire had the excuse of being flat on her back and incapacitated – she was just supposed to take things easy for the last week or so before the baby arrived. She had what was called pre-eclampsia – pregnancy-induced hypertension. Though Davina'd never been pregnant, she had become an expert on the subject through private study.

As she wrestled with a tape-gun to seal the envelope, Rick Durham thumped on the side of her divider. 'Keeping busy, Davina?' he asked, all breath spray and hair gel. He had that established-partner gloss that Davina hoped one day to see on Claire. Partners' secretaries got an immediate pay raise, a slightly larger cubicle, greatly increased status in the lunch room. Their photocopy requests were filled promptly and their business machines readily and cheerfully serviced.

Rick was being groomed to take over as Managing Partner whenever old Mr Biltmore (son of one of the firm's founders) decided it was time to step down. Though Mr Biltmore was still very much the beaky, eagle-eyed solicitor, there were moments – increasing in number over recent years – when a certain vagueness overtook his eyes and his mouth slackened as though he were wondering, suddenly, where he was and what he was supposed to be doing. It was times like this that gave the junior lawyers great hope and optimism about the future.

'I was about to send a rush courier to Claire, actually,' Davina told Rick. 'She's working from home, busier than ever it seems.'

'She's doing well?'

'Great. Like I said, busier than ever.' Get your hammy hands off my divider, Davina thought. I'm not impressed by your flashy college ring; I don't want to count the hairs on your fleshy knuckles. She cleared her throat and scowled at her envelope, as though offended by something on the front of it.

'But no baby yet?' Rick was still smiling.

'Claire thought her water had broken this morning.' Davina imagined that the remark would motivate Rick to push off. He couldn't deal with references to body functions, especially female ones. But surprisingly, he didn't move. What was he waiting for? Pressing up against her upholstered divider? 'It wasn't her water though.' Davina typed Claire's address on the label for the envelope. 'It was just her mucus plug – that's what came out in the end.'

'Really.' Rick's smile was fading nicely.

'Yes, it was only the *mu-cus plug*.' Davina watched with satisfaction as Rick's pinstriped backside hustled off down the corridor.

But Davina remained unnerved by the encounter. What business was it of his how busy she was? Or how busy Claire was? It used to be that no one at Bragg, Banks and Biltmore bothered too much about what the secretary was supposed to do for the four, six, sometimes eight months that their bosses took off to have a baby. But things were changing. In the worst cases – two secretaries whom Davina cringed to remember – the lawyers never came back *at all*. One of those girls was still pounding Bay Street, résumé in hand; the other had given up trying to find work altogether and was sitting at home, hoping to become pregnant herself.

Even when the return of the lawyer from maternity leave seemed assured, it was dangerous to let oneself get confident. The trick was to make sure you looked busy, so that no light bulbs went off in any legal or management heads telling them you had time to spare. If that happened, a girl could find herself pressed into serving another lawyer (Mr Biltmore, for example, who still expected his secretary to take dictation and bring him coffee on a silver tray) or worse, becoming a *floater*, drifting from cubicle to cubicle, filling in for any secretary on vacation, trying your best to do unfamiliar work and getting nothing but complaints for your efforts. Floaters were disconnected, unprotected, and at the mercy of a sharp-eyed personnel manager who would put them at the top of her list for firing whenever the firm decided it needed to down-size. This was *never* going to be the fate of Davina Lipshitz. She had suffered along with Claire Cunningham for too many years.

Just then Shelagh Tyler, an associate a few years younger than Claire, stuck her head over the upholstered divider. 'Any baby yet?' Her pencilled eyebrows were raised practically into her black hair, the grey roots of which were lengthening noticeably. She was beginning to look like a skunk. 'Nope,' Davina said. 'Still no baby. But you'll be the first to know.'

'Well. Hardly.' Shelagh's brows descended slightly, but Davina could tell that she was flattered.

'But it's a good thing Claire's away.' Davina pulled towards her a stack of 'dog files' that Claire had given her to be closed. 'Gives me a chance to start getting caught up.'

'Is that so?' Nails, like daggers, tapped against Davina's divider. 'I'm *totally* swamped. I've got to get this package out to Claire right away.' Davina picked up the roll of tape and tore off a long strand.

'You know, it doesn't look like you're swamped, frankly. It seems pretty quiet around here.'

'That's because we're so organized.'

Shelagh regarded Davina for a moment, in silence. 'Well, you let me know when you get through putting sticky tape all over that envelope. I could use some extra hands.'

'If I ever get caught up with everything, I'd be glad to.' Davina nodded agreeably and turned to the files, busily putting first one on top, then another, scribbling meaningless notations in the front cover of each, holding her breath, until she felt Shelagh move away, like a current of bad air.

3

Jolly Giraffe's Daycare Centre was situated on the busiest north–
south thoroughfare of the Beach, in a house dating from the
thirties, with the small rooms and gloomy dark-panelled interior
that real estate agents described as having 'lots of gum-wood'.

The closeness of the air inside made Claire want to hold
her nose. The toilets were plugged with diapers in each of
the two bathrooms on the main floor, she noticed, as she
trailed after the owner – a woman by the name of Kravitch
– past a cramped untidy kitchen where another woman was
boiling something on a stove top. 'We make sure the kids
get a hot lunch every day,' Mrs Kravitch said as Claire followed her broad, swaying rump up the creaking staircase to
her office – a cramped messy space under the eaves, where
'Cunningham – Boy' was about to be added to the waiting list
for fall enrolment.

'I have a few questions first,' Claire said. 'About the playground, for one thing. It's right out there on that very busy
street . . .'

'It's well fenced. And the children stay inside mostly. They
get to watch a video each day, so when your little fellow gets
old enough to have a favourite, we would encourage you to
bring it in.'

'I'm not sure I want Harry inside watching videos all day . . .'

'I said once a day, not all day.' Mrs Kravitch smiled thinly.
'And infants don't go out much, in fact. Two walks a day, at
ten-thirty and two. We have strollers that take five babies at
a time. It's a lot of you-know-what that babies need all that
fresh air.'

Claire looked down at the fee schedule that Mrs Kravitch had pushed into her hand. 'Eleven hundred a month?'

'It's the going rate. Government-set.'

'I'm a bit surprised, I guess. At the cost of daycare. Where did I get the idea that daycare was cheap?'

'It is. For those who qualify for a government subsidy.' Mrs Kravitch's eyes flickered over Claire's clothes. 'The fees go down as the child gets older. But infants need the most care, of course.'

'How many babies are there to each staff person here?'

'Three to one, until they're a year old.'

Three demanding Harrys with only one person to look after them all? 'Is that standard?' Claire asked.

'It's the law. And a lot of you-know-what, if you want my opinion. Five to one would be more than adequate.'

'But what if they were all crying at once? If they all needed feeding? Or changing? Or . . . comforting?'

'Some of them would just have to wait their turn, wouldn't they?' Mrs Kravitch tried, with a half-smile, to lessen the impatience in her voice.

'Well, I guess I have no more questions. Thank you for your time.' Claire rose to leave.

'Do you want your name put on our list or don't you? You'll never get your baby in if you don't put your name down now.'

'I'll have to think it over. Thank you. I'll let you know soon.'

Feeling numb, Claire had turned and groped her way down the dim staircase, then through the house past a group of pre-schoolers watching television in what was the original front parlour of the house. Outside on the dusty grass, another group of children fought amongst themselves as they swarmed over an inflated inner tube while clattering trucks and noisy cars, trailing blue oil smoke, roared along the street. There was no one supervising the children, as far as Claire could see. Perhaps, the day being so hot, the staff were all watching from inside . . .

The Sunshine Children's Village was certainly aptly named, she thought, a little while later, making a visor with her hand as she squinted across the sun-bleached courtyard – a sad scrap of yard with no toys except for a small slide, a single swing and a faded rubber ball, all of which were being ignored. Children cried and clung to the six-foot chain-link metal fence. Those who were old enough to talk wailed for their mothers.

'They're new here,' the supervisor told Claire, 'the ones making all the fuss. It takes a bit for them to adjust. Makes it hard on everyone though.'

The playground staff, two sullen young women with studded lips and eyebrows and wearing very tight T-shirts, sat under the single tree, avoiding the worst of the sun, watching the children in a desultory fashion.

Claire had just come from the Sweet Cloud Extended Daycare Facility, located in an office tower near her law firm. There, the children played outside – on a walled-in patch of asphalt twelve storeys above ground, overlooking the city's Go Train railway line and the cross-hatching of street-car cables that swung over the street. 'You can drop your baby off as early as seven a.m.,' the owner, a fattish, fortyish man by the name of Mr Sweet, informed Claire, 'and leave him as late as seven at night. There's an additional charge, of course, for late pick-up.'

What a good idea! Claire had thought, her arms protectively hugging Harry to her. And if I pay you enough, I might never need to come and pick him up at all.

'I'm not sure we want a European girl,' Claire said. 'If we do, I'd like to get one I can relate to – a Ukrainian, or an Austrian.'

'They have poor ideas about nutrition,' said Ben. 'Too much sour cream, too much cholesterol in their diets. Look at your dad. An educated man, a physician even, and what's his favourite snack? Lard on bread.'

'And the lard has to be twice as thick as the bread, and you have to eat it with a raw onion, the way you'd eat an apple.' She watched for Ben's reaction, was satisfied when he shuddered. He often expressed incredulity, even disgust, over the culinary habits of Eastern Europeans. When Claire was in a wicked mood, she exaggerated these, or recounted heirloom family recipes that involved things like jellied pigs' feet. 'Just be thankful Dad isn't agitating to name the baby Ihor,' she said, 'or Bohdan.' Today she couldn't be bothered to slip into their usual silly debate over the merits of her muddled European background versus his Waspy one, in terms of the baby's genetic legacy.

With her French first name and Ben's last, few people realized that Claire was, at heart, a 'nice Ukrainian girl'; her maiden name Wolaniuk. Though she hadn't used the name for almost twenty years, she was beginning to wish she'd never let it go. True, it was hard to pronounce and even worse to spell, but at least it wasn't funny, like Cunningham, which suggested a pork picnic shoulder, scampering away on little legs, congratulating itself on its cleverness. As for her first name, it would be a good brand-name for a pimple cream. 'Banish those blemishes. With Claire.' Or else it suggested clairvoyance, which she certainly didn't have. Claire de Lune? Too abstract. Claire the Loon? Better.

'And look at your mother,' Ben was saying, his enthusiasm for an attack on her parents' culinary habits heightening.

'Mother's Austrian, not Eastern European.'

'But the way she lays on the butter and cream. Sachertorte from hell.'

'You don't even know what Sachertorte is.'

'Knackwurst. Whatever. My arteries harden just thinking about that stuff.'

Too bad that's all that's hardening around here these days, Claire thought. She gave her husband an appraising glance. 'Maybe we should hire a girl from the Philippines. Everyone says they're very hard-working, kind, patient, all that good stuff.' She took a can of paint from a shelf above the laundry-room sink and unwrapped the stiffened paint brush from the plastic wrap she'd wound around it. She was half-way through painting over Ben's old waterbed for Harry's nanny, for she and Ben had agreed that finding a nanny was the only realistic solution to the child-care problem. The daycares were not only expensive, they were brimming with bacteria, Ben pointed out, crawling with viruses. Did they want Harry picking up every little bug that went around? 'Nanny,' Claire said. 'What a stupid word. It sounds so phoney, so elitist.'

'It does make you think of Mary Poppins.'

'As if we could afford Mary Poppins.'

'Why are you painting?' Ben seemed to become suddenly aware of what Claire was doing. He had taken a break from his paper and was leaning against the laundry tub, watching her. 'Paint fumes aren't good for the baby. Or for you. I hope that's not oil-based.'

'All of the windows are open. Besides, if I don't paint it, who's going to? You?'

'It doesn't need painting. I liked the natural pine better. And I don't have time to paint.'

'And I do? Maybe you haven't noticed that mountain of manilla envelopes piled on the kitchen table. I get two or three a day from Davina. I see more of that Go Speed courier than I do of you.'

'Tell her to stop sending you stuff. You're on maternity leave. Davina should butt out. Your secretary works for you, not the other way around.'

'She's only doing her job. She's very territorial.' And more to the point, Claire thought, I'm scared to death of her. Davina'd been fired by her previous employer – another lawyer at the firm – because he couldn't tolerate her editing his letters. 'But his writing was so verbose!' Davina'd explained, when Claire interviewed her. Claire had been impressed by her spunk, especially since English wasn't Davina's first language.

'You've got to start letting go,' Ben was telling her. 'You can't keep up the level of productivity you're used to. You've got other things to focus on.' Part of the problem with being married to a younger man was that he imagined himself to be older, in terms of common sense and emotional maturity. To prove this point, he often adopted a pedagogical role with Claire which was especially irksome when he was right. 'One of the agencies has a Swedish girl we can see,' he said casually.

'No.'

'The least we could do is interview her. We don't have to hire her.'

'You've got that right.' Claire pried the lid off the paint can with a quarter she kept in her overalls pocket for that purpose. She could feel her blood pressure rising. 'This conversation may be hazardous to my health. Besides, with your busy schedule I'm surprised you've had time to call employment agencies.'

'We've got to find the best person for Harry – is there anything more important?'

Claire said nothing, resenting afresh his rightness. (Or was it righteousness?)

'Swedes are simple and good-natured,' he said. 'They like to stay home and raise kids.'

'And I don't?'

'You think you would?'

'Did you ever bother to ask me?'

Ben stared at her. 'If you want to stay home with Harry, quit your job – great. I'm behind you a hundred and ten per cent.'

Claire rolled her eyes and dipped her paint brush into the can. That's what hockey players were supposed to give to each game: a hundred and ten per cent. She wondered whether now, with inflation, it shouldn't be a hundred and twenty per cent. Or a hundred and fifty. 'Well, I'm still thinking about it,' she said. 'Work or not work. It's my career, isn't it?'

'But you've almost got your partnership at the firm.'

'No one's said that – not exactly.'

'It's certainly been implied though, hasn't it?'

'That was before I got pregnant.'

Ben was silent for a few moments as Claire continued painting. Perspiration popped out on her forehead and upper lip. 'We'd have to sell the house,' he said at last, 'but Harry'd be fine in an apartment for a couple of years. Until I get my practice rolling. Maybe by then we could try to get into the real estate market again. Recover from the beating we're going to take on this place.'

The Sweet Cloud Extended Daycare Facility, with its dizzying view of the railway yards, drifted into Claire's brain just then. What would it be like to give up their house? To have no backyard for little Harry? No front walk to push him along in his stroller? But then, it wouldn't be her pushing it anyway, would it? It would be a stranger – some nanny person. Because Claire would have to work to keep the house. 'Maybe you're right about painting,' she sighed, 'the fumes are making me dizzy.'

'And we might want to get Harry a dog, some day,' Ben said. 'We couldn't do that in an apartment.' Another pause. 'Swedes love animals, you know.'

'You can't generalize about an entire race like that.' Claire added a final dab of paint onto the headboard of the bed, then wrapped the brush again in its gooey Cellophane wrap. The waterbed was the only piece of furniture Ben had when she met him, apart from an unfinished Ikea desk (from which she got slivers in her behind one adventurous afternoon in his room). He'd been a touchingly young twenty-six, not even knowing how to write out a cheque, and with only one suit (brown, three-piece, chalk-striped, with flared trousers) which he kept stuffed in a plastic shopping bag in his hospital locker. It was hard to believe this often cranky and overworked surgeon was the same person, or that Claire had ever shared an overheated waterbed, and scratchy polyester sheets, with him, without complaint. Before she could paint the bed, she'd had to scrape off all sorts of stains from flavoured love oils and blobs of candle wax. Baby Harry had been conceived on this waterbed and soon his nanny would be sleeping on it. There was a certain irony there. She spent a few seconds trying to decide if it was irony or the natural progression of things, but soon gave up, frustrated and mentally fatigued. Being slow and stupid was another pregnancy symptom she'd been unable to avoid. 'Well, I've never heard this theory about simple, baby-loving Swedes,' she said. 'Minding babies would have been the last thing on your mind when you lived over there. You were just out of college – hardly in the market for a nanny. You were sure you'd never even get married. At least, so legend would have it.'

'I was hardly a legend,' Ben said, looking pleased.

Claire glanced at him. 'All I've ever heard about Swedish girls is that they're blonde and very liberal, sexually speaking.'

'Now who's generalizing?' Ben hooted. 'For your information, lots of Swedes are brunettes, and it's the Netherlands that has no censorship laws. Sweden is actually a very uptight country. Income taxes are out of sight, and the price of booze keeps everyone sober or sends them paddling over to Denmark. And look at Volvos. The most boring car on the market, but also the safest. Where is it made? Sweden.'

'If it's such a dull place, why did you stay there for two years?'

'I had a job.'

'You call collecting facial scars a job?' To an outsider, this might have seemed a low blow, but Ben was proud of the fifty-two stitches on his face, as he was of his twice-broken nose. And Claire loved his face, though she often wondered what he really looked like, minus the scar tissue. Sometimes, in private, she studied his high school and early college photos. Was his nose really aquiline once? His lips a perfect cupid's bow? These questions were of interest in assessing Harry's gene pool. And she loved Ben's body, as well as his face, and that had survived the hockey years intact, except for a patch on each shin where hair refused to grow after years of being stripped bare by the friction from tightly laced skates. *Concentrated man,* was how she thought of him. He was short, muscular, apparently invincible, and the world's greatest cuddle. It was the main area of difference between Ben and Simon, the Greek god, Mr Please-don't-bother-to-iron-my-shirts-Babe-I-need-them-done-right. Ben was also a tireless sexual athlete, always eager to please. That had been a major attraction during the early part of their relationship, but over the past year, Claire had been finding the idea of sleep a lot more attractive, most nights. On occasion, his boundless sexual energy actually appalled her. But now, scant days before her due date, in one of life's horrid little ironies, she was looking at him with renewed sexual interest. She wiped her forehead and upper lip on the sleeve of one of his cast-off shirts. 'Anyway, I have pregnancy-induced hypertension. If you make me mad enough, it could poison Harry.'

'I am aware of your condition. I diagnosed it.' Ben always got huffy when she used medical terminology, something she felt entitled to do, having come from a doctor's family.

As Claire fitted the paint can lid on to the can, she considered what argument to make next. It wasn't that she didn't trust Ben, or that the idea of a blonde and probably pretty nanny in their home was threatening. She was a professional; she wouldn't hire or not hire a secretary because of her looks, would she? 'If Swedes are so simple-minded, why do we want one of them looking after Harry?' she said finally. 'Don't we want him to be stimulated?' She sat down on the paint can, sealing it shut with her weight.

'I said they have simple values. It's got nothing to do with intelligence. Besides, we're not going to get a Harvard *cum laude* to look after our kid, let's face it.' Ben ran his hands through his hair, as he did when he was perplexed or annoyed. He had a wonderful mane of it – thick, black and wavy – and he wore it long even though, by the end of each day in the hospital, he suffered from severe OR head, his hair pushed up into a comical cone-shape by the snug-fitting surgical cap. As an intern he'd worn his hair short: it was either that or put on a hairnet and have patients confuse him with the kitchen staff. He'd complained a lot that year about physical weakness and shortness of breath, and Claire was never sure if he was kidding. 'Anyway, I told the agency we'd see this girl, along with a few others who are *not* Scandinavians. Minus any representation from Eastern Europe, I've lined up a mini-United Nations, just for you. Why don't you see them all? Then you decide. I'll leave it entirely up to you.' He paused. 'As long as your decision isn't totally bizarre.'

'Meaning?'

'Meaning, you have to show some judgement.'

Claire sighed wearily. She was having palpitations. Why couldn't he just drop it? Was he trying to kill her? Or Harry? She looked at her watch. 'I should bill you for this tiresome conversation. Let's see, at my rate of two twenty-five an hour, you've just racked up an account for sixty-seven dollars and fifty cents.'

'And the cost of a repainted waterbed just hit two grand.'

Once again, Claire found it hard to argue with his logic. 'I can't interview anyone on Wednesday. I'm meeting Christine for lunch. Don't look at me like that, it's her treat. And then I have a dental appointment at three.'

'I thought you were worried about your blood pressure. Seeing Christine could be fatal.'

'It's you who finds her so aggravating, not me. And she won't be around much longer. Bernardo's taken some job in the States – they're moving.'

'Doing what? Has anyone in your family ever figured out what that guy does? Or Christine?'

'He's some sort of entrepreneur. And she's in public relations.'

'But why this lunch? I thought you didn't want to be seen in your condition.'

'We're meeting at an out-of-the-way place.'

'Where's that? Kingston?'

'Can we talk about all of this later? I feel awful, like I'm going to have a CA.'

'A what?'

'A CA. Cardiac arrest.'

'That's an MI. Myocardial infarct. CA means cancer.'

'Well, if you keep hounding me about getting some Swedish babe, I'll probably get stressed into getting CA, maybe wind up DOA.'

'No one says DOA any more. It's VSA. Vital signs absent. It's more accurate. As a lawyer, you should appreciate that. And the link between stress and cancer has never been established. It's purely anecdotal at this point.'

'Thanks, Doc. I feel better already.'

'Anyway, Wednesday's not a problem – I've set up some interviews for tomorrow.'

'What's the big rush? We only just decided to look for a nanny yesterday. We don't even have a baby yet.'

'Claire, the process could take months. We aren't going to find the right person just like that. Be realistic. We've got no time to waste. Here, let me help an old lady to her feet.' He took the paint brush from her and put his arms under her armpits to hoist her to her feet. 'My dear God! Soon we'll need a hydraulic lift for you.' He brushed a strand of hair from her forehead and kissed her on the nose.

'Please don't cutify me. I hate that.'

'You are cute – I don't have to do a thing except watch you. But I do have to get another few pages of my paper done today. And I'm preparing a child-care questionnaire for the nanny applicants.'

'That'll be interesting.'

'So you'll at least talk to the Swedish girl?'

'Only if she's fat. With a huge overbite. And facial hair.'

'Hirsute.' Ben squeezed her arm and bounded up the basement stairs. 'Like I said, it's your decision,' he called back.

Claire watched him go, trying to analyse why she was so

bothered by their nanny discussion. She was reconciled to the fact that they would have to give up their privacy and hire a 'live-in' nanny. A 'live-out' would charge three hundred dollars a month more than a live-in – three hundred more than they could afford. The going rate for a live-in nanny was, surprisingly, less than one of those heart-breaking daycares. And the Cunninghams' house would be cleaned, their meals prepared. There was no alternative, really. And Ben was right: Claire couldn't consider giving up her work. Not for years. Even if she wanted to.

She'd never given a thought to ethnic background or nationality of their nanny-to-be, but she had been picturing a diligent, hard-working and (though she was ashamed to admit it, even to herself) *homely* young woman, who would be grateful to have a cheery and clean apartment to retire to each evening. Maybe she would even want to iron Claire's blouses or Ben's shirts (which they would never ask, nor expect, her to do of course) while she was down there watching *Jeopardy* or chatting on the phone to her (equally homely) nanny friends. But a Swedish girl! Was she secure enough to handle seeing, first thing in the morning, a lanky blonde, with pouting bee-stung lips and tousled hair, coming down the stairs from the nursery, cradling Harry – Claire's baby – in her slender, sun-browned arms? And why would she want someone hanging around all day saying *ja* this and *ja* that, writing dots and little circles over the vowels of words when she made out the grocery list? And they left the tops off sandwiches, didn't they? Hadn't those open-faced things driven Ben's room-mate wild in Sweden? In frustration, Mike Hoolihan – that was his name – had always taken two of them, slapping them together, filling to filling, to make one decent and proper sandwich.

All things considered, having a Swedish nanny could be profoundly annoying. And if Swedes were so attracted to babies, wasn't there a risk that the nanny might try to appropriate the baby for her own? After Claire returned to work, Harry might forget about her, or worse, reject her whenever she tried to take him in her arms. She'd heard about cases where that exact thing happened. A nanny was basically a babysitter, not a surrogate mother. Claire would be cordial and fair, but not overly friendly; she would not be the girl's advisor or confidante. She would be her employer. Period. After all, she wasn't interested in adopting a daughter, especially one who looked like Britt Ekland.

She struggled up on to a footstool and peered into the blackness above the furnace to see if there were any Peek Freans up there. There was just one left in the bag: a Bourbon Cream. As she munched, dribbling chocolate crumbs down her chest, she checked her workmanship on the bed. It didn't look great, but it would do. This was a nanny apartment she was furnishing, not the Ritz. Cheap and cheerful was the goal.

Humming tunelessly and wishing there were more cookies squirrelled away in the house somewhere, Claire turned off the basement light and, taking a firm grip on the banister, hoisted herself up the stairs, reminding herself that her condition was temporary, and that in no time at all she would return to her normal size seven.

Back in the kitchen, panting, she eyed the pile of nicely thick brown envelopes that Davina had recently sent over, feeling the familiar twitch of excitement. There was billable work in there, letters of instruction, maybe something from a new client. Feeling guilty, like someone cheating on a diet, she opened the top one and pulled out a handful of yellow telephone message slips. Trying not to make too much noise, she shuffled and cut them. Most, she noted with disappointment, were from a man named Mike Potochnik – the client from hell – the only referral she'd ever had from any of her relatives. He was the son of her father's best friend from the Old Country. A Ukrainian – *nashyj* – one of their own. Referrals from family were destined to result in disaster: a complaint to the Law Society, ruined friendships, feuds that would span generations. She had told Davina to send Potochnik's file to accounting, to be billed out and closed. And new work from that direction wasn't something Claire was keen to get. Still. She studied the message slips, some of which had the 'urgent' box ticked off. Business was business. She was about to reach for the kitchen wall-phone when Ben suddenly reappeared.

'As your house doc, I'm ordering you flat on your back.' He snatched the message slips from her hand.

'That kind of talk used to be a terrible turn-on,' Claire smiled, trying to hide her annoyance.

'And I'm confiscating your precious pile of envelopes as well.'

Claire watched, licking her lips, too hot and tired to fight him for them. 'I ought to at least see what's in there. What if it's something important?'

'You'll find out about it in three months. Whatever it is, it isn't worth risking your health. Or Harry's.'

When he had bustled back upstairs, obviously pleased at the way he'd taken charge of the situation, Claire leaned against the kitchen counter, arms crossed over her belly. Inside her, Harry started to hiccup, a rhythmic beating that could go on for hours. Ben was right again. She undid her watch and put it on top of the microwave. There was no 'billable time' when one was on maternity leave. And Harry did deserve the best. She would start taking better care of herself, forget about the office and concentrate on finding him the perfect nanny: a capable and caring employee. And keeping an emotional distance from the nanny would be easy for her. But would it be so easy for Harry? And worse – try as she might, Claire couldn't discount the awful suspicion – would it be so easy for Ben? Maybe, if she weren't old enough to have once been mistaken for Ben's mother, the idea might never have entered Claire's head.

4

Claire soon realized that Ben's quiz was going to be a major obstacle in their search for Harry's nanny. In fact, he seemed to have designed it to ensure they never hired one at all.

Over a dinner of grease-spotted cartons and steaming foil trays (they'd ordered in Chinese food, Ben expressing concern over the safety of Claire's garden bounty), he presented her with his hand-written list of issues he thought they should discuss before they started interviewing. Claire sat across from him at the kitchen table, belching painfully and popping antacids, enduring a massive heartburn prompted by the Moo Shu Pork, and frowning at his list. Did they want Harry to get any sun? That was the first question.

'Hm,' she said, 'I guess a little wouldn't hurt.'

'Wrong!' He looked at her triumphantly. 'I just read the latest dermatological study on early sunburn. It's a big risk factor for malignant melanoma. Very scary.'

'I thought a person needed sunshine for vitamin D.'

'Ha! Do you know what a minuscule amount of vitamin D you actually need?'

'So what is this? Some kind of test?' Sulking, Claire went on to the next question. 'Should the nanny answer the phone when alone with the baby, or let the answering-machine do it?' She puzzled over that for a moment, sensing Ben's gloating satisfaction at her dilemma. 'If I get the answer wrong do I get an electric shock?'

'There is no wrong answer.'

'Could've fooled me.'

'I just wrote down some things I thought we should talk about. Don't take it personally.'

'Well then, she *should* answer the phone – that's my answer. What if I were calling about something important? I'd go nuts if all I got was a machine to talk to. Besides, I'd never know where Harry was – whether they were in or out, or where to look for them.'

'A valid point.' Ben nodded, but Claire knew he was being condescending. 'Look, you don't have to come up with all the answers right now.'

'I thought these were timed, skill-testing questions. You mean you're letting me off the hook? Gee, thanks, Doc.'

'I want to get on to the *coup de gracy* – la questionnaire.' He passed some neatly typed pages across the table to her. 'It's taken me hours of research in my paediatrics and emerg medicine texts. I'm going to read the questions out loud to each girl – that'll give us the advantage of the surprise effect – she won't have time to think about a response, just like in a real emergency.' He leaned forward, excitedly.

'You're tipping the table.'

'Read.'

Apprehensively, Claire read through the quiz. It presented a series of complex, life-threatening scenarios that made her stomach churn with alarm. What if Harry fell down the stairs and were lying at the bottom, not moving, turning blue? What if he tripped and hit his head on a sharp corner and was not bleeding heavily, but just whimpering? What if he stuck his tongue in a light socket? She was aghast that poor little Harry, not yet even born, was already being injured and maimed in so many creative ways. What sort of man – father – could conceive of so many terrible things happening to his infant son? Even if Ben truly was only concerned about Harry's welfare, and determined to get the right person for the job, he'd still had to sit around, dreaming up these unspeakable calamities, thinking the unthinkable. She regarded her husband through narrowed eyes. Inside, Harry hiccupped. On the other hand, she worried, was Ben's ability to confront these tragedies as potentially real disasters, an indicator that he would make the better parent? There it was – that word again – the more *mature* one?

Ben's matter-of-fact attitude about life and death constantly amazed Claire. After spending all day cutting people up, rearranging their features and 'harvesting' (a concept she found particularly distasteful) tissue, he would come home to unwind by watching movies on the late-night pay channel – the more grisly and violent the better. She would have thought the last thing he'd want to see was more guts spewing out all over the place. What did this say about him as a doctor? As a surgeon? As a father?

'I don't know myself,' she finally sighed, feeling hopelessly inadequate, the Chicken Soo Guy repeating unpleasantly, 'I have no idea what I'd do in any of these ghastly situations.'

'You're kidding, of course.' He gave her a gimlet-eyed stare.

But she wasn't. Or rather, it wasn't that she didn't have a clue about what to do but she was afraid of what she would likely do. Panic, scream, forget even how to call 911 – probably dial 411 and get Directory Assistance. 'What city please?' she would hear on the other end as baby Harry bled and whimpered all over the floor. Then the receiver would clunk to the floor as she passed out. She looked over at Ben and swallowed.

'Obviously,' he said, 'you need to take an infant and child CPR course. And PDQ.' The disappointment and concern in his eyes was heart-breaking. Claire had to look away.

It was hardly surprising that no one they interviewed, in the first two days, managed to pass Ben's test. Mostly, the candidates sat on the Cunninghams' lumpy chesterfield and looked uncomfortable, uncomprehending or scared as he read out the hypothetical situations. Claire also got the feeling that, from the way the women looked at her – from under lowered lids, or sideways – they perceived something odd and shameful about the man of the house doing the interviewing, doing the woman's work. Was the wife addled? Gone soft in the head? Would they be expected to change *her* diapers, as well? They'd cast surreptitious glances to where Claire sat, hands clasped across her enormous belly, swollen feet up on an ottoman, flushing with hypertension and embarrassment.

In addition to failing Ben's quiz, all applicants failed miserably in other aspects of the interview as well. Neither Claire nor Ben could imagine any of them being entrusted with Harry's care, or living in the Cunninghams' basement apartment. There was the stone-faced Irish girl who'd hugged a Bible to her chest and pronounced that children should not be allowed to become attached to their nannies, though there had to be little danger of that, Claire imagined, in her case. Then there was the lady from 'the islands' in lace stockings and stiletto heels who cautioned that, as she would be living with them, they should know that she wasn't too crazy about eating lobster. She was followed by a local girl who confessed to having visions – though nothing bad, of course – and boasted that she was a faith healer, able to cure just about anything by a laying on of her hands. Next, they interviewed a pedigreed English nanny, complete with papers, who recounted her entire life story, boyfriends included, and who knew other nannies back home who had worked for 'the Royals'. But she didn't want a position like *that*, she assured Claire and Ben. She'd like to feel welcome to come upstairs in her bathrobe of an evening, to share a glass of wine with them and a nice chat.

After her came a two-hundred-pound college student who wanted to take a couple of years off her studies to work as a nanny. She was pleasant enough, and even had her ECE certificate, but Claire and Ben were concerned about the cost of feeding her, and of the dietary habits she was likely to pass along to Harry. They discussed her, worriedly, after she had gone. Were they being unfair? Prejudicial? To someone who merely had the bad luck to be horizontally disadvantaged?

Lastly, they interviewed two Filipino girls, though they'd expected only one and were never sure which of the two was actually applying for the job. Their boss – the man who ran the agency – waited for them in a car outside. They'd spent most of the interview holding hands and giggling at each other, and the salary that Ben quoted seemed to strike them as particularly funny.

Frustrated and fatigued, with no one else to interview that day, and upset by the idea that they might never find anyone suitable for Harry, Claire decided to go shopping.

Before she became pregnant, clothes had been her passion. She had so many it was embarrassing. Some days, it made her want to vomit to think about them, let alone look at them. She'd even devised a rotation system – clipping numbered tags over each padded satin hanger – to ensure that all of her outfits were given equal wear. Seeing those dresses, skirts and pants in her closet now was depressing. They looked as tiny as doll clothes; she couldn't believe she'd ever squeezed into them, or that she ever would again. Her brassieres, small as training bras, she'd hidden away at the back of her underwear drawer, amazed that anyone with breasts that fitted into them would bother with a bra at all.

Some mornings, in her pre-pregnant state, she would change her clothes several times before leaving for work. Even deciding on a pair of earrings was a time-consuming but pleasurable chore. There was a woman in her head – Claire liked to think of her as her Dresser – who was always there, helping with her daily selections, giving her fashion tips and advice. Did that scarf *really* work with that blouse? Wasn't that hose more appropriately a summer sheer? The yellow in that skirt was just a tad off, if she was trying to co-ordinate it with that sweater. And Claire might want to rethink that handbag. Her Dresser was coolly polite, but critical and not easily pleased. She would have a restrained tantrum over anything stained or sloppy or mismatched, and wouldn't let Claire out of the house until she looked as close to *done* as she could get.

But her Dresser had abandoned her by the end of her first trimester. Realizing she had a hopeless case on her hands, she wouldn't have wanted to be associated with a woman who was going to float through her pregnancy like a fully inflated dirigible, littering herself with cookie crumbs and grease spots, coming apart at the seams, frayed around the edges. 'Why not just wrap an old chenille bedspread around yourself?' Claire could imagine her acid remark.

At times, she felt an enormous relief, blithely waddling past the beckoning shop windows, knowing she was free, that there was no point in even looking at clothes, and that the salesgirls would, like her Dresser, ignore her – if they saw her at all.

Unable to justify buying herself clothes (other than a few maternity outfits which were either shockingly shoddy or outrageously expensive – and looked awful on her no matter what), Claire was obliged to seek out other shopping vistas. Her urge to shop was like a fast-flowing sewer which had suddenly been plugged at one end. Eventually, new waterways had to appear or there would be an explosion from the built-up pressure. Happily, Claire's pipe had sprung a variety of minor leaks which quickly gushed into raging torrents.

First was the redecorating of the house, beginning, of course, with the nursery. Animals would be the theme, she decided, since she'd already poured so much anguish and energy into the Noah's Ark wall hanging. She papered the walls with bright, multi-coloured stripes, adding a border of jungle animals peering around bright green foliage. Then she ordered bumper pads, a crib skirt and window valences custom-made out of contrasting fabric. She found a tiny goose-down duvet, with a paw-print cover and co-ordinating sheets, pillow cases, an area rug.

'You bought goose-down for a baby?' Her mother frowned. 'What if he's allergic? Or when he spits up? You can't just throw goose-down in the laundry. The down has to be taken out, specially washed, dried somehow. It's very expensive.'

'Hmm,' Claire had said, examining the label sewn into one seam, 'do you suppose that's why it was on sale?'

After tramping through all three locations of Storkland, her legs throbbing and shoes pinching, she found an irresistible nursery lamp with circus animals trooping around the base while it tinkled 'The Lion Sleeps Tonight', in music-box notes, and – surprise! – there was a matching switchplate for the wall, as well as a night light.

'Where are you getting the money for all this?' Ben wanted to know, looking up from his *Surgical Anatomy of the Nose* as two delivery men grunted and cursed their way up the narrow staircase with a nursery rocking chair and matching footstool, knocking chips of paint off the banister and spindles as they did so.

Claire had tossed her head and laughed as if Ben had made a witty remark. She really had no idea how they were going to pay for any of it. But, curiously, this only encouraged her to embark upon even more elaborate shopping adventures, more cunning means of subterfuge.

She'd gone on to redo the kitchen – red vertical blinds,

checkered wallpaper with a saw-tooth border, and a kitschy wall clock in the shape of a cat that rolled its eyes from side to side as the seconds were ticked out by its swinging plastic tail.

The dining-room was next. Although she had completely lost interest in entertaining, even after the morning sickness subsided, she took an afternoon off work to stand in a miserable driving rain, with a few hundred other people, waiting to be allowed into the Great Hall of China warehouse clearance. After almost two hours, she'd finally fought her way inside, only to find there was nothing in there she wanted. But, caught up in the contagion of frenzied purchasing, and refusing to leave empty-handed after getting wet feet and a flu-like chill, Claire spent five hundred dollars on liqueur glasses, brandy snifters and champagne flutes. All of this sparkling crystal made the dining-room look shabbier than ever, so she bought yards of fabric and swagged a huge sagging valence across the top of the windows, then hung a set of Victorian-style floral prints that she trimmed with gold cord and tassels.

'Harry'll have a good time swinging from that curtain thing', and 'Those pictures'll look nice splattered with rice cereal', were Ben's only comments. His research paper had been accepted for presentation at an international Head and Neck meeting in San Francisco, but it needed revisions, so he had less time (and interest) than usual to admire, or question, Claire's efforts.

When there was nothing else she could imagine doing to the house, she began to realize what a range of goods beyond the decor of his nursery she would need to look after Harry properly. She had a complete list from a helpful salesgirl at Storkland, called *Layette CheckList*. Some things on it were a trifle off-putting – the nasal mucus pump, for example. Others were puzzling. What was a receiving blanket, for instance? She needed four to six of them, apparently. Were they blankets in which one received the newborn baby, as in, from the nurse or doctor? Or did one wrap the baby in them when one was 'receiving' – that quaint old-fashioned term for having visitors over to the house? Or were they blankets that the new mother would receive from others, as gifts? (And if the latter, why would they be listed as things she was supposed to buy?)

Most of the list was easy enough to figure out, however,

and Claire was grateful that someone had taken the trouble to write it all down. She bought bottles, soothers and teethers, a vaporizer, booties and hats, hooded bath-towels. She ordered a high chair, crib, a change table and chest of drawers; she bought strollers, a wind-up swing, a potty and a bouncy exercise jumper that could be hung from any standard-size doorframe. Their 1911-built house had only two such standard frames, Claire was disappointed to discover: one at the top of the basement stairs, the other in the front hall coat closet. As Harry couldn't very well dangle at the top of a flight of stairs, he would have to do his jolly jumping in the closet.

Finally, she bought safety locks for the kitchen and bathroom cupboards, covers for every electrical outlet in the house, sun shades and a child restraint seat for the car, remembering Ben's quiz and congratulating herself on her foresight in warding off infant disasters, yet at the same time bothered that safety devices had not been her primary concern.

After giving it a lot of thought, and reading some sobering articles about the takeover of the planet by garbage – passed along by Ben's mother Prue – Claire decided to use cloth diapers on Harry. Interviewing the nanny applicants reminded her that she didn't yet have any. What if Harry arrived early? Would he have to go around bare-bummed, or innocently polluting the environment with paper diapers, until she managed to get organized?

'Cloth diapers?' Elfriede gasped over the phone. 'I used to wash your diapers by hand, for both of you kids. Ask me about cloth diapers sometime.' Claire didn't ask – she knew her mother's opinion would come out on its own, but she wasn't going to let it change her mind. Times had changed. After all, in her mother's day, breast-feeding was something that only desperately poor women were forced to resort to.

But this business of diapering wasn't as simple as Claire'd expected. There were several stores right there in the Beach dedicated to the covering of babies' bottoms with various types of fabric. There was a myriad of decisions to be made – one didn't just slap a diaper on the kid and be done with it. Would she use pins, or diaper covers? Would the covers be terry cloth? Designer fabric? Would they have Velcro fasteners, tie-ons or snaps? What about liners? Did she want shaped, pre-folded, reinforced, plastic-covered or regular cloth? Had she thought about washing them? What about disinfectants? Anti-fungal agents? Deodorants? Had she thought about *who* was going to wash them? (She decided not to mention the diapers in the nanny interviews, unless one of the girls specifically inquired. She had a suspicion that pre-soaking, washing and folding cloth diapers would not likely be viewed as a perk.)

After spending an hour in the diaper store, perspiring over all the options, Claire settled on five dozen pure cotton pre-folded diapers, and ten snazzy Hawaiian-print, plastic-lined, Velcro-fastened covers. The covers were actually part of a set that included a matching diaper bag, change pad and mosquito net. She bought them too.

Her small car low to the ground with the weight of so many bags and packages, she pulled into the driveway of 67 Pine Beach Road just before five. There was a car parked in front of the house – an old, bottle-green sedan – with a man sitting inside. There was something vaguely familiar about him, Claire thought: the pronounced curve of his forehead, the hunch of his shoulders. She glanced back in her rearview, trying to get a look at his face, but he was bending over the seat, just then, as if searching for something on the floor of the car.

She parked in the garage at the side of the house, debating whether to go back out to the front to find out if she really did know the man. Probably, she was just imagining she knew him. Still . . . She peeked around the side of the garage and saw, with relief, that the sedan was pulling away from the house. There were always people sitting around in cars doing nothing; they were like subway mumblers – a fact of city life. She wouldn't give him another thought. Besides, she had more pressing problems at the moment, such as figuring out how to get her bags and parcels into the house past Ben.

It was hard to tell if he was home, since they kept the blinds down during the day to keep out the summer sun. Beyond the house the lake sulked, grey and hazy, with a few sailboats lining the horizon like ducks in a shooting gallery. As Claire approached the house, the air conditioning clicked on and began humming loudly from behind the shrubbery, advertising its damage to the environment. Otherwise, all was quiet.

As a precaution, Claire decided to leave most of her purchases in the trunk to smuggle in later, in case Ben was home and taking a break just then from his research. She didn't feel like being confronted with questions about what was in those bags and how she expected to pay for whatever it was, even though all she'd bought were absolute essentials. '*Diapers* for heaven's sake,' was how she'd phrase it, if challenged, 'hardly a shopping spree.'

With all of this in mind she was, therefore, extremely surprised on opening the front door of the house to see Ben sipping a beer in their living-room and chatting with a young, very blonde and exceptionally pretty woman.

'Claire!' He bounded out of his chair as if he'd been jabbed by the devil's pitchfork, his drink sloshing over the sides of his glass. 'This is Brita Edvardsson,' he beamed. 'She had a mix-up with another interview and had to come today, on short notice. I didn't know how to reach you, I called up all of your usual watering-holes—'

'Watering-holes?' Claire wiped the sweat from her upper lip. 'What do I look like, a buffalo?'

There was a moment of embarrassed silence in the room. Then, still grinning idiotically, Ben grabbed her arm and pulled her towards the girl, who had unfolded from her chair and was smiling shyly. She held out her hand. Huge blue eyes – they were dark, almost navy – met Claire's hazel ones. A fine gold bracelet – a chain of dangling gold stars – tinkled on her wrist, with a sound like tiny wind-chimes. She was wearing a loose cotton sweater with the sleeves rolled up – her boyfriend's possibly – and jeans. It was impossible to see what her figure was like exactly, but Claire thought she could make a pretty intelligent guess.

'*Jag heter Brita*,' she said, with one of those typical musical lilts to her voice, 'I am Brita.'

Claire took her hand, smiling remotely. 'I've been out shopping for diapers,' she said. 'Cloth diapers – the kind you have to wash.'

'*Ja*,' said Brita, 'of course. The baby must have some diapers.'

'Some?' Claire said pleasantly. 'Try five dozen.'

Brita nodded emphatically and turned to Ben, seeking confirmation that *ja*, indeed, the baby did need them, and giving
what Claire thought was a rather gummy grin. There were
spaces between Brita's teeth – not large ones, but there none
the less.

'You're not going to believe this,' Ben said, 'but Brita's almost
an old friend of mine. Well, not her – but her family. She was
just a kid when I was over there in Sweden.'

'Let me guess. A gangly kid with freckles and braces?' Claire
smiled thinly.

'Oh, *ja*,' Brita rolled her eyes dramatically, 'I was very skinny.
Too much skinny.'

'Her mother is a great cook. I did some mean freeloading off
her family. They were big hockey fans.' Ben chuckled. 'What
a co-inky-dinky. I couldn't believe it when she started telling
me about her family. I didn't even recognize her. But then it
suddenly hit me.'

'Do tell,' Claire said, thinking that suddenly hitting him was
a mighty appealing idea just then.

'I told her she could start a week Monday, if that's okay with
you of course.' He seemed suddenly perplexed by something in
his beer glass. Brita was frowning out of the window at the lake,
as if she too were puzzled – by the line of sailboats, perhaps.

Claire stared at Ben for a moment, breathing hard. 'Really?'
she finally managed. 'Could you help me bring in some things
from the car?'

'Let me do it. I will help.' Brita sprang to the front door, her
shag of blonde hair swinging enthusiastically.

'See? Brita wants to help already,' Ben beamed.

Reluctantly, Claire followed Brita on to the front porch. When
she turned to look back at her husband, it was to see him
grinning at her over his beer and rocking on his heels. Did I
just do something terrific or what, his expression said. Never,
Claire thought, had the man managed to look as grotesquely
handsome as he did at that particular moment.

5

The spot Christine had chosen for lunch was hardly out of the way, unless fifty floors above the major business intersection of the city could be called remote. As for the anonymity Claire had been hoping for, within minutes of entering the plush blue velvet interior of the lounge she recognized two people, both of whom she associated with some unpleasantness in the past. One was a short, buxom woman who'd always reminded Claire of a pigeon, not only in appearance but by the way she clucked and pecked over her company's legal bills. She was now a former client, having recently fired Claire and her firm, using the often employed explanation that her company thought it best to 'spread its work around'. The other was an abrasive young man, a recently called lawyer who was still naive enough to think he knew something about the law. He was on 'the other side' of one of Claire's slumbering-dog files that had woken up that past spring to become a howling nuisance. Fortunately, neither of these individuals appeared to see Claire, or else didn't recognize her in her mammoth condition, for there was no glint of acknowledgement in response to her wooden smile.

She squeezed herself into a banquette by a window, ordered a club soda, and settled back to watch a sea plane landing at the island airport. But her own reflection, in the polished glass, kept intruding upon the view. For a second, she was shocked to see her mother in the window – minus the usual beads or string of pearls, perhaps – but it was surely her. Claire stared. No. It wasn't Elfriede, it was Claire herself! She'd never believed the people over the years who'd told her she was the image of her mother, until now. Her father was there too, in the face that looked back at her, in the pregnancy-induced heaviness of it and in the wide Slavic cheekbones. Claire had always thought of her face as a rather ordinary one, pretty basic, a melting-pot face – although several times in her life someone or other had said triumphantly, 'I was sure you were Ukrainian!' or 'I knew your last name couldn't really be Cunningham!' Her nose was a bit too wide to be considered pert, and upturned just short of being pug. Her best feature was her eyes – large and round with hazel irises. She also had 'full, sensuous lips' according to Simon, who liked to read soft-core porn that he hid in dusty piles under their bed. As for her hair, it was baby-fine, perpetually a mess, slightly wavy, but only in directions Claire never wanted it to go, and brown. There was no other word for it. It wasn't auburn or chestnut or ash. It was brown.

As her sister approached, lifting a finger in recognition and smiling her aloof public smile, Claire regretted having accepted the lunch invitation. Christine, in her black linen suit with the pale silk camisole peeking coyly out from the neckline, looked, as usual, polished to perfection, *done*. She even had on a hat! Boater? Claire wondered. Panama hat? It was a smart straw thing with a grosgrain band. Looking *done* was something Claire never managed to achieve, even with the help of her Dresser and no matter how much time and money she spent on clothes and cosmetics. Maybe it was because she found manicures excruciatingly boring, abhorred the thought of paying some woman to yank out her underarm, leg or pubic hair with melted wax, and had never got the hang of fashion jewellery, all of it essential in attaining that illusive state of *doneness*. And she would never have dared wear a hat, except in the winter, or in the privacy of her garden, and then only out of necessity. She would have felt ridiculously overdone under a summer hat. On her sister, however, it was perfect.

Christine went in for all of the personal services, even to having the tiny spidery veins in her legs injected with saline to make them fade. She'd spent five years in France, pretending to study the cello, and come home Frenchified and snooty, an Italian husband in tow. They thought of each other as exotic beasts: she was wowed by the colour and drama of Rome; Bernardo was proud of possessing a blonde wife. Now, a decade later, Christine had lost much of her snootiness and no longer struggled to find the right English phrases, but she'd managed to retain both the French style and the Italian man.

'I can't believe Ben's hired a Swedish nanny,' were her first words to Claire. 'I was totally shocked when you called. A *Svenska*! And while you were out diaper shopping! That's grounds for divorce, in my book.'

'You've never been divorced, so that's easy for you to say. If this marriage doesn't work out, that's it for me. I don't have the energy to go through another one.' Claire was surprised to hear herself say this in such emphatic terms. Had her subconscious been busily at work deciding this? Assessing the pros and cons, the possible net return, of yet another marriage? She couldn't recall having thought about it at all.

Christine tossed her head, making her earrings rattle. They were complicated intertwined loops in pink, white and yellow gold that matched her necklace, as if part of it had leapt up from her neck to dangle from her earlobes. Her hat remained precisely in place. 'Come on now, don't be so negative. Let's be constructive. You need action. What are you going to do about this hideous development?'

'Nothing.' Claire studied her menu. 'It sounds like she'll be great for Harry. She passed Ben's wretched nanny quiz. And she's even taken some child care courses.'

'So *he* tells you. You weren't there for the interview, remember?'

'Well, I'm not going to get paranoid over this.' Claire was wishing she'd never confided in her sister.

'The problem, if you want my opinion,' Christine began, as soon as the waiter had taken their order, 'is that you married a party animal. Even the way you met – wasn't it at some party?'

'He called to invite me to one. I was on his list.'

'When you both lived in that wild apartment building with the hot tubs and tanning beds. Did you ever go to his party?'

Claire shook her head. 'He was just trying to sell me a ticket – for fifteen bucks. Dream on, I told him, I don't pay to go to parties. That seemed to intrigue him enough to keep me on the phone for six hours.' Claire had to smile at the memory.

'Six hours! Obviously, you had a lot in common.'

'Sex, mostly. But that was back in the self-indulgent eighties. When AIDS was just a rumour.'

Curiously, Ben remembered their first meeting quite differently. It hadn't been by way of a phone call at all. In his version (which had come back to Claire via several friends), she had been scantily clad, lying face-down by the edge of the kidney-shaped pool in the building's courtyard. As he told the story, Ben had dived into the water, swimming with great determination to pop up by Claire's side where he gently traced a finger along one of her thighs. 'Next time, I'll use my tongue,' he claimed to have whispered, before disappearing again under the water. Claire had no memory of this incident. She had to have been asleep at the time. (If it happened at all.) Otherwise, she would have called the police. She and Ben had had the same silly conversation about it at least a hundred times. But what was so wrong with the real story, she suddenly wondered, watching Christine bite into the olive from her martini. Not sexy enough? Not glamorous or exciting?

But it was more than sex, more than heavy-breathing phone conversations, that had drawn Claire to Ben. She never told Christine how much she admired him for the way he would study far into the night, wearing a set of headphones to block out the noise of his room-mates drinking or entertaining women in the adjoining rooms. She also never told her sister how different Ben was from most of the other young men who lived in the glitzy singles' high-rise – the losers, the salesman, the consultants – all of them terrified of losing their hair and their hold on the lonely divorced women who also lived there. They expected the women to buy them presents, to take them places. But not Ben. In all the months between Halloween and Victoria Day, Claire couldn't remember ever leaving the apartment with him. He had no money with which to take her out, and he refused to let her pay. Instead, he littered her apartment with love notes, flowers from street vendors, small stuffed animals. He messed up her bathroom, made playful fun of her decorating. He was like a wriggling, tail-thumping puppy who was not quite paper-trained, but whose wild pink tongue and genuine eagerness to please made up for whatever he lacked in social graces. As Simon's wife, Claire had been the clutter, the organic mess in his pristine ledgered world. But Ben's world was all mess and bodily excrescences, at the centre of which was his intense drive to succeed.

'Hello?' Christine was saying, tapping her swizzle-stick on the edge of her glass. 'Earth to Claire.'

'Sorry – it's the hormones. I keep having these lapses.'

'Well, as I was saying, it's not just that Ben is a party animal, but he's one with a *past*. Capital P. And a *hockey* past. What could be worse? Think about the influences he was exposed to during his formative years. The drinking, the screwing of anything that moved . . .'

'He doesn't drink any more. Maybe a beer occasionally.' Claire wanted to change the subject but it seemed her sister had an agenda.

'And what about the head injuries? I can't imagine how he ever made it through med school.'

'And won the silver medal.' Claire was anxious to come to Ben's defence although Christine was right about him being a party animal. He was a 'swell guy', often a victim of his own gregariousness and taken advantage of by a lot of friends, former friends and friends-of-friends. He was a work-hard, play-hard sort of regular guy who was always up to date on the latest hockey, baseball and football scores. He never read a newspaper or turned on the radio, as far as Claire knew, but was plugged in to that mysterious jungle telegraph by which men always seemed to know who was playing whom in any given sport, on any particular day.

He thought of himself as having a rollicking and ribald sense of humour, too. Why else would he waste money, year after year, buying those awful joke gifts for Christmas and Claire's birthday? At first mildly amusing, they had become a source of irritation in recent years. She never knew what to do with them. Usually, she hid them at the back of a closet and threw them out later, when he'd forgotten about them. They weren't things she even wanted to keep in the house. A toilet paper-holder that played 'Swannee River' when a piece of tissue was yanked from the roll; a plumber's helper with the head of the Prime Minister, cast in iron, welded to the top; the plastic button that read: 'This is My

Husband's Idea of Jewellery!' It seemed the deep belly-laugh
Ben enjoyed at Claire's discouraged sigh each time she opened
one of these, was worth the ridiculously high price of the gift.
Was it his own juvenile sense of humour that he relished? Or
was he spitefully enjoying her disappointment? Other women
got diamonds or cars; she got tacky joke gifts as thanks for
putting him through med school, internship and now residency.
Though she tried not to let on, she was growing more sour with
each passing year.

And what did it mean that she could imagine her husband
capable of such cruelty? And if he was, why was she starting
a family with him? Just then Harry rolled over inside her, as if
alarmed by the suggestion of discord between his parents. Claire
massaged her belly, hoping to reassure him.

'Are you feeling okay?' Christine applied a smear of butter to
the end of her seven-grain roll. 'You've had a frown on your
face since I walked in the door.'

'Don't take it personally. I think it's permanent. Every time I
see my reflection in a mirror or window, I'm frowning. Either
that or I see Mother.'

'Well, stop frowning. It's no joke that it will become permanent – Ben can confirm that. And you look more like Dad. But
what's this about Ben getting a medal?' She bit into her roll, her
green eyes challenging.

'The silver medal in medical school. I've told you many times.
You just like to forget when it's convenient.' Claire shifted in
her chair, trying to relieve the sensation of Harry squeezing her
diaphragm. 'You've never given Ben much credit.'

'You're right – now I seem to remember something about an
award of some kind. That's what made him so amazing to all of
us – the hockey player turned medical whiz-kid. That's what sold
Dad on him, too, even though he kept telling you there was no
future with him . . . because of your age difference.'

'Ben's not that much younger. He's thirty-two.'

'And you're thirty-nine.'

'That's only seven years.' Claire tried not to think about a
certain car rental clerk. 'You want the Ford Escort?' he'd asked.
'Your son over there asked for the Mustang.' Ben had rushed to
assure her afterwards that the man had to be blind, or incredibly

stupid. 'In order for him to think you're my mother,' he argued, 'I would have to look about twelve years old, or you'd have to look about fifty. Hardly likely.' Sitting in the Escort a little while afterwards, Claire had twisted a crumpled tissue and sniffed, grateful for his support, but it was the first time she'd ever considered that they might make an odd-looking couple and that people might wonder how, or if, they were related. They would struggle to find some familial resemblance between them, as she and Christine had often done, digging each other in the ribs and whispering, 'I sure hope that's his daughter!' Claire had recently bought a book about older women marrying younger men. *Robbing the Cradle*, it was called. It had been thrown together by a well-known journalist who bragged on the flyleaf about the number of younger lovers she'd had, as if that made her an expert on marrying or living with one. Mostly, the book tackled amusing minor irritants: what to do when your younger man won't stop wearing your clothes; when he won't turn off the ball game or remove his baseball cap when you're making love. It didn't deal with real problems, like how to react when you discover you've got more in common with his mother than you do with him. And that while you and she belt out the lyrics to 'Bicycle Built for Two', he's out trying to find the new *Frozen Bitch* CD.

'Ben's too cute to be a doctor,' Christine was saying. 'In a sea of Wallabies and corduroy pants with droopy behinds, he really stands out. That's your typical doctor, isn't it? Wallabies and baggy cords?'

'You called him a Wanabe Wallaby after you met him.'

'Not to his face!'

'Yes you did.'

'Did I really?' Christine laughed delightedly. 'I don't remember that. But I do remember thinking that at least his pants fit his cute little tush. Too bad he's so short. He'd be perfect, wouldn't he? If he had a few more inches?'

'He's got the inches where it counts.'

'Excuse me?'

Since Christine's French experience, she liked to pretend prudery, when it suited her, trying it on now and then like an outdated hat from her closet. The French, it seemed, could get offended by just about anything. Claire flushed, seeing herself through her sister's eyes: gross and sweating and making vulgar implications about the size of her husband's penis. Her feet were throbbing. Under the table, she eased off one of her shoes, then the other, thinking, too late, that she might not be able to get them on again.

'You know,' Christine began carefully, 'I have a friend who's five years older than her husband. She thinks it's just a matter of time before he leaves her for a younger woman. She used to be terrified but now she's resigned to it. You don't have that feeling about Ben, I hope.'

'He's too busy to go looking for another woman. Sometimes it takes him hours to answer my page.'

'You know who checks Ben's pager, don't you? When anyone pages him?'

'He does.'

'Not when he's in the operating room.' Christine shook her head, knowingly. 'I've been finding out a lot about doctors lately. More than some people might want to know.' She looked pointedly at her sister. 'Ask Ben some time. About his pager.' She dug into the seafood fettucini with her usual gusto as Claire nibbled, mouse-like, at the edges of her salad. Why was it that she was eating less and less but getting bigger and bigger? What she ate seemed to have no relation to how much she gained, and hadn't from the start of her pregnancy. And what did her sister mean about Ben and his pager? And how had she suddenly become an expert on doctors?

Christine was examining something deep-fried on the end of her fork. 'I hope that's not calamari,' she said. 'Did the menu say there was calamari in this?'

'I don't know. I wasn't interested in seafood.' Claire studied her sister's profile as Christine looked around for a waiter to complain to, wondering for the thousandth time whether she'd had something done to her nose while she was in France. Surely it was less Ukrainian-looking now. It was almost beaky. Ben said he couldn't tell, since all the snipping and suturing would have been done on the inside, leaving almost no external scarring. 'So tell me about this new job Bernardo's got; and what you'll be doing. It's got something to do with doctors, I presume.'

Woman's Work •

'Well,' Christine seemed to forget her complaint about her meal, 'he's got a job with an international consulting firm, based in San Francisco, as a head-hunter. And he'll be head-hunting *doctors*. Canadian ones – like your little hubby. For private hospitals and clinics all over the world. And listen to this – it pays twenty grand a head – net!'

'Get out!'

'Seriously. Many parts of the US, for example, are desperate for doctors. He gets a bonus for specialists, and double for a sub-specialist. And you'll never guess what I'm going to be doing. I'm going to be a consultant on Canuck-talk. It's a serious problem. There are major differences in lingo between Canada and other parts of the English-speaking world. Bernardo's company is very concerned about making Canadians feel comfortable. I'll be doing a lecture series – presenting the Canadian psyche.'

'And bending it over to be kicked.'

'I'll have to talk about our zany postal code—'

'Britain's got the same kind.'

'And I'll be doing comparisons of everyday terminology. We don't say "Huh?", like the Americans, we say "Eh?" That's an obvious example, but there are tons of others. Like "soda". No one up here says "diet soda"; it's "diet *pop*". We have soda water, club soda. England is another story altogether. They use dustbins, Americans have trash cans, and we have garbage pails here. English women use sanitary *towels*, isn't that wild? I keep trying to picture myself stuffing one of those huge bath sheets between my legs.'

'It's not something I have to think about these days,' Claire said.

'And the Brits get a pay rise, not a raise. And they don't get fired, they get sacked.'

Claire looked away, the idea of being fired not something she cared to contemplate at the moment. 'Gee,' she said, 'you're a regular Henry Higgins.'

'And don't even get me started on Australia!'

'Okay.'

'Laugh if you want, but it's a great opportunity. I won't tell you what they're paying me because it would make you ill, while you slug it out up here with your law practice, docketing your six-minute time blocks.'

51 •

'The whole idea is nauseating. You're selling out this country, draining its brains, that we taxpayers paid to educate. You want to leave us baby boomers to grow old and decrepit without enough doctors to go around.'

'Oh, please! That's me you're talking about, that beleaguered taxpayer. We've been in the over-fifty per cent tax bracket for long enough. It's time to cash out. If we stay here, we could never afford to retire. Don't look at me like that. I don't feel the least bit guilty. And if you think about it, you'll see what I mean.' She went back to picking through her seafood, carefully examining each morsel before deciding whether it merited eating. 'Of course, we'll keep our Canadian citizenships. If one of us ever gets sick, I mean really sick – touch wood – we'll have to come back here.'

'That reminds me of something that happened last night,' Claire said. 'There was a man going around door to door, selling something. And he was smoking – I noticed because he flicked ashes all over our porch.'

Christine's eyes widened. 'And it's such a fire trap, isn't it?'

'That's not the point. He told me he goes to the States to buy cheap cigarettes. I reminded him that it's Canada that will have to pay for his medical treatment when he gets lung cancer. He thought that was great – a perfect arrangement. He laughed about it. Isn't that sickening?'

'Really? Well, that's the Beach for you. No one dares sell anything door to door in our neighbourhood.'

'You don't see a certain parallel there?'

'With what?'

Claire studied her sister for a moment but decided not to pursue it. Conversations with Christine could quickly degenerate to nastiness, leaving bad feelings that lingered, to surface later at family gatherings, like a gone-off potato salad for their mother to sniff out and worry over. Wolaniuk reunions were unpleasant enough. They were loud, argumentative, and would seem rank with hostility to anyone who didn't have roots in Eastern Europe and know that this was how family members related to each other as they drifted along from one meal to the next. Bickering was the Eastern European equivalent to

Waspy polite chat about the weather – largely irrelevant, but it passed the time.

'So what can you tell me about this research Ben's doing?' Christine cocked her head at Claire. 'Is it exciting? Something new? Maybe we could lure you two to the US. We'd get about fifty grand for Ben, once he's finished his training. Maybe we could cut you in for a bit.'

'There'll be three of us, remember? And no thanks.'

'Come on. Think of the shopping. Remember how Mom used to take us to Buffalo or Detroit before school each year? And we had to wear everything back to elude Canada Customs? Coats over sweaters over blouses.'

'And boots over socks over tights. We really used to sweat it out,' Claire chuckled. 'And Mother thought she was being so crafty. As if the customs guys didn't notice all these Michelin children waddling back over the border, bundled up like they were heading off to Siberia—'

'At a hundred and ten in the shade.'

It was moments like this, Claire supposed, that enabled her to put up with Christine – this delving into the bag of shared memories to find those unpolished jewels of Wolaniuk family history. It was a ritual, this mutual groping, and no meeting was complete until they'd dug out and held up to the light at least one of these gems. 'Anyway, I really don't know much about Ben's paper except that the last letter Davina typed for him was a request to Pathology for fresh cadaver heads. He's trying out some new rhinoplasty techniques.' She looked pointedly at her sister.

'I hope you remind him not to bring his work home.' Christine gazed levelly back, her eyes revealing nothing about her nose nor any procedure ever done to it.

'And he's given up his half "down day" each week. We used it to sneak off to the movies last winter. But this year he wants to use it for rat surgery.'

'Rat surgery? Well, better than another woman, as Mother would say.' Christine slid an object off her fork on to the side of her plate, then wiped the tines with her napkin. 'Speaking of other women, let's get back to the real subject of this lunch – Helga or whatever her name is.'

'It's Brita.' Claire hesitated, wishing she'd never confided in Christine. 'And I said I refuse to get paranoid about this.'

'Paranoid? Let me spell it out for you, then. Ben lived in Sweden for two years, basically goofing off, getting laid a lot and being well paid for it. He's never gotten over those glory days – that's the impression he's always given me. And now he's brought a little piece of Sweden into your home – someone he actually *knew* when he lived there.'

'She was just a kid then.'

'She still is a kid – she's half your age! And you're thinking of allowing this situation? Are you insane? And just when you're at your worst? You're big as a house. I wasn't going to mention it – I mean, I know how lousy you must feel – but you don't look well. What does your o.b. say? Isn't he alarmed?'

'He only likes rare and interesting problems in pregnancy. Getting fat is too banal.'

'Well, maybe you should change doctors.' Christine poked her head under the table, sat up again and flicked back her shoulder-length hair. Still, her hat didn't budge. She was the only blonde in a family of brunettes, and the only one with green eyes – so green most people assumed she wore tinted contacts. She was cool and pale and in control, an enigma in a family where red-faced fussing and fulminating was the basic level of self-expression. Maybe she'd been mixed up with the real Wolaniuk baby in the hospital nursery when she was born. 'You don't have any ankles left at all. I didn't swell up like that with Anita. I hope you'll be able to get your shoes back on.'

'You had Anita in winter. Water retention is a lot worse in summer. Besides, that was six years ago – you just don't remember the details.'

'Oh yes I do. One never forgets. You can forgive – I mean, you don't hold it against the baby forever – but the husband? Him you never forgive.' She laughed. 'Come on, have some wine.'

'It's not good for Harry.'

Christine refilled her glass and pushed her plate aside. 'You've got to be realistic about this Brita person, stick to your guns. Do you really want Darryl Hannah lounging around your house in her bathrobe? Getting Ben to come down to her room to change a light bulb in the middle of the night?'

'Uma Thurman is more like it. You should see her.'

'I don't have to. Ben hired her while you were out. That says it all. And sure, you trust him, but why tempt him? You'll have enough to worry about with the baby. Why ask for trouble? Invite it into your own home? *Pay* for it?'

'But the others we interviewed were hopeless.'

'You interviewed for one day!'

'So I'm supposed to fire Brita because I'm afraid Ben has a thing for Swedish girls?'

'You're not afraid he has, you know he has. Like most men. And there's a simple solution – interview more. See dozens of nannies. You're on maternity leave – you've got the whole summer to find someone who suits you. It's your home and your baby. Get the right person for you.'

'But what'll Ben say? Brita hasn't even started. I don't have just cause.'

'Stop talking like a lawyer and start talking like a woman. And forget Ben – he'll get over it. You're the one who has to be comfortable with the girl you hire.'

'He thinks she should start right away.'

'Of *course* he does!' Christine hissed. 'Claire, Claire. How much does it take to make you see what's going on right under your nose?'

'But it makes sense. She could help with the gardening. It's really too much for me.'

'The gardening? That little weedy patch you've got behind your house?' Christine settled back into the banquette. 'You're being an idiot but do what you want. You have my opinion. The only Swedish nanny I'd allow in my house is one over six feet tall named Sven. Or Bjorn. Maybe Lars.' She took a gold-plated compact and lipstick – heavy enough to make good weapons – from her handbag, powdered her nose, reglossed her lips, then leaned across the table. 'I'm so glad I only need a housekeeper now that Nita's in school full-time. Did you ever think about how easily we working mothers turn over the keys to our homes and hand over our children to the care of strangers? What do we really know about these people we hire? Are they thieves? Psychos? It's insane when you think about it. I heard a story the other day about a woman who strangled her nanny with her bare hands. Killed her. The nanny went to answer the phone and left the baby alone in the tub. He drowned. And the irony of it is, it was the *mother* who was calling, just to see how things were, feeling guilty probably. With her bare hands, can you imagine? How many of these nannies realize that their lives are at stake? There aren't many jobs where a mistake gets you strangled with someone's bare hands. But how's a mother supposed to react? Say – oh, the kid drowned? No problem, we'll just get another?'

Claire was suddenly claustrophobic, suffocating, her blood pressure soaring. There were shooting pains up and down both arms. 'I really feel sick now,' she said, dry-mouthed, as she signalled madly for the waiter. 'I need some air.' Under the table, her feet groped for her shoes.

'You're not in labour, are you?' Christine seemed to recoil ever so slightly.

'I've never been in labour before, so how should I know?' Struggling to bend down around her girth, Claire tried, without success, to force her swollen feet into her shoes. The waiter arrived with their bill and Claire hurriedly pulled out her credit card and threw it on to his tray, forgetting that lunch was supposed to be Christine's treat. 'I can't get my shoes on,' she said, stricken. 'What am I going to do?' She was desperate now to get outside. Her face was flaming and her breathing short and wheezy. She picked up her shoes. 'I'll just carry the damn things.'

'You can't walk out of here barefoot! Claire, this is Bay Street.'

'To hell with Bay Street!'

'Look, honey,' Christine was ineffectually trying to help her to her feet, 'I'm afraid I've upset you. But please don't misunderstand my intentions. It's an imperfect system but we all have to take our chances – do the best we can.'

Claire shook off her arm, signed the credit card slip, grabbed her shoes and plunged through the blue velvet lounge, packed now with business lunchers, hurrying for the elevators.

'Even when I was on maternity leave I was always putting Nita in her crib and going down to the basement to scream into a pillow.' Christine was talking rapidly, following close at her heels. 'I mean, it's better than child abuse, right? I was so frustrated. And bored. I could never give up working to stay home with a kid. I'd be nuts within a week. So would you. A nanny is really the only option for women like us.'

Claire knew her sister would be anxious to bolt before things got messy. What if her water broke and Christine had to take control of things? What would happen to her *hat*? 'I don't want to talk about nannies any more, okay?' she said as the elevator plummeted soundlessly towards earth. Suddenly, her lower lip began to quiver. Then, without warning, as the elevator doors slid open, she burst into tears. She fumbled in her handbag for a tissue, eventually producing a crumpled wad. Christine took her by the arm and steered her gently out on to the street, into the shade of an office tower.

'I hope that's not toilet paper,' she said, when they had stopped.

Claire looked down at the strand of tissue that dangled from her hand. 'What if it is?'

'We're on Bay Street, sweetie. You have clients – Bernardo and I have contacts. That's your law firm's building right over there.' Briskly, she opened her handbag and took out a linen hanky with a scrolled C embroidered in one corner. 'Here, honey.' She dabbed at Claire's eyes, peering into her face. 'Are you going to be all right?'

'Yes, sure,' Claire sniffed. 'I'm okay. I'm just at such a low point right now. If Harry doesn't come soon I'm going to lose my mind.'

'I know how it is – the waiting – especially at the end.' Christine gripped her firmly by the shoulders and leaned forward to kiss her – a little French *buss* on one cheek. 'Are you sure you're okay?'

Claire nodded, pressing the scented hanky to her eyes. 'Yes. I feel better now.' One of her shoes dropped to the ground.

Christine bent to snatch it up, then pushed it back into Claire's hand. 'Look, are you really sure you're all right?'

'I'm sure.'

'Well then, you go straight home, promise?'

'I have a dental appointment.'

'You can't drive like this.'

'I'll get a cab.'

'I'll call one for you. Which kind do you like? Diamond? City?'

'I need some air first. I think I'll walk for a bit.'

'But Claire – you've got no shoes on.' Christine grasped the sleeve of Claire's shirt.

'So? I'll buy some!' Several passers-by turned to see what all the fuss was about.

'Okay, okay.' Christine smiled nervously. 'A walk would be good for you. Just don't go too far. You never know when something might . . . start. Happen.'

'I won't,' Claire mumbled into the linen hanky. It was scented with *L'Air du Temps*. She gagged.

'And listen to your big sister. This is probably the best advice I'll ever give you. Ditch the *Svenska*. And if you don't have enough nerve, give me a call and I'll do it for you. It'd be my pleasure.' She adjusted her hat slightly, whisked her hanky out of Claire's hand and snapped her handbag shut. Then she slid into a cab that was double-parked and seemed to be waiting just for her, and was gone.

6

After Christine had gone, Claire stood in the shade for a few minutes, practising what she thought might be Lamaze breathing techniques, until she felt, if not better, then at least less likely to have a stroke. She wasn't in labour, of that much she was sure, and if something else was about to happen to her – well, it would make itself known eventually.

But she was reeling from the lunch with her sister that was supposed to have confirmed that her fears about Brita were ridiculous. Away down Bay Street, in the slow-moving snake of traffic, Claire could still see the crown of Christine's hat, in the rear window of the taxi. She fanned her reddened face with one of her shoes – (she didn't, at that moment, give a damn who saw her though she knew she would care, and quite a lot, some time later) thinking that the relationship between sisters was indeed a strange one.

Ben would likely be at home, she thought, and could come and get her. But she had a feeling that seeing him wouldn't do much to cheer her up. They would only start talking about nannies and child care and end up having a huge heated debate about Brita. And his pager. What on earth had Christine been going on about? No, Claire decided, tucking her shoes under one arm and her handbag under the other, there was only one thing that could be counted on for solace in dark moments such as this. She lifted her chin and turned in the direction of the downtown department stores.

It would only be window shopping, she reminded herself, since she was so far overdrawn at the bank that the instant teller machine had spat back her card, refusing to cough up even ten dollars. She'd recently refinanced their credit card debts with a demand loan, putting up with her bank manager's stench of Brut, menthol cigarettes and dirty stories about the indiscretions of his tellers (who were all nymphomaniacs, if he were to be believed). In addition to that loan and a mortgage, the Cunninghams also had a capital loan, a home equity loan plan, a chattel mortgage on their car and a fully extended line of credit. They were facing an avalanche of debt, armed with only a fistful of money-saving store coupons for things like Tie 'N' Toss Garbage Bags and Looney Tunes Meals. Each decade, Claire read a few financial articles – case studies about couples who were tucking away money for their nest-eggs, squirrel-like and far-sighted, a healthy chunk of each pay going straight into the bank. And with each decade, Claire fell further behind this mythical, penny-pinching couple who leaped ahead, gleefully compiling interest on their interest, socking money away for their children's educations and congratulating themselves on how *they* would never be a burden to anyone.

Claire was a feckless spendthrift, inheritor of the bad seed that plagued both her parents but had either skipped her grandfather's generation, or been temporarily disabled due to a lack of things to buy in the Ukrainian village where he spent much of his life. He'd been forced to leave his farm when it was collectivized by the Russians, and had come to Canada at the age of fifty, to work as a janitor, managing to save almost two hundred thousand before he died. He never paid a penny of interest and laughed contemptuously at those who did. Claire paid nothing but. If he could see the way she lived, it would kill him again.

At the moment, however, it was footwear and not interest payments that was her most pressing concern. Claire began walking along Bay Street, picking her feet up, nimble as a Lipizzaner, flinching from the scorch of pavement and sidewalk. Without so much as a glance she passed the glass and granite office tower that housed Bragg, Banks and Biltmore. (Had any of her colleagues been in the restaurant when she bolted, barefoot and pregnant, for the elevator, she worried. Had any *clients* been there?)

The first store she came to, and into which she ducked,

gratefully, was Woolworth's – a small shabby place dating back to the forties, complete with soda fountain, swivelling padded stools and lunch deals with names like Rib-B-Q Platter for only three dollars and thirty-three cents. Woolworth's had survived the brutal snobbishness of the financial district because it was the only place, within screaming distance of King and Bay Streets, that sold anything practical: needles and thread, bathroom tile caulking, Crazy Glue. Just inside the door was a dusty bin of beach shoes that Claire quickly dug through to find a pair of yellow thongs, size large. She undid the rubber band that held them together, eased them on to her stinging feet, and flip-flopped towards the cash desk to pay for them, feeling much better. Thongs were a marvellous invention – so comfortable, so airy and non-confining. Why had she never appreciated them before?

Leaving Woolworth's, well pleased with her new footwear, she walked a few blocks further uptown, a short while later stepping into the scented coolness of a giant department store. Claire's spirits soared. She'd only been off work for a few days, but already she'd been feeling disconnected, out of tune with the business and working world, cut off from the fluorescent glow of the shopping catacombs below her office tower. Now she was back! (If only for an hour or so.)

She traversed the main floor, trying to rid herself of the faint but unpleasant aftertaste of the lunch with Christine. She would be revealing her insecurity if she did as her sister suggested, gave in to her paranoia, and fired their new nanny. Didn't Ben deserve to be trusted? And Brita? Why should she be condemned as marriage-wrecker simply because she was beautiful? And shouldn't Claire's marriage to Ben be tested, if it came to that? If some domestic trauma as minor as hiring a nanny could split them apart, if Ben's commitment to her were not fundamentally sound, wouldn't it be better to find out now? Before they had more children? While Harry was young enough not to know the difference between a one- and a two-parent home?

Claire strolled past a rack of scarves, thinking briefly about Davina, then paused at a display of summer hats, remembering Christine's. She picked up a pale, straw-coloured one with a cluster of silk cornflowers at the back. Large people in hats only looked ridiculous, she reminded herself, like Petunia Pig or Elsie the Cow. And she was a large person now. She put the hat back on the mannequin.

Avoiding a rack of skinny belts, she bent to inspect a showcase of summer gloves – white, floral, fish-net and lacy. In case the Queen dropped in for tea, she supposed, or to wear to an IODE luncheon. Her hands were easily a full size larger than usual, she thought, holding them out, splay-fingered, above the glass of the counter. Two rows of cocktail sausages, they looked like – one of them with a wedding band cut deeply into the casing.

It was clear that finding something for herself was going to take a certain creativity. Since perfumes were still nauseating, she held her breath to detour past a bored-looking salesgirl who was standing by the escalator, waiting to spritz shoppers with an atomizer of the latest scent.

Discouraged, Claire turned around in a slow circle, trying to ensure that she'd seen all there was to see. There was nothing else on the main floor except for men's underwear and bathrobes. And cosmetics.

She flip-flopped over to a counter where an assortment of phials and test-tube-shaped bottles were arranged, picked one up and read its label, marvelling at the pseudo-scientific names given to these products. Ordinary words like 'cream', 'powder' and 'lotion' seemed to have been replaced by 'gels', 'balms' and 'benefits'. And all of them promised to stop, eliminate, or actually *reverse* the aging process. Reverse it! A fountain of youth for less than fifty bucks!

She opened a bottle and sniffed its contents, wondering about the legality of the claims on the label. It wasn't her field, advertising law. She and her clients conceived of trademarks – the names for all sorts of new products – that Claire then searched (making sure no one else had used them) before undertaking the tedious bureaucratic process of legally registering them. 'Age Reversal'. That was a good one. Too bad it wasn't one of hers. 'Wrinkle Attack Balm', however, was the brainchild of one of her clients – a good one too – with its intentional pun on the word 'bomb'. But the 'Age Soothing Gel' was even better. Its name conveyed the quintessential advertising message: promising a lot but delivering nothing. 'Age Soothing'. Claire turned the frosted glass bottle in her hands, agape with professional envy. One had to laugh, really, at the pathetic gullibility of some women. Claire bought a jar of it, about the size of her big toe (early-morning circumference) for sixty dollars.

It looked as though 'youth' was a dirty word in the cosmetics business, muscled aside by all sorts of 'anti-aging' products, as if the cosmetics industry had thrown up its hands and cried, 'Okay, ladies, we admit we're no longer young, but by God we're doing something about it!'

From the next counter over, a pleasant, smooth-faced man gave her a friendly, come-hither wave. 'Please par-*don* the nail colour,' he said, holding out a hand for her scrutiny. 'I had a lady who wouldn't try it on herself – she made me do it. Who would believe me in fuchsia!' He seemed in no great hurry to take the polish off and Claire suspected he would do the nails on his other hand too, when he had a chance. He studied her critically. 'Did you want something to perk up your complexion?' He lifted his precisely arched brows. 'Do you exfoliate regularly?'

'That's kind of personal, isn't it?' said Claire.

'Maybe you'd rather work on your make-up a tad. Now, this product – I was just showing it to another lady –' he squeezed some creamy white lotion on to a fingertip – 'is absolutely a-ma-zing. It's a base for your eyeshadow and lipstick – makes it stay perfect all day. It really works.'

'How would you know?'

'I use it myself.' He closed his eyes. 'See? I've had this shadow on since six this morning and it's not creasing.' He was right. No crease. And his mascara was perfect too. Not a smudge. Taken aback, Claire wondered what his mother would think if she could see him now. Might this be Harry in eighteen or twenty years? 'This product line has a fabulous moisturizer too,' he continued enthusiastically. 'Here, let me touch your face.'

Reluctantly, Claire offered him a cheek.

'I knew it!' He let out a little scream. 'Your skin is *crying* for moisture. And you with a baby on the way.' He clucked and shook his head. 'You need to take better care of yourself, pamper yourself. You're all you've got, you know. Here, touch

my face, luv.' He grabbed Claire's hand and stroked his cheek
with it. 'See how good it feels? Sort of springy?'

'You're a few years younger than I am.' Claire withdrew
her hand.

'Doesn't matter. I drink, I smoke. I party all night.'

'Shame on you.'

'But that's how *your* skin should feel. Moist. Tacky. This is one
place where tacky is good.' He sighed, those arches of concern
once more rippling over his nicely tacky forehead. 'So what are
we going to do for you today?'

Claire eventually decided on an intriguing gel with mysterious
blue threads swirled through it – the 'age-dedicated microsomes',
foot soldiers in the war against aging – and a 'Time Smoothing
Day Block, SPF 40'. Both of these, the young man assured her,
would make her skin more 'manageable'.

'Have you got a card for our products?' he asked. 'If you buy
two hundred and fifty dollars' worth, you get a free tote-bag. It's
vinyl but everyone will think it's patent leather. I had to sniff it
myself to be sure.'

'No, I don't have your card,' Claire said, though she had a
wallet already bulging with a pantyhose card, a haircut card,
a movie rental card, a coffee card, a bagel-with-cream-cheese
card. She even had a card card, from the card shop in the second
sub-level of her office building's concourse.

The young man cheerfully filled out a small rectangle of pink
cardboard, entering in the amount of Claire's purchases, then
folded it over and pressed it into her palm. 'There you go,' he said
warmly, 'you've got a good start on your tote-bag already. But
I'd save up the points if I were you. After five hundred dollars,
you get a real washable silk kimono.'

Claire thanked him for his advice and left him to finish doing
his nails. Then she drifted, barge-like, to another counter where
the salesgirl gave her a sympathetic look. 'Any day now, eh?' she
said, indicating Claire's belly.

'Yes, thankfully.'

'Your first?'

Claire nodded.

'Wow. That's so exciting. I hope someday I'll have a little girl.'
She looked again, wistfully, at Claire's enormity.

'It's a boy,' Claire admitted, feeling absurdly apologetic.

'I'd want a boy too, eventually. You're so lucky. And you already know what it is. That's so great. But I'd want to be surprised.'

'It was a surprise.' Claire noticed there was no wedding band on the girl's finger. She bought a 'PM Time-Zone Repair' that smelled like Estée Lauder's armpit and had to be applied to the skin around her eyes with a glass eye-dropper. She wanted some nail polish but it seemed to have been replaced by 'Liquid Nail Wraps' full of 'Calcium-bonding Complex'. How many complexes did the modern woman need, she wondered.

'Treating yourself today?' The girl smiled, totalling up Claire's bill. Claire nodded, perspiring heavily. 'Good. You deserve it.' She slid the charge-card slip over the counter. 'Just sign here, Mrs . . .' she tilted her head to read the name, 'Cunningham. And listen, good luck with that baby!'

Claire's purchases, so far, totalled one hundred and eighty dollars. She felt better – a lot better. She knew her exhilaration was only temporary, and that as soon as she unpacked the rustling tissues, slid off the gold cords, peeled back the silver seals and found herself with only a small pile of plastic tubes and a mountain of new debt, she would come crashing down to new lows, just like a junkie. But at that moment, she was enjoying the discovery that there were all sorts of things that a heavily pregnant woman, with a much younger husband who'd just hired a gorgeous Swedish nanny, could justify buying on a torpid summer afternoon. She still had almost an hour before her dental appointment. A lot could be accomplished in very limited time, when a woman had a strong sense of purpose.

Her purchases rattling, clattering and tumbling in the thin plastic bags that the store had provided, Claire waddled blithely over to the bank of public telephones near the elevators. Why not check in with Davina, she thought, see what was up back at the ranch. Ben need never know. After all, she was back in *her* world now, even though it was just temporarily.

Davina's phone was snatched up midway through the first ring. 'Claire! Thank God you called. Listen. They want your general file on the Coastal Bank,' she said, sotto voce.

'Who does?'

'*They*. Rick Durham and Mr Biltmore. God knows who else.'

'Well, give it to them.'

'I don't have to give it. They *took* it!'

'It's not as though I can do anything with it, is it? Besides, it's a dog file. One of those hounds from hell.'

'But that's not all that's going on around here.'

Claire swallowed. Her hands, gripping the department store bags and telephone receiver, were damp. 'So?' she said lightly. 'What else is new?'

'Someone's been into your office—'

'Davina, lots of people will be in my office over the summer. You've got to accept that—'

'And measured it!'

'Measured it?' Claire said faintly.

'*Yes! They measured it!* With a tape measure! Look, I've got to go – someone's coming.'

The line went dead, leaving Claire to gape at the receiver and clutch her shopping bags as if they were a lifeline. Silly, Davina was being silly, she told herself. She had a flair for the melodramatic, that woman did, always had. This sort of thing was exactly what Davina craved: lots of cloak-and-dagger intrigue over missing files and offices being measured and what-not. Ben was right. Davina was bad news for the diastolic pressure. Claire tried to laugh, then wondered who else she might call. Shelagh might be in – but she didn't feel like talking to anyone else from the office, not really. Not any more.

Harry did a giant flutterkick just then, as if to remind his mother that he was still around and anxious to be born. Claire put down her bags to give him a loving rub, then took up the telephone receiver again and dialled her home number, longing to hear Ben's warm voice, with its endearing boyish crack. But Ben didn't answer. He would be studying of course, Claire reminded herself, with those headphones over his ears. Her own annoying voice invited her to leave a message. She hung up, then dropped another quarter into the coin slot and dialled the number of Ben's pager. It vibrated, she knew, and was usually attached to his belt – even with headphones on he would notice a call. Happily, she punched in the numbers of the public telephone for him to dial back. When he phoned, she meant to ask him what he thought Christine could possibly have been talking about when she'd gone on about doctors' pagers, making sinister and puzzling suggestions about who answered them. Claire smiled to herself as she waited, anticipating Ben's voice, his surprise at her call, his eagerness to chat. But though she stood there for fifteen minutes waiting for him to return her page, the telephone never rang back.

Eventually, hoisting the bags of cosmetics over her shoulder and no longer smiling, Claire flip-flopped out of the department store to stand on the street corner where she waited, through seven traffic light changes, until she managed to flag down an available cab to take her to her dentist.

7

VOLUNTEER AT LARGE it said on his badge, and he was eyeing Claire's suitcase with suspicion. 'I hope that ain't as heavy as it looks,' he said.

'Don't trouble yourself,' said Claire. 'I can manage.'

'You're a lot younger than me. I didn't volunteer to be no red cap. I volunteered to be a Volunteer.'

Feeling vaguely guilty, though she was the one in labour and carrying not only the heavy suitcase but an extra sixty pounds of baby, amniotic fluid and fat, Claire plodded after him down the hospital corridor. As they waited for the elevator, the Volunteer scowled again at her bag. 'So what you got in there? Books?'

'I do have a few,' she confessed, 'but they're small . . . paperbacks. Baby books mostly. Some files too.'

'Files? You mean, like work?'

'They said it could take a while, having the baby. I like to keep busy.'

The Volunteer shook his head. 'When my wife went in for her kids the only kind of file she would've had with her was a nail file.' He jabbed irritably at the UP button of the elevator. 'Some people bring a whole library with 'em when they come in here. I can't deal with that. I'm an old man.'

It was his job to show Claire to her room on the labour floor and it was hard to imagine a less appealing tour guide, or labour floor. The corridors were dingy – a greyish-blue with wan pink borders – someone's idea of making the place look cheerful and baby-like, Claire supposed; and perhaps it had had that effect back in the sixties when it was last painted. Bits of faded tinsel decorations from some long-ago Christmas clung to the walls with aging yellowed tape.

Claire's room had the same grimy paint, but two of the walls were papered in a bright floral, and an attractive butterfly mobile floated over the birthing bed – a padded, sectional table at the end of which a pair of stirrups jutted, and over which someone had popped a pair of striped oven mitts. To help get that bun out of the oven, Claire thought with a nervous smile. Also over the bed was a large convex mirror, the kind convenience store owners use to watch for shoplifters. Claire wondered why anyone would want a mirror over this particular type of bed. She should have known, but she'd avoided pre-natal classes and hospital tours, not wanting to hear other women's horror stories. She was a worrier, and the less she knew about what was going to happen to her, the better. She would deal with whatever happened, when it happened, as she dealt with most things in life. Somehow. The childbirth books were disturbing enough – the photographs of husbands ineffectually holding up pastel teddy bears; the agony on the women's faces in labour; the blissful mental wasteland afterwards.

Beside the birthing bed was a square machine that was humming in a businesslike way, with a strip of paper threaded across the front of it and a twinkling panel of lights; behind that an oxygen mask and IV pole, neither of which Claire would have any use for, she decided. Then she was suddenly aware that the Volunteer-at-Large was still there in the room with her, as if waiting for a tip.

'Could you open a window for me?' she asked, thinking she should give him something to do.

'They're painted shut,' he replied peevishly.

'It's so stuffy in here, I thought—'

'Air conditioning don't work neither.' The Volunteer grinned, looking satisfied. 'Well, I'll be getting along. They keep us volunteers busy around here. Too busy, if you want my opinion.'

Claire thanked him as graciously as she could for his help, though he hadn't been of any, and she was rather offended by his attitude. She was, after all, the patient – a woman in labour – and she didn't see why anyone who *volunteered* to help out in a hospital needed to be so cranky about it.

She put her bag down and went over to the window to twiddle ineffectually with the air-conditioning knob. It was a clear summer day outside, perfect to introduce Harry to the world. She felt a surge of happiness, the crabby Volunteer forgotten. The hospital's parking lot was directly below her window. She couldn't see Ben, or their car. She wondered what was taking him so long.

She'd woken up suddenly, at four in the morning, to find herself in soaked sheets. Trying not to panic, she'd nudged Ben awake. He'd gone into the bathroom, stumbled around finding his medical bag, and returned with a strip of chemically treated paper to confirm that it was amniotic fluid there all over the bed. 'But it can't be!' Claire had protested weakly. She wasn't ready for Harry; he wasn't due for another few days. 'Better bring forward that date in your diary,' Ben yawned as he'd climbed back into bed. Then he rolled over and, patting her hand and telling her there was no rush, was soon snoring lightly. Shivering with excitement, Claire had gone into Harry's room to twitch smooth his bassinet sheets, realign his pile of folded diapers and pick up bits of lint from the carpet, as if expecting some very particular house-guest. She did a load of laundry, then turned the dishwasher on – something she never did in the daytime. Ben got up to take a shower – she heard him curse as the hot water dribbled to nothing – but when he came out of the bathroom, a towel around his waist, he was whistling. He got their camera from where it was waiting in readiness by the front door and steered Claire into Harry's room to photograph her from several angles, standing beside the bassinet and doing her best to smile.

Claire's contractions, if that's what they were, were no more than a vague cramping and pulling sensation – too diffuse to time. They felt strange, but were not actually painful. According to Ben, they hadn't really started at all, but Claire didn't see what he could know – really know – about it.

Feeling calm and in control of things now, she got undressed and put on two hospital gowns, one open at the back, the other at the front, so that her girth was completely covered. She had to wonder at all the fuss about childbirth – all that screaming, panting and eye-rolling, the clutching of bed-posts and sheets she'd seen in movies and heard about from friends and relatives.

There was nothing to it, she thought, as she folded her clothes and put them in the dented locker at the opposite end of the room. Beside the locker was another padded table, with an incubator-type lamp hanging over it. On top of the table was a clear plastic tub, weigh-scale, measuring tape, tiny white toque and flannel gown, a stack of blue flannel (receiving?) blankets and a paper diaper. No point making a fuss over the diaper, she decided, one or two paper ones couldn't do much harm. She approved of the determined optimism conveyed by the arrangement of things on that table. Of course Harry was on his way, of course he would be healthy and need a flannel gown and diaper, of course he would have only one head, need only one toque . . . There were also two blue wristbands on the table, one large, one small. She picked them up. 'Cunningham, Boy' it said on each one, 'Mother – Claire'. The bands were joined together. The symbolism of that made her lower lip quiver, so she quickly put them down and climbed up on to the bed, drawing the curtains around it. Then she lay back, her head and shoulders propped on a lumpy foam pillow. Harry seemed to be going crazy, jabbing and poking at her, impatient to get out. As she watched her stomach roll and twitch and rumble, the bed-curtains were jerked apart by a harassed-looking nurse.

'You're all settled in, I see,' she said. 'Has the doctor had a look at you?'

'No.'

'They'll be along eventually. You're not in active labour yet.'

'How can you tell?'

She gave Claire a knowing glance. 'You're not in enough pain.' Then she went about being brisk and nurse-like, ripping apart the wristbands and snapping the larger one on to Claire's wrist, taking her pulse, blood pressure and temperature, buckling across Claire's belly the fetal monitor belt that was attached to the humming machine. She switched on the monitor and the paper tape started to move across it, a needle-like pen graphically recording Harry's heartbeat.

'How do you know I'm not in enough pain?' Claire said. 'Maybe I have a high pain threshold. You can't feel what I'm feeling right now, can you?'

The nurse ignored her. From her pocket she took a scrap of

paper on which were some scribbled notes. The grubby pink stethoscope slung around her neck had a baby's ID bracelet twined around it: a strand of pink, blue and white ceramic beads.

'Can I get a bracelet like that for my son?' Claire asked, feeling a sudden urge to shop.

'They don't make these any more. Too dangerous. The baby could choke on a bead if the string broke.' Both legs of her pantyhose had runs, Claire noticed, as she leaned across the bed to reposition the oxygen mask on its pole. 'Have you talked to the anaesthetist about your epidural?'

Claire had been anticipating such a question. 'I'm not having one,' she said firmly. 'My doctor and my husband have been given strict instructions. I don't care if I beg and plead, I don't want one. Millions of women have given birth without an anaesthetic. I don't see why everyone just assumes a woman wants an epidural. In my office, all of the women expect to have C-sections – as if that's now the normal way to give birth. They want them booked in advance.' Claire twitched her hospital gown smooth, feeling very much on the moral high ground.

'We'll see what you have to say a little later.' With another smug smile the nurse left, her crepe-soled shoes making sucking sounds on the tiled floor.

Claire knew her game: she only wanted her anaesthetized so Claire would be less trouble, to make her own life easier. Hospitals had the wrong attitude. The health of the baby and mother should be most important, not the convenience of the staff. And the nurse was obviously mistaken about her labour not being active. As she settled back against the blocky rubber pillow, sulking about having been assigned a labour room nurse who obviously didn't know what she was talking about, a telephone rang. It was on the wall by the locker. It couldn't be for her. Could it? She undid the monitor belt and struggled down off the bed to answer it.

'Thank heaven I caught you!' It was Davina. 'I hope you're not in the middle of something . . .'

'I'm in the hospital – in labour. What's the matter?'

'I was wondering if Mr Potochnik ever got out to see you. He keeps calling. He's making me crazy. I knew you were touchy about having your phone number given out, so I gave him your address.'

'You gave my address to a stranger?'

There was a pause on the line. 'I thought he was an old friend of yours.'

'His father knows my father. We're hardly friends.'

'Well, sorry. I didn't think you'd mind. I thought maybe he was going to bring you a baby gift. He came in demanding to see you – he was upset when I told him you were already on maternity leave.'

Potochnik. Claire frowned. 'I gave you his file to close out. And I gave him the name of another lawyer if he needed anything else done.'

'He wouldn't talk to anyone but you. Hold on.' Silence. There was no music, no a.m. radio, no beeps to indicate that Claire was still on hold and hadn't been cut off. Her bare feet were cold on the tiled floor. 'Sorry – there was someone hovering around my desk. And that's another thing. Am I supposed to just hand over any of your files to anyone who wants them? This is not a one-time event. It's happening practically every day.'

'Someone has to look after my practice. No one can do my work without seeing my files. Besides, I've got nothing to hide – they're all in good shape.' She thought uneasily about the odd grocery list that slipped in between pieces of correspondence now and then; the tampon that had rolled out of a file while she was standing in the middle of the office. 'You dropped this,' one of the (young) (male) (single) lawyers said, scooping it up and handing it to her. 'What is it? Some kind of pen?'

Claire shifted the receiver from one hand to the other, wiping her free hand on her hospital gown. 'I can't get involved in this sort of intrigue right now, Davina. I'm supposed to stay calm.'

At that moment, Ben arrived with a pile of fashion magazines, a grease-spotted deli bag and a large brown envelope. 'What do you think you're doing?' He grabbed the receiver from Claire's hand. 'Buzz off, Davina,' he said into it. 'Your boss is in labour, okay? Call back in about six weeks.' He hung up and prodded Claire back into bed where he rebuckled the fetal monitor, grumbling about Claire's health and Harry's well-being. 'What would you do without guys like me,' he said, 'you type-A women lawyers?'

'Actually, I wish you wouldn't interfere with my practice.'

'The one you want to give up? That one?'

'I never said I was giving it up.' Claire's thoughts were flitting anxiously from client to client, lawyer to lawyer. Who was it who was always wanting her files? She hadn't had a chance to ask Davina. Her belly was twitching and cramping, Harry doing what seemed to be a dance of rage in there, pummelling his mother, demanding her attention.

Then the nurse materialized again to confiscate Ben's deli bag. Claire was not to eat anything, she warned, in case there were complications.

'Isn't starvation a complication?' Claire joked.

Ben and the nurse looked at her as if to say they didn't think she was in much danger of that, but a few minutes later a lady wearing a blue smock and a hairnet brought in some high-protein Jello and a cup of weak tea. Claire sipped the tea, tasted a spoonful of the Jello and pushed the tray away. 'I've gained sixty pounds in the last nine months and now they want to put me on a diet.' She paused. The nurse was speaking to someone in the corridor. 'They've already started pushing the epidural,' she told Ben in a low voice.

'I warned you.'

'I'm not having one. You know that.'

Ben was silent.

'Well? Isn't that what we agreed?'

'It's up to you. You're the one who has to go through labour.'

'I'm doing it without an epidural. Let's not discuss it any more. Pass me a magazine, please.'

Together, they flipped through the magazines, then filled out the hospital's menu card, though Ben said Claire would be discharged long before that particular meal showed up. Then they tried to time Claire's contractions. They felt like strong menstrual cramps, about twenty minutes apart, ebbing and flowing – nothing that a couple of extra-strength Tylenols couldn't relieve. Claire's excitement was beginning to wane, especially after the nurse told her that things could continue on in much the same way for hours, unless she wanted to be put on an oxytocin drip to speed things up. She didn't. She picked up a magazine again. Maybe, she thought, Harry was a phlegmatic baby who would reward her for her patience by popping out easily with a minimum of fuss and bother – and sleep through the night from day one. But they didn't want him too phlegmatic, did they? She felt a small tingle of fear. What if there was something *wrong* with him?

Ben leaned across her bed and studied the long strip of paper, like ticker-tape, that was looping out of the fetal monitor and piling up on the floor. 'How many trees died to record young Harry's heartbeat?' he mused, studying the jagged ink lines. 'Looks like it's slowing down a bit.' He frowned. 'No – there, it's up again. Poor little fellow. What a trauma.' He sat down again. 'How do you feel?'

'Fine. A bit bored actually.'

'Things'll pick up. Especially if you go for the drip.'

'I won't.'

'Harry could be out in a couple of hours if you did.'

'No.'

'We could order a pizza after.'

'Haven't you ever heard of letting nature take its course?' Claire opened her magazine. 'What's wrong with you medical people?'

Ben just yawned and opened his brown envelope to shake a few slides on to the bed. 'I picked these up yesterday from the photo lab. Some of them are beautiful. Want to see?'

'I wish you'd put them away, Ben. Can't we share this time together? Without your slides?'

He sighed and scooped up the slides, pausing to admire a couple before dropping them back into the envelope. 'You're going to be too busy to care about what I'm doing. Screaming, swearing.'

'Hardly.'

'But if you don't want me to make good use of my time I'll just sit here like a dummy. Maybe look through this *Vogue* again.' He settled back on the naugahyde chair to give Claire a mournful look. He was wearing his hospital greens – baggy drawstring pants, a loose-fitting V-neck shirt with short sleeves in which no one could possibly look good – all of it approximately the same colour as the chair. 'One of the staff guys is going to take call for me for a couple days after Harry arrives. He doesn't have to – it's very nice of him.'

'Ben?' Claire looked up suddenly from a fashion photo of a scowling stick of a woman, dressed in a beaded evening gown, knee-deep in mud, a dead fish on her head. 'Who answers your pager when it goes off?'

'I do.'

'Even when you're in surgery? When you're scrubbed?'

'No. You can't touch anything when you're sterile.'

'So who presses the button and reads you the pager message?'

Ben cleared his throat. 'One of the nurses – usually.'

'But where is the pager when you're scrubbed in?'

'What do you mean, where?'

'Is it on a table? Is it in the operating room?'

'It's where it always is. On my belt.'

'On your pants. At the front. Above your fly. There?'

'On my greens. So what? Where is this line of questioning going, Counsellor?'

'So – how does this nurse person get it?'

'The *nurse person* just grabs the pager, turns it on and reads it. What's the big interest in my pager all of a sudden?'

'Let me understand this,' Claire barrelled on, wishing she could stop herself from putting to him the inevitable question, 'your pager goes off – and some nurse – reaches up under your shirt and grabs it from the front of your pants?'

'That's about it.'

'So you get felt up every time I page you.'

'If that's the way you want to think about it—'

'And sometimes I have to page you three or four times before you answer. And each of these times some nurse person has her hand down your pants?'

'Claire. Come on. If you'd ever been in an OR you'd know it's not like that – how crazy you sound—'

'So a four-pager must mean the nurse is attractive. When you answer right away, she's no day at the beach? Am I right? Or else it's a male nurse – the one-pager?'

'You'd laugh at your fears if you could be there—'

'Fears? I'm not *afraid*. I'm just surprised that this sort of thing goes on in an operating room.'

'What *sort of thing*?'

'And that you've never bothered to mention this detail of

your work until now – until I mentioned it, until Christine brought it up.'

'I might have known she was behind this.'

'Why not let your wife relax for a while?' The nurse, who'd never really gone anywhere, was checking the monitor again. 'Go downstairs, buy a box of chocolate cigars. I told you this could go on for ever without much change. The doctor'll be up in a few minutes.'

'Do you want me to stay?' Ben asked Claire.

'I guess not. If it's going to be a while . . . you don't have to.' Claire's attention was suddenly focused again on the daunting reason she was there in that birthing room. The pager issue would have to be stored away in a corner of her mind to be examined later, when there was less pressing business at hand. 'If nothing's happening, you might as well go get some food for yourself. But don't go far, okay?

'Doctors are never any good when it comes to their families, are they?' Claire said to the nurse after Ben had gone. 'Especially surgeons.'

The nurse whisked the curtains closed around the bed, clearly unimpressed by hearing that Ben was a surgeon. With a lawyer wife in labour. It was probably her worst nightmare. She would be pitying the obstetrician, the residents, herself. Maybe she would be lucky and go off shift before the delivery. 'Now, you give a holler if the contractions start coming faster,' she said. 'They're going to talk to you about the drip and the epidural. Your OBGYN's not on tonight – the one covering for him has a dinner party – so they'd like to get things over with. Dr Butt would.'

Claire scowled. Butt? A dinner party? Get things over with? Induced labours were rougher, she knew that much, the contractions uneven and too close together. And she was expected to endure that because of some doctor's *dinner party*? 'Tell him I won't be needing him then,' she sniffed.

'She,' the nurse said. 'Doris Butt.'

Claire chewed her lower lip from one side to the other, trying to digest the unpalatable idea of an induced labour with the sadistic Doris Butt manning the oxytocin drip, anxious not to miss a single chilled shrimp or watered-down drink at her dinner party. 'Forget it,' she said.

The nurse wheeled the IV pole closer to Claire's bed and checked her watch. 'I'll go and see if Dr Butt's on the floor yet.'

Less than an hour later, Claire was spread-eagled, her bare feet straining against the striped oven mitts, purple-faced and pushing hard enough to blow an artery while a gaggle of nurses, interns, residents, and Dr Butt stared at her crotch and engaged in a sometimes acrimonious debate over whether or not *The Phantom of the Opera* was really a true opera. Claire clung to Ben, gripping his greens in her teeth, sobbing that she couldn't live through another contraction, begging for an epidural. But it was too late. Her body was a runaway train over which she had lost all control. It was screaming on towards the station, turning Claire inside out with the force of it.

'Come on, Claire! Work at it,' Ben was urging.

'You've got to work hard!'

'You can do it, Claire!'

'Okay! Claire? Don't push yet!'

'Now! Push now!'

'Work! Work at it! Push!'

Then Harry's head was crowning between her legs – a tiny, fuzzy red dome she could see in the mirror above where she lay, spread out like one of Ben's lab specimens. She was pushing and swearing and sweating so hard that she didn't even feel the snip of the scissors cutting her flesh – the dreaded episiotomy, another thing she'd decided never to allow.

Ben produced a video camera from somewhere and began recording *cinéma vérité* footage.

'Look at that lovely strawberry blond hair,' someone remarked conversationally. Claire barely had a chance to yell at Ben to get the fucking camera away from her crotch before Harry plopped out, with a lusty primal scream and a gush of body fluids.

It would be some time before Claire realized that that lusty primal scream, and those fluids, had been her own.

8

They brought Harry home on the first of July, though Claire wouldn't have known what day it was, if anyone had asked. She'd only been in the hospital for forty-eight hours, but had ceased to care about time, and the fact that June had slipped into July entirely escaped her notice. She would later look back on that summer and remember it only in terms of events that occurred either before Harry, or after.

Outside the hospital, the world was too bright, glaring with an intensity that hurt her eyes. As soon as she passed through the revolving glass doors, Ben behind her clutching Harry in his car seat, she wanted to scurry back into the cosy security of the hospital with its grimy corridors and churlish staff, and burrow into the soiled sheets of her unmade bed. She leaned on Ben – though not enough to endanger Harry's safety – as they crossed the dazzling expanse of asphalt parking lot, like desert survivors making their tedious way towards a twinkling mirage of parked cars.

As they drove east from downtown, Claire fretted over Harry's comfort, fiddling with the sun shades Ben had stuck to the car windows with rubber suction cups. The shades were a nuisance, tending to roll up suddenly with a 'flubbata' sound, or pop off altogether. Even when they stayed in place, the sun always seemed to come into the car at such an angle that it smacked Harry in the face, making him blink and frown in consternation.

Claire and Ben had been rather taken aback at first by the look of their son – his tiny head elongated from the squeeze down the birth canal, patchy tufts of downy red-blond hair, a large purple bruise in the middle of his forehead and one eye glued shut with the ointment that had been squeezed into it within seconds of his appearance. By early evening, however, his face had settled into a perfect oval shape and his bright blue eyes were looking inquisitively at them from below the knitted white toque that had been popped on his head to keep him warm.

'I've been thinking,' Ben said from the front seat, 'about Brita.'

'What about her?'

'About her room, actually, not so much her.'

Claire bent her head over Harry, rubbing his cheek with hers, waiting to hear what Ben had to say.

'I thought maybe we should get her a new TV. The one that's down there is pretty gross, and there's no cable on it.'

'It works, doesn't it?'

'But it's black and white.'

'We don't have the money for a new TV. Cable maybe. Besides, she's not our house-guest. She'll probably be going out a lot at night, not sitting in our basement watching *Wheel of Fortune*.'

'Maybe. But I want to make sure she's comfortable, happy with us, so she'll stick around. You're the one who'll have to start interviewing to find a replacement if she quits. My next rotation's going to be very busy. Very busy.'

'Rotation. What a word. I always picture you residents as a bunch of spinning tops, rotating here, rotating there, in your white coats, pockets stuffed with rubber mallets.'

'Reflex hammers. And surgeons don't carry them.' Ben drove in silence for a few moments. 'My point is, I won't be there to help if you run into trouble with nannies quitting every other week. And we were lucky to have found someone as good as Brita so fast.'

'If she quits over something as trivial as a television set, who needs her?' Claire tucked Harry's blanket more snugly around him. The way he was bundled up – a sleeper, a shawl and blanket, a lacy crocheted cap and tiny mittens to keep him from scratching his face – one would have thought it was the dead of winter outside. Though he didn't seem to mind. Harry was going to be the quintessential nice guy, Claire decided. He'd hardly cried at all since he was born.

'I was only thinking of you,' Ben said.

'So I'll consider your suggestion,' Claire said, 'one of these days.' As she spoke, a blue helium-filled balloon – a great bunch of them had been sent to the hospital by Christine – bobbed into her face. IT'S A BOY!! the lettering screamed. 'These silly balloons . . .' She pushed it away.

'I don't know why we had to bring them home—'

'Only three.'

'They're obscuring my rearview.'

Claire grabbed the ribbons that trailed from the balloons and tugged to pull them down from where they were clinging to the roof of the car. On the seat beside her were Ben's flowers – a tight-packed, symmetrical arrangement of carnations and roses, the carnations dyed blue to match the IT'S A BOY! plastic scrollwork sign, the whole thing stuffed into a ceramic container shaped like a catcher's mitt. It seemed that everywhere Claire looked over the past two days something shouted IT'S A BOY! at her. Shouldn't it properly say HE'S A BOY, she'd mused as a toy wagon, piled high with booties, bibs, plush toys and candy – a gift from her firm – was wheeled into her room.

Also on the car seat beside Claire were Ben's other gifts: a pair of earrings in the shape of diaper pins and an over-sized T-shirt with a screaming baby and THE CALL OF THE CHILD lettered on the front of it. 'That's to replace your WOMB WITH A VIEW shirt,' Ben had chuckled. Finally, there was a wall plaque with a wood-burned line drawing on it of a man and woman in bed, both wearing night-caps and looking panic-stricken. At the top of the plaque were the words I GOT UP LAST! IT'S YOUR TURN! and below the bed was a dial that was to be turned to point at either the mom or the dad. UP NEXT! it said. 'I had it glued to stick permanently on the *mom* side.' Ben had given one of his hearty belly-laughs as Claire tried to move the pointer. She'd looked at him, wondering which of several replies she had in mind he most deserved. At moments like that, she had to struggle to avoid comparing him to Simon, with his knack for finding elegant and romantic presents and composing rhyming couplets or haiku to go with them. But then, if she were with Simon he'd still be researching the diaper pail – with or without a holder for the deodorant pellet? With or without a snap-on lid?

A pedal mechanism? They'd have argued bitterly over the baby's name, over whether to have a baby at all . . . She looked at the back of Ben's head and sighed happily.

'Oh yeah,' he said, 'did I mention that Brita's already started with us?'

'Since when?' Claire was shocked.

'Yesterday. She was kicked out of her friends' place early. They decided to go away for the summer and wanted to close up their house. She said she could find somewhere else to stay, but I didn't see any problem with her starting early.'

'But Ben, we talked about this. We agreed she would start in September. We can't afford to pay her for July and August. And we don't need her. I'm going to be home with Harry.'

'Listen to this – she's willing to help you out for *free*, just to have a place to crash and stash her gear.'

'Crash, gear, stash? She used those words?'

'She's young. Give her a break. Besides, you should be glad. Wait until you see the house. Think how nice it will be for you to have everything cleaned, meals made, from the minute you get home with Harry.'

Claire didn't think it sounded at all nice; it sounded more like a horrid, unwelcome intrusion. 'So she's there now? She'll be there when we get home?'

'Waiting with open arms to take Harry and let you get some rest.'

'I don't want her to take Harry. I don't need any rest.' Claire's emotions were on the rise; it wouldn't take much to push her into hysteria. 'I want some private time alone, just the three of us. You've only got a couple of days off.'

Ben sighed, tapping his wedding ring on the steering-wheel. 'If that's how you feel, I'll tell her to find somewhere else to stay. It's as simple as that.'

Claire's eyes met her husband's in the rearview. 'Isn't that how *you* feel?' she said.

'In a way.'

'You could have warned me, you could have *asked* if it was okay with me.'

'I thought I had . . . told you. Look, she's a foreigner, and she's our responsibility. I mean, we hired her. And her room was all ready. I didn't think it was such a big deal.' As usual, when Ben knew he'd done something wrong, his mood turned quickly to anger. 'You're hormonally overloaded, Claire. What woman in her right mind would complain about having *free help* for two months? I thought you'd be thrilled about the great deal I negotiated on your behalf. It was going to be a surprise.'

'You just said you thought you'd told me! You didn't mean it as a surprise! I may be hormonally overloaded but I'm not as stupid as you obviously think!' Claire seethed in the back seat, her hand on Harry's steady-breathing warmth. She swallowed, self-pity yanking at her, her jaw tightening, a lump in her throat. Her eyes, as she looked at her new son, misted.

Ben glanced at her in the rearview. 'Please don't cry, Claire. I'm sorry. Look, I'll stop the car right now. I'll find a phone booth, call Brita and tell her to pack up and leave before we get there.'

'Of course you can't do that!'

'I can and I will.' Ben slowed the car down and flipped on the four-way flashers, looking for a place to pull over.

Claire closed her eyes. 'Don't stop the car. I can deal with this. We can't throw Brita out.'

'I'm pulling over.' The car swerved to the side of the road.

'I said *don't*! It's too dangerous!'

A passing motorist, confused by the erratic movement of the Cunninghams' car, blared his horn at them and yelled 'Asshole!' through his window. Ben turned off the emergency flashers and sighed. 'It's up to you.'

Harry, who'd been quietly dozing, opened his eyes suddenly, screwed up his face and let out a shriek of rage. His eyes glistened with fury as his face changed rapidly from pink to red to purple.

'Can't you do something?' Ben said anxiously.

'Like what?'

'Nurse him!'

'I can't nurse him now! He's in his car seat! And I fed him just before we left the hospital. He can't possibly be hungry.' Claire watched her son in alarm. He'd cried in the hospital but not like this, with such intensity. She jiggled his car seat. Harry screamed louder. 'Just get us home, Ben. Okay?'

They made good time on the expressway, though its whizzing cars, clattering tractor-trailers, tangle of exit and entrance ramps and forced lane changes left Claire haggard with anxiety. Everything was moving too fast, careening on towards certain disaster, carrying the three Cunninghams in their little car away with it.

The traffic was more congested than usual as they finally turned off the expressway towards the Beach. 'What are all these people doing out here?' Claire demanded, struggling to be heard over Harry's cries.

'It's Canada Day.' Ben was tight-lipped with tension. 'We were nuts to buy a house at the end of the Beach.' Frustrated, he eased into the right lane and turned on to Queen Street. They bumped slowly along, Harry's howls subsiding marginally.

Canada Day? The thought depressed Claire. Hardly surprising since just about everything seemed to have that effect on her lately. She'd sobbed over the wording of Harry's birth announcement in the newspaper, broken down at the sight of a premature baby in the hospital nursery, and wept a pailful of tears over Harry's circumcision, which Ben maintained was essential for health and sanitary reasons (and, more to the point, Ben was circumcized himself).

But wasn't there something inherently sad about Canada Day? Maybe because it was so unimaginatively named. Calling it Canada Day was so lacking in imagination, like the flag. A red maple leaf with a couple of borders tacked on for symmetry. Why hadn't they used *Castor canadesis*, the Canadian beaver? Surrounded by shimmering sea-to-seas, a panoply of maple leaves, a criss-cross of wheat sheaves, a border of lingcod? With the aurora borealis boldly rendered in the background? The Cunninghams' house had a flag holder built into the front. Where did one buy a flag, Claire wondered. Was there a Ministry of Flags and Official Symbols somewhere? If so, they would likely be out of flags; they would have been on back-order for months; no one would have any idea when the next shipment would be in. And where were they coming from anyway? Korea? Taiwan? All Claire had was a tiny lapel pin of the Canadian flag that she'd pinned on Harry's diaper bag. It was a thank-you bonus the book store gave out for buying a Canadian author. In hard cover only.

Despondently, she stared at the crowds waiting outside Lick's for ice-cream and jamming Kew Beach Park, lining up at the band shell for fifty-cent hotdogs and Cokes. She felt a cry coming on, desperately wanted to hang her head out the window and howl. Blinking rapidly, she looked over at Harry, new Canadian, wailing miserably in his car seat.

'Are you okay?' Ben asked, with another worried glance in the rearview mirror.

Claire only shook her head, knowing that nothing she said would make any sense to him. How could it, when it barely made sense to her?

Their house, as they pulled into the driveway, looked shabby, almost menacingly so, as if not-nice things were going on behind those drawn vertical blinds. Flies buzzed and settled on the garbage cans at the side; the front walk looked more cracked and uneven than Claire remembered it. The lawn was a carpet of weeds; the front porch on the verge of collapse. Was this the best that they, a doctor and a lawyer, could do for Harry? The safest, most pleasant environment they could provide?

And things were not right inside the house; something was different; there had been changes. Claire noticed as soon as she crossed the transom. Minor things perhaps, but they were important to Claire. The tea-towels in the kitchen, for instance, were damply folded, neatly piled – she could see them on the counter from where she stood. She always hung them over the oven door handle. How else could they be expected to dry? The dishwasher was churning industriously, squirting and spinning. Claire never used it in the middle of the day. It made the kitchen too hot in summer, for one thing, putting unnecessary strain on the air conditioner, and it made more sense to wait until the end of the day, when the dinner dishes could be added to the load. In the living-room, the back cushions on the love seat had been turned to stand up on their corners in three dizzying diamond shapes instead of the neatly aligned squares that Claire preferred, and one of her best place-mats had been turned into an antimacassar for the back of a wing-chair. There was an unfamiliar scent in the air, a faint perfume. Her house had been personalized in the two days that she'd been gone. With someone else's personality.

Gripping Harry in his car seat – he had stopped crying but was looking at her crossly from below his crocheted cap – she took a step towards the kitchen as Ben tied the helium balloons around the newel post of the staircase. Claire sniffed. Furniture polish too. Suddenly she froze, gripping Harry tighter. 'Has this floor been *waxed*?' A wave of panic washed over her.

'Looks like it,' Ben beamed. 'Brita's been hard at work. I knew you'd be pleased.'

'Pleased? That someone's booby-trapped my house?'

'What are you talking about?' He lugged her suitcase in from the front porch and put it down on the gleaming hardwood, wiping his forehead with his sleeve. 'What have you got in this thing anyway? Encyclopedias?'

'Waxed floors are treacherous. What if I slip carrying Harry? Or *she* does? I never put wax on the floors.' Claire didn't move, terrified of taking another step. 'Brita has to wash it off, that's all there is to it.'

'But it looks great – you can practically see yourself in it. It's the first good cleaning this floor's ever had. And the wax'll wear off soon.'

'Not before someone's had an accident.' Claire hugged Harry close. He was sound asleep again, snoring with faint wheezy noises, occasionally mewing, or rubbing his face with his mittened hands.

Ben puffed out his cheeks, letting his breath expire with a strained, asthmatic sound. 'So I'll ask her to wash it off. Or I'll do it myself.'

'But how will I get upstairs? I have to take Harry to his room. He needs to be changed. He'll get a rash. He's been in the same diaper all day.' Claire's eyes were filling again. 'And we don't have any cream to put on a rash – I didn't have a chance to buy any yet.'

'Look, try and relax. I'm wearing runners, I won't slip. Let me take Harry upstairs.'

'No!' Claire clutched the baby fiercely. He stirred, opened his eyes, blinked once, then wound up and let out a fresh scream of rage.

'See what you've done?' Ben reached to take him but Claire pulled him back.

'*Kan jag hjalp dig?*' Brita had suddenly appeared out of nowhere, quiet as a cat. Or maybe she'd been there all along, watching them, judging, forming opinions. 'Please. Can I help?' She was smiling broadly, holding out her arms for the baby. Claire glared at her, then at Ben, feeling an insane urge to toss Harry into the air, like a football, to see who'd get him before he landed. She let out a snort of mad laughter as Ben and Brita exchanged looks.

'Yes, you can help, Brita,' Claire said, serious again, not wanting Ben trying to pack her off for some post-natal psychiatric assessment. 'You see,' she said slowly, but too loudly, as people often did with foreigners, thinking that volume somehow increased their ability to understand, 'I want to take Harry up to the nursery. The baby's room. But you've put wax on this floor! *Wax!*' She tapped her foot for emphasis. 'And I'm afraid of falling. Because it's slippery.' She shuffled her foot to demonstrate. 'Capeesh?'

Brita looked stricken. 'Vax? Ah! *Jag forstar!* I am so stupid. *Ursakta mig.* I did not think.' Her deep blue eyes seemed to darken a shade as she looked sorrowfully at Claire.

'Yes, well – I'm sure you didn't. It was a mistake, that's all. Anyone could have made it.' Claire was beginning to feel ashamed of herself. 'There's no real harm done, I suppose, but I've got to stand here with the baby now, until someone gives this floor a thorough scrub.'

Harry seemed to be withholding his screams until further notice, but was flailing his mittened fists and squirming under his load of blankets. He was obviously put out, and his lacy cap had slid down over one eye, giving him an incongruously jaunty, cock-eyed look.

'So I will wash it now? This floor?' Brita bit her lower lip – a charming picture of consternation.

'We would be grateful,' Ben said. 'I'll help you as soon as Claire gets settled.'

'The pail? Is in the basement, *ja*? Near to my room.' She turned and hurried down the hall. 'How can I be so stupid?' she muttered.

Claire watched her go, feeling hot and cross and fat – Cinderella's stepmother, sending the lovely girl into the dungeon to get a mop and bucket to scrub the floor, because of some hormone-induced, irrational fear of wax.

'You don't think you've over-reacted a bit?' said Ben. 'She was only trying to please you.'

'I thought you were the one who was so big on child safety. I can't believe you let her wax this floor. Look at it, it's like glass.'

'I guess I wasn't thinking either. We wanted you to be pleased with the house, knowing how you'd be feeling. Well, let me at least take your suitcase upstairs, since you don't trust me with Harry.'

We wanted you to be pleased? It was established now, Claire thought, that neither Ben nor Brita had spent much of the week-end thinking about the safety of her or Harry. But what had they been doing instead? Brita had waxed the floor, but why? Was she trying to kill Claire? Harry? And she'd obviously squirted some furniture polish around. But what else had she been up to, besides that and cosy chats with Ben about Claire's emotional state? Carefully, she put Harry in his car seat on the floor, not wanting to risk dropping him, then smoothed down her shirt, trying to regain her equilibrium, to feel at home in her own home.

The biggest shock of the childbirth experience was discovering that she was just as big now as on the day before Harry's birth. Her weight had dropped only a disappointing sixteen pounds, and she actually looked much worse. Before, she'd been firm and smooth and round, like a gigantic watermelon, her enormity excusable to anyone who saw her. Now, everything below her massive breasts was pale, loose and flabby, like cottage cheese or bread dough. She was only permitted one exercise by her obstetrician (other than rotating her ankles while lying down) which was to sit on the toilet and contract all the muscles between her legs, as if she were trying to hold in a pee. It was hard to imagine working off forty-four pounds that way.

For her bringing-home-baby outfit, she'd chosen a pink and white shirt and co-ordinating slacks. 'Perfect for a new mom!' the salesgirl had assured her. Claire bought the long cardigan and the pink pedal-pushers as well, not bothering to try any of

it on, confident that it would fit, since it was all a size nine, and
she was normally a seven. But as she was getting dressed to leave
the hospital, she'd found that she couldn't pull the slacks up
higher than mid-thigh. She'd been obliged to come out wearing
what she'd worn going in – an out-of-shape T-shirt beneath a
voluminous denim jumper, the classic maternity bag.

Had Brita worn *jeans*, with a *tucked-in* shirt, to make her feel
bad? To make her look worse? She was disappointed to discover
that the loose cotton sweater Brita had worn when Claire first
met her hadn't been hiding a few extra rolls of flab, a button or
two that couldn't be done up. Any considerate person, who'd
thought about it at all, would surely have realized that the last
thing a new mother wanted to be confronted with was some little
stick-figure in *jeans* and a clingy knit shirt that was *tucked in*.

'I unpacked some of your stuff,' Ben said, coming back down
the stairs. Brita could be heard rattling around in the basement:
probably trying to figure out which end of the mop to use, Claire
thought, then was again ashamed of her pettiness.

'Well,' she sighed, 'I guess I can't stand here all day. Maybe you
should take Harry upstairs after all. But be careful.' He seemed to
have settled again – his eyes were closed and he was breathing
with rapid shallow breaths. He let out a tiny mew, then a healthy
hiccup, before spitting up a stream of breast-milk.

Claire watched Ben climb the stairs with him, then skated
cautiously into the kitchen to get a glass of water. The big
summer tumblers – the ones with the Skydome on them –
were not in their usual place in the cupboard. She shut off
the dishwasher, opened it and noticed, with surprise, that the
crystal champagne flutes were in there. There were just two of
them. Nestled together on the bottom rack.

As she stood there, staring, someone banged on the front door.
She made her way cautiously back over the polished floor. It
was a delivery boy, bringing another bunch of flowers. How
kind people were when you had a baby, she thought, pulling
off the thin florist's paper. More carnations. Pink and blue.
Whoever had sent them obviously didn't know whether Claire
had had a boy or a girl. Still, one had to be touched by the
gesture. She set them on the hall table and took the small card
out of its envelope. 'Congratulations!' someone had written on

the card. 'Let's hope you make a better mother than you do a lawyer!'

She read the card again, not fully comprehending its meaning. Then, feeling as though she'd been kicked in the stomach, Claire stood at the bottom of the stairs and howled, 'Ben? Could you come down here, please?' She sank on to the bottom step. Ben's anxious footsteps hurried along the upstairs hall as a blue balloon, loosed from its moorings, floated up to bump against the lop-sided hall skylight. There would be no way to get it down; it would continue to yell IT'S A BOY!! up there until it finally exploded from the heat which built up in Mr Proctor's improperly installed dome of glass.

AUTUMN

9

Harry's eyes popped open. 'Ah. Ha-ha,' he said. He reached up his hand – fingers splayed wide apart, a small, sweet, sticky starfish – and tried to seize the mobile that hung over his crib, just beyond reach. 'Dow!' he told it. A pony, dog and chicken chased after each other, swaying gently. A plush cow with flaring nostrils and a stuffed gold star between its front hooves hung over the side of his crib. The string that dangled from it was pulled down, with a ratchet-like sound, and began to recede into the cow again. 'Catch a Falling Star', the tinkly notes played.

Crossly, Harry rubbed his eyes as the venetian blinds of the nursery window were opened and sunshine played across his face. 'Da-day-day,' he complained.

'*God morgon*, Harry! You are sleeping so late today! What a lazy boy! *Alskling snuttis!*' The voice was soft but its tone was excited. There was another tinkly sound, like tiny wind-chimes, as Harry's designer-covered duvet was shaken out and thoroughly fluffed. 'How is Brita's little prince this morning? It is a beautiful day. A bee-oo-tiful day. *En san underbar dag.* Can you say this? Can you? *En san underbar dag. Underbar* is wonderful. That's what you are.' The side rails were popped up, then lowered into place. A tangle of pale blonde hair dangled into Harry's face, tantalizingly close. He reached out, grabbed a fistful and tugged.

'Ah! Harry! No, no. This hurts Brita.' Gently, his fingers were pried open, the golden fleece freed. A small teddy, made from a striped sock, was offered as consolation. 'Here is your bear. *Leksaksbjorn*. In Swedish this means the teddy bear. Is he not the most handsome bear in the world? For the most handsome baby?'

'Woo-chay!' Harry stuck the bear's ear into his mouth and gummed it.

'Woo-chay? Is this your teddy's name? This is a funny name. This is not Swedish. Shall Brita teach the prince to speak Swedish? We must call your bear something else. Nils or Oscar. Oscar is good I think.' Harry's fat little neck was covered with kisses and he squealed and squirmed with delight. '*Pussgurka*,' Brita cooed, chucking him under his chin. But then his face clouded over and he scowled, concentrating fiercely. There was a pause: his face darkened.

'What? Is the most handsome baby making the most handsome poo for Brita?'

Obligingly, Harry filled his diaper with a wet, explosive noise.

'Boy,' Christine said, 'he can really let it rip. I'm glad I'm not the one changing him, never mind washing those diapers. I still can't believe you're using cloth. Is it because of pressure from Ben's mother? She's some kind of Green Peacer, isn't she?'

'Prue has nothing to do with it. It was a personal decision.'

Christine and Claire were sitting at Claire's kitchen table, drinking tea and sampling Elfriede's poppyseed cake. A lot of amplified rustlings crackled over the nursery monitor, along with Brita's chortles and Harry's grunts. 'Brita sounds okay, but she knows we're listening. Don't kid yourself. That little prince routine . . .' Christine rolled her eyes.

Claire reached across the table and snapped off the monitor. 'I feel like a hideous sneak, eavesdropping on her. It's an invasion of privacy.'

'Have you got a toothpick? These poppy seeds are a social embarrassment.' As Claire got up to get a container of toothpicks from the cupboard, Christine added: 'You're not eavesdropping. You're only taking an interest in your son's care-giver. As his mother, you'd be negligent if you didn't. When is it you go back to work?'

'Monday.'

'Sneaks up on you fast, doesn't it?'

Claire nodded. Her stomach jumped. She'd left Brita alone

with Harry often enough – usually when she desperately needed some time to herself – but never for a whole day. And this wouldn't be for just one whole day; it would be for a series of whole days stretching on, with no end in sight. Even when Ben was finished with his residency, he still had to study for and pass his exams, spend a year or two doing fellowships, then a couple of years establishing a practice. She couldn't even consider part-time work for at least five years. By then, Harry would be in kindergarten, going off to school, the brass buttons on his Osh'kosh overalls twinkling, handkerchief tucked in his pocket, taking an apple for his teacher. Harry gone. Her eyes started to sting. How had summer slipped by so fast? Was it possible that she'd used up her four months' leave already? Stroller wheels had turned endlessly, miles of boardwalk planks (sun and shadow, sun and shadow) had unravelled under her feet. She'd spent long dreamy hours in Harry's room, peacefully gliding in the nursery rocker as her son nursed, making small whooping sounds, like a tiny dolphin. 'I'd whoop too if a breast the size of my head was coming at me,' Ben had laughed, in reply to Claire's worried question. And then there were the diapers. There was always a pail full of them waiting to be done; every day the Cunninghams' ancient Maytag squealed in protest as it struggled to agitate and spin the heavy load. Brita always seemed to be busy with something else when it came time to rinse and wash those diapers.

'I'll miss the park,' Claire said sadly. 'I've met some wonderful women this summer. Stay-at-home moms. They never got too friendly with me though – I guess they think I'm not one of them since I'm going back to work. I get a sympathetic nod whenever I mention that. They avert their eyes.'

'Brain-dead,' Christine said. 'I bet none of them has had an original thought in a decade.'

'That's not fair, Christine.'

'It's true. What do most of them talk about? The best way to clean a high-chair tray? Which store is having a good sale on diapers?'

'We talked about books a lot, actually.'

'Dr Spock? *What To Expect the First Year*? Penelope Leach?'

'Look, I don't have to defend them. I'll miss them. They've

all had interesting lives, terrible problems. One has Hodgkin's disease and a brand-new baby – she can't breast-feed because of the chemotherapy. Two of them are single mothers. It's horrible what some women have to endure.'

'Forget them, Claire. They're not like you. You're an alien being. You'll never be one of them. You work.'

'*Outside* the home,' Claire corrected her.

'I hate when people say that. Anyway –' Christine was clearly not interested in hearing more about the stay-at-home moms in the park – 'you shouldn't worry about going back to work.' She looked at Claire with narrowed eyes. 'I'm sure Brita's quite adequate as a nanny.' Deftly, she extracted a poppyseed from between her incisors.

'She's better than adequate. Though maybe not so much on the housekeeping end of things. And Harry adores her. His first real smile was at her.'

'So *she'd* like you to believe.'

'It was. I taped it.'

'You made a video of his first smile at Brita? How awful for you.'

'I'm glad he likes her,' Claire said irritably. 'What mother wouldn't want her baby to like his nanny?'

'Oh well, in that case,' Christine shrugged and sawed off another slice of cake, 'I'm glad to hear she's so perfect. You're lucky you found her.'

'She's not perfect. I didn't say that.' Claire sat down at the table again and studied her sister, debating whether to pass her the morsels for which Christine had the real appetite. 'One thing that annoys me is that Harry always smells like her. There's some perfume she wears – sort of medicinal-smelling. Something Swedish. Loganberry, I don't know.'

'Tannis root?' Christine said archly. 'Have you thought about that?'

Claire gave her a look.

'So why don't you tell Brita her perfume bugs you? Just say quit stinking up my kid. Or fire her – that's your best solution.'

'I don't want to fire her. I just told you she's good.'

'Claire, I don't know how this could have escaped your notice but Britt Ekland is a hag compared to her.'

'Well, I can't fire her because of her looks.'

'It's the best reason I can think of, but then I never would have let Ben hire her in the first place.'

'I have no problem with having an attractive nanny for my son. I'm glad, actually.' Claire dug a knife into the poppyseed cake, cut off a large wedge and took a bite, showering the front of her shirt with crumbs. She had thought that, pregnancy over, she would no longer be a slob, but if anything she seemed to have become worse in that respect.

'Attractive? You and I are *attractive*. But she's gorgeous.'

'Oh, I don't know. With all that shaggy white-blonde hair, she reminds me of an Afghan hound.'

'Sure, she's a real dog. A howler, I bet she makes pit stops at every fire hydrant. And what about Harry? He's imprinting on her. For the rest of his life he'll want a woman who looks like Brita. *His* Brita, his beautiful nanny. No one less will ever do. He'll probably be in analysis for years; he'll be all screwed up, forever wanting the unattainable – a Swedish sex goddess. Where is he going to find a woman like that over here?'

'What absolute nonsense. He's not even three months old. And who says she's a *sex* goddess? Besides, he sees more of me than he does of Brita.' It wasn't quite true, but Claire didn't feel like mentioning how Brita seemed to have taken over Harry, subtly nudging Claire aside, leaving her to do the routine chores, as often as she could.

'But that's going to change, isn't it? Starting Monday. Harry's hardly going to see you at all, is he?'

Why are you doing this to me? Claire thought, looking at her sister, feeling that jump in her stomach again. For a moment she didn't say anything. She cut another hunk of Elfriede's cake and stuffed it into her mouth. She should be upstairs with Harry now, on her second to last day of maternity leave, not down here in the kitchen listening to Christine's malicious paranoic blather. She thought about asking her to leave, then decided she couldn't. Not with Christine moving to the States in a couple of weeks. Bad feelings festered all the better over long distances. 'Well,' she said, 'for all Brita's good looks, her personal habits could use some improving. Her toenails are always dirty, for example. I see them all the time because she wears Birkenstocks.'

'Disgusting,' Christine said happily.

'And she has a bit of BO, to be blunt.'

'Most Europeans do. They don't take baths as often as we do. I noticed that in France. And Italians? Don't get me started about Bernardo when I first met him.'

'And she has hairy legs and armpits.' Claire's mood lifted as she warmed to the subject of Brita's physical shortcomings.

'But all of that just makes things worse,' said Christine. 'Here she is, gorgeous but earthy. Attainable. A real woman. Who wants to have sex with a celluloid centre-fold?'

'Who said anything about having sex?'

Christine hesitated. Her eyes met her sister's. 'I only meant that facing up to the fact that she is fashion-model stunning is the first step in dealing with this beast. I wasn't implying anything else. It was just loose talk.' She shaved off a sliver of cake, making the edge of the loaf even. 'This cake's a bit dry. How can Mother suddenly screw up the recipe after making it for thirty years?'

'Even if Brita is gorgeous,' Claire continued defensively, 'it's hardly her fault.'

'Maybe not that she was born that way, but she could've done something about it. Let herself get fat, say, or dye her hair mouse-brown.' Christine laughed.

'She'd still look great,' Claire sighed. 'I can't fire her, especially now, just as I'm about to go back to work. But I have to admit, when I see some of the other nannies in the park, I wish I'd hired a different type of person.'

'But *you* didn't hire her at all, remember?'

Claire ignored her. 'They're so peaceful, so patient. The Filipinas all sit together, murmuring in their language.'

'Tagalog.'

'And then there's our Brunnhilde, crashing through the underbrush like an Amazon, singing at the top of her lungs. She really cuts loose when she's in a good mood. And instead of cleaning up around here, she rearranges things. It's like living with a poltergeist. She's jumbled up everything in my kitchen cupboards – she never puts anything back where it belongs. It took me an hour to find the coffee pot last weekend. She even moves furniture. I almost broke my leg one night when I went down to the living-room to turn off the air conditioning.

She'd moved a table for some reason. I had a bruise the size of a grapefruit for weeks. So I told her to knock it off. She sulked for a while, but she's stopped.'

'What does a twenty-four-year-old know about arranging a room? All they care about is where to find the mattress. Maybe she moves things so you won't notice she's stealing. Ever thought of that? If you can't find anything anyway, you won't be surprised when something disappears.'

'Really, Christine, you should be writing fiction – you're wasting your talents on that Canuck-talk business of yours.'

'So what else does Brita do that bugs you?' Christine leaned forward, almost visibly salivating.

'Nothing else – nothing major. She yacks on the phone for hours – all night if she doesn't go out. I feel like we've adopted a teenager. I don't know how she's managed to make so many friends in the short time she's been over here. Ben thinks we should get her a private line.'

'Maybe she's talking to her fence. Or her pimp. What if she's a call-girl and just does this nanny stuff on the side? As a front? Have you seen anything interesting when you've gone through her things?'

'I've never gone through her things!'

'Like hell you haven't.'

Claire looked away. 'Well, I might have peeked at her room once or twice. This is, after all, our house.'

Christine nodded encouragement. 'What did you find?'

'Nothing. I only looked at the room, that's all. I didn't *find* anything. Except a mess. And a Swedish flag draped across the ceiling. It'll probably take the paint off – I think she used duct tape to stick it up there.'

'And of course if doesn't go with your decor. Blue and yellow.'

'No,' Claire frowned, 'the flag's red. With a yellow cross.'

'That's not a Swedish flag then.'

'Of course it is. Brita is Swedish.'

'I'm no flag expert, but I don't recall the Swedish flag having any red in it.' Christine rewrapped the poppyseed cake in its tin foil. 'Haven't you got an atlas? Usually there's flags in there. You should check it out. Maybe you'll discover that Brita's really

Transylvanian. So come on, let's go through her things – I bet we find some interesting stuff.'

'Like what?'

'Penicillin prescriptions for the clap, blood work requisitions. Handcuffs. A gun. Who knows?'

At that moment, Brita startled them by pattering lightly down the stairs, Harry in her arms. Claire stared at them, her cheeks flaming. With the monitor off, she'd forgotten that Brita was still in the house. How much had she overheard? Christine seemed busily occupied refolding the tin foil wrapper around the cake.

'I will now take Harry to the beach,' Brita said, 'is this okay?' She smiled and gave him a big kiss on the cheek. 'He needs the beautiful sunshine.'

'Don't forget the sun-block,' Claire said faintly.

'*Ja*. Of course.'

Brita looked radiantly healthy, and she seemed happy – not like someone who'd just heard herself assessed as a possible thief and prostitute. Probably she hadn't overheard anything, Claire thought with relief, or hadn't understood what she'd heard. 'I should get out myself,' she said. 'I could use some fresh air.'

'Why not come with me and Harry? That would be very nice.'

'Maybe I will. I'll come and find you later. On the board-walk.'

'Don't stay in on my account.' Christine stood up, watching Brita narrowly. 'I was just leaving – unless, Claire, you want me to help you look into that matter we were discussing . . .' Her eyes flickered over Brita.

'I don't.' Claire took Harry and bounced him nervously on her knee as she waited for Brita to warm a bottle of expressed breast-milk that Claire had laboured to produce, using a crude suction pump that seemed to drag the milk out of her more than pump it. Brita then packed the bottle in the diaper bag along with extra diapers, a floppy-brimmed sun-hat and a tube of sun-screen. 'Good God, Christine,' Claire said, after they had gone, 'what if she heard us?'

'Then she'd quit and all your troubles would be over.'

'They'd be just beginning. The last thing I need is to have to find a new nanny on short notice.'

'How does Ben like having Brita around?'

'They have the odd exchange in Swedish, but Ben's is pretty bad.'

'I bet he's trying to brush up on it though. And Brita's giving him all the help she can, in her cute broken English?'

'Wrong,' Claire lied. 'Besides, you know Ben. He works so hard – I've hardly seen him at all this week. I can't really say how he's reacting to her.'

'Did you ask him about his pager?'

'Yes, I asked him,' Claire sighed. 'And it's all too stupid to waste time thinking about.'

'I bet you page him a lot less now, don't you?'

'No,' Claire lied again. 'I do exactly what I did before.'

Christine gave a little snort. 'Well, just as long as Ben's not here when Brita's also not here . . . that's when you should worry. And I'd get myself a Swedish dictionary if I were you. Make sure you know what they're talking about. I think it's pretty rude – speaking in another language when there's someone else in the room who can't understand it.'

'I wasn't. I mean, the times I heard them I don't think they knew I was there.'

Christine shot her a penetrating look. 'Really?'

'So why don't you show me the pictures of your new house?' Claire said. Her sister's brow smoothed instantly, Claire's dilemma (if it was one) already old news. She opened her handbag to retrieve a photo shop envelope. 'What's this style called?' Claire studied the pictures, amazed by the scale of the place. 'Hacienda?'

'Ranch, sprawling ranch. Look at the size of it – you could drive a herd of cattle through the living-room.'

'Not bad – if you don't mind living on a major fault line.'

'With a house this big, we can afford to let half of it drop into the bay.'

'The fountain's a bit much, don't you think?'

'Fountain! That's just the bird bath.'

'It would take up our whole yard.'

'The actual fountain is in the back. Here. See? Aren't those urinating cherubs darling? And here's the fish pond and the swimming-pool.'

'I don't see the barbed-wire fence and the search lights.'

They sparred a bit for a while, a silly conversation about life in the States versus life in Canada. Christine would expect lots of visits from her only sister, she said, as she gathered her things to leave. And she would call often. Sure you will, Claire thought, standing on the front porch and watching as she slid into her car, remembering the time she'd visited Christine in France and how enchanted she'd been by her sister's acquired elegance. She'd become strongly attached to her during her three-week stay; for the first time in her life feeling a real sisterly closeness. When it came time to leave, Claire had been sniffling and teary at the airport, but Christine had only gazed back at her, dry-eyed, puzzled and embarrassed by her red-nosed effusiveness. She was cool-burning, as icy blue as a gas flame. But there was little danger of tears this time, Claire thought, as Christine's champagne-coloured BMW rolled silently away down Pine Beach Road.

She went back into the kitchen and sat for a while at the table, wondering how her life had suddenly become so complicated and laden with worries; when it was that it started to slip out of gear. She still had no idea who had sent her that malicious card with the pink and blue carnations. They'd arrived in an unmarked van and there hadn't been a florist's name on the card or wrapping. She and Ben had worked through the benign explanations: it was a mistake; it was a joke. But they both knew it was neither.

Now that she had Harry, Claire also had a full voting membership in the paranoia club: suddenly and acutely aware of the number of twisted psychos (Harry snatchers) out there; the frequency of newspaper stories of child abuse and neglect; of how often people screamed, fought and smashed beer bottles on Pine Beach Road and surrounding streets. She saw how many transients, sociopaths and other undesirables were drawn to the Beach in summer. Ever since those carnations arrived, she'd been waiting for something else to happen, something truly awful. It hadn't – yet – but the fear of it stained her summer days with Harry, tinging them grey around the edges.

As for her work, once a source of strength and solace, and the very thing that defined her, the thought of returning to it filled her with dread. Had her practice been sucked down the toilet while she was away? Had her clients, fickle at the best of times, tossed her aside for some other (probably male) lawyer who was waiting and eager to help when they needed something done? 'Could it be a client who sent you those flowers?' Ben had asked. 'One with a major grudge on? Over your account, maybe?'

'Clients are always incensed about their accounts. But they don't go sending hate mail to lawyer's homes.' Of course, she thought, if you scratched the surface of any client, you would likely find a grudge of some sort against his or her lawyer. But they seldom took it personally. It was business. It wasn't as though anyone ever went to prison, or sat around on Death Row, as a result of Claire's practice. She did trade-marks and licensing work for heaven's sake. What could be more innocuous?

'Well, what about this guy Protochniak?'

'Potochnik.'

'Has he got all his oars in the water? Does his elevator go to the top floor?' Ben had studied her closely. 'Does he have some reason to personally dislike you?'

'Of course not. I helped the guy out. I actually saved his bacon. He'd be sunk now if it wasn't for me.' And it was true. The only thing Potochnik could fault her on was not returning his calls, or being unavailable when he wanted to see her. But he was a closed file, as far as Claire was concerned, and he must have been content with consulting another lawyer while Claire was on leave since he'd stopped trying to contact her.

But now she had Christine's insinuations about Ben and wild fantasies about Brita to add to her load of anxiety. A hooker, a thief. Really, she had to laugh. She got up from the table and tried to, as she carried the dirty dishes to the sink to rinse them. She needed to go down to the beach, find Harry and play with him for a while. It would clear her head, make her happy again. Christine was absurd, possibly even evil, a truly wicked sister. Claire shut off the tap and watched the last drops of water plunk down on to a china plate. What if, just for the sake of argument, Brita really were up to something illegal? There was another worrying thing about her that Claire hadn't bothered to tell Christine. Brita didn't seem to care about her pay and had waved off all offers by Claire and Ben to start paying her before Claire went back to work. Yet she went out a lot, bought loads of junk food, clothes and cosmetics. Didn't that indicate she had some other, more lucrative, source of income? That her nanny job was just a front? Christine would have relished this information, would have insisted they go through Brita's things immediately, charging down into the basement like a pit bull to sniff out and clamp down on the truth.

With a creeping sense of shame, Claire left the kitchen and made her way down the basement stairs, telling herself she was only about to do what any good mother would do. She couldn't be expected to go back to work and leave helpless little Harry with a criminal, could she?

The sitting-room part of Brita's apartment was in general disorder – littered with Harry's toys, a dirty diaper and a number of forgotten bottles, now ripe and cheesy with bacteria. Claire found one beside the chesterfield, another on top of the television. They would have to be thrown out, she thought, looking with distaste at the thick yellow sludge inside them.

Brita hadn't bothered to clean up her bathroom either. The tub mat was puckered and furry with mould, the sink drain clogged with blonde hair, the water in the toilet scummy. Claire unhooked the child-proof latch on the cupboard, took out a can of drain cleaner and dumped half of it into the sink, the other half into the toilet. The noxious chemicals hissed. The drains moaned and gurgled. Too late, Claire noticed the warning label on the can: THIS PRODUCT NOT FOR USE IN TOILETS. She shuddered and, closing the bathroom door on the tortured hissing and moaning, wandered back through the sitting-room, towards Brita's bedroom, chewing her nails.

As she opened the door, the huge red and yellow flag fluttered against the ceiling. Christine was right – red didn't seem like the right colour somehow; it looked too aggressive for Sweden, sort of Red-Squarish. She made a mental note to dig out their atlas and check on the flag colours. Otherwise, Brita's bedroom looked much the same as the other rooms – maybe a little messier. Framed photos, knick-knacks, a jumble of make-up brushes and pencils, inexpensive bracelets, hair clips and rings littered the bureau. Claire picked up one of the photos and studied it. It wasn't a very clear picture, had obviously been taken with a cheap camera. It was of Brita herself, younger than she was now, dressed all in white, with a crown of lighted candles on her head. Some Swedish tradition, Claire supposed. It looked like a fairly hazardous endeavour. She put down the picture and picked up another. Brita again – another blurry photo – this time leaning against a sports car, one hand on her hip, the other resting on the fender, an amused expression on her face. She was pleased with her photographer, whoever he was. Claire was fairly sure it would have been a he. Probably, they'd just finished having sex when the picture was taken. In that sports car perhaps.

How odd, she thought, that Brita would display framed photos of herself. It wasn't as though she were likely to forget what she looked like, was it? Wouldn't it be more natural to bring pictures of her parents, her cat, her boyfriend or her home in Sweden? Brita didn't have any siblings, she'd once told Claire sadly. Maybe that's how it was with only children – they became self-absorbed. Claire didn't want that to happen to Harry.

She looked around the room, fearing, but at the same time hoping, that she would see something shocking, off-putting or sickening. But the only thing she could place into any of those categories was the mess.

Brita's wicker garbage pail was overflowing with Swedish Marabou chocolate bar wrappers and crumpled nacho bags; and there were wads of dried chewing gum cemented to the side of it that Claire knew would never come off.

In the closet were piles of clothes, untidily half on and half off their hangers. Other things weren't hung up at all, but had been dumped on to the floor, balled up with a tangle of shoes, boots, belts and bags.

Like most people who had acquired something at no cost, Brita was careless with her looks. She didn't seem to own any good-quality clothes, but Claire had long ago realized that women who looked like Brita, especially at Brita's age, didn't need to spend a lot to look great. It didn't matter what junk she hung from her ears or around her neck or wrists, or what rag she threw on, she always looked terrific. Claire knew this because, in her younger years, she'd tried to imitate other girls whose appearance she admired, thinking that copying their clothes was the key.

・ Sylvia Mulholland

There was a set of twins – Maureen and Marleen Blaber – who'd gone to the same ballet school as Claire when she was in junior high – Mr Heatherfield's School of the Dance, run out of an IOOF hall on Tuesday nights. Claire was so in awe of those gamine-like Blabers that she was forever scrutinizing them, making covert notes, hoping to replicate that certain something they possessed, wanting desperately to be like them. The twins were marvellous, they were cute, everyone loved them. Even endearing was the unco-ordinated way they struggled to follow the sprightly Mr Heatherfield, whose pockets were always heavy with loose change and keys that jingled and sometimes fell out as he demonstrated a *grande jetée* or an *entrechat*. Though Mr Heatherfield wasn't much of an attraction – a sort of Father-Knows-Best in grimy leather ballet slippers – his daughter-in-law, Miss Vivian, who taught tap-dancing, was of absorbing interest to Claire and the other girls. Dazzling and long-legged, wearing clingy high-cut leotards, she hoofed through 'This Diamond Ring' played on a Seabreeze portable, twirling a paper parasol – a sort of enlarged version of the type found in exotic cocktails. Miss Vivian, however, was clearly out of Claire's league, so it was the Blaber twins she tried to model herself after. But no matter how close she came to replicating them, even as far as pencilling a sprinkling of freckles over her nose, she never looked like one of them: no one ever confused her for the third Blaber, the missing triplet.

It was the same thing with Brita. If Claire put on her cheap sweaters, her thin cotton T-shirts, her grungy windbreaker and Birkenstocks, she would only look like a middle-aged woman who shopped at the Goodwill. But Brita in Claire's clothes, in her silks and suedes and cashmeres, guided with a firm hand by Claire's Dresser – that would be something. Something Claire really didn't care to see.

She shut the closet door and quietly pulled open the bureau drawers, one by one, hot with shame. They were mostly empty but for a few stray socks, some greying bras and panties, a hairbrush cloudy with blonde hair. The bottom drawer was crammed with paper – dozens of letters and postcards to and from some place called Goteborg, tied in bundles with ribbons or string, bearing intriguing stamps with SVERIGE printed somewhere on each one. Well, Claire thought, a snoop she might be, but she drew the line at reading someone else's mail, never mind that it was illegal to do so. (And that it was in Swedish.) There was a limit to what she, as a concerned mother, was entitled to know, wasn't there? At the back of the drawer a fat wad of printed pamphlets, bound up with two rubber bands, caught her eye. They were red, with a yellow cross at the top – a miniature version of the ceiling flag. SKANE!! it screamed on the cover, followed by dense-printed text replete with the double-dot and tiny circle accent marks that characterized the Swedish language. There were lots of exclamation marks too. Whoever had authored the text had been pretty fired up about something; there was a strong political flavour to it. Could Brita be a communist? A religious fanatic?

There were so many of the pamphlets in the bundle, Brita would be unlikely to miss just one. Claire reached out to extract the top one but quickly pulled back her hand. Brita's light step had sounded on the front porch above her.

10

At half past eight on the morning she was due back at work, when she should have been on the expressway, breezing towards her office, excited about returning to work, Claire was lurking in the Cunninghams' garage, spying on Harry's nanny. There was no nicer way of putting it. She stood peering through the garlands of cobwebs on the cracked garage window at the grimy window of the kitchen that was actually a sun porch, crudely remodelled by Hookman-Nailman-Screwman. Claire could see Brita moving around in there, then picking up the telephone receiver and dialling a number. Who could she be calling? Claire had barely left the house. What could Brita possibly have to say to anyone so early in the morning? That the coast was clear? And what was Harry doing, that he didn't need watching? And if he was happily occupied in his swing or Jolly Jumper, why wasn't Brita unloading the dishwasher, doing a load of diapers or any of the multitude of other things that needed doing at 67 Pine Beach Road?

Claire had left the house in a frenzy, several outfits, complete with accessories, scattered in her wake, and a dense clutter of cosmetics and appliances crowding the bathroom sink. Her Dresser had been on her back the whole time, preventing her from enjoying her last precious moments with her son, appalled that nothing fitted Claire properly, that she hadn't lost all her pregnancy weight and had nothing new to wear.

During Claire's frantic and frustrated clothing changes, Brita had watched with an expression that was alternately puzzled and frightened, jiggling Harry in her arms and trying to keep out of Claire's way. She could see herself through Brita's eyes –

a muttering madwoman who stormed up and down the stairs, crazily pulling laundry out of the basket, sniffing it, discarding it, then scrambling to iron another blouse and skirt, smearing nail polish on the ironing-board cover and snagging her pantyhose on a chair leg before staggering out to the garage, fumbling with her keys, her lunch bag clenched between her teeth, her eyes wet with guilt and sorrow over leaving Harry.

As she watched Brita talking on the telephone, Claire picked at her cuticles, doing further destruction to her fresh polish, and trying to recall whether she'd left her hair-dryer plugged in beside the bathroom sink. What if Harry got hold of it somehow? Pulled on the dangling cord? Or pushed it into the sink? She took a step towards the garage door, frowning. Framed by the kitchen window, Brita pushed her fingers through her shag of hair, then reached into a cupboard, took something out and popped it into her mouth. Nachos or taco chips, probably. For breakfast! What sort of slap-dash nutritional habits was she likely to instil in Harry?

She'd better go back in there, Claire thought, find out exactly what was going on. As she debated doing this, Brita hung up the phone and disappeared from view. Though relieved – Brita'd obviously gone to see to Harry – Claire continued to watch the blank square of kitchen window, depressed and anxious. Harry was going to grow up without her, starting today. In a flash of time he would be a man, with a family of his own. She might well not live to see any grandchildren. If Harry waited until he was thirty-nine to have children, as she had done, she would be seventy-eight. *Seventy-eight!* A wheezing, rattling hair's breadth from eighty! What possible use would she be to him then? Harry and his wife would never trust her with babysitting her own grandchild: they would be afraid she might keel over and fall down the stairs while carrying their baby; that she would break her hip and never get up again, unable even to crawl to the phone to call for help. She would be a liability, of no use to them. Unless she were dead. They would wait impatiently for her to croak to collect whatever money she hadn't squandered by then. 'How much longer is the old witch going to hang on?' Harry's wife would whine. (Claire disliked her already – some cool blonde with a name like Ashley who would never be good enough for her son.) Or maybe they would keep her prisoner in her own home, locked in the attic, tied up with skipping ropes and fed cat food – elder abuse, it was called. Ben, of course, would still be alive and just nicely into his prime – a vigorous seventy-one, barely out of his sixties. He would have moved into a swank condominium by the waterfront, still able to drive his own snazzy car to take his grandchildren to the zoo or to visit Claire in the nursing home. If they bothered to put her into one. If they bothered to visit. If she were still alive.

Ben would outlive her, Claire knew, even though he was seven years younger and men had a shorter life expectancy than women, and despite his frequent joking that he would have a massive infarct at the age of forty, climbing out of his Lamborghini, an expensive Cuban cigar between his fingers.

And here she was now, almost forty, and what had she accomplished? She was not even a partner yet at Bragg, Banks and Biltmore. The rising stars at the firm got their partnerships early, at age thirty-five tops. And here was Claire, hanging in at thirty-nine, anxious now that her short maternity leave (not nearly long enough to enable her to bond inextricably with Harry) might still have been long enough to wreck her partnership chances for years. The serious lawyers, the women who had some clearly understood *future* at the firm, worked right on through their labours, their secretaries trotting files and phone messages in and out of the delivery room. Leaving the hospital after a day, they worked at home for a few more, telephone receivers cradled under their ears, baby under one arm, efficiently hooked up with modems and faxes and e-mail so as not to miss a beat in the forward stride of their practices. They were back in the saddle within a week (haemorrhoids be damned), pushing plants or chairs across their office doors to keep out intruders while they diligently pumped out their breast-milk behind their desks at ten o'clock and at two.

Or else the women lawyers in the firm simply stayed unmarried, gave up on the idea of ever having children, wholeheartedly embracing the law as the jealous mistress she was reputed to be.

Was partnership such a great accomplishment anyway, Claire wondered. And what was there to accomplish, *really* accomplish in life? Immortality was a joke. The jury was still out on heavyweights like Mozart and Michelangelo. In the span of all eternity, they had been famous for a mere speck of time, a crumb, a freckle. What hope did she, a mere lawyer and mother, have of doing anything of lasting impact? Who, even a month after she left her practice (or died) would remember her for registering NAPPY SACK as a trade-mark for diaper bags? Her clients would probably look upon her sudden departure as an opportunity to have their accounts reduced, or written off – for all the inconvenience they would be put through by Claire's inconsiderate demise, they would believe themselves entitled to substantial discounts.

Needing some normal everyday activity to drive these troubling thoughts from her head, Claire got into her car and pulled out of the garage and down the driveway. Then she hesitated. She stopped in front of the house, letting the engine idle. Maybe she should just stick her nose in the door, see what Brita was up to and give Harry one last teary kiss and a squeeze. She could pretend she'd forgotten something – an envelope, her watch. Or would her sudden reappearance be nothing more than a cruel and self-indulgent act, upsetting Harry's precarious equilibrium? As she sat there, pondering, Brita opened the front door to retrieve the morning paper. Startled, Claire beeped the horn and waved. Equally startled, Brita returned her wave, then stepped out on to the porch, frowning and looking puzzled. Feeling like an idiot, Claire waved again and, grinning imbecilically, pulled away from the house. Brita would now realize that Claire, idiot or not, could pop up unexpectedly at any time: she would be on her best behaviour and Harry would be safe. Or would the idea that Claire was spying on her only make her more devious and cunning? And resentful?

Claire pulled the car around the corner on to Queen, heading west towards the centre of the city, mired in feelings of bitter envy. Brita would get to stay there in Claire's house all day, with Claire's baby. She would read the morning paper out in the sunshine on the deck, munching nachos or chocolates as Harry gurgled happily in his portable baby seat. Claire was about to take her cell-phone from the glove compartment to call Brita to remind her to put lots of sun-screen on Harry, but realized she'd been too disorganized to remember to bring the phone. Would getting it be a valid reason for going home? A justification for unsettling Harry? She glanced at the last bit of Pine Beach Road in her rearview, her throat tight. All she would see of Harry now was at weekends. And the dreaded night shift.

Christine had once described her daughter, Anita, waking up in the morning as 'unfolding like a flower'. But Harry, sad to say, had quickly passed through his unfolding-flower stage. After over two months of relative docility, and periodically sleeping through the night, he'd undergone a radical personality change a week before Claire's scheduled return to work. He now exploded with a pterodactyl shriek of rage, hot and sweaty and smelly; pissed off with the world in general and Claire in particular. And he didn't wait until morning for these scenes. Even with her earplugs in, a pillow over her head and her bedroom door closed, she would be startled awake by his every cough, hiccup or whimper, yanked back from the edge of sleep like a dog on a choke-chain, obliged to stagger down the stairs to take a bottle of formula from the fridge where she kept several lined up, like a row of sentinels, decorated with trucks, Sesame Street characters or hockey club insignia. Once the bottle was warmed in the microwave, she would stumble back upstairs with it, on feet as heavy and clumsy as tree stumps, shaking the bottle and slopping formula on to her arm to make sure it wasn't too hot. By the time she got back to bed she was wide awake, and would finally drop off to sleep only moments before Harry's next outburst. Completely neurotic about it now, she doubted she would ever sleep properly again. Finally, she'd begged Ben for sleeping pills. She had several kinds now: an arsenal of hypnotics in the bathroom cabinet. There were the turquoise tablets, bitter as arsenic and hard enough to crack a molar; the pale yellow, chalky-tasting pills; the speckled green capsules. All of them stunned her into a sudden dreamless stupor, but left her irritable and woolly-headed in the morning. Some of them even had interesting side-effects unrelated to her mental state. The green ones, for example, made her hands tingle randomly; the turquoise ones left her mouth dry and her tongue thick and furry.

Really, she thought, she should have been relieved to be going back to work, should have fallen on her knees to give thanks to the gods of full employment. Except that going back to work meant she now had a day shift to add to her night shift. Two jobs for the pay of one. On the floor of the car was Claire's briefcase, heavy with a bewildering assortment of brochures, instruction booklets and forms that had to be filled out for Brita: for her government health tax, her unemployment insurance, Canada Pension Plan and Workers' Compensation. Claire hadn't yet been able to muster the mental energy to tackle those forms, and worse, to calculate (and make) the payments required to the various levels of government.

There would be no more afternoon naps for her, she thought, no lying on the couch with a cold cloth over her eyes to ease her fatigue. It would be business as usual. Her clients wouldn't care that she'd been up all night, and she wouldn't dare tell them. They would worry about her competence, her response time to their problems. They would think about finding another lawyer. If they hadn't already. Ben had offered to share the night shift with her, or take it over entirely when he wasn't at the hospital, but it was more work trying to wake him than it was to just get up herself. Even if Claire were to turn Harry's monitor up full blast and attach it to Ben's head with a rubber band, he wouldn't wake up. He was usually so exhausted himself that he passed instantly into unconsciousness, responding only to the beep of his hospital pager. And being with him during an evening was like living with an old man, or a narcoleptic.

Brita, too, slept like a stone, like the dead, in a tousled blonde coma, sunk deep in Ben's waterbed. She was never bothered by Claire's thumpings, the beeping of the microwave or Harry's impatient yells. The world was divided into two camps, in Claire's analysis: those who wore shower caps, and pyjamas and socks to bed, and those who didn't. She belonged to the former group, Ben and Brita to the latter. They fell asleep instantly, simply passing out whenever they felt like it, while Claire and the others in her camp took hot baths, downed mugs of warm milk and fiddled with foam, sponge or wax earplugs until dawn.

Tired, cranky, and again in a state of high anxiety over Harry, Claire slunk into the underground parking lot of her office building at quarter to ten – midday to the hard-working types at Bragg, Banks and Biltmore.

She made her way to her office by a circuitous route, slipping first into the Java Hut, the Bagel Hole, then the women's washroom where she took several gulps of water and lots of deep breaths and tried to steady her trembling hands. She looked at herself in the wall of mirrors to see an exhausted middle-aged woman in a navy-blue linen suit that was bunching and straining in places it had never bunched and strained before. 'You're back,' she said to her face. 'You should feel terrific.' And she did. Terrifically miserable.

As she hurried along the carpeted corridor to her office, she hoped no one would notice her. She needed some re-orientation time; a chance to figure out where – and who – she was again, to get used to the translating of time into dollars and the charging of every six-minute block to a seven-digit file number. But her office was not where she remembered it. Or, more accurately, it was in approximately the same place, but it had shrunk. The heavy chemical smell of carpet glue and fresh paint assaulted her in the area near Davina's cubicle.

'They moved your wall,' Davina said, following close at her heels into her office.

'They? Who they?'

'Management Committee. We've got three new lawyers. They had to make room for more offices.'

'Why didn't you tell me?' Claire put her briefcase down and slowly turned around, trying to orient herself in the remodelled space. Her furniture was all there, but it had been squeezed into half the floor space. One of her two windows was gone. 'This looks awful. You could have called me.'

'I was instructed not to bother you with my telephone calls,' Davina sniffed.

'Who instructed you?'

'Your husband, that's who.'

Claire sat down in her desk chair, feeling light-headed from the carpet glue and paint. 'Well, I suppose if they needed the space—'

'No one else got their office cut down. Just you. I tried to warn you, I told you they were in here taking measurements.' She was holding a bulging accordion folder full of papers, a couple of computer disks, a wad of telephone message slips. Clearly, she was anxious to get back to their normal routine. 'And what about me? I had to *float* for the last two months.'

'Oh, Davina. I'm sorry. I thought you could just keep on doing my work for whoever took over the file.'

'Well, it didn't happen that way.'

Claire nodded, thinking how hard it was to have a secretary and how close to impossible it seemed to keep her happy.

'Your voice-mail overflowed last week. That's why we're back to using these message slips.'

'What do you mean it overflowed?'

Davina shrugged. 'Ask Tech Support. Maybe there was too much on it. It backed up somehow, like a toilet. A lot of messages got lost. These are all the new ones. Also your mail. And some draft affidavits you're supposed to review for one of Rick's clients. Better do those first. Rick's the new Managing Partner, surprise surprise. It's on your e-mail or in a memo somewhere. Unanimous vote. Mr B. is staying on as Counsel to the firm – I had to work for that bastard for six weeks. Well,' she looked at Claire, her eyes bright with anger, 'as you can see, there've been a lot of changes around here in the last few months. A lot of changes.' She thunked the file folder, computer disks and messages down onto Claire's desk.

'Could you give me a minute to get settled?' Claire indicated her styrofoam cup of café au lait, the grease-spotted paper bag from the Bagel Hole. 'I haven't had a chance to eat anything yet today. I need to think about all this you're telling me, read my mail. And I need to call home, see how Harry's doing.'

'Didn't you just leave home?'

'Yes. But it's not that simple.'

'I guess it isn't, is it?' Davina pulled Claire's door closed with slightly more force that was necessary, leaving Claire to her breakfast and the pile of work on her desk. Alone, she swivelled in her chair, still wondering whether she should call home. What would she do if there were no answer? Panic, she thought. All reasonable explanations – Harry was being bathed, Brita had taken him to the beach – would fly immediately out of her head. Better not to call. Not yet. No matter how desperately she wanted to. She eased the lid off her coffee and took the buttered bagel from its bag, then regarded her newly down-scaled office, impressed suddenly by the sense of order it conveyed, despite its size. Davina had done a nice job of reorganizing everything. There was a pile of neatly labelled colour-coded files, stuck all over with sticky notes reminding Claire of what needed to be done, the discreetly ticking clock, the high-tech phone with its multitude of programming options. Sure, there might be chaos lurking below this superficial order and control, but on the surface, things looked good. And the practise of law had a lot to do with how things looked. Even the decor wasn't half bad really, despite a sense that there was too much furniture crammed into too little space. At least, Claire thought, no one had appropriated her oriental rug or her Morris Louis print, a weirdly organic abstract that reminded her of a pair of lungs. Beyond her single window, she could see a thin scrap of lake, peeking from between two glass and concrete towers. As she watched, a sailboat slipped across that scrap of lake, then disappeared. It was a hell of a view. She began to enjoy the silence in her office, the privacy, the feeling that she was once more in control. Of course, her kingdom was a small one – the number of people who were paid to do things for her was limited to Davina, the mailroom boy, her accounting clerk (when she wasn't in a bad mood) and an articling student or two, if they weren't otherwise occupied with a project for a more senior lawyer. At home, Claire reigned over only two subjects – Harry and Brita – neither of whom seemed to pay much attention to her. Maybe being back at work wouldn't be so bad.

After licking the last crumbs of bagel from her fingers, she took some time to arrange the framed photographs of Harry she'd brought in with her: some (the cutest) she set up on her desk, so she could gaze at them, close up, all day. The others she put on her book-case. Anyone walking into her office would think she had six kids, instead of just one, judging by the number of photos. To make room for so many Harrys, she was obliged to move the lone photograph of Ben. Taken only a few years earlier, it was his med school graduation photo that had once prompted the mailroom boy to ask if the guy in the picture was Claire's son. 'No, it's my husband when he was a boy,' she should have laughed, 'isn't it a riot? His mother sent it to me'; or 'No – the picture came with the frame, I really must put something else in there.' But she'd been too upset, at the time, to come up with such a flippant response. She placed Ben's photo on the bottom shelf of her book-case. Then she picked up one of Harry's, suddenly missing him desperately. What was he doing right now? Was he happy? Was he missing her too? Could a three-month-old baby truly miss anyone? Yes. His mother. She picked up the telephone receiver, then put it down again. Then she remembered the hair-dryer which she might have left plugged in beside the sink. She dialled her home number and listened anxiously to the succession of tiny beeps, then four rings and her own voice, apologizing for not being able to answer the phone. They must have gone out. It was a warm sunny day, but would be windy by the lake. Would Brita have the sense to put a hat on Harry? To bundle him up properly? Claire called back and left a message on the answering-machine about the hat; called again to add another about the hair-dryer. Then she sighed and pulled the accordion folder of mail towards her, determined to stop worrying about Harry and concentrate on her floundering law practice. She hesitated. Either that, or she should drive home. She could be there and back in an hour – that small effort could save Harry's life. She looked at her watch. If Brita and Harry were outside, he wouldn't be anywhere near the hair-dryer, she reasoned. She should just keep calling, every fifteen minutes until she got through. That's what she would do. She programmed her home number as number one, using the 'speed dial' function on her telephone, and turned her attention to the file folder.

The first document in the folder was a memo to all lawyers and staff announcing Rick Durham's sudden elevated status in the firm. Claire should have expected it, but she hadn't. At times, her lack of awareness of what was going on in the firm amazed and troubled her. Two other lawyers, or staff (or a combination) could be having an affair right under her nose – they could fornicate on top of her desk while she was sitting there dictating a search report – and she would later be dumbfounded to find out about the liaison. 'No kidding,' she would say, standing by the coffee machine in the lunch room, 'who would have suspected?' (The answer would probably be 'Everyone but you'.) Christine was the intuitive one in Claire's family. She could pick out in a crowded room exactly who was having it off with whom. She had a sort of x-ray eye for infidelity. Shelagh Tyler had the same uncanny geiger counter for sexual activity, and it was Shelagh who, a moment later, opened the door of Claire's office to welcome her back. 'Back in harness already?' she smiled. 'Stand up, let's see how you look. Are you skinny again?'

Claire's blue suit – French, double-breasted, with an elegant little kick-pleat in the skirt – was slimming, as her Dresser pointed out, but the waistband was too tight, so Claire had to leave it unbuttoned.

'Come on,' Shelagh coaxed, 'come out, come out, wherever you are. You can't hide behind that desk forever.'

'Why not?'

'I can already tell you look great. Come on, stand up.'

Irritably, Claire stood up.

'Wow. You look fantastic. You got your figure right back, didn't you? That's amazing. In just over three months. Have you been working out or what?'

'No, actually. I haven't had time.'

'You don't just zap back into shape like that without trying!'

'I'm not back in shape.' Claire sat down again, tired of being scrutinized and lied to. Shelagh's hair had been freshly coloured, her nails perfectly manicured. Claire held her own ruined nails behind her desk, with the rest of her anatomy she didn't care to display at the moment.

'That's quite a stack of mail you've got there,' Shelagh said, giving Claire the impression that she was envious. 'Must have been nice to have had the whole summer off.'

'Summer off? It's hard work having a new baby. It wasn't exactly a vacation.'

'You mean you didn't get in any tennis? Or golf? I thought you had a nanny.'

'I do. But she sulked if I didn't let her take Harry, so I ended up doing everything else a lot of the time. The diapers, grocery shopping. But is that the attitude around here? That I had a four-month paid holiday?'

'Relax. No one thinks that.' Shelagh paused. 'There's a bit of

envy in the air, that's all. The golfers mostly. Men, of course.'
Another pause. 'I wanted to let you know that there's a memo
in your mail you aren't going to like much. You have to do a
seminar later this week. A freebie. Word's come down from on
high. For a couple of Durham's clients. Big boys. So you better
not screw it up – not that you ever would of course.'

'Seminar on what?'

'Marketing, protection of trade-marks, the usual. Since you've
been away, Rick figured you wouldn't have much on your plate
for the first couple weeks. Besides,' Shelagh gave her a wink,
'you weren't there at the meeting to say no, were you?'

Claire would later wonder if Shelagh, with that prescient
ability of hers, could have known then that the day of the
seminar would turn out to be the worst day of Claire's life. And
the sudden news that she would have to prepare a seminar, on
such short notice, for some very important clients, completely
erased the other matters that had been on her mind just then:
first, calling Brita, and second, that she'd meant to go to the firm's
library to look up the colours of the Swedish flag.

'Good morning, gentlemen.' Claire beamed at the suits around the granite-topped boardroom table. 'As you know, I've been asked to quarterback this presentation.' (Male clients loved sports metaphors, she'd reminded herself when she'd hastily thrown together the presentation.) The reports she began passing around the table were slick, Tory blue-covered and glossy. The firm's printers had done a nice job at very short notice. Never mind that the reports didn't actually *say* much. Claire experienced a heady surge of self-confidence. She really was *back*. Back in her world. In total control. 'So I would ask all of you to please tee-off by turning to page one of the report to the recent case law, where you'll note that . . .' She paused, stricken: 'It's not there.' Not only was the first page missing, but page two had been inserted upside-down. 'Sorry,' she said, 'looks like couple of fielding blunders here – maybe we should just go on to the slides. Could somebody dim the lights, please?' She turned on the projector, expecting the slides to be in the wrong way up and backwards, as they invariably were, no matter how carefully she loaded them into the carousel, but what she wasn't expecting was the murmur of disgust that swept through the room. On the boardroom screen was one of Ben's reconstruction sites – a man's face, mid-surgery, the skin peeled back over the skull, the eyeballs dangling from venous threads, a leering grotesquerie. She snapped off the projector. 'That was one of our clients who didn't pay his account.' Silence. 'No, just kidding. That was a federal trade-marks examiner. So the moral of our story is, don't try this stunt at home, folks.'

An hour later, Claire was sitting in Rick Durham's office – an over-decorated corner suite with a private WC complete with shower. Rick was a litigator, crowned prince of the interlocutory injunction; his wife, Jocelyn, liked to dabble in interiors. He was leaning against his bleached oak desk, arms folded, legs crossed. His brass blazer buttons had fox heads emblazoned on them. They were a Waspy classic; Claire had read about them in a men's magazine once. Rick belonged to a mysterious Anglo world where men wore argyle socks, penny loafers and amusing suspenders. He would have been raised on things like junket and bread pudding, both of which Claire always thought were meant to be put out for birds in winter. Ukrainian girls knew that real pudding came powdered, in waxy packets, in either the instant or five-minute cooking variety, and that it was flavoured vanilla, chocolate, or best yet, butterscotch. But not bread. Bread was bread. Eaten at the end of a meal, after dessert; sometimes served with salt on Ukrainian special occasions, or as an edible base for lard.

Rick started to pace. He had his mad face on. The pennies in his loafers glinted as he walked. Though she was in big trouble, and she knew it, Claire couldn't help but wonder if Jocelyn buffed Rick's pennies and fox heads each morning. On a small oval table was a photo of his children in their private school uniforms, and another of some Old Boys doing Old Boys' things. Claire frowned, trying to make out what those Old Boys were doing. Punting on the Thames? Cricket? They were not things that round-faced women of Eastern European descent were privy to.

Rick seemed in no hurry to say anything, preferring to let the tension build in the room. He picked up a silver putter from where it leaned against the wall in one corner of his office. Claire wondered, with a tingle of fear, whether he meant to hit her with it. Litigators were famous for going berserk when the pressure got too great. But Rick merely aligned himself for a shot at an imaginary golf ball. What was he going to shoot it into? All Claire could see were a pair of toe rubbers, yawning hugely from the floor beside his office sofa. Toe rubber golf, she marvelled, with a silver putter no less. It was another Anglo pursuit she would never properly appreciate.

Rick swung his putter, delicately but with confidence.

'Fore?' Claire ventured.

He gave her a peeved look. 'You seem to be somewhat confused about why you're here.'

'Here in your office?' Claire said apprehensively. 'Or do you mean here at the firm?' She tried to look politely interested in what he was about to say next, but her knees were shaking. She wanted to sit down.

'You're here so that I can tell you how *pissed off* I am with you and your presentation. If Mr Biltmore had been in that room, you wouldn't have a job right now. If there was ever a scheme designed to make our firm look bad in front of our clients, this would be it.'

'It wasn't a scheme. It was an accident.'

'And that crack about the clients' accounts? Way out of line.'

'It was just a joke – I was as embarrassed as anyone else. More so.'

'Why don't you have a chat with our Accounts Committee to find out how funny they think receivables are? These are tough economic times. But we can't go around suggesting we use physical coercion to collect our fees.'

'Rick, I didn't know what else to say – it was a major upset in the first period. I have no idea how that slide got into my carousel. It was one of my husband's surgery slides. I was putting the whole thing together last night – it was pretty late. Then Harry, our son, kept me up the rest of the night.' She paused. 'He's started teething. It's very early – normally it's nine months or even a year before they start. Teething.' She drew in a deep breath. 'I'd say I got everyone's attention though, wouldn't you? And the rest of the presentation went off pretty well. It wasn't a hat-trick, I'll admit that – but still, I toughed it out to the final whistle, didn't I? But it's rough when your fourth line generates the most action in your other team's end.'

Rick examined his putter, looking perplexed. 'You know, Claire, sometimes I have absolutely no idea what you're talking about.'

'I can see that.' Claire nodded. 'You're a golfer. I tried to include a golf reference or two. But I get all my coaching from my husband. He played pro hockey for a while.'

'That right?'

'Years ago.'

Rick nodded thoughtfully. 'Look, have you ever considered taking some time off?' He gave the face of his putter a brief caress with his thumb, then replaced it in its corner.

'I've just come back from maternity leave.' Claire laughed nervously. 'What is this? The big heave-ho?'

'Of course not. You've always been an important part of our team. We could just arrange a sabbatical for you, for as long as you think you need. Practising law can get to a person after a few years.'

'But I just got back. I was off for almost four months.'

'Don't you want to spend more time with your new baby?'

'We have a good nanny. And I'm a lawyer. I like what I do. I don't think I could stay home.'

Rick stroked his beard, so neatly clipped and shaped it reminded Claire of a topiary hedge. She knew what he thought of her, could read it in his dark brown, bottom-line sort of eyes. She was a hormone-crazed, breast-feeding, neurotic working mother. Unbalanced. A liability. Someone to be 'handled'. 'Well, I'm not prepared to push the issue,' he said. 'As long as you can assure me that you're not going to start making mistakes that could be costly to the firm.'

'Of course I'm not,' Claire said, her colour rising. 'I've never made a mistake . . . that I'm aware of. I've never been reported to the Law Society, or made an insurance claim. You won't see any mistakes coming out of my office.' Small though it is, she added mentally.

'Atta girl,' Rick said. But he didn't look entirely convinced.

Having no appetite for lunch that day, and shaken by both her presentation and her Managing Partner's questioning of her competence, Claire went shopping. When the dressing gets down, the tough dress up, she told herself.

There really wasn't anything she needed to shop for, except maybe a short half-slip, now that hemlines were, once again, on the rise. But even without a definite purchase in mind, she could always cruise the shops under the guise of doing legal, or market, research. After all, her business was trade-marks, brand-names, new products, packaging and labelling. She could almost be considered negligent if she didn't keep up on popular trends, hot products, consumer preferences.

'A chemise!' the salesgirl in the lingerie shop cried. 'Every woman should own at least one. Forget about half-slips. Once you try on a chemise, you'll never go back. So feminine. Just feel this. It may seem like a lot of money, but you have to look at it as an investment.'

Claire wanted to laugh, recalling that old joke about one's money being tied up in investments like rent and food. 'Is it silk?' She turned the garment inside out, checking the label.

'Polyester.'

'For a hundred and fifty bucks?'

'It's a very good polyester,' the salesgirl sniffed. 'Feels and looks as good as silk, but you can throw it in the wash. And the dryer too. It's perma press. But not like the old perma press. You can feel the difference. This is a true miracle fibre.' She ran her vermilion nails over the fabric, as if it somehow proved her point. 'So you should splurge on yourself a little. You need more in your life than work and diapers.' She watched carefully for Claire's reaction. She'd felt the nibble, the tug on the line. It wasn't every day she could sell a chemise. 'Especially now that you've got your figure back,' she added shamelessly. She was one of the salesgirls who had snubbed Claire while she was pregnant.

What sort of woman, Claire wondered, could make her living by lying to other women? Although it was true that she had her figure back, sort of. A flabbier version, perhaps, but she was again a size seven. She had Brita to thank for it. No matter how little food Claire served up on her plate, it was always too much. Brita would gesture vaguely at her stomach, say: '*Nej tack. En liten portion,*' her eyes fearful, as if Claire were some apple-cheeked farm woman who was deviously trying to fatten her up, or the witch in *Hansel and Gretel*. Once, Brita'd looked in amazement at Claire's loaded plate. 'Ah,' she'd smiled broadly, '*smaklig maltid*! You have a very good appetite.' Embarrassed, Claire had forced herself to leave half her food on her plate at the end of the meal, though she'd lain awake most of the night, her stomach grumbling, as a result. She didn't want to be known for having, or being, a '*smaklig maltid*'. Eating less had become a sort of contest between her and Brita, each of them trying to out-do the other, like silly Southern belles who considered eating a shameful act, a publicly disgraceful activity. It had reached the point where they each took smaller helpings than Harry did, at a sitting. Once, after Brita had eaten a laughably small portion, Claire had removed her empty plate, offered a refill that was refused, then said, 'Brita, you can't possibly be full.'

'I am not *full*,' Brita had replied, rolling her eyes – a remark that was followed by gales of laughter from both Brita and Ben.

'Full means "drunk" in Swedish,' Ben had explained, still chuckling.

'Thank you so much for pointing that out,' said Claire, scraping the food off her plate and into the garbage.

'It's not every woman who can wear a chemise.' The salesgirl had sensed Claire's distraction, and was anxious to snap her back on course. Claire pictured legions of disappointed women, Andy Warhol comic-strip tear-drops trembling in the corners of their eyes, sobbing over that chemise, buried deep in their lingerie drawers, owned but unwearable.

It was a relief to know she wasn't one of them, she thought a little later, as she nudged the pink lingerie shop bag under her desk with her foot. She never liked anyone in the firm to know she'd been out shopping. Shelagh had already accosted her in the elevator, seized her bag and dragged out the chemise. 'Cute slip,' she'd said.

'It's a chemise,' Claire informed her.

'A what?' Shelagh'd spied the price tag. 'A slip for a hundred and fifty bucks? You've got to be kidding. And it's not even silk. Did you know that?'

'It's better than silk. Every woman should own one.'

'At that price, this is one woman who won't be.' Shelagh'd stuffed the chemise into the bag, and handed it back to Claire with a look. The articling student, a pimply-faced youth with a huge overbite who was with Shelagh on the elevator, had laughed uproariously. And quite inappropriately, Claire thought.

She unwrapped the poppyseed Danish she'd picked up from a

deli, and put her feet on a cardboard box of dead files she kept under her desk. Davina was still at lunch, and would be for another ten minutes, thank God. She had finished the pastry and was surreptitiously picking poppyseeds from her teeth with a paper clip, trying to sort out her feelings about everything that had happened that morning, when the telephone twittered.

She looked at it apprehensively. She could understand how lawyers could come to dislike what they did for a living. It was often unpleasant, and usually stressful, and much of her work involved play-acting – puffing herself up like a porcupine or an alley cat, to seem fierce to the lawyer on the other side, a trademarks examiner or hearing officer; or pretending to her own client that she knew the answers to 'intriguing' legal questions, when she didn't.

'I want you to know that you lost me the deal,' said the voice on the other end.

'Pardon?' She didn't have to mentally flip through her rotary card file to identify the caller. She could tell by the accent. Mike Potochnik.

'You lost me the deal. The big deal with the US fried chicken chain? For my software? And the six hundred keyboards? Is that clear enough for you? Remember how you swore they would come crawling back to offer me a better deal? Well, they didn't. They walked. They're going with the competition. And expanding into Mexico and Europe. They said I was too greedy.' He sniggered unpleasantly. 'I guess I should expect a big bill for this, eh? A real whopper. A zinger. Or maybe you lawyers don't charge for ruining a person's life. Maybe you just do it for fun.'

'I'm sorry,' Claire said, 'this is Mr Potochnik, isn't it?'

'It's me all right – Potochnik the schmuck. Remember what you told me? You don't need a lawyer to sell yourself down the river?'

It was one of Claire's favourite lines for clients who wanted to jump at any deal that was coming at them too fast, especially from the States. They were too easily dazzled. Mike Potochnik had designed a software program for fast food fried chicken restaurants and he was good at what he did. His product could log sales of thighs, legs, breasts and wings like nobody's business. It could convey to the cooks the exact timing needed to produce an entire order, garlic bread and salad included, fresh and finished at precisely the same moment: the bread piping hot, the salad crisp and cool. But the American chicken chain had been playing hard ball, trying to blindside Potochnik and get everything for nothing. They virtually demanded his first-born, served up on a styrofoam tray with a side of coleslaw.

'Well,' Claire cleared her throat and shifted in her chair, 'I may have said something along those lines. But I didn't sell you out. I simply advised you that, in my opinion, it was not a good deal. You would have lost control of your product.'

'No, not *something along those lines*. You said exactly that. *Exactly*. And I'm never going to forget it, believe me.'

'All right, so maybe I did. When did all this happen?'

'Just after you left for your summer off. I haven't heard from them since. Or you. But I don't need to tell you that, do I?'

'Was it you who sent me that malicious card?'

'Malicious? I sent you nothing malicious. I merely expressed my best wishes for your new career as a mother.'

'Thanks for ruining my summer.'

'A ruined summer's not much compared to a whole life, is it?'

'I did not ruin your life.'

'Well, I want to complete that excellent bit of advice that you gave me.'

'Okay,' Claire hesitated, 'I'm listening.'

'The way I see it, you maybe don't need a lawyer to sell yourself down the river.' He paused. 'But it sure as hell helps.' He gave a short, ugly laugh, then hung up before she could reply.

Claire stared at the receiver for a few moments, her heart thumping unpleasantly as she struggled to rein in her wildly galloping fears. An unhappy client not only meant a lot of bad press, but she could expect the Accounts Committee on her back (since he certainly wouldn't pay her last bill) and maybe the Law Society. A complaint made to that governing body of the profession meant endless paperwork: letters documenting the problem (from the client's often muddled and overwrought point of view) and the lawyer's butt-covering responses. All of it was non-billable, dead time. But worst of all, what if Potochnik were right? Had she sold him out? Been too impatient to negotiate the terms properly, to do the best job she could? She'd been pregnant at the time, almost eight months. It was unseasonably hot during those couple of weeks in May during which the negotiations had taken place. She remembered how irritated she'd been generally, unable to sleep at night. Potochnik had been a pest, the way one-file clients tended to be, calling her several times a day, demanding an explanation and re-explanation for every phrase, word and comma in the thirty-page document prepared by the dozen in-house attorneys at the chicken chain's head office in Texas. It was no good telling him she had no patience for fine print: fine print was her job.

As she sat slumped in her desk chair, stewing about Potochnik and waiting for the inevitable phone call about him from her mother, Harry popped suddenly into her mind. She pressed the speed call button on her telephone, needing to hear the sound of his endearing babble, and Brita's assurance that he was safe. But there was no answer. It was two-fifteen – Harry's nap time. As she puzzled over where they could be, the phone twittered again.

'*Hjalp!*' It was Brita. '*Hjalp*. It's Harry,' she wailed.

'What's wrong with him?' Claire struggled for breath, so scared she couldn't take in enough air. This was it – a mother's worst nightmare. Harry was dead, or kidnapped by some twisted child molester. She would see his sweet face on every bus shelter poster, on every milk carton and cable television bill, until they finally found him . . .

'He's in hospital!'

'What? Why?'

'Is his – his *blindtarm*! They say is his *blindtarm*!'

'Blindtarm? What do you mean? His arm? He's blind? What? What are you trying to say?'

'No, no, *blindtarm. Blindtarm!* Oh, what is the word in English? In the stomach!'

Claire took a deep breath. Harry wasn't dead; he hadn't been kidnapped. He would be all right. He had likely just swallowed something that disagreed with him – a bug, a dustball a marble – they were probably pumping his stomach now. She had to try to be calm, understand what Brita was saying and take control.

'Okay, Brita? Now, listen. Tell me which hospital you've taken him to.'

'Yes – the big one – for children.'

'Okay. You're at Sick Kids'. That's good. Now, have you paged Ben?'

'*Ja*. He's here, Ben is.'

'Ben's there? With you at the hospital? Why can't he talk to me? Put him on the phone. Brita? Go and get Ben!'

There was a muffled, scuffling sound, then a clunk, as if the receiver had been dropped. Claire pictured it hitting the wall, then dangling from its twisted silver cord as her voice bleated helplessly in the pale green vacuum of the hospital corridor. 'Brita? Brita, come back! Brita? Get Ben! Please! I need to talk to Ben!'

'He'll be fine,' Ben said shortly. He'd called back as Claire was darting frantically around her office, bouncing off the walls in a confused panic, unable to think even how she would get to the hospital. 'I can't talk right now. They're just doing a work-up on him.'

'A work-up?'

'Some blood tests, urine samples. Routine stuff.'

'Blood tests? For what?'

'I've got to go – I'm being paged. Harry's out of danger. You don't really need to come over.' Then the line went dead.

In the taxi – Claire was too rattled to try to drive herself to the hospital – she sat in the back seat, twisting a tissue in her fingers, then tearing it to shreds. Out of danger, Harry's out of danger, she repeated silently to herself. Then suddenly, inappropriately, her Dresser materialized and began blathering on about the polyester chemise that Claire had left in the pink bag under her desk. She was deeply concerned about Claire's wardrobe, she said, her standards. A chemise was all very well and good but this move towards polyester . . . well, it gave her pause. And of course Harry was all right – thank God! – but what if there had been a, well, an occasion that called for dark clothes – and God forbid there should! – would Claire have had anything – suitable? What did she have in basic black, for instance? What about a good bag and shoes? Had she thought about a hat? A veil? This was probably a good time to stock up – after all, look at

Basil and Elfriede. They were both a tad long in the tooth. There was no telling when either of them might decide to shake off this mortal coil, as the saying went. Wasn't it better to be prepared? Than to just show up at a significant funeral dressed in any old thing?

It was at that moment that Claire realized that her Dresser wasn't merely a dresser. She was a salesgirl! She had calcium-bonded nails, tons of eye make-up, a toothy, artificial smile, and she was firmly in control. She was Claire's worst nightmare, a hideous composite of all the pushy saleswomen she'd ever encountered. And she'd taken up residence in Claire's head!

Despite the cursory and unhelpful telephone conversation with Ben, Claire had to believe him. It was inconceivable, unthinkable, that anything serious could ever happen to their baby. Harry was out of danger; he would be fine.

Her Dresser had raised an interesting point about Claire's wardrobe, though. She really didn't have anything suitable to wear to a funeral. And, at that moment, as Claire imagined the cosy, mutually supportive scene going on right then in the hospital waiting-room, she realized that she did have a particular funeral in mind, that she would want to be sure and look good attending. Or perhaps two of them, to be more accurate.

12

'*Mein Gott*,' Elfriede said. 'How did he get this hernia? Was he doing heavy lifting?'

'It was an inguinal hernia, Mother. Nobody knows why babies get them. He was born with it. It was painful – that's why he's been screaming so much lately. Poor little fellow. I should have noticed that his nuts were purple and swollen. Somehow I missed that . . .'

'But he's out of hospital? He's in no danger?'

'The hernia's been repaired and Harry's bounced right back. He didn't even have to stay overnight at Sick Kids. But I'm a wreck, of course. Especially after the way Brita carried on. I was scared to death.'

'I'm very relieved.' There was a short silence on the line. Elfriede cleared her throat. 'But I also wanted to ask you about something else, Claire.'

'Let me guess. Mike Potochnik?'

'Isn't there something you can do for him?' Elfriede's voice was wound tight with anxiety. 'His mother is very upset about what you did.'

'What I did? I merely pointed out to him that what he was being offered was a bad deal. It's my job to tell these hard truths to clients.'

'But do you have to ruin their lives to do it?'

'I did not ruin Mike Potochnik's life. I wish people would stop saying that.'

'Maryna says his wife wants to leave him, take the children.'

'If that's true it's not because of me. If you knew Mike Potochnik better you'd realize there are probably a dozen reasons why his wife might want to leave him. But the fact that he didn't sign a terrible deal for the licensing of his software is not one of them, believe me . . . Unless he gave her unrealistic expectations.' Of course, Claire realized, that was exactly what he'd done.

'Maryna says he would have been a millionaire by now. That chicken chain just opened thirty new restaurants in the United States, and twenty more in Mexico and Europe. It was in the paper yesterday.'

Claire could picture the entire Ukrainian community of Toronto studying the *Report On Business* every day, eager to find clues to the magnitude of Mike Potochnik's loss, and the Wolaniuk family shame. 'He wouldn't have been a millionaire – it's not possible under the deal he wanted to sign. I've never seen such a one-sided agreement. I know my business. He would have had marginally more money than he does now.'

'They were going to pay him two hundred dollars for each restaurant.'

'He told you that?'

'He's told everybody.'

'Well, that's peanuts, two hundred dollars. They should have offered him ten times that amount.'

'But two hundred times fifty is a lot of money. And in United States dollars.'

'If Mike had taken the two hundred, he would have been hamstrung. He couldn't have sold his software to anyone else, ever, in any version. He'd be suing me right now – that's where his money would be going. To pay some other Bay Street lawyer to come after me because I let him sign a lousy deal. His program is good. Tell Maryna to stop worrying. Tell everyone to stop panicking. He'll get another offer for it.'

'Opportunities don't come along like street-cars – not from the United States. Not for Canadians. And Ukrainian Canadians?' She hesitated, her anxiety almost audible. 'So there's nothing you can do for him?'

'I'm meeting him for lunch. Maybe we can figure something out.' It was blind optimism. All Claire was going to do was let Potochnik take shots at her for an hour, then try to convince him not to take his complaint to the Law Society. It wasn't because she'd done anything wrong that she'd agreed to talk to him, she just didn't need the aggravation of having to report the complaint to the firm's insurers, explain it to the Executive Committee and discuss the whole mess with Rick Durham, especially after the way she'd gone on recently about there never having been a claim made against her. She also didn't want to have to talk about it, endlessly, with her mother.

'But you won't charge him for this meeting?' Elfriede fretted. 'I promised I'd ask. Maryna says Mike's afraid he'll get a big bill from you after the lunch. Is that really what lawyers are like? Maybe you'll send me a bill for this telephone call? Your own mother.'

'No one's going to get a bill. Why should I send him one anyway? He didn't pay my last one. Tell Maryna I'll even buy his lunch. All the holubtsi he can stuff into his face.'

'Try to be nice to him, Claire. The Potochniks are Dad's oldest friends. They went to school together, in the Old Country. A one-room school-house—'

'I know, with a thatched roof and storks nesting in the chimney.'

'So promise you'll be nice to him?'

'If I can get through natural childbirth, I can probably get through lunch with Mike Potochnik.'

The Pysanka Café was a small, clean, cafeteria-style restaurant in the west end, directly across from the spot where the nature trail started in High Park. It was owned and operated, with extreme pride, by three generations of the Smychych family. The food was basic Ukrainian, jazzed up a little to widen its appeal to vegetarians and other non-ethnics. As Claire's father liked to say, there was no such thing as a vegetarian Ukrainian. If there were only vegetables on the table, it just meant there was no chicken sick enough to kill.

The Pysanka's menu made a big deal out of the high-fibre content of the holubtsi, the all-natural ingredients used in the borscht, but Claire was relieved to see that the café was licensed.

The choice of restaurant was Potochnik's. He was sick of Bay Street, he said, and doubted he'd ever have a reason to go there again, after the way he'd been treated. The High Park area,

• Sylvia Mulholland

home to a large number of Ukrainians, Poles and other Eastern Europeans, was famous for its delicatessens with many styles of rye bread, cheesecake and sausage. Claire's parents lived there, so had her grandparents and so did their family dentist. Her uncles had taken her to feed the ducks on Grenadier Pond, and the earliest pictures of baby Claire pulling the heads off tulips were taken in one of the Park's many gardens. Since she was expecting to need a drink or two to get through the meeting, she'd left her car at the office and taken the subway to the café. She arrived twenty minutes late, irritable, nauseated from the lurching stops of the train, and in no mood for either Ukrainian food or trying to humour Mike Potochnik. But he was nowhere in sight. The café wasn't very busy, so he obviously hadn't been turned away for lack of a table.

She went up to the counter and ordered a half-litre of wine, deciding to give him another fifteen minutes to show. Probably, he'd read some book about getting the upper hand in business meetings and about how being late was a good way to start – demonstrating to your adversary that you were too busy for the meeting. The book would also have advised that he insist on meeting on his own turf. Potochnik had an apartment around the corner from the Pysanka. Since he lived so near, was unemployed, and had been the one to request the meeting, his lateness was insulting on several levels.

Claire carried her wine to a table near the back of the restaurant, as far away from the other patrons as she could get. If Potochnik was going to make an embarrassing scene, maybe dump sour cream on her head, she wanted as few witnesses as possible.

She sat down, facing the door, so as to be prepared to greet him, and sipped her wine uneasily, wishing she'd brought something to read, or some work to do. The Pysanka had a newspaper rack, but it contained only Ukrainian papers that Claire couldn't read. As she was pouring herself a second glass of wine, Potochnik flung open the café door, sweeping in a litter of autumn leaves, his long scarf swirling in the wind. No doubt he imagined himself a romantic figure – the young poet Taras Shevchenko, perhaps. He looked more like a young Kruschev – he was pasty-looking with the high forehead and round face that

• 138

Claire believed was typically Ukrainian, based on a sampling of the four others she knew so well – her father, her two uncles and herself. The most distinctive aspect of Mike Potochnik's face, however, was a long scar on his left cheek, close to the jaw-line.

He unwound his scarf and hung his jacket over the back of the chair across the table from Claire. 'Well, I see I'm a bit late,' he said as he sat down.

'That's okay,' she smiled.

'Hey, don't get me wrong. That wasn't an apology.'

Claire nodded and sipped her wine. 'Would you like something to drink?'

'No wine, that's for sure. I haven't had wine for years. Too much lead. It's in that foil cover they put over the necks of the bottles. Lined with lead. The lead makes contact with the cork, the cork makes contact with the wine. You figure it out.' The fluorescent lights overhead caught the lenses of his eyeglasses, turning them into flat Orphan Annie disks. 'I might have a beer,' he said, looking around, as if expecting to see one waiting for him somewhere, 'at least it's made by giant conglomerates that have the money to pour into proper crop research. Not like coffee. Those poor bastards just dump on the *Raid*. They can't afford to care. Maybe I'll just have water.'

Claire nodded again, and tried to look agreeable.

'Or nothing,' Potochnik added. 'Water has its own problems. That filtration plant near your house in the Beaches, for example. Ever been inside it? Feh.'

Claire's eyes met his. An image of an old, bottle-green sedan presented itself to her. It had been Mike Potochnik lurking in his car outside their house that day she'd come home to find Brita in their living-room. 'Well, go ahead, Mike,' she said. 'Please. Have whatever you want. It's on me.'

'I guess it would be.' He laughed shortly, and settled back in his chair. 'You know, I'm really intrigued about why you insisted on this meeting.'

Claire looked at him in surprise. Of course, the mothers were behind all of this – making Claire think Potochnik wanted the meeting, and vice versa – throwing them together in the hope that they would work things out, once they were face to face.

'I mean, there I was,' he continued aggressively, 'sitting at home not doing much of anything – waiting for another big offer to come in from the States, or for my welfare cheque to drop through the mail slot – and I get this call from my mother to say that the famous Bay Street lawyer, Claire Wolaniuk – oh, sorry, Claire Cunningham – wants to have lunch. With me! With a small-time computer programmer who can't even sell his software. I was impressed, let me tell you. I said, okay, Ma, but I hope she doesn't want to see me just to collect her bill, because I don't have the money. But that should come as no surprise to her, I said. I would have had the money, if she hadn't lost the deal for me.'

'Forget about our account.' Claire smiled thinly, trying to sound gracious.

'What?' Potochnik slapped his forehead and threw himself back in his chair. 'Did I really hear such blasphemy?' He pretended to clean out his ears. 'From a Bay Street lawyer? What would your Rick Durham say if he heard this?'

Claire stared at him, her lips still frozen into a vague smile. It would do no good to toss her wine in his face and stomp out of the restaurant. He was an unhappy client, no more, no less. She had expected him to insult her. His reference to Rick was unsettling, however. Had he been researching the firm? If so, why? Maybe he was going to write a letter of complaint about her to Rick and Mr Biltmore. 'Why don't you have that beer, Mike? Let's try and be civilized about this.'

'Civilized? You need to say that? What am I? Some cabbage roll? Some country bumpkin just fallen off the hay wagon? With shit on my boots?'

Claire looked around to see who might have overheard. The restaurant had gone completely silent. Even the cashier was leaning on her register, watching them. 'Maybe we should take a walk. Would you like to do that?'

'A long walk off a short pier? Isn't that how the expression goes?'

'That's not what I meant,' Claire said, thinking, however, what an excellent idea it was. 'I only meant that if you're going to get so angry, maybe it would be better not to disturb the other people in here.'

'I'm not going to assault you,' he glowered. 'Why don't you give me a little credit?'

'Then please, why not have a drink? Or some food?'

'I notice you're not eating.'

'I'll have something later.'

He stood up suddenly. 'Okay, I'll eat. Some good Ukrainian food. At least I know what's in it.' He strode over to the counter, grabbed a tray and began loading it with an assortment of dishes from the self-serve counter. For the benefit of the other patrons, Claire looked down, chuckling into her wine as if he'd just said something terribly witty.

'My mother tells me you had a baby boy, is that right?' Mike's tray was crowded with steaming platters and a hefty side order of sour cream.

'I guess you didn't know that when you sent me those flowers.'

'No. I didn't. And in retrospect, I suppose it wasn't a very nice thing to do – sending you that card. I should have handled my complaint more professionally. But tell me something about this baby of yours.'

Claire frowned, concerned by this sudden change in tactics. She preferred being openly abused to answering questions about Harry. Potochnik cut a pyrohy in half with his fork, then loaded a mountain of sour cream on top of it. 'These are stuffed with sauerkraut. Not as good as my mother's, but you should try some. So, have you got a picture? Of your boy?'

Reluctantly, Claire took her wallet out and retrieved a photo of Harry. It was an early one, taken at the hospital the day he was born. Potochnik would have a hard time identifying him from the picture.

'Cute.' Mike handed it back after a cursory glance. 'He gets the red hair from your husband, I suppose.'

'It's very blond now, actually. But I don't see why you want to talk about him, frankly.'

'Don't get paranoid.' He squirted some vinegar from a bottle on the table on to his drahli – boiled pigs' feet, onions and carrots, encased in yellow jelly. He'd taken a huge, pale and quivering slab of it. 'I'm not going to sit out in front of your house in my car, if that's what you're worried about. Stalking – isn't that what it's called?'

'Like you did in the summer?'

'I only wanted to talk to you, since you were too inconsiderate to return my calls. But I changed my mind when I saw you. You didn't look so good. Anyway, you don't have to worry – I had to sell the car. I couldn't afford to keep it on the road.' He paused. 'I only asked about the Beaches because I think you should read the report that's just out about people who live close to the Great Lakes. Serious health problems. Especially bad for kids. Did you know that?'

'No.'

'You'd be better off in Sudbury or someplace. But then, it's probably too ethnic for you up there. Anyway, I'll send you a copy of the report, for your kid's sake. If I can afford a stamp, that is. I've always been interested in the pure sciences.' He continued to eat, relentlessly.

'Really?' Claire sipped her wine and began to relax. If she could keep the conversation on Potochnik and his interests, perhaps the meeting wouldn't be so bad. People loved talking about themselves. 'I have no head for sciences myself. People who do always amaze me.'

'Funny that it's you who has the job right now. Not me.' He scraped his fork around his plate. 'Anyway – he's a cute kid, your boy. What's his name?'

'Harry.'

'Pretty Anglo, eh? Harry. Do you cal him Hal? Like in William Shakespeare?'

'Henry,' said Claire. 'Prince Hal was Henry. Not Harry.'

'There's a difference?'

'Of course there is.'

'It's not Zynoviy or Lubomyr. That's my point.'

'And your name's not Myroslav,' Claire bristled.

'It is, actually.'

'Oh.'

'I shorten it – trying to get ahead in this country. It doesn't help, having a name like Myroslav Potochnik. I'm sorry to say.' He shook his head. 'And with legal representation like I had, being called Mike didn't help either. I don't know why I should be surprised that you called your kid Harry. Your parents named you Claire. Anti-Ukrainianism runs in your family.'

'That's ridiculous and unfair.'

'So, are you going to send little Harry to Ukrainian summer camp?'

'I hadn't thought about it. He's not even six months old yet.' She tried, but failed, to picture Harry in an embroidered shirt plucking a bandura.

'There's a waiting list,' Potochnik snickered. 'You can't sign him up too early.'

'Well, Ben – my husband – is not Ukrainian. And neither is my mother, as you know.'

'Of course not.' He smiled unpleasantly.

'But if Ben were—'

'Sure, sure,' Potochnik waved a chunk of rye bread at her, 'you don't have to explain. Maybe Upper Canada College will have a summer camp for toddlers by the time your Harry is old enough.'

'Did you go to Ukrainian camp, Mike?'

'Every year until I was sixteen. I had to learn the dancing – that Cossack stuff. All that jumping around in boots and baggy pants.'

'Really? And that scar on your cheek – I couldn't help noticing – I don't mean to embarrass you, but is it from a sabre?'

'When I was fourteen,' he said gloomily. 'A zit. A big one. I should never have picked it.'

'Oh, I'm sorry, I thought—'

'Anyway, getting back to that dancing, the girls always irritated me, you know, they had it so easy. Just a little hopping and skipping around with flowers and ribbons.'

'I've always admired that dancing by the men. It looks awfully difficult. You must have been in terrific shape.'

'Oh sure, it was great. My knees will never be the same.'

Claire nodded, knocked back the rest of her wine and refilled her glass, feeling a pleasant buzz. 'I suppose I better get some food.'

'You mean there's something here that you would eat? They do a pashtetyky of brains that's not half bad. Why don't you try that?'

'Look, Mike,' she flushed, 'if you're hoping to gross me out, it won't work. I was raised on this stuff. And I don't know where you're getting this idea that I'm anti-Ukrainian, but I'm getting tired of that type of comment.'

'That so? Why don't we change the subject to something less sensitive then? I'm sure you didn't call this meeting to rediscover your ethnic roots, anyway.'

'No, I wanted to talk about your software, and how we could effectively market it, get you a fair deal. Failing that, we could discuss how I might be able to find something for you with my firm.'

'*Find something*?'

'A job . . . is what I was thinking.'

'Like what? Janitor? That's usually where you people expect to find Ukrainians, isn't it?'

Claire thought guiltily about the cleaning lady she often saw, replacing the toilet paper and towels in the ladies' room at her office, and Oksana, whose job it was to keep the firm's kitchen tidy and prepare tea and coffee for clients. They reminded her, poignantly, of her grandmother, with their too-tight knee-high stockings, their rubber flip-flop shoes, incongruously dyed hair and bobby pins. She often caught their eye, suspected they watched her with a certain grudging sadness, knowing she was one of them, a closet Ukrainian who thought she was cleverly disguised by the name Cunningham. But they knew. Her cheekbones gave her away. 'I meant in computer systems,' she said, 'programming or something. We employ a couple of guys in Information Systems – IS it's called. We could use some real expertise. There's a person you could talk to – Ross Owen.' Ross was a lawyer, and the firm's information systems analyst. He often stopped by Claire's office, bringing her software updates and memos about training sessions and networking – none of which she ever read. He was Mr Hard Drive, while Claire was strictly a floppy diskette: short on memory, low on power. Ross was forever DOS this and RAM that. Claire's private nickname for him was Baba Ram Dos (or Baba DOS Ross) – a sixties joke Ben wouldn't have been able to appreciate. 'His sister works for us too, in word processing,' she added. 'She used to have her own business, selling cubic zirconium, but it didn't do too well.'

'Cubic Zirconium,' Potochnik snorted. 'Did you know that was invented by the Russians for use in their spacecraft? What irony. It now dangles from the earlobes of cheap Western women. The real meaning of perestroika.'

'My point was that we try to help people out – at the firm. We take care of our own.'

'Sure. I'm living proof of that.'

'Anyway,' Claire sighed, 'if you like, I can speak to our office manager, set something up – an interview.'

'Don't bother. I don't need your job creation program. I'm keeping myself busy. I've written a book on programming. Trying to get it published – that's a full-time job in itself. Know why I'm having trouble? Because of my name. No one wants a book on computer programming written by a guy named Potochnik – they figure it has to be thirty years out of date already.'

'I'm sure that's not true.'

'It is. But I refuse to change my name.' He looked at her accusingly. 'You think Claire Wolaniuk would be working in a Bay Street firm?'

'Of course.'

Potochnik shook his head. 'Don't kid yourself. You'd be doing labour law somewhere – Winnipeg maybe. Or real estate out here in the west end. Maybe collection work for the Ukrainian Credit Union. Except that you don't even speak the language. You'd have fallen between the cracks, so to speak.'

Claire nodded, wishing she'd got a full litre of wine instead of half. 'Well, think over what I've said about a possible job with the firm.'

'No, Bragg, Banks and Biltmore would be too big a switch for me. My program is for chickens. You can't expect me to switch to rats.'

'What do you mean, rats?'

'You're a smart lady. You figure it out.'

'Well, I guess we don't have anything else to talk about.' Claire reached under the table for her handbag, stood up and pulled on her trench-coat.

'I still intend to write to the Law Society about you, make no mistake about that. I might even sue you, I haven't decided.

I'm not sure I want to make that much of a time commitment.'

Claire leaned across the table. 'You do what you have to do, Mike. But I know I gave you good representation. I even came up with a trade-mark for your program, for free, when you couldn't think of anything.'

'Good name? *Road Runner*? That's now half my problem. Who wants to buy a chicken program called *Road Runner*? Might as well call it *Road Kill*.'

'It's better than *Speedy Chicken*, which is what you suggested. It sounds like hens on amphetamines.'

'I'm not going to continue this silly debate.' Potochnik picked up his scarf and wound it around his neck, glaring at Claire as he did so.

'And I can document everything from my file,' she said. 'It won't get you anywhere, reporting me, trying to make trouble.'

'No, but it will force you to think twice next time some poor immigrant's kid comes to you for help.'

'I gave you excellent advice.'

'Your heart wasn't in it. Your mind was on other things. I wasn't a big money-maker for you – you didn't want to waste your time.'

'That's not fair. Most of my practice is individuals or small companies with untested products.'

'Well, I'm going to teach you to take more care with those clients. If you have any left, that is.'

'I really wish you wouldn't do this. You *will* sell your program, Mike. It's good and you know it. I'll even review your next agreement for nothing. Come up with a new name too.'

'No thanks.' He laughed shortly, unpleasantly. 'You've done enough already.'

'Well then, think about our families. They've been friends forever. Why do you want to start a feud?'

'I know,' Potochnik said sadly, 'this will probably kill my mother. But sometimes one has to put personal feelings aside. I'm a man of principle. Besides, I didn't start all this. You did.'

Claire tied the belt of her coat and pulled on her gloves. She had to get out of there before she started to cry. Or maybe that was what she should do: throw herself at his feet, confess that he was right, that she was losing her mind, hormonally overloaded and psychotic from sleeping-pill abuse, that her son's nanny looked like Uma Thurman, was possibly a criminal and engaged in private jokes with her husband that she could not understand; and that if she lost her job they would have to sell their house and move into a squalid student apartment near Ben's hospital. They wouldn't be able to afford the Beach, Harry would never again be wheeled along the boardwalk to grin and point up at the seagulls. She looked at Potochnik, her eyes filling. 'Please,' she squeaked.

But he avoided her eyes, staring down morosely at his grease-streaked plate. 'Don't worry about getting the tab for lunch. I'll even pay for your drinks. You go back to Bay Street and make some more money.'

With a small strangled sob, Claire turned and rushed out of the café. The wind on Bloor Street smacked her in the face as she leaned into it, making her tedious way towards the subway station. She was so distraught that she boarded the westbound train instead of the eastbound, and had gone as far as Kipling – the end of the line – before she noticed her mistake. As a final insult, the car she was on was taken out of service and she was obliged to get off and sit, shivering and sniffling, on the windy platform for almost half an hour, until the next train came along to pick her up and carry her back downtown.

WINTER

13

Every year, Claire got infected by the Christmas spirit in early November, just after Halloween. Halloween itself had turned out to be a bit of a bust, at least where her expectations for Harry were concerned. She'd looked forward to it as the first year when she wouldn't want to turn out all the lights, close the blinds and pretend no one was home. This year they had Harry, and an endearing, almost painfully cute cow costume that Claire had ordered through the Neiman Marcus catalogue from New York.

Thinking about Harry going out on his first trick-or-treat had brought back memories of her own childhood experiences: of rain, and glitter and sparkles that washed off the synthetic costumes; of Claire's mother struggling to make angel wings for her girls, from coat hangers and the fabric from an old tulle party dress; of Mrs Fedorchuk on their street who, nonsensically, gave out fresh jelly doughnuts that ended up at the bottom of the kids' bags, squashed flat and studded with peanut shells, and of her poor daughter, Irene, who was never allowed out on Halloween because she suffered from migraines. Claire also recalled the arguments she had every year while married to Simon, who insisted they hand out only healthy treats: miniature boxes of raisins, peanuts-in-the shell, apples – all of which made them the most unpopular couple on the block and earned them a thorough window-soaping for their caring and concern.

Of course, Harry, at four months old, was far too young for trick-or-treating, or to eat any of the sugary goodies Claire and Ben collected on his behalf, but he was not too young to be taken around to the neighbours and shown off. The cow suit had cunning stuffed horns on the hood, and a swishy tail dangling from its rear. It was a black and white cow – a Holstein. Harry, however, had been less than impressed by it. He had a cold, for one thing – the snot from his running nose had mingled pathetically with the black and white grease-paint that Claire had carefully dabbed on his face. He'd whined at the first house Ben carried him to, whimpered at the second, and by the third was bawling miserably, flinging his small decorated paper bag of candy on to the sidewalk and struggling wildly to get the cow hood off his head. And later, the sight of other children crowding the front porch in brightly coloured costumes and often horrifying masks had pushed him into hysteria. Ben made up a bottle for him and hustled him off to his crib, leaving a discouraged Claire to distribute (or eat) all of the miniature chocolate bars by herself.

Brita had gone out with friends for the evening. There was no such thing as Halloween in Sweden and she was wanting to see the annual drag show down Yonge Street. In Sweden, children dressed as witches at Easter, going from house to house with brooms and coffee pots – a sort of marauding hardware store was how Claire pictured it – and giving out cards with drawings of chickens on them in exchange for candy or money. This custom struck Claire as bizarre, but was probably no more so than any of those celebrated in Canada, as Ben pointed out.

Halloween had seemed to bring out the worst in the Beach. Late in the evening, two women showed up, canvassing in aid of a single mother in their apartment building whose child had recently died.

'Of what?' Claire wanted to know, appalled.

'Leukaemia,' they chorused with downcast eyes, after a slight hesitation. 'We're taking up a collection to help her out. Anything you could spare would be appreciated. She's on welfare.'

Claire hurried to get her purse, acutely aware of the big S they must have seen in the middle of her forehead. Not sure she believed their story, she had to resist the impulse to cross-examine the women. What if they were telling the truth? Her probing questions would be met with scorn and hatred, as though she were some female Ebenezer Scrooge. Are there no workhouses? No prisons? Flushing, she'd pushed a ten-dollar bill into their jar and closed the door. Christine had been right: there was no telling who would show up at your door in the Beach.

Christmas, however, was sure to be a success. Even though Harry was too young to get much out of it, it would be terrific fun: the Cunninghams' first Christmas together as a family.

By early December, having already been steadily shopping for a full month, Claire was beginning to lose track of the presents she'd bought for Ben and Harry and where she'd hidden them in the house. And as the calendar rolled on towards the 25th, she began to lose her Christmas spirit altogether, dreading a pile of gifts under the tree with her name on the tags; knowing that under the wrappings would be things she didn't want, didn't need and didn't like, but couldn't take back. A fresh selection of joke gifts from Ben was what she had learnt to expect. She would rattle and squeeze the mysterious parcels, hoping to feel the blue velvet cases from Birks Jewellers, but sensing, somehow, that the cheery wrapping concealed only the thin cardboard boxes from the Tacky Shop or Preposterous Presents. 'Gee, thanks, honey,' she would say, 'how did you know my old whoopee cushion had a hole in it?'

Her Dresser was applying pre-holiday spurs to Claire's rump with a vengeance, and had been joined by a number of others as well. Harry now had his own diminutive Dresser – a Cuteness Counsellor, actually – and lately, a spritely Christmas Consultant had crowded into Claire's head, urging her to buy things like cedar rope, door wreaths (front and back), star-shaped guest soaps, fingertip towels, pot holders, fridge magnets and simmering potpourris. There was even a pouting James Dean sort of Sex Expert in her head, who kept reminding her – in his taciturn manner – of the decline of her libido, implying that she needed more elaborate (and uncomfortable) underthings as he made lewd suggestions about winter evenings with Ben in front of the hearth (which they didn't have). But by mid-December, Claire was fed up with the lot of them. She had become a true Christmas Grinch – embittered, exhausted and aghast by the amount of money she had spent. Ben, who often broke into spontaneous renditions of 'Good King Wenceslas' in midsummer, had been 'cranking the stereo with Christmas tunes', as he put it, since the beginning of November. If Claire was obliged to listen to the 'Hallelujah Chorus' one more time that year, she would go mad, she told him one night when she was feeling particularly piquey.

A few days before Christmas – a grey and slushy afternoon – she found herself in one of the big downtown department stores, cross and perspiring and trying to find socks for Harry on the third floor that had recently been rearranged (she was sure) for the sole purpose of befuddling her. The store had an upbeat atmosphere, jazzed up 'Jingle Bells' was blasting out of everywhere, jangling Claire's nerves. What was the marketing theory behind all the noise, she wondered. That shoppers would be so rattled they would lose track of what they'd meant to buy, and consequently buy a lot more? Or that they would forget to count their change? It was more likely to send them screaming out of the store – something she was seriously considering as she made another tour, diagonally, across the vast sales floor, still searching for Harry's socks and losing hope of ever finding them.

Suddenly, she heard a 'Ho Ho Ho', so deep, so genuine and profoundly merry that she thought, for a moment, it must be St Nick. She wheeled around and followed the sound until she found him, sitting on his throne, all alone, during a lull in the children's photo-taking. This Santa was as perfect as his laugh. His hair and beard were real – long and silky, and a sort of yellowish-white – none of that cottony stuff typical of department store Santas. His eyes really did twinkle (drugs? Claire wondered, at the same time despising herself for her cynicism) and his mouth was truly that perfect little drawn-up bow that Clement Moore had described in *The Night Before Christmas*. He seemed so patient and kind, so benign, that she had to go right up to him and tell him what a superb Santa he was. He winked at her, chuckling another bowl-full-of-jelly chuckle. 'Why don't you come sit on Santa's knee?' he said. 'No one's ever too old for telling Santa what they want for Christmas.'

Claire studied him for a moment, uncertainly. There was no one around but one of his helpers, an attractive young woman in a red velvet mini-skirt and fake fur-trimmed jacket who jingled a ring of bells, encouragingly, at Claire. The woman had a lot of hair – several times more than she actually needed, Claire noticed – she had almost as much hair as Brita. Claire was acutely conscious of other women's hair lately, since hers had started falling out just as Harry turned the corner of four months. Great handfuls came out when she washed it, when she moussed and dried it, when she so much as looked at it. A good third of it had gone – possibly forever – and venturing outside in a stiff breeze had become a source of stress and embarrassment. Female pattern alopecia, Ben said it was: it was likely post-pregnancy-induced (in which case her hair should grow back in) but it might also be attributable to Claire's age (in which case it wouldn't). That word 'alopecia' somehow made it sound much worse than it was.

Feeling suddenly impetuous, Claire stepped up on to Santa's platform and settled gingerly, on the edge of his lap. 'So,' she said, colouring a bit, 'what do I want for Christmas? I'll have to think about that for a minute.' She drew in a deep breath, let it out slowly. 'How about time? Can you get me some more of that? I meant to bake Christmas cookies with Harry, my son, this year – really I did. But I've been so busy at work . . .'

Santa shook his head.

'You're right,' Claire sighed, 'it was my own fault. I spent too much time shopping.'

Santa said nothing. Only his eyes twinkled.

'But I suppose I shouldn't expect any sympathy from you on that count. You work here in this department store. If it weren't for Christmas shoppers you wouldn't have a job.' She sighed again. 'Well, how about giving me ten years of my life back?' Santa shook his head sagely, his eyes still twinkling. 'Take a year off my husband's residency? Or what about energy? I could use more of that. Or make me a better mother. More patient with Harry.' Santa stroked his beard reflectively. 'Okay – I'll be reasonable. Just send me a new nanny. Maybe one of your elves wants to be retooled – needs a career change.' Claire's hazel eyes met Santa's blue ones. 'So just bring me some more hair,' she said finally, 'or anything from the Tacky Shop.'

Santa laughed heartily, putting so much zest into his 'Ho Ho Ho!' that Claire almost fell off his knee as the camera's flash bulb popped in her face.

The resulting picture, which she never bothered to take out of her handbag after a cursory glance, didn't show her with the impish, devil-may-care expression she'd expected to see. Instead, she looked tense and pale and pinched, sitting edgily on Santa's knee, as if afraid he might have a hard-on beneath that expanse of cherry-red velvet.

Ben, along with all other residents, was expected to take part in a Christmas entertainment for the staff at his hospital. As a result, Claire saw even less of him than usual in December. He would arrive home late, his hair pushed up into its usual cone shape. Grouchy and haggard, he would spend a few minutes tossing Harry on the bed, exciting the requisite number of gleeful squeals from his son, before disappearing to be alone with his slides. Claire would watch him head for the study, wishing he'd put as much time into extracting gleeful squeals from her. The Christmas Caper at the hospital was to be a slide-show parody of *How The Grinch Stole Christmas* – the Grinch being the Minister of Health who was pushing to reduce doctors' fees, province-wide. From what Claire had seen of Ben's script, it was conventionally scatological – lots of ribald toilet humour meant to embarrass senior administrators and department heads – the kind of thing hospital staff supposedly delighted in. Claire could understand how they might find it funny at the end of a night of heavy drinking, but the Christmas Caper was to be presented during early morning rounds, at 7 a.m. What could possibly be funny at that hour, she wondered.

The organized holiday festivities, from Claire's end, consisted of a party for the entire firm at a downtown hotel – to which no spouses were invited – and a smaller party at Shelagh's condominium, to which only the lawyers and their spouses were invited. Shelagh's party would be a good opportunity to meet the 'new kids on the block', the three lawyers who had recently joined the firm. One of them, a woman named Gillian something-or-other, Claire was quite prepared to dislike. She had red hair for one thing (and therefore a bad temper, Claire concluded, knowing she was being pigmentally prejudiced) and pale blue-grey eyes that reminded her of an Alaskan Mala-mute's. Gillian also 'did patents' – something no one else in the firm understood – and the reception area of Bragg, Banks and Biltmore was suddenly populated by a number of *characters*, or 'loopy inventors', as Shelagh called them, with prototypes of their inventions poking through shopping bags or bound up with string or Cellophane tape.

On the morning of Shelagh's party, Claire looked out of her bedroom window to see that an avalanche of snow had been dumped on the city, and that still more was coming down. Ben had left very early – he would have missed the worst of it, she realized with relief. After watching one of their neighbours spinning his car wheels in the drift at the foot of his driveway, Claire decided to take the day off work. Harry would have his home-made Christmas cookies after all. And she – his mother – would bake them.

Despite the evils it brought to the city and its drivers, the snow was pretty and Christmassy and it had the effect of jettisoning Claire back into the mood she'd lost during her tiresome Christmas shopping. She hummed parts of the 'Hallelujah Chorus' as she dug through her recipe box to find the battered cards of Wolaniuk family favourites: Medivnychky, Cossack's Kisses, Pfefferneusen, and the old-fashioned Waspy kinds as well, like the (essentially tasteless) sugar cookies that would be lavishly decorated with red and green sparkles and jaw-breaking silver balls. She felt cheerful and optimistic: Brita was a great nanny; Potochnik would forget his vendetta against Claire, sell his software to some giant conglomerate and get on with his life. She might even go out and take some photographs of the snow, she thought, after another glance at the winter wonderland, and send them in to one of the local newspapers for possible publication in its *Toronto By Lens* section.

Harry sat in his high chair by a kitchen window, mesmerized by the falling snow as Brita bustled about, feeding him cereal and mashed banana, treating it as a special occasion – Claire staying home for the day. An act, Christine would say it was, but Claire had no interest in that sort of joy-sucking cynicism today. She felt cosy and companionable, liked the feeling of being safe and warm in their house while the white stuff continued to pile up on the windowsills and blanket the yard.

With a surge of good will, she realized that she liked Brita, truly *liked* her.

'Does all this snow make you feel at home?' she asked.

'Oh, *ja*. We have a lot of snow at home. But not so much last year – I don't know why – what's going on with the weather.'

'But usually you have a lot? This much?'

'Much more. Sometimes it comes as high as the windows and we must climb out the windows to go to school. We always must go to school. Snow is no reason to stay home. Unless we can't open the windows. Then we can stay home.'

Brita would be spending Christmas with some Swedish friends in Toronto, which meant there would be less picking up after her for Claire to do. That in itself would be a holiday. And even better, Claire would be alone, finally, with Ben and Harry. 'Do you have Santa Claus in Sweden?'

'*Nej*. We have Lucia. The girls dress in white with candles on the head. There is Lucia in every school, every town, every church. There is one for all of Sweden. It gets a bit ridiculous, to tell the truth.'

'Oh, Lucia,' Claire nodded. 'That picture you have downstairs? That's you as Lucia, isn't it?'

'My picture?' Brita looked at her in surprise.

'I had to take a man down there to the basement,' Claire said quickly, 'to read the gas meter – it's in your closet. Don't worry,' she laughed, 'I wasn't snooping, if that's what you're thinking.'

'Yes,' Brita said without expression, 'that picture is Lucia. She was an Italian saint. Silly. We aren't even Catholics in Sweden. Lucia is for light – the festival of light. Because it is so dark in winter.'

'But isn't it dangerous, putting lighted candles on your head?'

'They put a napkin on the head, under the candles – something like that. Now they use electric lights mostly – not so much candles any more.'

'What about presents? Does Lucia bring presents to the children?'

'The *tomten*. He brings the presents.' Deftly, she spooned some banana into Harry's mouth. He swallowed, his eyes fixed on her, evidently mesmerized. 'He comes to the door on Christmas Eve and asks if there are any nice children inside. Then he gives out the presents.' She frowned. 'I think they are already there under the tree – but he gives them out, I think. And my father always misses him. He always must go out to mail a letter, so every year he misses the *tomten*. Dad, you missed him again, we say every year.'

'Do you miss your home, Brita?'

'Some things. The food. The fish. There is not so much junk food in Sweden.'

She was one to complain about junk food, Claire thought. But she said, 'So what else is different here in Canada?'

'We don't have so much sky-scraping buildings. And there is more space. The houses are not so crowded together. With the tiny backyards.'

Then Brita was lifting Harry out of his high chair, snuggling into his neck, calling him *pussgurka* and giving him noisy kisses. Jealousy washed over Claire, her jolly mood ebbing away. 'How would you like to make some Christmas cookies, Brita? While I take Harry out to see the snow?'

'*Nej*. No. Please. I am not so good making cookies.'

'But surely you have some great old family recipes. Make something Swedish for us. Or use my recipes. Any one in this box.'

'I rather not. I can take Harry out. He should be changed now – he has a wet diaper – his pants too, they are wet.' She kissed him again. 'It's better you make cookies.'

'Well, no – I don't want to. Not right now. I mean, here I am with one precious day off to spend with Harry, and I'm not going to waste it by rolling cookie dough.' Suddenly, unreasonably, childishly angry – why couldn't Brita make herself scarce for once? Wash some of those diapers she was always talking about changing? Why did she have to be so clueless? Couldn't she sense when Claire needed some private time with her son? Claire snapped shut the lid of the recipe box and turned to put it back in the cupboard. She would simply buy Christmas cookies, like any other working mother, she decided. Harry wouldn't know the difference – he only had one tooth, for heaven's sake. Next year would be the year to start on Christmas traditions with him. She wouldn't waste a single second on housework or cooking or other drudgery. Today, she belonged to Harry. Alone. 'And speaking of Sweden, Brita,' she said, 'I've been meaning to ask you about that flag you've put up on your ceiling downstairs.'

But as she turned around, she saw that Brita and Harry had gone. From upstairs, she heard the sound of Harry's bureau drawers being opened and closed, the lid of the diaper pail banging shut. More work for Claire was what that meant.

Discouraged, she gazed outside at the Cunninghams' yard – backyards weren't all *that* tiny in Canada – at the poor little junipers that were bowed over under the heavy snow. She should go out there, she thought, shake them free before their branches got damaged. Still feeling petulant about Harry and scheming about how she would get him away from Brita, Claire put on her boots and jacket, grabbed a broom and waded out into the deep drifts to nudge and poke and shake her trees.

By noon it was clear that the city was under siege. Would it become known as 'the Great Storm', the stuff of legends? Inside again, Claire turned on the twenty-four-hour weather channel and watched the blue strip running across the bottom of the television screen. 'Severe Winter Storm Warning' it said, over and over. On another channel, the weather man was chuckling sardonically, advising people to stay home, or clear off the roads as fast as they could. He always seemed to be in fine form when he had dire predictions to make, as if he never got invited out anywhere, or had any plans, and resented those who did. So much for Shelagh's party, Claire thought; so much for the green velvet she meant to wear, so much for her husband's admiring glances.

The telephone and hydro wires, networked across the backyard like giant clotheslines, swayed and sagged. On the deck, the planter boxes were piled high with snow – they looked like huge, just-risen loaves of bread, still in their pans – and more snow was mounded on the corner posts, forming perfectly rounded ice-cream scoops, as though decorative finials had been added to them.

This type of snow was ideal for making hard-packed snowballs that could put out a person's eye, but useless for anything else. It was too wet for tobogganing; too heavy to shovel. Great clumps of it banged and thumped on the roof, falling from the oak tree with a sound like overweight reindeer landing. For the first time, Claire felt a tingle of fear, no longer thinking about missed Christmas parties. Ben would be stuck at the hospital: there was no way he'd be able to get home that night – he would be in real danger if he tried. She considered all the nurses who would be similarly stuck there with him, keeping him company through the long winter night. It might be days before they were able to dig themselves out. She thought about paging him, but decided not to. Not yet.

Instead, she marched boldly upstairs to the nursery – whose house, whose baby was it, anyway? – telling Brita that she would be taking Harry out, ignoring her sullen looks, then bundling her son in multiple layers of clothing to carry him outside and watch him experience his first big snow. He frowned as it came down thick and fast around him, clinging to his long eyelashes, making him blink. A viciously pointed icicle dropped suddenly from the roof and plunged into the mound of snow below. With a gasp, Claire pulled Harry out of the way and sat him safely on his sled in the middle of the deck. The snow was no longer the picturesque and benign matter she needed to reactivate her Christmas spirit. It had become malevolent and threatening. She tugged Harry back and forth across the deck a few times, but rather than cooing and gurgling and making other delighted-baby sounds, he only scowled and looked perplexed as he was juddered and jerked through the sticky snow.

Then Brita banged on the window from inside, holding up the telephone receiver. It was Ben, calling from the hospital between cases, to ask what time they had to be at Shelagh's. He was unaware of the snow and didn't see how it made any difference to their plans. The party was still on, wasn't it? True party animals didn't let something as insignificant as a snow storm stand in their way: it never entered their heads that someone (almost always someone *else*) would eventually have to get behind a steering-wheel and try to navigate an obstacle course of car pile-ups, police spot checks and slippery streets. He would try to be home before seven, he said. And of course he would be careful.

It was almost five when the snow stopped coming down. The city's ploughs were making a speedy progress, the news service reported, efficiently clearing the main arteries to make getting around the city possible.

The party was still on, Shelagh told Claire over the phone, and she was thrilled by the atmosphere that had been created for it. How lovely her place would look with all that dazzling white in the background, the outdoor lights of the surrounding condo balconies softly glowing. She'd even hired a pianist to play favourite carols and songs on her baby grand. Atmospherically, at least, it seemed that the Lord had smiled down on Shelagh's party and Claire's green velvet dress.

14 ∫

Ben and Claire arrived at Shelagh's place an hour late, along with a number of others from Claire's firm who had also been held up by the bad weather. The smell of expensive perfume and damp furs mingled with a lot of foot-stamping, complaints about the driving, and compliments to Shelagh on the splendour of her Christmas decorations. The preference for outdoor lighting in the swank, uptown area where Shelagh's condo was located, was for tasteful twinkly white fairy lights strung on balconies, over potted evergreens and inside, on the ubiquitous *ficus benjamina* trees. The Beach was for showier stuff: beaming light-up Santas, deliriously flashing multicoloured strings of oversized bulbs that outlined the garages, house windows and doors; giant red ribbons tied around front porches; miniature reindeer, frozen in midprance, with Rudolph's nose glowing hallucinogenically from various rooftops.

Shelagh, in a sheer black blouse over a velvet bustier, with silver sequinned harem pants clattering about her legs, grabbed their coats and steered them into the dining-room which had been set up with a full bar and a tuxedoed bartender. 'So,' she turned to Ben, 'Claire tells me you plastic surgeons can go up to twenty hours on one operation.'

'A reconstruction, sure. Not a face-lift.' Ben laughed.

'I can't even imagine doing something I absolutely adore –' she gave him a coy wink – 'for twenty hours.'

Ben chuckled, raising his eyebrows, nodding and pursing his lips.

'So how can you stand it?' Shelagh pressed. 'And what could possibly take you that long? I mean, do you guys just wade in there, muck around for seven or eight hours and then say, "Geezus, look at this bloody mess" and spend the next ten or twelve hours trying to patch things up?'

'Basically. Something like that.'

'So come with me for a moment. I need to talk to you about a couple of things.' She tucked his arm under hers and pulled him conspiratorially into an adjoining room which served as a small library, the walls lined with book-cases. 'We can talk better in here.' She hadn't seemed to notice that Claire had arrived with Ben.

One of the firm's partners, Alexander Spears, was standing morosely in the vestibule, close to the front door, glowering into his scotch on the rocks. He was a brooding Jewish intellectual who had interviewed and hired Claire at Bragg, Banks and Biltmore, three years earlier. Claire had always found him attractive, and the admiration, she knew, was mutual. Until her pregnancy. 'So, Alex,' she said, stepping over a pile of leather boots and toe rubbers, 'you look lonely out here. Didn't you . . . bring anyone?' He was notorious for always appearing at firm functions with a good-looking woman (who was never more than half his age) on his arm.

'My girlfriend's at my place. With the dog.'

'You got a dog?'

'*She* got a dog. I said no for three months, but in a single moment of weakness I broke down. She's going to have to look after it – I told her I wasn't going to do a thing.'

'I didn't know you were . . . living with someone.'

'At the moment,' he said drily. 'For allowing that dog I should be shot and pissed upon.'

'Well, if it's piss you're after, I'd say a dog was heading you in the right direction. Or you could try a baby.'

'Thanks for that note of levity.'

Claire struggled to manoeuvre some slippery spinach dip on to a large button mushroom – a platter of raw vegetables had been put out on an antique table in the vestibule. 'Well, look on the bright side. At least you'll never have to follow the dog around with a plastic bag over your hand – you'll be spared that indignity since your girlfriend's going to do it.'

Alex swirled his ice cube irritably in his glass. 'There is no bright side with a dog. The damn thing swallowed a sock the other night.'

'A sock? Isn't that too dry to swallow? Bulky?'

'It was wet, a wet sock. We'd just done the laundry. So I called up the vet, I mean, I didn't know whether it was something to worry about or not. The dog seemed okay, but the vet freaked, said we had to give her hydrogen peroxide to make her vomit up the sock. Well, she vomited all right. She vomited everything she'd ever eaten in her whole life. Anyway,' he took a quick swallow of his drink, 'that was two nights ago and the dog's still puking – blood now. She might need surgery.'

Claire nodded, trying to think of some way to commiserate. 'We have a baby, you know, there's a lot of cleaning up to do with him too.'

'So how's the kid anyway?'

'Great. Harry's great. And I'm finally feeling like my normal self.' She looked into Alex's eyes, seeking affirmation that she looked like her normal self as well – perhaps even better? – but he only nodded and continued to reflect upon his drink.

'This dog will live forever,' he said, 'I know it. It'll live to shit on my grave.'

Claire looked around for Ben to help ease her out of this unhappy loop of a conversation, but Shelagh, who'd been joined by three other women, had him securely cornered. She was turning her profile towards him, indicating her neckline and making a small flapping gesture with her hand. Ben would cope, Claire thought, he was used to it. Women always accosted him at parties, as soon as they found out he was almost a plastic surgeon, shamelessly offering up their moles, wrinkles, bulges and stretch-marks for his scrutiny. It was an occupational hazard that Claire suspected he enjoyed.

The only thing anyone ever asked, after discovering that Claire was a lawyer, was 'criminal law?' Their eyes would light with momentary interest. Over the past few years there'd been a flood of books on the best-seller list, all of them courtroom thrillers with titles borrowed from criminal law: *Presumed Innocent*, *The Burden of Proof*, *Beyond Reasonable Doubt*. Everyone wanted to hear about courts and criminals, judges and corruption – any lawyer ought to have a few real-life titbits that could be shared at parties. But when Claire admitted she was just another Bay Street hack – ha ha – who practised an arcane form of law – intellectual property – paperwork, a desk job, strictly solicitor's work – the face of her listener would sag with disinterest. Trade-marks was what she specialized in, she would add, like Coke? Nike? Kodak? But her listener's eyes would have already glazed over and talk turned to the weather as a topic far more engaging than what Claire did for a living. She liked to try to imagine writing a novel, based on her own practice. There could be *Deceptively Misdescriptive* – a tear-jerker about a trade-mark that just couldn't cut it, or perhaps *The Retroactive Extension* – a pot-boiler about a churlish trade-mark examiner who refused to grant extensions of time to meet statutory deadlines. Or maybe someone could write a book about the gutsy realism of a law practice: *The Aged Invoice, The Write-off, Receivable! And over Ninety Days.*

'Nice balcony lighting Shelagh's put up,' she said to Alex, standing on her toes to peer over a sea of suit-clad shoulders at the tiny fairy lights that blinked off and on beyond the sliding glass doors of the condo. 'And all that snow makes it so pretty, doesn't it?'

'You should see my neighbourhood,' Alex said. 'Mine is the only house with no lights. I might as well have put JEW on the roof in big red and green bulbs.' Claire and Alex looked at each other in silent acknowledgement that there was nothing left to say.

'Well,' she finally said, 'I guess I better go check out the buffet before there's nothing left.' And rescue Ben, she thought. Wherever he was. Alex neither objected to, nor acknowledged, her leaving. Such a rude man, Claire thought, her cheeks hot. Why did she even bother trying to make conversation with such an unpleasant person? Attractive though he was.

She wandered over towards the piano, listening in on snippets of other people's conversations. As she passed the kitchen she heard the shriek of the blender, a demand for more tequila. Someone was whirling up a pitcher of margaritas, apparently.

She stopped at the end of the short queue of people who were waiting to help themselves to food at the buffet. Over the tinkle of ice-cubes beside her, a woman was complaining that she never wore her fur coat any more because she was afraid of being spray-painted by animal rights activists. 'I put it on to come over here tonight,' she said, 'first time in two years. I wore it from the house to the car, from the car to the front door. That's it.'

'What kind of fur is it?' her listener asked.

A slight pause. 'Wolf.'

'Arctic wolf?'

'I don't know – just wolf.'

'So you're pretty sure it was caught in a leg-hold trap then.'

A longer pause. 'Well, I never really asked . . .'

Someone else was bemoaning the fact that his sister-in-law was threatening to buy him a bathroom mirror for Christmas. 'I told her not to,' he was saying, 'I mean, we just bought the house and I'm fussy about what's going in it. But now my wife's pissed off at me for hurting her sister's feelings, so we'll be getting a mirror for sure. Christmas as the ultimate revenge.'

'So retaliate. Give her a fruitcake.'

Behind Claire, someone else was saying, 'Shit and puke. Years of cleaning up shit and puke. That's what you get when you have kids.'

'And don't forget the screaming, the tantrums. And years without sleep,' another voice added.

'But surely that's not all there is to it?' a third person said, with a nervous laugh. Claire turned to look at her – a hugely pregnant woman who was running her hands uneasily over her belly, evidently alarmed. 'It's not so bad,' Claire wanted to tell her, but that would have been an admission that she was eavesdropping.

'How's your nanny working out?' Shelagh had come up behind Claire suddenly. 'I hear she'd drop-dead gorgeous.'

'Who told you that?'

'Oh, a little bird.'

'A little bird named Ben?' Claire managed a wry smile, to indicate that she wasn't threatened.

'Not saying. But it wasn't him.'

'Well, she's not gorgeous. She's attractive. And very good with Harry. That's what really matters.'

'Harry – what a riot. He was so cute that day you brought him in to the office, and he dumped your coffee all over your files. Is he getting any serious hair yet?'

'He's got a bit of stuff – not much, though – ten hairs doing the work of thousands.'

'Where would he get blond hair from? You're both brunettes, you and Ben.'

'I don't know.' Another wry smile. 'But people do keep asking us that.'

'Better watch out. Everyone's going to think your nanny is Harry's mother.'

'I guess they might,' Claire chuckled, as if she found the idea amusing. Far from being amused, however, she was remembering one afternoon when she was exhausted from a sleepless night (Harry had had the croup) and had come home early, hoping to steal an hour's snooze before dinner. She'd been surprised to see Ben's car pull into the driveway a few minutes later. His case had finished early and he'd come home to take Harry out before his bath, down to the boardwalk, maybe to Lick's for an ice-cream. Claire didn't feel like going. But Brita did. Together, Ben and Brita wheeled Harry out towards the beach as Claire watched from the kitchen window, noting the air of easy intimacy the three of them conveyed. They looked like a charming little family. Certainly, the last thing anyone would suspect was that Brita was Ben's employee. Was that what Ben hoped? Her head throbbing with a tension headache, Claire had watched until they dwindled to tiny specks on the boardwalk, feeling like a dried-up, cast-away husk; an old brood mare put out to pasture with nothing to look forward to but the glue factory. They were gone for over two hours. Claire never did get her nap that day.

'You should see our nanny.' Rick Durham's wife, Jocelyn, had suddenly appeared to join Claire and Shelagh. 'Ugly as sin, but great with the kids. We interviewed a Danish girl first – drop-dead gorgeous, like yours. She seemed great and I would have hired her – I actually would have – but Rick said no way. He didn't need that kind of temptation in the house.'

'He said that? Didn't it bother you that he would admit it?'

'He's a man who understands his own weaknesses. It's better that way.' She tilted her head to one side and studied Claire, waiting for her reaction.

'I'm starved,' Claire said. 'This food looks wonderful. A meal I didn't have to cook myself.'

'Our nanny cooks too. Like a dream. She could do a buffet like this without any help.' Jocelyn stayed close behind Claire, identifying the various dishes.

'You're so lucky. Our Brita can't cook. But she's great with Harry. And that's what counts, isn't it?' Claire wished Jocelyn would go away, but knew she had to be pleasant to her. She was, after all, the Managing Partner's wife now.

On the table was a hot chicken dish with puff pastry circles on top, a wild rice casserole with porcini mushrooms, two kinds of salads – one of them with mandarin orange sections and almond slivers on top – a silver filigree basket of delicate golden rolls and butter pats shaped like sprigs of holly.

'The chicken is to die for.' Shelagh was there again, squeezing Claire's arm. 'But your hubby is the main attraction here tonight. He'll pick up a lot of business in this crowd – we'll be beating down the door of his office before he's had a chance to hang out his shingle. He'll do well – he's so cute. He even got a smile out of Sandra Johnson.'

'Hey, I'll be first in line when he opens that office,' Claire said, wondering how many times she'd said that over the past four years.

'Talk to you later. I better go do my hostess thing.' Shelagh clattered off in her sequins, leaving Claire to eavesdrop on more conversations. Ahead of her, there was more nanny talk going on. 'It was one of our best pots,' a woman was complaining, 'that we'd got for our wedding. And instead of simply admitting she'd let it boil dry, she hides it in the back of a kitchen cupboard – under the sink – with a dish-towel inside it. Like we're going to take out the pot – assuming we ever found the thing – and go to use it without noticing there's a dish-towel in the bottom of it. Does she think we're stupid?'

The listener, another woman, clucked sympathetically. 'Well, we've been renovating our bathroom and one day *ours* asks us what we're going to do with the old bathroom cabinet. She wants it. So I say, sure you can have it, but what do you need it for? You live with us.'

'I'm telling you, she wants to live out. I've seen the signs. She's furnishing an apartment somewhere. She'll hit you with it when you're least expecting it. Live out or she quits – that'll be the ultimatum. And live out is three hundred more a month, don't forget. Just count your towels when she leaves – that's all I can say. I bet she's got a husband somewhere. Has she got her open permit yet? You should call Immigration and find out.'

Though she wasn't feeling the least bit hungry and would have preferred to spend the rest of the evening getting drunk, Claire piled some chicken, rice and salad on her plate, admiring Shelagh's silver serving pieces. She had a collection of lovely antique mismatched china, too – an eclectic mix left to her by her grandmothers, and a set of water glasses etched with designs of thistles and wild flowers. Claire thought about how much she herself used to enjoy entertaining: all that fussing over menus, the shopping and cooking, the decisions over centrepieces, flowers and candles, the starching and folding of linen napkins into the shapes of swans, fans or tulips. She had two books on creative napkin folding, and dozens of cookbooks: Greek, Italian, Thai – the entire United Nations huddled together in the cupboard above the fridge. But she had no time to cook anymore. Nor energy. She'd started buying things like Hamburger Helper, something she hadn't resorted to even in her student days. Why couldn't Brita cook? she grumbled to herself. Any idiot could read a recipe. All Brita ever made was fish sticks in the microwave.

She carried her plate back into the living-room, exchanging scraps of small-talk and polite smiles here and there, heading for the only vacant chair. Rick – the man who couldn't trust himself with a Danish nanny – was standing beside it, talking to Pete Johnson and Ross Owen, two other partners in the firm.

'Claire.' He pressed his lips together, drawing them out at the sides in what was undoubtedly meant as a smile. 'We were just discussing the Ukrainian situation.' He was wearing green and red suspenders, with Santa heads patterned all over them. Jocelyn liked to buy him wacky suspenders and socks, Claire had heard.

'Really?' she stood uneasily, her hands occupied with plate, wine glass and cutlery, wondering if it would be rude to sit down, and who had told Rick about Potochnik. Had Mike sent out his hate letters already? 'I've been meaning to come and talk to you about that situation,' she said. 'I'm sure I can handle it. I

just haven't had the chance to get to it, with the holidays and all
. . .' Actually, she hadn't heard from Potochnik in almost a month
and had been hoping he'd dropped his idea of filing a complaint
with the Law Society. Or suing her.

'You're Ukrainian yourself, aren't you?' Ross Owen said.

'My father is, yes.'

'That should be a big help,' Peter added.

'Actually, I think it's more of a problem.'

'Really? I was hoping that wouldn't be the case. Well, my door
is always open, as you know.' Rick studied her for a moment. 'It's
going to mean a lot of work, you know. Most of it unbillable.'

Most of it? Claire tried to imagine billing *any* of the time she
would have to spend sorting out Potochnik's mess, to Mike
Potochnik. He would blow an aneurism if she tried. Did the
Executive Committee seriously expect that she was going to
bill for it? Had it already been discussed? Decided? She looked
up again, dreading the line of questions that was sure to follow,
but Jocelyn had grasped one of her husband's suspenders and was
pulling him over to join the carol sing. She was wearing a set of
Christmas-light earrings that flashed on and off, alternating from
side to side.

The group having broken up with no more discussion about
Mike Potochnik, much to Claire's relief, she decided to take
her food into the library, hoping to find Ben there. But the room
was empty. She sat down in a comfortable armchair and ate
steadily, in silence, listening to the sounds of her chewing for a
while, then slurping some wine. Ben would be out there mingling
in the crowd, giving free plastic surgery consults, drumming up
business, being witty and charming and generally the life of the
party. He hadn't said anything about Claire's dress. Perhaps it
was too conservative. Ben liked clothes that were wild and sexy
– or at least he used to. But Claire hadn't felt like dressing up as
an adolescent tonight. She was a mother now, hoping soon to be
a partner in Bragg, Banks and Biltmore. It couldn't help to dress
in any way that could be considered unseemly, especially with
the Potochnik problem threatening her practice and possibly her
partnership prospects. In her Dresser's opinion, the green velvet
was a 'good, though conservative choice – borderline elegant.
And best of all, it was (that dreaded word) *slimming*. Now, if

Claire could just manage to shed that little puddle of flab around her waistline. It had, after all, been six months since Harry was born . . . surely enough time to get her figure back completely. And what about having a chat with Ben about hair transplants? They were supposedly doing some marvellous things these days – that "plug" look was no more, if you saw the right specialist of course—'

'Shut up!' Claire told her Dresser, and was startled on looking up from her chicken to see someone watching her from the doorway of the library.

'*Det var en utsokt maltid.*' It was one of the new lawyers, Gillian whatever-her-name-was.

'Pardon?' said Claire.

'*Det var en utsokt maltid.*' Her pale eyes blinked at Claire. 'I heard someone say you're Swedish.'

'We have a Swedish nanny, for our baby. How can people manage to mix things up like that?' Irritably, she pushed a piece of chicken around on her plate. And why was everyone talking about their nanny anyway? Gillian really did have the most disconcerting eyes, Claire thought, glancing up at her again. 'You speak Swedish?' she said.

'Not really. I had a Swedish grandmother – I only know enough of the language to praise her cooking. I just said "That was a great meal." It's about all I know. Well,' she looked around, 'this is obviously the most interesting room in the condo. But that row of books at the top looks fake – one of those wallpaper strips you buy at the paint store that looks like a row of book-spines.'

Claire smiled. 'You seem to have Shelagh's number already.'

'Sure. I've worked with her already.'

'And you do patents,' Claire said.

'I know it doesn't sound very interesting, but it is to me. And I get to hang out with creative types, which I like.'

'Your clothes are certainly . . . creative.' Claire gave her a quick appraising look. 'Great jacket.' It was black satin, patterned with huge pink cabbage roses. Below it hung a brief edge of floaty chiffon. And Gillian was wearing, incongruously, heavy black army surplus-style boots.

'I know I'm not conventional Bay Street,' Gillian said, 'but I don't want to be. Career suicide I'm sure, but hey – that's life.

Vive la différence and all that. Bay Street's got enough suits.' Her untidy red hair fell over her eyes as she bent to peer at a row of books. 'I wonder if there's anything worth reading in here. Seem to be a large number of sex books . . . She's not married, I take it? Shelagh?'

'No.' Claire had a sudden thought. 'Since you've got some Swedish in your background, maybe you can answer a question for me.'

'I can try.'

'What colour is the Swedish flag?'

'Blue. With a yellow cross.' Gillian's long fingers were tracing over a row of encyclopedias. 'Here – there'll be flags in here. I'll show it to you. Under f – for flags—' Claire put her plate and wine glass down on the desk as Gillian passed her the open book. 'Flags of the world . . . Europe . . . Scandinavia. Here.'

'That's weird,' Claire said. 'I don't see any red flag with a yellow cross.'

'Why do you want that?'

'I just saw one somewhere.'

'Well, Denmark has a red flag – so does Switzerland. but the cross is white.'

'Yes. I can see that.' Claire closed the book, frowning.

'Maybe you got the colours wrong.'

'I guess I must have.'

'Anyway. I know I've seen you in the hallways at the firm, but I should introduce myself. I'm Gillian Lawrence.'

'Claire Cunningham.' They shook hands. 'Sorry – I should have come around to see you. Our firm's not very good at making new people feel at home.'

'I don't mind. I prefer to be left alone, really. Mine is an insular sort of practice. Very technical.'

'Really.' Claire could feel her eyes glazing over. 'So that was quite a storm today, wasn't it?' she said.

'I can't wait to get away to San Francisco,' Ben said, leaning his head back on the head-rest as Claire struggled to ease the car out of the snow drift in front of Shelagh's building. 'How about you?' He patted her knee through the thickness of her heavy wool coat.

'Right now, I'm more concerned about getting home.' The air inside the car was heavy with the sweetish smell of alcohol. Claire, who'd only had two glasses of wine, was, as usual, the 'designated driver'.

'You'll manage – you always do.' Ben closed his eyes with a sigh. 'California's going to be great.'

'Don't expect it to be hot, just because it's California. It's San Francisco we're going to, in February.'

'I don't need heat, I just want to get away from this snow. And the hospital. And be alone with the woman I love.'

'Too bad she won't be there,' Claire joked.

'How do you know she won't?' he returned.

'Oh, touché.' Unable to come up with any better response, Claire drove on in silence for a few minutes. 'I noticed you were accosted by Jocelyn Durham,' she said. 'What is it she wants done?'

'Can't say. Doctor–patient privilege.'

'Seriously?'

'No. She'd never be a patient of mine – she's the type with unreal expectations.' He yawned and closed his eyes. 'Anyway, just think, in a little over a month you and I are going to be sitting in the hot tub of a luxury hotel, maybe sucking back some raw oysters, watching dirty movies on the Pay-Per-View. I can take a few rounds out of you and we can sleep in till noon. No baby, no diapers.'

'I thought you had to present a paper.'

'That's only for one hour. The rest of the time, I'm yours. Think you can handle me?'

'I ought to be able to do more than that.' Claire tried to ignore his hand, wanting to pay full attention to her driving, peering into the night through the small space cleared in the windshield by the car's inefficient defroster. Much as she wanted to continue the banter with Ben, Rick's reference to Mike Potochnik was bothering her. A lot. She still hadn't told Ben about the problem she was having with him. Normally, she confided everything to Ben, but he was so busy lately, so preoccupied and tense. She didn't want to worry him needlessly. And besides, what could he do about it? How could he help? It was her practice, her problem. If she couldn't handle it alone she wasn't much of a lawyer. And what if Ben thought less of her if she told him? Maybe he would side with Potochnik, agree that she really was incompetent, had been careless. 'I had an okay time tonight,' she said, pushing thoughts of Potochink out of her mind. 'Met one of the new lawyers. Gillian Lawrence. She does patents.'

'Oh yeah,' Ben said without interest.

'She's sort of intriguing. A bit of an oddball. Bizarre clothes. We need a few like her around the firm, I guess.' Ben yawned hugely. 'She has a Swedish grandmother – so I asked her about that flag on Brita's ceiling. It's not Swedish, she tells me. The Swedish flag is blue, not red. But you would know that, wouldn't you, having lived there?' No answer. 'Ben?'

She looked sideways at him and was disappointed to see that he had fallen asleep. 'My very own Christmas *tomten*,' she sighed, with another glance at his cherubic face. Then she wiped a mittened hand across the steamy inside of the windshield and decided that discussions about flags could wait and she'd be better off concentrating on her driving.

15

Since Ben had the luxury of being off call for both Christmas and New Year's Eves, he was expected to pay for it by being on call for the next two days. Claire spent Christmas and New Year's Day in much the same way: wheeling a squealing and delighted Harry up and down miles of hospital corridor on stray gurneys or wheelchairs, waiting while Ben checked patients on the floor, answered the intern's questions or popped into the operating theatre to give an opinion on follow-up reconstructive work. *My child is going to grow up playing with hospital waste the way other kids play with Lego blocks,* she thought, steering Harry away from a cart full of dirty bed linen that had attracted his attention.

A number of times, Ben took her and Harry around to various nursing stations to show them off. 'Where did that blond hair come from?' the nurses would always ask, looking at Harry, then quizzically from Claire to Ben and back again. Whatever answer she came up with – her sister was a blonde, one of her uncles had sandy-brown hair – Claire always felt they suspected her of lying, that Harry wasn't her son, or that Ben wasn't Harry's father.

Aside from a few nurses, interns, and the odd, unlucky staff doctor, the hospital was pretty well deserted. As many patients as possible had been cleared out for the holidays. The overheated corridors echoed with the rumbling of the gurney's wheels as Claire and Harry rolled along, waiting for Ben. The cafeteria was reduced to a grumpy skeleton staff, and the choice of meals was limited – Claire ate her Christmas lunch straight from a vending machine. Harry loved the slots and levers and the bright glow of the machines, so he was well entertained as Claire slurped microwaved soup from a can. As good as a home-cooked meal, she thought wryly. All I need are a couple of fish sticks and I'd have a real banquet here. She tried not to feel sorry for herself, and to stop thinking about an old John Prine song, 'Christmas in Prison', the lyrics of which kept repeating in her head. Lunch finished, Claire and Harry had to wait still longer to see if Ben were needed for a finger replant, or whether the digit was too badly mangled to save. Guiltily, Claire was relieved to hear that it was, indeed, too far gone and that all Ben had to do was clean up the stump – a half-hour job, as opposed to twelve or thirteen. By the time they got home, however, it was almost six; Harry was cranky and tired and it was too late to cook the turkey. Ben and Claire had a glass of wine and gave Harry a bath together, agreeing that what was really important was not turkey and stuffing and cranberry sauce, but that they'd spent Christmas Day together – their first as a family. Brita had already gone – after a prolonged and tearful goodbye to Harry – to stay with her friends over the holiday. She was looking forward to some large gatherings with people she hadn't seen since she'd left Sweden, as well as something called Knut Week at Ikea, when some character named Old Knut apparently capered about the store wearing an outlandish hat, giving out candy and playing tricks on customers, an experience Claire was glad she wouldn't be expected to share.

Ben made her wait until Christmas night to give her her 'significant' present. As soon as Harry was asleep, he scampered upstairs and returned carrying a blue bag, with a famous silver trade-mark 'B' on the side. But Claire wasn't about to get excited about it – it was likely that the bag contained some hideous practical joke and that concealing it in a jewellery store bag was Ben's idea of making the set-up (and Claire's reaction) even funnier. Apprehensively, she pulled out a flat, rose-coloured box and traced her finger across the top. She sniffed it. It was real suede. Ben was practically hopping up and down with excitement. 'Hm,' she said, 'it looks too flat to contain a joy buzzer ... Something isn't going to jump out at me when I open it, is it?' Cautiously, she lifted the lid of the elegant oblong box. There, displayed on more suede, was a heavy gold link necklace: sixteen inches long, eighteen carats.

'Like it?'

'We can't afford this.' It was bad enough that Claire was a hopeless spendthrift. Ben was the one who could be counted on not to spend a dime unless he had to. Had he suddenly gone berserk with their credit card?

'Don't worry,' he chuckled, 'it's paid for.'

'How could you possibly pay for this?'

'Aren't you going to try it on?'

'Ben – I don't mean to sound ungrateful – I'm overwhelmed by this. But can we afford it?'

His face darkened. 'I got five hundred bucks for publishing one of my papers, and I did a seminar for a drug company on wound dressings. Plus, I got food money reimbursement from my last rotation. Satisfied?'

'Yes. I'm sorry. Don't be pissed off.'

'Well, if you don't try it on soon I'm going to have to conclude that you don't like it.'

'How could anyone not like this?' Claire picked up the necklace and undid its complicated clasp.

'That's called a lobster trap,' Ben said, 'the way it hooks together there.'

It's lobster *claw*, Claire thought, but didn't bother to mention it.

'See?' he continued. 'I'm learning about these things. I was going to get you pearls but I couldn't believe how much they cost. I could only have bought you about five pearls. I couldn't even have afforded to have them strung.'

'No, this is gorgeous. Perfect.' Claire blinked, misty-eyed. His food money! He'd spent his food money on a necklace for her jealous, ungrateful, suspicious neck.

'Nothing's too good for my woman.' There were spots of pink high up on his cheeks and a stray lock of hair curled down over his forehead. He was perspiring a little.

'Help me with this clasp.' Claire waited while he put the necklace on her, watching the lights of the Christmas tree. She thought about the night they'd trimmed the tree – she and Ben. And Brita. Then she remembered something she'd tucked away in a back corner of her mind, afraid of examining too closely. She'd gone out to the kitchen to get some eggnog for the three of them and returned to stand in the entrance to the living-room, stunned as she watched Brita pass a glass ornament to Ben, with a gentle murmured comment in Swedish. There was something going on between them. At that moment, Claire had known it with a certainty. She hadn't felt like finishing the tree after that but had sat in a corner, brooding, then, soon after, gone up to bed. Alone.

'Did you get anything for Brita?' she now asked, reaching up and fondling the necklace, noting how quickly it took on the warmth of her skin. She had given Brita a pair of flannel pyjamas, some sheepskin slippers and a collapsible umbrella: all useful, practical and thoughtful gifts, since Brita didn't seem to have much of anything in those categories.

'Nothing, really.' Ben kissed the side of her neck, then got up to fiddle with the lights on the tree. 'A stupid thing. I gave it to her the other day, before she left for her friend's place. Why?'

'Just wondering. I got her a load of stuff myself so I'm kind of surprised that you bothered.'

'It wasn't much.' He got down on the floor and reached in behind the tree. 'One of the bulbs on the green string is burned out. I better unplug the whole thing before I try to change it – I don't want to electrocute myself.' The tree lights blinked out, and he and Claire were suddenly sitting in darkness. 'I guess that wasn't very smart.' A few of the glass ornaments tinkled as he sat up again, brushing the lower branches.

'So what did you get her? Brita?'

'You would have hated it. A gag gift. You know, the kind that makes you gag.' He grinned, his teeth shining in the dim light coming through the windows from the streetlight in front of the house.

'But what was it? Something from the Tacky Shop?' Claire knew the sort of lewd thing that store carried, along with its ever-popular line of toilet humour: panties built for two, studded condoms, mugs shaped like breasts, night-shirts that say I LOOK BETTER NAKED or LET ME CALL YOU SWEETHEART 'CAUSE I FORGOT YOUR NAME across the front. 'I thought gag gifts were reserved exclusively for me.' Her eyes were getting used to the darkness and she could see her husband quite clearly now.

'You've moved up a couple of rungs in my esteem,' he said. 'You've given me a son – now I don't have to have you beheaded.'

'I've become a sort of queen dowager, is that it?' Other terms sprang to mind: kicked upstairs, bought off, given the golden handshake. Nervously, she continue to fondle the necklace.

'I guess you could put it that way. But I don't know why you'd want to.'

'I feel sort of hurt that I didn't get a joke gift this year, that's all. Silly.' She made an attempt at a light laugh.

Sitting on the floor beside the Christmas tree, Ben put his face in his hands. 'What do women want, Lord?' he moaned.

'I only meant that it's become a sort of tradition with us, hasn't it?'

Before he could answer, Ben's pager beeped intrusively. He got up, turned on the living-room lights and spent the next twenty minutes on the phone, arguing with an emerg doctor about whether a drunk who'd been in a bar fight should be admitted by the plastics or orthopaedics service, and whether Ben would have to be the one to go in to the hospital to do it. Claire watched him from the couch in the living-room, noting his aggressive pose as he leaned against the kitchen counter, the angry hunch of his shoulders. The gold necklace felt too heavy suddenly around her throat, as if it just might tighten, constrict, and finally choke her.

She never did have a chance to make amends with Ben, or find out what he'd given Brita for Christmas, since he left for the hospital a few minutes later. By the time he returned, some time after midnight, she had already knocked herself out with sleeping pills.

16

'The way a man packs is so aggravating.' Claire was lying on her stomach, stretched out across the bed, her head propped in her hands, watching Ben. Beside her was a pile of clothes that she thought, tentatively, she would take to San Francisco. 'Men put one suit in a garment bag, toss in a couple of shirts – all nicely packaged by the cleaners – a couple pairs of socks and jockey shorts and they're set. You don't even need to remember your razor. You can always pick up a disposable at any airport newsstand.'

'If it's so annoying, don't watch.' Ben was preoccupied with sorting through an El Producto cigar box in which he kept his meagre collection of jewellery – a man's Gucci watch that had once been Claire's, his college hockey ring that they'd nicknamed 'Shazam', joking that it gave him supernatural powers, and the wedding ring he seldom wore because he had to scrub so often for surgery. He also kept, for sentimental reasons, a pierced earring: a dangling portrait of Salvador Dali and two soft-watches in plastic laminate. He'd had one ear pierced in first-year medical school, shortly after he met Claire, despite her horrified objections. He'd let the hole grow over six months later, but he was glad he'd done it, he said – it was something to tell the grandchildren, to let them know their old grand-dad wasn't a total geek way back when. Claire would have enjoyed buying him some new jewellery – a Rolex watch, some gold cufflinks and a fine leather case to keep them in, but she'd given up on shopping for Ben – if she bought him something, she could hardly hide it, and he was getting so cranky about her spending that the pleasure she got from buying was entirely erased.

'What's really irritating is how everything men do is so abbreviated,' she said. 'How does a man wash a dirty pot? He fills it with water and leaves it in the sink. How does he make a bed? He throws a bedspread over whatever mess there is. Of course, he just assumes that some woman is going to trail around after him, tying up his loose ends, picking up his droppings. And while women carry around saddle-bag purses full of cosmetics, pills, tissues, teething biscuits and bottles for the baby, what's the male equivalent? A skimpy wallet, with not even a change purse or a place to hold a cheque-book, just enough room for a swatch of credit cards and an outdated picture of the kids. The wife's photo gets tossed at about the time of the first baby.' She didn't bother to mention Ben's photograph still on the bottom shelf of the book-case in her office. Claire enjoyed these occasional tirades against the tyranny of men; the folly of women. 'You should see what I've been going through to pack for this trip. I've had everything laid out for a week – and I still haven't a clue what to take. If the blue knit dress goes, I need to pack the blue shoes and bag. If I take the red one, I need the strapless bra and the red shoes. Will there be a cocktail event? A formal one? Do I need some business clothes? You haven't told me much about our itinerary.' Even her Dresser had been daunted by the prospect of advising her on what to pack for a trip which had no clear agenda. 'But you? You'll just wear the same suit for a week, maybe change your shirt a few times. It seems like everything I own needs completely different underwear and accessories.'

'Now I know why we're so broke.' Ben seemed distracted, as he always did before a conference. This one, in San Francisco, was a big one, and the fact that his paper had been accepted for presentation was a major career coup.

'Then there's all the other paraphernalia that women have to drag around when they travel,' Claire continued, 'blow-dryers and curling irons, hair gel, sprays, eye creams.' When she was growing up, she'd believed that women had a tremendous advantage – there was so much they could do to improve their appearance, all within socially acceptable limits. They could dye their hair, put in eyelashes and eyebrows where nature had skimped. They could wear structured bras, slimming panties with hidden 'tummy control' panels, sheer stockings that gave their legs a shimmer and made a sexy swishy sound when they crossed them. She could recall exactly her first pair of *nylons* – Cinnamon Spice – and the lace-trimmed garter belt that kept them up. Now she saw all of it for what it really was – an unfair advantage that men had, not women. Men didn't have to waste all that time shopping for these things, then applying or squeezing into them. They got on with more interesting or profitable concerns. Sure, some men were dabbling in vanity and so-called appearance enhancement: they were dipping their toes in, testing the water, buying face bronzers and getting hair transplants, but they would never wholeheartedly embrace it the way women had. They recognized it for the trap it was.

Despite her grousing, she was looking forward to their trip and having Ben all to herself for a week. They could drink champagne on the flight, get loaded – maybe he'd feel her up under the airline blanket. It would be their first time away together since she became pregnant.

'No one's forcing you to wear make-up or anything else,' Ben said, folding his underwear up into neat little parcels that he then stuffed into his dress shoes. 'In fact, I don't really like make-up at all, if you want my opinion.'

'Since when?'

'Since always. Especially that stuff you put under your eyes. It makes you look tired or depressed.'

'So? I'm usually both.'

He looked at her with irritation. 'When are your parents blowing in?'

'Tomorrow morning.'

'You know,' Ben said after a moment's hesitation, 'we do have another solution to the Harry problem.'

'I wasn't aware we had a Harry problem.'

'I meant with the babysitting. We could take Harry with us. For free. The airline doesn't charge for babies.'

'Ben, I want some time together. How are we going to go out if we have to look after Harry?'

'We would take Brita, of course. She could get a room with Harry—'

'Are you insane?'

'Why? Lots of people take their kids and nanny when they go

on holidays. Just think about it for a moment. I've checked with the airline and there's still a few seats available. And the hotel has a single room, believe it or not.'

'You've called the hotel? The airline?' There they'd be in the hot tub, happily drinking champagne and getting to know each other again, when they'd hear a tap on the door. Claire would look up and see Brita in a white terry robe, loosely belted, with Harry in one arm. *'Kan jag komma over?'* (or some such thing) she would ask, pouting prettily. 'My room has no *varmt bad,'* she would add sadly. 'Hey, Brita, come on in. Move over, Claire,' Ben would say effusively. 'There's even room for Harry. Isn't this the life, girls?' Brita would be there at breakfast, with them at dinner – they could hardly *not* ask her to join them, could they, Ben would argue – she would be at the side of the pool, towelling dry her yards of pale blonde hair as Claire struggled up the pool ladder, her own mousy hair stuck flat to her head.

'Of all the monstrously obscene idiotic ideas you've ever had —' Claire began.

'Hey! Hold on. You don't have to go ballistic on me. I thought you'd like the idea. You wouldn't have to worry about Harry—'

'I don't want Brita with *us* on *our* vacation! *Forstar ni?* Or do I have to spell it out for you? In Swedish? I can do that. It seems that's all you choose to understand these days.'

Ben was holding his breath, sort of squinting at her, obviously planning his next words. 'Okay. Forget it. It was an idea, maybe a dumb one. But I still don't know why we need your parents here. Brita can look after Harry on her own for a week.'

'After that *blindtarm* incident? No way. She's too short on common sense.'

'It was no *incident.* Brita just got scared when she saw that his testicles were purple and swollen. Frankly, I'm surprised Harry's own mother didn't notice them first.'

Claire ignored the jibe. 'Well she didn't have to over-react. Screaming *hjalp*! *hjalp*! over the phone. Especially since you were there with her. I almost had a heart attack.'

'She did a great job that day. She took him straight to Sick Kids' and paged me immediately. I'd rather have someone overly cautious than someone who tries to treat Harry herself.'

'You don't know what she put me through. I thought he was dead, or poisoned and having his stomach pumped. And I'll never understand why you couldn't have given me the full story over the phone. *Blindtarm* means appendix, for God's sake. And his appendix wasn't even involved.' She sat up, hitting her head on the low-sloping ceiling, then jumped off the bed and started throwing clothes into her open suitcase.

Four months had passed since the day of the *blindtarm*, but she and Ben still argued intermittently over who was the best, or least, able to deal with an emergency. It was a sort of contest. 'Good Parent–Bad Parent' Claire called it in her head.

'You're lucky I didn't fire Brita,' she said.

'I'm not *lucky* you didn't. If you want to fire her, go ahead. Break Harry's little heart.'

'As if he'd know the difference. All he cares about is that someone feeds and burps him.'

'That just shows how little you know. Why don't you try reading a book about babies sometime? You might learn something.' Ben was tossing things into his suitcase as fast as Claire. 'So be my guest. Fire her. Just make sure you get a good replacement. I'd like to hear one of your friends' nannies try to tell you over the phone that Harry needed a hernia repair, if you think you had trouble with Brita. Someone else might have tied a tourniquet around his nuts and permanently ruined his sex life. Or done a faith-healing number on him. You should try another nanny, then maybe you'd see how lucky we are to have Brita – but by then it would be too late. Someone else would have snapped her up and we'd never get her back.'

'Christine thinks Brita might be a hooker. We both think it's odd that she never seems to need her pay.'

'No, you know what's odd? What's odd is how much time you two spend thinking about her. Is a beautiful girl so threatening that you have to find something wrong with her? Make her into a whore or put her down in some other way?'

'She's not beautiful.' Claire was disgusted to hear herself say something so obviously untrue.

'She worked as a model in Stockholm, modelling underwear and sporting goods.'

'Underwear and sporting goods? Together? You mean like garter belts and riding crops? Split-crotch panties and spurs? Did she have a black bar across her eyes?'

'Of course not.'

'So if she's such a hot ticket as a model, why is she working here as a domestic? And besides, how do you know all this about her recent past? I thought she was a gangly goofball with braces when you were over there.'

Did he hesitate, just for a moment, before answering? Claire's eyes met his.

'She told me, of course,' Ben said. 'How else would I know? And no one ever said anything about braces – that's your fantasy.'

'I didn't realize that "underwear model" was part of your Berlitz vocabulary. How would you translate that? Would it be in the *Sweden for Voyagers* phrase book? What would it be under? The Hotel Services section? Excuse me, bell-hop, could you recommend a good underwear model? It's right after *var ar kontakten for rakapparaten*?'

'What are you talking about?'

'That means "Where is the plug for the razor?" I know some Swedish too, see?'

'You really are losing it, Claire – if you have to snoop through a Swedish phrase-book for kicks.'

'Why? Because I want to make Brita feel at home? Just like you do?' She opened the door to her side of the closet (a joke actually, since her Dresser had long ago muscled Ben's meagre wardrobe into a corner), raked a few hangers along the closet pole, yanked off a green cardigan and threw it into her suitcase. 'Maybe Brita didn't actually tell you about her underwear modelling. Maybe she just demonstrated – with body language. Simple Swedes are supposed to be good at that.'

'When did you get to be such a jealous threatened bitch?' Ben's eyes had their yellow look. If he were a cat, he would have laid his ears back at that moment, Claire thought, feeling a little afraid of him. 'And don't give me this crap about how you want to make her feel at home. She knows you don't like her. She's told me that much – *i engelska*.'

Abruptly, Claire sat down on the edge of the bed. 'Look, maybe I shouldn't go to San Francisco after all. If we're going to fight the whole time, I'd rather stay home. At least we'd each have some relief from this constant bickering. We've been at each other's throats since Harry was born.' More accurately, it was since Ben hired Brita, but she didn't feel like pointing that out just then.

'So stay home if you want. I thought it would be a good chance for us to get away from here and get to know each other again –'

'Sure,' Claire snorted, 'while joined at the hips with our Swedish nanny.'

'But the way you've been acting lately, I'm not sure I want to know you any better. And what the hell – your plane ticket was only four hundred bucks and we're loaded, aren't we? We can afford to just throw it away.'

'Just like we could throw away another four on Brita. Plus the cost of a hotel room. But what's a thousand bucks when it comes to our superlative super-underwear-model nanny?'

Ben checked over the contents of his shaving case, his lips pressed together in a grimace, then stuffed the case into his carry-on bag. Claire watched him, thinking that she'd never seen him so angry. But what right did he have to be enraged? Because she wouldn't agree to take his *mistress* along on their vacation? They had to be having an affair. Didn't they? Or was she really 'losing it' as Ben suggested? Was he really only concerned with Harry's well-being? Perhaps he truly didn't want to leave his son and go off to another country. And if that were true, shouldn't Claire be grateful to be married to such a caring and concerned man? Instead of reacting like a spoiled neurotic nit and throwing a tantrum because of her own pathetic insecurity?

When was it that they'd both lost their sense of humour, she wondered, as she watched Ben zip up his suitcase and place his bags along one wall of the bedroom.

'I'm going to wake up Harry,' he said. 'We can't let him sleep all day. I want to take him for a walk along the boardwalk.'

'It's too cold.'

'It is not – it's like spring out there. And you can thank Mount Pinatubo for our totally screwed-up weather patterns.'

'What has Mount Pinatubo got to do with anything?'

'You figure it out.' He left the bedroom and was soon in the nursery entertaining Harry – talking in that squeaky, all-purpose falsetto he used to amuse his son or to imitate the women in Claire's family.

Claire continued to sit slumped on the bed, trying to sort out her feelings over the trip that was supposed to function as their second honeymoon. Not only were she and Ben quarrelling constantly, but Ben was right about not wanting to leave Harry. She panicked about it too, when she let herself think about it. Her parents were well intentioned, but without their hearing aids, they could sleep through a sonic boom. And Brita was, well, Brita. Who would hear Harry when he yelled in the middle of the night, wanting a bottle, needing to be changed? Would the three of them put together have enough common sense to deal with a diaper rash, let alone a real emergency? Would any of them even notice that an emergency was happening? And was it even fair to ask her parents to be responsible for Harry? After all, they hadn't had to care for a baby for almost forty years. From San Francisco, Claire would be reduced to frazzled impotency, as on that day of the *blindtarm*, a faint frantic voice over the telephone line, only this time, thousands of miles away, instead of a few city blocks.

She'd tried to tell Ben about these feelings the night before, when they were in bed and he'd finally closed and put *Cancer of the Face and Mouth* down on his bedside table. But he only reacted with impatience. 'If we don't go now, cut the strings, we'll never go anywhere,' he'd said. 'Are you going to wait until Harry's twenty-one before you'll leave Toronto? Apart from your plane ticket, this is a free trip – it's being paid for by the Plastics Department. We can party all night, get in the Jacuzzi together like we used to do. I can tie you up with surgical dressings, like in the bad old days. Hmm? Remember?'

Compelling arguments indeed, Claire reflected. But now that leaving Harry was an impending reality, wasn't Ben changing his tune? Wasn't he as worried as she? Perhaps it explained this bitter argument they'd just had – the worst ever, as far as Claire could recall.

With a weary sigh, she got up off the bed and began taking things out of the suitcase again. Her Dresser would pull through for her eventually, if only to make Claire go out and buy those accessories she lacked to align every piece of her wardrobe with every other piece – the domino theory of dressing. Just minutes earlier, her clothing dilemma had seemed funny, and Claire had anticipated that Ben would share in the humour of it. There was a time when he would have enjoyed a silly digression into the packing habits of men versus women. Now the situation only depressed and frustrated her as much as it apparently bored and irritated him.

Nobody had warned them that having a baby would eliminate any easy-going tendencies they had; that they would never again sleep, or get up, when they wanted to; never lounge in bed on a Sunday morning or spontaneously go out for a beer on a hot summer night. 'Enjoy your freedom while you can,' was the only pat piece of advice they got, from every direction, while Claire was pregnant; as if they should go out every night, party till dawn and somehow bottle every moment of the experience to swill and savour later, when they were stuck in the house with a baby and no sitter. For all her expressions of love for Harry, Brita never hung around much in the evenings, and usually made a face when asked to stay late and babysit. On occasion, Claire came home to find her standing in the window, jiggling Harry and waiting impatiently, jacket on, handbag slung over her shoulder, so that she could bolt out the door as soon as Claire showed up to take Harry.

In the past month, it seemed, this feeling of being trapped had hit them hard, and Claire and Ben had turned on each other, often hurling accusations of incompetence or gross negligence when it came to Harry's care. *Somebody* left this switchplate uncovered; *somebody* didn't wash this bottle properly; looks like *somebody* forgot to buy more formula. That *somebody* almost always seemed to be Claire.

And no one had told Claire that she would start fantasizing about sleep the way she had once fantasized about sex: always anticipating it, hoping it would just naturally happen; never getting enough; daydreaming about being able to sneak a quickie in the afternoon. Worst of all, the things that had once appealed to her and Ben about each other had become the greatest

• Sylvia Mulholland

sources of irritation: Ben's youthful energy Claire now viewed as juvenility; her sophistication he saw as cranky middle age.

Profoundly depressed, Claire went down the hall and stood watching Ben in the nursery as he played with Harry, holding him up to bat at the Little Bo Peep mobile. The sheep – three white, one black – were light and fluffy, and each time Harry grabbed for one, it bobbed up and away out of his reach. He made excited gasping sounds as Ben held him up, undaunted by the futility of his efforts. Claire had to smile. 'Ben?' she said.

'Hmm?' He didn't turn around.

She felt like apologizing, but she didn't know for what. For memorizing innocuous Swedish phrases and hurling them at him in a jealous rage? For suggesting that Brita was a prostitute? For having too many clothes? For being herself? 'If you're going down to the beach,' she finally said, 'would you take a look at the retaining wall? I think we've got a new Proctor on our hands – the east side of it especially.'

'Great.' Ben held a squirming Harry up against his chest and riffled through the bureau drawers to find him a sweater. Neither he nor Claire, it seemed, was going to bother making the usual jokes about Proctors, and Ben obviously wasn't going to invite her to join them on the boardwalk. 'See you in a bit,' was all he said as he disappeared down the stairs with Harry.

Claire gathered up the litter of toys strewn about the nursery, then went into the bathroom. Peering through the small shuttered window, she could see her discouraging garden below, and the sulky sludge of lake beyond. Ben had Harry in the umbrella stroller and was trying to manoeuvre it over the uneven ground in the wreckage of Claire's vegetable patch. Brita hadn't been much of a help with that garden; in fact, Claire had been shocked to see how little she knew about making things grow. Brita was an expert on things that didn't matter: MTV and *Fashion Television*, or gelling her messy blonde hair into spikes. So much for the nurturing-Swede theory.

Swedes are uncomfortable with the urban scene, according to *Sweden For Voyagers*, *greatly preferring a retreat to the fields and forests where they hike for miles, collect mushrooms and loganberries, or simply revel in the tranquillity of Mother Nature.*

What a howler. Brita spent most of her leisure time listening

• 192

to head-banging heavy metal CDs and munching on those chocolate bars she got from Ikea. She wouldn't know a loganberry if one hit her between the eyes.

Wishing she hadn't bothered to allude to her recent forays into *Sweden For Voyagers,* Claire watched as Ben jabbed his foot into the crumbling mortar of the retaining wall, shook his head in disgust, then lifted Harry in his stroller, up over the top of it and on to the sand below. The boardwalk didn't reach as far east as 67 Pine Beach Road, so they had to drag or push or carry Harry in his stroller through gravel and sand for a few hundred feet. It was a distance Ben always negotiated with ease.

Never had the seven-year age difference between them seemed so apparent as it had over the months since Harry's birth. At times, Claire imagined what it would be like to find someone her own age, or older, who had confronted his mortality but bravely struggled on, tinged with sadness about the ultimate uselessness of human endeavours. He would wake up every day, as she did, in a panic over the passage of time, wondering which part of his body was going to give out next and how much the damage control would cost. Maybe it would be a tendon, shot like an old brassiere band; a tooth that was chipped or cracked; perhaps a mysterious, alarming lump that had suddenly popped up in a groin or armpit or appeared as an ominous shadow on an x-ray. So far, Claire hadn't had anything really serious go wrong with her, but there was always something niggling and incurable – back pain, headaches, a sour stomach. Like their house, Claire's body was brimming with Proctors that lurked just below the surface. Ben, on the other hand, was still young enough to deflect the thought of death with some glib saying, like 'When your number's up, it's up', and believe he meant it. If Harry ever had to choose between them, he would be better off with Ben, Claire realized suddenly, beginning a wade into the deep quagmire of self-pity. Ben was the one who could save Harry in an emergency, perform CPR, the Heimlich manoeuvre or a lightning-quick tracheotomy. He had the youth, the energy, the strong back; and he was a Fun Dad. Claire was just an *aged prima gravida,* according to her hospital chart. She had scoliosis, molars stuffed with mercury-leaking amalgam fillings. She was the pill-popping insomniac. And now that she was no longer needed for breast-feeding, she was the one who could easily be replaced with paid help. Christine was probably right: it was only a matter of time before Ben left her for a younger woman.

She turned away from the window and left the bathroom, heading back to deal with the mountain of clothes on their bed, in her suitcase. All things considered, their second honeymoon was off to one hell of a lousy start.

17

'San Francisco. I haven't been there since 1967. I was only fourteen. Dad rented some kind of tour-on-tape for the car. We had to cruise through Haight-Ashbury, windows rolled down, with this tape blasting out: "Here we are in the colourful Hippy district! Just look at all the weird individuals!" And then the guy on the tape starts laughing. All those acid heads sitting out on their blankets must have thought they were on a major bummer. Christine and I hid on the floor in the back seat.' Claire took a swallow of champagne. 'Of course, you wouldn't remember much about 1967 – you were still in diapers.'

'Still wetting the bed at least.'

'I'll never get over the fact that I married someone who was born in the sixties. But then, you lied when I met you, telling me you were born in 'fifty-nine.'

'That was my big mistake.' Ben gave Claire's hand an affectionate squeeze.

'Well, if we hadn't gotten together, there'd be no Harry now. I miss him already. Don't you?'

'Like a cluster migraine.'

'Seriously?'

'Sure, I miss him. But I'm glad he's not here. Harry's a great baby. But he is a baby. We need some time alone.'

Claire didn't want to tell him again how worried she was about leaving Harry. She'd posted signs all over the house for the enlightenment of her parents: MAKE SURE TO KEEP CRIB RAILS UP; CAREFUL OF HOT COFFEE!!; DO NOT USE FRONT BURNERS ON STOVE; KEEP BLIND CORDS TIED UP!!! Then she'd decided that wasn't safe enough, so she'd hidden the coffee-maker in the basement and removed the front burners of the stove altogether. There wasn't much she could do about the blinds except redecorate, but she'd kicked herself for having put them up in the first place. Ben had notified every resident at the Sick Children's Hospital – all were poised to receive a frantic call from Elfriede; ready to bump Harry to the front of the line in the emergency room. The Cunninghams had left their car, with Harry's car seat properly installed, pointing out of the garage (so that Basil and Elfriede wouldn't have to take needless risks by backing out of the driveway) and attached a diagram to the car seat illustrating how Harry was to be buckled in. They could have brought Harry with them – *without* Brita, of course – but Claire's imagined air travel horrors were worse than those she could concoct if he stayed home. There was Harry, being torn from her arms as the plane plummeted towards earth, seconds before it burst into flames; Harry being shunted down the escape chute – a shrieking, terrified bundle; Harry's oxygen mask failing to drop down from the compartment when the cabin pressure decreased – and Claire losing consciousness after putting hers on him; Harry being snatched by a psycho at the airport while Ben and Claire searched for their baggage or struggled to lug it off the conveyor belt. He had to be better off at home with Claire's parents. And Brita.

She knocked back the rest of her champagne and peered over the row of seats ahead of her to catch the attention of a flight attendant. 'Well, I miss Harry a lot,' she said, 'I need to drown my sorrows in drink. Let's get some more booze.' She turned to Ben who was intent on reading something he'd taken from his carry-on bag. 'What are you doing? This is supposed to be fun time.'

'I wanted to look over the brochure for the conference. I see Bernardo and Christine will be working the exhibits room.'

'Yes, I know. I wasn't sure how to break the news to you.'

'What is it she's hawking again?'

'Canuck-talk.'

'Jesus.' He sighed heavily. 'I hope they won't expect us to spend any time with them. Things have been so peaceful since they moved.'

'They'll be too busy making money to care what we're doing.

But I'd like to have one dinner with them. We should see their house. It's supposed to be amazing.'

'If your taste runs to sickening ostentation.' Ben slid the brochures back into his bag. 'I guess you'd take it personally if I spent half an hour reviewing my paper.'

'Considering this is our first time away together since Harry was born, yes. Look it over when we get to the hotel. Tomorrow.' She had finally managed to attract a flight attendant and order more champagne. When it arrived, she said, 'Now, drink up so I can take advantage of you.'

'Up here at a cruising altitude of forty-seven thousand feet?' Ben's nostrils flared slightly.

Claire hesitated. 'Sure – why not?' Her head was spinning a bit, from the booze and the altitude. 'We haven't had any turbulence. We need to shake things up a little.'

'So,' Ben put his hand on her knee and massaged it gently, 'what did you have in mind?' He looked dazzled.

'I don't know.' In truth, Claire didn't know what she had in mind. Could she really be feeling this sudden desire for Ben here? In an aircraft? Somewhere above Saskatoon?

'If you don't want me to work on my paper, you're going to have to come up with something pretty diverting.' He leaned over and nuzzled her ear. 'How about we do it in the can?'

'The can?' Claire swallowed, staring straight ahead.

'You know? The john, the loo? Do we need your sister to translate?'

'But there's no room in airplane bathrooms. They're tiny. Besides,' she craned her neck to see over the seats behind them, 'look at all the people waiting to get in.'

'Sure, they're all lining up to do it in there too. We just have to wait our turn. And be resourceful.'

'What if they flash the "Return to your seats" sign while we're in the thick of it? What if we get trapped in there and the plane goes down?'

'I can't think of a better way to go, can you?' He nuzzled her ear again, tickling the inside of it with his tongue. It made the roof of Claire's mouth tingle. She shivered. 'All we have to do is wait until they turn the lights down and start the movie. Nobody goes to the can when the movie's on.' His fingers inched up from her knee, tracing circles on Claire's thigh. 'It's an old comedy. Something about a dog. I don't want to see it anyway.'

For a moment, Claire's fledgling enthusiasm fizzled. What if it had been a movie he wanted to see? Would the idea of sex with her have come in a far distant second? Or not even rank for consideration? She cleared her throat. 'Well, I'm not really sure I'm that kind of girl. Maybe I'll just read the airline magazine. There's an article on Napa Valley wines . . .'

'Claire, you're at your sexual peak. You're supposed to be able to wear out guys my age.'

'Is that why you married me?'

'What do you think?' He took her hand and placed it on his crotch. Ben could get an erection over just about anything: a hole in a fence, a pencil sharpener. He seemed to have a hard-on more often than he didn't. And it was true that when he met her he'd been thrilled by Claire's sexual appetite, her willingness to experiment, even with some rather offbeat 'variations' (as the skin mags called them) involving ties, surgical dressings and spatulas. Now, six years later, he had to be feeling swindled.

She pulled her hand away and took a deep breath. 'Well, okay. As soon as the lights go down I'll go. You wait about three minutes, then follow me. Just bang once on the door and I'll let you in.'

'I'll be banging more than the door.'

They sat together in silence, feeling warm and agitated, sipping champagne and anticipating the carrying out of their outrageous plan. The flight attendants took forever to pick up the dinner trays, then fumbled for an eternity getting the movie started. There was some trouble with the sound, and for a while it looked as though there wouldn't be any on-board entertainment of any kind.

'This is the last time we're flying Air Canada,' Ben muttered as the lights were finally dimmed and the movie started, with warbling sound and a fuzzy picture.

'So, what should I do when I get in there?' Claire asked, as she struggled out of her seat and climbed over his knees.

'I'm sure you'll figure it out.' He patted her on the backside as she stepped into the aisle. Her progress towards the rear of the plane was unsteady. She wondered if she'd lost her mind, and half hoped there would be a long queue of people waiting to use the facilities. But there was no one back there, not even a flight attendant on the fold-out seat beside the microwave.

She stared, for a moment, at the brightly-lit VACANT/LIBRE sign on the lavatory door before opening it, feeling weak-kneed and woozy. Once inside, she studied the lay-out of the cramped and airless cubicle, puzzling again over what, exactly, she was supposed to do. Ben seemed to think she should know. Was it some kind of test? If she failed, would it mean she was hopelessly repressed, a failure as a woman in her sexual prime? A missionary-position flop? The space certainly didn't seem to lend itself to anything more involved or long-lasting than *coitus interruptus* of the most unsatisfactory kind. In fact, it was hard to imagine the two of them fitting in that space together, let alone doing anything more acrobatic than breathing.

Were the three minutes up? She should have made it five. Or ten. What would Ben think if he arrived, primed and raring to go, and found her standing there, peering into the mirror above the basin, perhaps squeezing a blackhead? She'd better do something to look interested in this venture. And she was. Sort of. It was going to resuscitate their marriage, wasn't it? But what would her grandmother have thought? 'You be *kurva*. Feh!' she'd hissed at Claire the summer she turned up on her baba's porch, having just hitchhiked back from the west coast, barefoot, and carrying a yowling cat in a basket. A *kurva* was a whore – a slut. Although, in retrospect, it was probably the cat more than anything else that had set her grandmother off, the entire family still remembered and talked about the incident, no matter that it happened more than twenty years ago; despite how staid and successful and responsible a person Claire believed she'd become. There was no statute of limitations, it seemed, on embarrassing familial situations. It was a good thing her grandmother wasn't alive to hear about Mike Potochnik.

Slowly, Claire turned around in the cramped space, trying to work out the various possibilities for coupling. There certainly weren't many. Vertical was the way to go, obviously. She could try and sit on the narrow counter, but then her rump would rest in the wash-basin, probably overflow it. AS A COURTESY TO OTHER PASSENGERS, PLEASE WIPE THE BASIN AFTER USE, it said, faintly disapproving, on a sign above it. She appraised the toilet seat next, marvelling at how casually she would have plopped herself down on to it, in her younger years, uncaring about how many of her body parts came into contact with it. Now, it seemed to swarm with bacteria, microbes, viruses. Feeling a sudden urge to pee, she lifted her skirt, pulled down her pants and squatted uneasily above the toilet seat, quadricep muscles protesting. She pulled her pants back up, flushed the toilet, and felt a small surge of panic as the blue water was sucked noisily away. Ben would be there any second – she had to get busy.

There wasn't enough room in there to do it doggie-style. She tried to bend over the small counter. Her expression, reflected in the mirror, showed not sexual excitement, but acute embarrassment. She couldn't go eyeball to eyeball with herself for the duration of *the act*, with Ben reflected over her shoulder, his face contorted by agony, ecstasy and exertion. She coughed. The things some women would do to pump some adrenaline back into their marriages! Then she tried leaning with her back against the door, putting a foot up on first the toilet seat, then the counter top. She imagined Ben puffing and banging away, oblivious to the thin door that would be trembling under the strain. The sign on the outside would flash from VACANT/LIBRE to OCCUPIED/OCCUPÉ, then back again, as Claire's backside bumped against the door latch.

Maybe Ben could sit on the toilet, and she could sit on his lap, facing him. He wouldn't care about microbes. But the seat had no lid. And wasn't there some danger associated with airplane toilets? Claire recalled something about suction, about a tremendous vacuum being created under certain conditions. DO NOT THROW OBJECTS INTO THE TOILET warned the sign above it. She and Ben were obviously too big to get sucked out through the toilet, but, infinitely worse, they could get stuck there, wedged into the bowl like the two humping dogs she'd once seen, welded together for hours on the front lawn of 67 Pine Beach Road, and have to wait until the plane landed to be freed.

There was a muffled thump on the door. Ben already! And she had done none of the things she was supposed to do to prepare for their adventure – whatever those things were. Hyperventilating slightly, she unlocked the door to let him in.

'You're not ready,' he said, looking disappointed.

'I wasn't sure, exactly, what to do.'

'Christ, Claire. It isn't that complicated.'

'Well, it's a bit hard to lie back naked under satin sheets in here – or maybe you hadn't noticed. And it's bright enough to do brain surgery. I'm having a bit of trouble getting into the mood.'

'I'll get you in the mood.' He pulled her close, breathing hard. 'Pitter patter, let's get at her.' He reached a hand up under her skirt, then drew back and looked at her in amazement. 'You've still got your underpants on.'

'Surprise.'

'Well, get them off. That's pretty basic, isn't it?' He started fumbling to undo his belt, then pushed his jeans and shorts down to his knees. His stiff penis waved in the air, searching, antenna-like.

'But where should I stand?' Mortified, Claire slipped her panties off and, not knowing what else to do with them, stuffed them into the waistband of her skirt. Then she hiked her skirt up. 'This is so romantic.'

'It will be,' he said, 'in retrospect. You'll get hot over this memory for years. Lean up against the door.'

'I thought maybe I could sit up on the counter . . .'

'Forget it. No room. No time.' He seemed to know what he was doing. Had he done this before? 'Put your arms around my neck, then wrap your legs around my waist.'

'You've got to be kidding.'

'Just do it, Claire. There's two guys out there with exploding bladders, desperate to get in here. If you keep diddling around, they'll break down the door.'

Claire put her arms around his neck, then, using what was left of her stomach muscles, and wishing she'd done some post-natal exercises to get back into shape, she gave a little jump and managed to get her legs around Ben's waist. Almost immediately, they began to slide down again. He gripped her under the thighs and hoisted her back up into position. 'Nobody said this would be easy,' he grunted. 'Grab on to me with your legs. Use your muscles.'

'I'm no fucking gymnast.'

'Well, I can't do it all.' He fumbled for his penis and, after a lot of rather comical struggling, managed to stuff it inside her. 'Man, you're dry. You could have brought some gel or something.'

'I don't normally carry lubricating jelly on me.'

'Let's not fight, okay?' He winced as he thrust harder.

'So, do you want to forget about this?'

'No way. This is great.' Another dry thrust. Then he stopped, his head on her shoulder, his hands digging into her thighs.

'Now what?' she said.

'What do you mean, now what?'

'I can't stay like this for long.'

'It won't take long.'

'What if they hear us outside?'

'Then they're lucky – we won't even charge them.' His eyes were closed, his brow creased with concentration as he laboured to get some in–out action going. 'This is wild. You're incredible.' Claire arched her back, trying to relieve the pressure on the door, afraid it would pop from its hinges and they would tumble out into the aisle, bare-assed, glued together. Ben opened his eyes to look at their reflection in the mirror. 'Hey, check us out. We look great. Too bad we can't see more.'

'Yes,' she said, 'this is so romantic. How will we ever go back to an ordinary bed?' What if he really did enjoy it? What if it led to more of such things, and he insisted they start *doing it* in all sorts of high-risk public places – shopping mall washrooms, hotel lobbies, underground parking garages? She clung to him, sweating with the effort of keeping her legs tightly around his waist. The muscles of her inner thighs, long since atrophied from non-use, began to tremble uncontrollably.

She leaned her head back, trying to squeeze some pleasure out of the experience. Maybe Ben was right – it would be a lot more enjoyable in retrospect. FOR YOUR PROTECTION THIS LAVATORY IS EQUIPPED WITH A SMOKE DETECTOR met her eyes.

'Christ, it's hot in here.' Ben thrust and pumped, thrust and pumped. Then he laughed abruptly.

'What's so funny?' Claire tried to smile into the forest of his thick black hair.

'That plug on the wall – beside the mirror.'

'What about it?'

'Look at the sign under it. FOR YOUR RAZOR.'

'So?'

'What was that Swedish phrase you said yesterday?' He pushed deeper into her, then withdrew with a clumsy jerking movement. Claire's vague smile faded. 'What was it?' he said. 'That phrase?'

'I can't remember.'

'Where's the plug for the razor? Say it.'

'No – really. I can't remember.'

'Come on,' he panted, 'it was funny.' He was perspiring heavily, pumping harder, working frantically.

'*Var ar kontakten for rakapparaten,*' she said through clenched teeth.

'Again!'

'No.'

'Please!' The sweat was trickling down his forehead as he thrust faster and harder. The door of the cubicle shook; the mirror trembled. The intercom system beeped. 'Does someone need assistance in the lavatory?' inquired a voice.

'Say it again,' Ben whispered fircely. 'I'm almost there.'

'But what if the whole plane can hear us? What if we're being broadcast through the intercom?'

'Just say it!'

'*Var ar kontakten for rakapparaten!*' She felt like pushing him down on to the toilet, so that some turbulence would create the necessary suction to catapult him out into the stratosphere.

'Oh! Oh, Claire! Oh, my God!' With a groan, he came, grabbing her face and kissing her hungrily. Then he collapsed, his weight slumped against her, breathing hard, moaning.

'I'm squashed,' she wheezed, her legs slipping down past his knees. 'I can't breathe.'

Someone was pounding on the door. 'What's going on in there? Do you need help? Are you all right?'

'More than all right, Buddy.' Ben pulled out of Claire, dropped her, then struggled to get his pants up over his sticky thighs. 'That was amazing. You're absolutely the best.'

'How do we get out of here now? With all those people

outside?' Crossly, Claire wiped off the insides of her thighs with a piece of rough brown paper towel.

'I'll go out and tell them you've been airsick and need a few minutes to get cleaned up.'

Claire pulled her panties out of the waistband of her skirt and stepped into them. She was trembling violently, would likely be unable to walk by morning. 'Oh, nice. I'm supposed to let everyone think I've been in here puking all over myself?'

'If you've got a better idea, let's hear it.'

When Claire returned to her seat a few minutes later, Ben had his chair back in the reclining position, his headset on, and his eyes closed. He was smiling dreamily – the high-altitude equivalent of rolling over with a fart and a snore. She sat beside him, sulking and leaking body fluids, wishing the movie would finish so she could get another drink, and fantasizing about strangling him with the wires of his headset.

Finally, bored with the silent antics of a slobbering St Bernard on the screen, she reached over and lifted off one of Ben's earphones. There was no sound coming out of it – he'd been pretending to be listening to something. 'So what was all that Swedish nonsense?' she demanded.

'Nothing. You're funny, that's all. You're a constant amusement. And amazement.'

'That so?'

'Yup.' He gave her hand a vigorous pat.

'I'm not sure that's a satisfactory response. Or that that was a satisfactory experience.'

'Sorry, counsellor. Why don't you just sit back and relax? Think about what we just did, feel wild and sexy and alive.' His eyes were still closed. 'That was just like the bad old days, wasn't it?' He pulled the headset back into place.

Claire sat and stewed for a moment, then pulled his headset off again. 'There's something I've been meaning to ask you.'

He looked at her, faintly exasperated. 'Shoot.'

'When I gave my presentation at work – that one for Rick's big clients – there was one of your slides in my carousel. A really horrible one. A man with almost no face. It got projected all over the wall.'

'That's bizarre. Must have been a shock. What did you say?'

'I don't remember – don't try this at home – something like that.'

'You said don't try this at home?' Ben laughed. 'To Rick's clients?'

'I didn't know what else to say. I was totally humiliated. And I'd like to know how that slide of yours got in there.'

'How should I know? Ben reddened. 'Are you suggesting I sabotaged your talk? Why would I do that? I don't want you to get fired. Look, if you want to think that, go ahead and sabotage mine, retaliate. Slip one of your slides into my carousel – the life cycle of a trade-mark or something. I'll deal with it.'

'I don't want to sabotage your talk. That's not the point. I just want to know who ruined mine. If it wasn't you, who was it?'

'I'm sure it was an accident. Maybe Harry was crawling around downstairs—'

'And he selected a grotesque reconstruction slide and just popped it into my carousel? Get serious. And it was the very first slide that came up. It practically killed my entire presentation.'

'Well, maybe he was crawling around and dumped out a tray full of slides and Brita got confused and didn't know where they should go.'

'Hardly likely. And even if that did happen, why wasn't she watching Harry while he was doing all this crawling around and dumping things out?'

'She can't be expected to watch him every second.'

'Why not? That's what we're paying her for.'

'What if she were putting in the laundry or something?'

'And what if he stuck a pair of scissors into an electrical outlet while she was so busy doing something else? Would that be excusable too? Would you overlook that so easily?'

'This is a stupid argument. I'm not going to get dragged into it. You just feel like fighting.'

'Can't imagine why. After being so sexually satisfied.' Ben gave her a look. She had his attention now. 'And while we're on the subject of Brita—'

'How did I know we would end up on that subject?' Ben sighed.

'I'd like to know what that flag on her ceiling is all about. It's not Swedish, is it?'

'I never said it was.'

'So what is it?'

'It's from a region – in the south. Skane.'

Skane? That's what was written all over those pamphlets in Brita's drawer. 'Isn't that where you lived?' Claire didn't feel like mentioning that she'd been through Brita's drawers. Ben's reactions to things were becoming completely unpredictable.

'I lived in Skane.'

'So this region has its own flag?'

Ben shrugged. 'I guess so.'

'You *guess* so? Why do I get the feeling you know more about it than you're telling me?'

'I don't know. Why do you?'

'Because you do.'

'Okay – there's a movement – they're sort of separatists. People in Skane think they're more Danish than Swedish. They want to separate from the rest of Sweden. The flag is a combination of the two countries' flags. The red is Danish, the yellow cross is Swedish.'

'Wait a minute, let me understand this correctly. Here's this beautiful Western country with one of the highest standards of living in the world and some group wants to get out of it?'

'I'd rather be Danish than Swedish. You'd understand if you lived there. Swedes can be pretty dour.'

'Ingrid Bergman, Britt Ekland and Uma Thurman are dour?' Claire snorted. 'Give me a break.'

'You can't judge a whole country by a few screen stars.'

'Dour.' Claire snorted again.

'Anyway, as I was trying to say – it's the Danes who have the *joie de vivre*. It boils down to the drinking laws, if you want the real story. People in Skane are fed up with having to go to Denmark to do any serious boozing.'

'You've got to be kidding.'

'No, I'm not.'

Claire didn't say anything for a moment. 'So Brita's a Skanish separatist?'

'I suppose she is. I haven't really talked to her about it.'

'So why didn't she stay there? Working for the cause?'

'I think things may be heating up a bit. Could be she had to skedaddle.'

'Skedaddle? That's how you think of it? Harry's nanny is some kind of anarchist – a political refugee – an alcoholic – living in our house, making bombs in our basement, organizing political rallies? She gets herself deported from Sweden and you say she just had to skedaddle?'

'I never said she was deported. And she doesn't even drink.'

'Maybe there's some rally going on right now in our house. They're doing all that wild drinking, thrashing each other with birch branches.'

. . . 'It's the Finns who do that.'

'And setting up a printing press to run off their political pamphlets.'

'You're talking crazy. And your folks are there, remember?'

'They're in the furnace room by now, bound up with duct tape. Ben!' She clutched his arm. 'We have to go back. How could we have been so blind?'

'What are you talking about?'

'Brita's got political pamphlets – red ones – down in her bedroom. In her bureau drawer. Hundreds of them.'

'You went through her drawers?'

'I had to. I had to find out what was going on. For Harry's sake.'

'No. For your sake. And I bet Christine put you up to it, too.'

'She did not.'

'I knew it.' Ben shook his head. 'What a sour bitch. You two are pathetic, you know that?'

When the plane landed, an hour later, they were still arguing about whether or not Brita should be expected to watch Harry every second, whether or not she was an anarchist, why Claire thought she should be entitled to go through her mail and other personal belongings, and what business any of it was of Christine's.

18

Things improved a lot once Claire and Ben arrived in San Francisco. Their hotel room overlooked something called the atrium – an enormous vaulted space that was meant to evoke the fragrant steamy sensations of a tropical greenhouse, interspersed with fountains and pools on several different levels. In the middle of the largest pool, around which the dining tables were grouped, was an island of glass block on which a pianist, in tie and tails, played Gershwin on a white baby grand.

For the first day, Claire luxuriated in the lack of things she had to do, in the obscenely thick towels and the complimentary bathrobes that were supplied, fresh and warm, each morning; in having their bed turned down at night, and in the gold-wrapped chocolate truffles, like the droppings of a tooth fairy, left on their pillows.

For the first night in months, she slept without pills – though her sleep was disturbed, full of startling dreams and strange physical sensations. She dreamed her father died and it took her mother three or four days to tell her about it. Elfriede was self-conscious about her slipping memory and afraid of repeating herself. 'Did I tell you that Dad died a few days ago?' she mentioned casually over the phone while Claire was mashing boiled carrots to feed to Harry. Claire awoke in a sweat, reaching for the phone, her arms and legs tingling as if with electrical shock. Ben patted her leg and rolled over. 'Your dad's strong as a horse,' he assured her, 'he won't croak for decades. Isn't this bed glorious?'

In the afternoon of the second day, Claire hobbled down to the hotel spa for a massage, asking the masseuse to concentrate on her stiffened quadriceps. Then she sat in the steam-room

• Sylvia Mulholland

wondering how she was going to pay for all the hotel extras. After that, she tried the sauna, for as long as she could bear it, ultimately concluding that both means of heating human flesh were vastly overrated pastimes. Ben could happily cook in a sauna for hours – a passion he'd acquired in Europe. The German ones were the best. Many of the public ones were co-ed. How often Claire had heard the story of his startled delight the time three long-legged frauleins – they must have been models! – walked in on him and casually dropped their towels. Brita, she imagined, would be big on saunas too.

The sauna is a most agreeable way to pass the time in Sweden, according to *Sweden For Voyagers. Enormously popular, the sauna combines the Swedes' innate desire to relax with their pursuit of good health, physical fitness and cleanliness. It even provides them with the chance for some relaxed pillow talk.*

How was that? Sitting at her desk in her office, Claire had read the words over again. (She usually read *Sweden For Voyagers* at work, carting it back and forth in her briefcase, from home to office.) Oh, it was *business talk*, not pillow talk, she realized, smiling at the workings of her overactive imagination.

After the sauna, the Swedes refresh with a cold shower, an invigorating swim or a roll in the hay.

Claire had stared at the text, appalled. How could they write such a thing in a guide book for tourists, many of whom would be elderly or, at least, terribly out of shape? Did the authors want to be responsible for dozens of strokes? How could they tell these people to broil in a sauna, raising their blood pressures to dangerous levels, then plunge into icy water and immediately engage in sexual intercourse? She'd called Davina in. 'Here, read this part about saunas,' she'd said.

'Takes all kinds,' Davina had shrugged, reading it then handing it back to Claire. 'I know lots of people who like them.'

'But don't you think it's a bit much? That last line?'

'Personally, I don't like snow – even when I'm fully dressed. Which they probably aren't, being Swedish.'

'Snow?' Claire read the passage again. Of course, the word was *snow*, not hay.

There were brief periods of time in San Francisco during which

• 210

she managed not to think about Harry, but the instant she did it was with a surge of guilt and a quickening of alarm. She called home first thing every morning and as late at night as she dared, aware that it was three hours later back east and that she was probably waking up her parents. As she dialled the number, she would brace herself for the worst. When there was no answer, she panicked; when there was, she struggled to decipher her mother's code language. When Elfriede said everything was *fine*, what did it really mean? When she said everything was *okay*, was that somehow less than *fine*? What did it mean when Claire could hear Harry wailing in the background? What did it mean when she couldn't?

Only once did Brita answer the phone. She was friendly enough but didn't seem eager to chat. 'I will get your mother,' she said. 'Mrs Wolaniuk?' she called, 'it's the *satkaring*. Your daughter.' Claire meant to look up *satkaring* in *Sweden for Voyagers* when she got home. Probably, it meant something like worrier, something to do with being a mother. Maybe *karing* was Swedish for caring. On occasion, she'd discovered, the languages were quite similar. If she spoke English with an affected German-style accent, she was often bang-on with the Swedish.

Ben was busier at the conference than he'd expected to be. There were some big names at the meeting, top surgeons from all over the world, and he wanted to circulate and meet as many as he could. The dinners Claire had with him took on a definite pattern, inevitably shared with some tag-along, spouseless surgeon whom Ben, in his usual gregariousness, had urged to join them. All of this bustling glad-handing was an investment that was important for his future – for their future. She should get to know some of the wives, he said, there were bound to be some interesting women there; or why not take some of the courses organized for spouses?

Though sceptical that there would be anything of interest to her, Claire dutifully got the spouse programme from the gosh-great-to-see-you girls at the information centre. There was a Breakfast at Tiffany's where champagne and chocolate-dipped strawberries would be served and where one could obtain a complimentary appraisal of one's own jewellery; later on, the chef de l'hôtel would demonstrate how to turn at-home entertaining into a *cordon bleu* event. Claire considered going to both: the first to see if her sixty-dollar wedding band was really worth as much now, six years after the fact; the second to see what the hotel chef had in mind for her to do with fish sticks.

Also scheduled was a day-long trek to a number of Californian vineyards, a Christian Dior cosmetic makeover, a harbour sail on which a line of designer cruise-wear could be purchased at cost. There were also a number of 'Spouse in the Office' courses for women who wanted to get more involved in their husbands' practices – seminars on income tax, investing, fee-billing software.

The remainder of the spouse program was designed to present the plastic surgeons' wives on a platter, ready for carving by the local merchants. There were daily cocktail parties, luncheons, fashion shows and shopping shuttles where the women were herded on to luxury coaches, plied with more champagne and bussed to the most exclusive shopping centres in Northern California. Claire was disappointed, though hardly surprised, to find that factory outlet malls were not on the agenda.

She went to one of the fashion show luncheons but it gave her a headache – too much rich food, over-amplified disco music, flashing strobe lights that hurt her eyes and made her feel frantic. Day-wear, cruise-wear, sportswear flashed by at a frenetic pace. There were outfits to wear while shopping, frocks for afternoon tea, twin-sets for your husband's office. There were society fund-raiser ensembles, togs for the beach, foul-weather gear for the yacht. During dessert, the cocktail gowns swished past Claire's table: a parade of jewels and shiny sequins that made her think of fish lures. Then there was the grand finale: a parade of dead animals; sheared, dyed and draped. No one in the crowd seemed particularly worried about being spray-painted by animal rights types. As Claire rose to leave, a woman beside her grumbled that the show's organizers would never be able to get the coats back to the store by the time their shopping shuttle arrived. Claire walked quickly out of the ballroom, head high. She knew when she was beaten. She couldn't have afforded so much as a single shoe worn by one of those models. Even her Dresser was muzzled into an awe-struck and brooding silence.

The next day of the conference was the one on which Ben was

to present his paper. Out of six thousand delegates, only about twelve hundred had signed up to hear his talk and Claire could tell he was disappointed. Every body would count, he'd told her. Claire, who could hardly imagine giving a talk to twelve people without her knees buckling, let alone twelve hundred, didn't see what possible difference her body could make, but she decided she would be the supportive plastic surgeon's wife and go to cheer him on at his presentation.

While she waited for his talk to begin – he was busy going over his slides in one of the prep rooms, she wandered around the Exhibitors' Hall, hoping to catch up with Christine, looking over the displays of glittering scalpels, scissors and tweezers, gelatinous tactile implants for the breast, for the face; luminous-coloured cold packs for post-surgical swelling and various styles of wraps and bandages.

A strolling violinist and accordion player were doing a rendition of 'Spanish Eyes', and at one of the booths, a man in a lab coat was cauterizing a chicken breast while another performed laser surgery on a slab of meat.

'This must be the gourmet cooking class,' Claire joked. 'Would that be top round or sirloin you're working with?'

'It's pork butt, actually,' he replied seriously. 'It's the closest you can get to human flesh.' Claire, who had just that morning indulged in a whopping American-size bacon and egg breakfast, decided not to pursue the subject. She wandered over to the next booth, to see the display of live leeches. 'Here, take these.' A curvaceous woman wearing rhinestone cat glasses pushed a business card and brochure at her. 'We're trying real hard to get ahead in this market.' With a shudder, Claire walked on, reading that leeches were being used to remove congested blood following tissue grafts – as many as a thousand in a single operation – and were making a big comeback in modern plastic surgery after their use fell into disrepute during the nineteenth century.

The booth set up by Bernardo's company was getting a lot of attention, judging by the crowd around it. Bernardo didn't spend any time in the booth, preferring to mingle and work the room, but Christine stayed put, loving the attention and babbling on with her hard sell about what the States had to offer

Canadian-trained doctors, or telling interested representatives from American health management organizations – HMO's – now to lure Canadians south.

'That right, eh?' Claire heard one of the Canucks say as he listened, obviously dazzled, to her sister. 'You say they call a pancake a *griddle* cake down here?'

'That's right,' Christine said, crinkling her eyes, 'or a flapjack.'

'Go figure,' he said.

'They also don't say "Go figure" – though it depends on what part of the States you're planning to go to. And that's where our company can help.' She spotted Claire over the man's shoulder and darted out from the booth to give her a quick kiss. 'So we'll see you tonight?' she said, her breath spicy with mouth-wash, giving Claire's hand a welcoming squeeze.

Ben's presentation was a great success. He was confident enough to lead into it with a joke; and lucky enough to get a laugh. Claire sat patiently in the back row, trying not to look at the projected images on the screen, watching her husband's dark head bobbing over the top of the lectern while twelve hundred plastic surgeons – a sea of surgical genius, the heal-with-steel crowd – watched in finger-twitching interest.

Afterwards, she had lunch with Ben in the hotel restaurant although he was distracted, flying high with his success, and they were constantly being interrupted by other surgeons who wanted to talk to him about his research. Claire listened with a polite, fixed smile for as long as she could stand it, then excused herself to go and find other diversions.

She didn't have much enthusiasm for the Cable Car Museum or the simulated earthquake on Pier Thirty-Nine, and she'd been warned away from a nostalgic return to Haight-Ashbury: it was a hang-out for skin-heads now, not a place for plastic surgeons' middle-aged wives.

She passed some time at FAO Schwarz, waffling over whether to buy Harry a talking tree stump, a set of wind-up dinosaurs or all the animal friends of Pocahontas, until the endless repetitions of 'It's a Small Small World' drove her back out into the street before she could decide. At a souvenir shop, she bought a music box on which tiny cable cars rolled over hilly streets to the tinkling sounds of 'I Left My Heart in San Francisco'. Then she marched up and down those hilly, windy streets for the rest of the afternoon, looking for something else to buy. Eventually, she ended up at Nordstrum, dizzyingly circling four floors of merchandise on the world's only spiral escalator. She bought herself two pairs of pants: one purple, one green, and a matching cotton sweater with silver threads running through it. She bought a black linen blouse, a pair of suede espadrilles and two leather jackets, because they were such a terrific buy, according to her Dresser. Then she picked up a couple of bottles of wine to take to Christine's and went back to the hotel room to wait for Ben, snip the labels out of her new clothes and try to figure out which she would declare and which she would try to wing through Canada Customs.

'What's that? Dalmatian dog?' Ben indicated the black and white hide draped over Christine's love seat.

'Pony skin,' she laughed, kissing the air on both sides of his face and taking his jacket. Bernardo was out with a potential client for the evening but had promised to join them later, in time for dessert.

'Wouldn't an endangered species be more *amusant*?' Ben continued to eye the love seat.

'Pinto pony is not endangered, but there aren't a lot of them around either.'

'There's one fewer now. Where do you go for those skins? A petting zoo?'

Claire wandered over to the enormous bay window in Christine's living-room, wanting to avoid the look she knew Ben would be trying to throw her way, and wishing Bernardo were there to ease the tension between Ben and her sister. 'Come over here and see this view, Ben.'

'You mean see this view and come.' He followed her to the window and slipped his arm around her waist. Since their in-flight adventure, and now that their boiling debate over Brita seemed to have settled into simmer (mostly because Ben was too preoccupied to talk about it) he had become quite amorous – the proverbial octopus man – lunging for Claire when they were alone in elevators, sliding his hands over her thighs in the hotel Jacuzzi, groping for her in the back seat of taxi cabs. She was enjoying the attention, but only to a point. It was a lot like the days right after they first met; the main difference being that, back then, she never got the urge to take a fly-swatter to him. She was also suspicious of the source of all of this *amour*. She imagined being interviewed on some crass daytime talk show. What is the secret of my successful marriage to a much younger man? She would smile cryptically and confess: I know how to ask for a razor in Swedish.

'Well, you two seem to be getting along well,' Christine remarked, an edge of envy to her voice.

'We had a great flight out,' Ben said.

'Oh?' She obviously wanted to hear more, but neither Ben nor Claire volunteered anything further. 'Well,' she sighed, 'I wanted to tell you about the view. This is what I call a real bay window. We've got a hundred and eighty-degree panorama of the harbour. Look at the lights on the bridges. That's the Golden Gate there, and the Bay Bridge over there. From the dining-room, you get a good view of Alcatraz too.'

'How appetizing,' said Ben.

'And you won't believe the storage space I've got, for my shoes alone. The previous owner would have put Imelda Marcos to shame. But the owners before her were a couple of pack rats. Guess how much stuff was found in this house after they died? Six tons! All the newspapers printed in San Francisco since 1900, including the ones in Chinese. They'd cleared little tunnels and passageways through all of the garbage, just so they could get around.'

'Sounds like our house,' Ben said.

'It's amazing there wasn't any structural damage,' Claire said, 'with six tons weighing the house down like that.'

'It was built in the twenties, a decade after the big earth-quake. They got smart after that quake, I guess. It's built like a bomb shelter. Have you done the simulated earthquake on Pier Thirty-nine?'

'She doesn't have to,' Ben said, 'I simulate an earthquake for her every night in our room.'

'Really?'

'But only if he's had beans for supper,' Claire added. She and Ben laughed.

'The humour you two share is beyond me.' Christine shook her head, her smile tight. 'Why don't you come into the kitchen? I'm just putting the finishing touches on the seviche.'

At that moment, Christine's daughter, Anita, appeared on the stairs, holding a pink-haired doll that looked a lot like Anita herself, Claire thought. She'd never really warmed to her niece – there was something remote and fishy about her.

'Nita!' Christine exclaimed. 'Come see your aunt and uncle. They've travelled all the way from Canada – where we used to live – just to visit you!' It was funny, Claire thought, how people always made long names shorter, but short names longer. Inevitably, the resulting nickname was two syllables in length. It was a sort of golden mean of names. Anita became Nita. Two syllables was perfect – a name like Harry, for example.

Anita plonked herself down on the pony skin and began pulling out the doll's hair, sending pink fibres into the air. Claire watched, wondering what effect it had on a seven-year-old girl to have to sit on a dead pony's hide, when other little girls were riding or petting them at zoos and fairs. She was missing Harry terribly, aching to feel his firm warm body in her arms and his sticky little fingers grabbing for her nose, trying to twist it off her face. She wanted to sniff his soft, *al dente* pink feet, nibble his fat toes, stroke his corn-silk hair.

'Nita's angry with me because I won't buy batteries for her Teddy Ruxpin,' Christine said. 'Remember that bear? I practically had to kill another mother to get the last one that Christmas when they first came out. I had it all packed up to give to the Goodwill when we moved – she hasn't played with it for years – but she grabbed it out of the box and insisted on bringing it down here. He takes four C-type batteries, and they last about a day. That Ruxpin was breaking us. Anita, stop pulling out your doll's hair.' Anita just glared at her mother and yanked out another tuft. 'Claire? Did I mention those andirons on either side of the fireplace? They're by Gilbert Poillerat.'

'It's essential to have a solid pedigree for one's andirons,' Ben said. 'Whatever they are.'

'You're joking, of course,' said Christine.

'Auntie Claire?' Anita's reedy voice interrupted them. 'Will you come upstairs and play with me?'

'Well, honey – I should stay and talk to your mother—' Claire knew that Ben would be signalling her like mad not to leave him alone with Christine but she didn't look at him.

'Oh, go ahead,' Christine said, 'indulge. She hasn't made any new friends here yet. She would love to have you play with her. I'm sure the doctor and I can find lots to talk about. Just take a drink with you and you'll have a good time.'

Sighing, Claire followed Anita up to her room, a vast chamber with its own separate dressing-room. 'So what would you like to play, Anita?' she said. 'House? Dolls?'

'Store.'

'Okay. I like playing store. When I was your age I made stores out of shoe boxes. I bet your mother's got a few of those around. I used to put Cellophane windows in them, and cut out pictures of all kinds of foods from magazines and then fill the shelves inside the store. Have you got some old magazines?'

'I don't want to play that kind of store. I want to play shopping. But we need to go into my mother's room.'

'Why can't we stay here?'

'There isn't as good a selection here. We're low on stock right now.'

Claire nodded. 'Why don't we give it a try anyway?'

'Well. Okay.' Anita opened the doors of her walk-in closet and started pulling out the drawers at the back of it. 'Were you looking for anything in particular? What can I show you today?'

Claire thought for a moment. 'I could use a belt.'

Anita continued busily searching through her drawers. 'Here's one.' She pulled out a slinky gold lamé with a snake's-head clasp, obviously an old one of Christine's, and brought it over to Claire, looping it around her hand, tilting it this way and that in the light. 'This is an excellent buy,' she said, 'see how it shines? And it goes with everything. You can wear it winter or summer. Dress it up, dress it down.'

Claire took the belt and pretended to study it, looking thoughtful. 'Well, I don't know. I'm not sure I like snakes all that much, to tell you the truth.'

'It's a classic. It'll never go out of style. These have been around since Cleopatra.' Then she fixed Claire with her fishy eyes, the colour of peeled grapes. 'Every woman should own at least one. Look at it as an investment.'

Claire stared at her, startled. 'I guess I'd better take it then.'

'Do you need anything to go with it? A blouse? A skirt?'

'Not today, thanks.'

'Shall I have it gift-wrapped?'

'No thanks, I think I'll just wear it.'

'That'll be two hundred dollars.'

'Two hundred? Isn't that a bit steep?'

Anita sighed. 'You get what you pay for.' She paused. 'Shall I put it back in the display case?'

'No. I guess I'll take it anyway – since it is a classic.'

'Will that be on your card?'

'No. Cash.' Claire pretended to take some money out of an imaginary purse and handed it to Anita.

For the first time, her niece smiled, showing a lot of gum and a number of missing teeth. 'Enjoy your belt,' she said.

Throughout dinner, Claire felt a lingering dysphoria over her game with Anita. Was that all the poor child aspired to do with her life? Shop? Could Harry turn out the same way, if Claire wasn't careful? Demanding reptile shoes, Boss shirts? Designer jeans? She thought guiltiy about her new leather jackets that she didn't need or even like all that much; the music box that Harry would immediately hurl down the stairs; the espadrilles that were a touch too tight.

While they ate, Anita lay under the table, kicking at one of the legs of it, making Christine's crystal wine glasses tremble. 'It helps release the bouquet,' she said gaily, 'just ignore her and she'll stop.' Eventually, Anita stopped, but only because she'd fallen asleep. After dinner, Ben carried her up to her room. Her doll, which now demonstrated female pattern alopecia to rival Claire's, remained face-down on the pony skin.

'Speaking of houses,' Christine said later, as she served a somewhat tough Pavlova, 'how is the Beaches love nest?'

'Holding out,' Claire said, 'but barely. We'll probably need a new retaining wall by the spring.'

'No thoughts about moving down here yet?'

'I think about it all the time,' Ben said. 'I'm totally sick of our health care system. It's a constant frustration. They've capped our incomes, and now they want to cut back the fees.'

'I know. It's a marketing dream for us.'

'As a resident, it doesn't really affect me. But next year I'm going to have to start thinking about it. Especially if Claire wants to quit work.'

'And do you?' Christine turned to her sister in surprise.

'I think about it now and then. Everything I make goes to pay for the house and the nanny – I'm beginning to wonder what I'm getting out of it. Harry's going to grow up without me. And I'm becoming fed up with practising law. I've got this problem client – former client – Mike Potochnik.'

'Potochnik? Dad's old buddy from the Ukraine?'

'His son.'

'Christ,' Christine said, 'that's like getting involved with a relative.'

'Worse. I think he might sue me.'

Ben moaned into his Pavlova. 'This is the first I've heard about him suing you.'

'He claims I lost him a big deal in the US. He would've been able to retire in two years, he says, if the deal hadn't fallen through. And it was my fault, according to him. He keeps saying I ruined his life.'

'And did you?' demanded Christine.

'Of course not. But now even Mother thinks I did.'

'Do you think he's dangerous?'

'I don't know.' Claire was disturbed to hear someone else voice her own fears, which she'd been telling herself were groundless. There was Harry, back home in Toronto, being looked after by her aging parents and a nanny with a shady past who was still practically a teenager, while a paranoic psycho could be lurking outside in the bushes, nursing his grudge against Claire, waiting for his chance for revenge. It would actually be easier for Mike to sneak around their property unnoticed, now that he didn't have a car. He could even climb up over the retaining wall from the beach. As soon as they got back to their hotel, she would call the airline, she decided, and see if she could get an earlier flight home.

'How is Brita doing, by the way?' Christine asked with a long look at Ben.

'Fine,' Claire said.

'Great,' said Ben.

'I'm so glad,' Christine smiled, her eyes flickering from Claire to Ben, then back to Claire.

Bernardo never did show up for dessert, or for coffee and liqueurs afterwards. The next morning, he sent a huge California fruit basket to Claire and Ben's hotel room, with a note of apology. He could well afford the fruit basket: he'd landed two Canadian surgeons that evening; one for a well-known teaching hospital in New York; the other for a private clinic in London.

That night, the Cunninghams lay in bed, fitted together, being spoons. Ben was the greatest spooner in the world, Claire thought happily. When she snuggled up behind him they were perfectly aligned: everything matched – hips, knees, ankles. Even her insteps were pressed up against the soles of his feet. She loved his smooth, solid warmth. He was always warm, like a trusty little furnace in their bed. She hadn't been able to get an earlier flight back, so she tried not to worry about Harry as she clung to Ben, telling herself they would be home soon and that, at least, their relationship seemed to be improving. It looked as though things were going to be a lot better between them. And, until they opened the front door of 67 Pine Beach Road a couple of days later, there was no reason to think otherwise.

19

'All happy families are alike but an unhappy family is unhappy after its own fashion,' wrote Tolstoy at the beginning of *Anna Karenina.* 'Everything had gone wrong in the Oblonsky household.' Claire would have several occasions to recall and ponder these opening lines the day she and Ben returned to Toronto.

'Now, before you react,' her mother said patiently, 'remember that I only thought I was doing what was right.'

Claire held Harry tightly in her arms – a hiccupping, sniffling bundle of misery. He'd broken out in chicken-pox while they were in San Francisco; her mother didn't want to worry her, so hadn't mentioned it when Claire called. His eyes were crusted over and his little face so obliterated by the angry oozing pox that there wasn't any clear spot that Claire could find to plant the many kisses she so desperately wanted to give him. As soon as she'd seen him, after rushing into the house dying to gather him into her arms, she'd burst into tears. Ben leaped immediately for the phone, calling Sick Kids', demanding to talk to the medical resident on call, then an ophthalmologist.

'Where's Brita?' Claire said anxiously.

'Well,' her mother said, looking uneasy, 'she and I had a difference of opinion. And she left in a huff. I don't know where she went.'

'Left? What do you mean left? She went out? She went to the store? Down to the beach?'

'I hope she didn't go out to the stores. That would be some shopping spree. It was three days ago.'

'She's been gone for three days and you didn't tell us?'

'What good would it do to tell you while you were in San

223 •

Francisco? I wanted you to enjoy your holiday. Dad and I managed Harry okay. We're both doctors, for heaven's sake. And anything we needed we just went out and bought. It's not like we're in Siberia here.'

Harry was looking up at Claire in silent misery. He blinked, his eyelashes thick with pus. 'Cookie,' he said.

'Did you hear that?' Claire was amazed. 'I think he actually said "cookie". Is that all you and Dad fed him?'

'Of course not.'

Although Harry looked terrible – he even had chicken-pox inside his ears – he didn't seem all that uncomfortable and had settled down in Claire's arms, resting his head against her shoulder, hiccupping occasionally. 'So what was the argument about? With Brita?'

'Your cloth diapers, that's what. She wanted to use paper ones the minute you were gone. But I said, Brita, that's not right – you can't sneak behind my daughter's back like that. You know Claire wants you to use cloth diapers, though God knows why. And who do you think is going to pay for paper diapers? I said to her. If you want to use them, pay for them yourself.'

'So what did she say?'

'I don't know what she said. It was in Swedish and I don't speak Swedish. Something rude. Sounded like s-h-i-t, but maybe not. "Forbidden sheet", that's what I thought she said. I made her repeat it because I wanted to know what she said to me so I could tell you.' She looked away, her mouth tight, eyes moist. 'Can you imagine? She talked to me like that? She's really something, that girl. Where did you find someone like her?'

'I didn't find her, Ben did.'

'She's *kurva*, you know what that is? Ask your dad.'

'Of course I know.'

'Anyway, for a couple days she used the cloth diapers, grumbling the whole time, and didn't do a single load of laundry. Well, those dirty diapers were starting to stink, I can tell you. And I wasn't going to wash them. I had four years of washing cloth diapers for you girls. By hand – I probably told you. I certainly wasn't going to wash them now, especially when you're paying so much money to have this nanny. That's her job. So I told Brita, go and do the laundry and snap out of it. That's when she packed her bags. Just like that. After calling me that rude name again, she was gone.'

'We can't take him in to the hospital because he's so contagious.' Ben had hung up the phone and was digging his medical bag out of the bottom of the front-hall closet, pushing aside boots, shoes, tennis racquets. 'Where's Brita? I need her to pick up a prescription for that eye infection, and we need calamine lotion for his itching.' He opened his bag, found what he was looking for inside it, and screwed together the parts of his ophthalmoscope.

'She's gone,' Claire said.

'What do you mean gone?' He flicked on the light of the ophthalmoscope, then peered with it into Harry's eyes, gently pulling up one of his eyelids, then the other.

'She quit,' Elfriede said, arms folded, leaning against the kitchen counter, 'just like that.'

'They had an argument about Harry's diapers. Brita wanted to use paper ones and Mother told her she couldn't.'

'I said if she wanted them, she could pay for them herself, that's all. She didn't want to pay for them and she didn't want to wash the cloth ones either. I think the diapers were just an excuse. These people have no loyalty. She probably found another job that pays a bit more.'

'Well, someone has to go out to get this medication for Harry. Let's get him into a bath. Poor kid. When did these pox come out?'

'The day after you left,' said Elfriede. 'He's been up all night every night.'

'You got up with him at night? How could you hear him?' Claire asked.

'Your dad did. Poor Dad. He's exhausted now. And he had office hours today.'

'Well, we're going to have to find Brita,' Ben said. 'She's our responsibility. We can't just let her wander around the streets. She could get killed. Or worse.'

'Don't kid yourself,' Elfreide said, 'that girl knows how to look after herself.'

'It's not only that,' Ben said irritably, 'we can't do without a nanny. We've both got to work tomorrow.' He gave Claire's mother a look which indicated he thought all of this was exactly what he'd expected to happen with her in charge. Then he started bustling around, getting out the baking soda to put in Harry's bath, phoning the pharmacy to get someone to deliver Harry's ointment.

Elfreide drew her sweater around her and settled down on to the chesterfield, obviously relieved that the house, Harry and Brita were no longer her concerns. 'So, Claire,' she said cosily, 'what did you buy in the States? Something exciting?'

'Not much.' Claire watched as Ben ran up the stairs to start the bath water, holding Harry protectively on her lap.

Elfriede was still waiting to hear what Claire had bought in San Francisco. 'I got a music box for Harry,' she said.

'And for yourself?'

'Nothing really.' Claire was amazed that the conversation was expected to slip so easily into trivialities. She continued to cuddle Harry. Her mother seemed to have forgotten that he was there. 'Christine convinced me to buy a sarong before I left.'

'A what?'

'A sarong. It's a silk rectangle, like a scarf only heavier.'

'Oh? What do you need another scarf for?'

'It's not a scarf. You wrap it around your waist.'

'For what purpose?'

'As a beach cover-up, or a short summer skirt. Everyone was wearing them in California.'

'What a strange idea.'

'It'd be great on a cruise.'

'You're taking a cruise?'

'Well no, not immediately.' Claire sighed. 'I got a couple of little things for you too – but I'll have to unpack to get them.'

'Well, I hope you didn't get me one of those sarongs. I don't even have a waist any more – it would be no good to me.'

'No, Mother, I didn't.'

'And how is Christine?'

'She's fine. She says she'll call you on Sunday. Their house is big, and expensive. You've seen the pictures.'

'And Anita?'

'Pulling the hair out of her dolls – the usual disturbed child routine. It's sad, really.'

'And Bernardo? Is he busy?'

'Away most of the time. He was just a blur at the conference. He didn't even show up for dinner with us. But he's getting richer.'

'So nothing much is new, in other words.' Her mother checked her watch. 'I don't know where your dad is. He was supposed to be on his way to pick me up.' Her bag was already packed, and waiting on the floor beside the front door. 'What a week.'

'Bet you can't wait to get out of here.'

'It's been a difficult time, that's all. Did you know you don't have a coffee-maker? We got up on Saturday morning to make ourselves some coffee and Dad tells me he can't find anything to make it with. Brita was no help, that goes without saying. I thought Dad was just not looking – you know how he is – but I discovered he was right.'

'I know, I'm sorry. It – broke. I should have told you.'

'So he drove from hardware store to hardware store and finally bought one – an old-fashioned percolator. I said why not one of those drip things, but there it is. You can keep it, since you need one.'

'Thanks,' Claire said guiltily. 'I'll write you a cheque.'

'Forget about it. It's a present.' Elfriede checked her watch again. 'Harry will be fine. But I wouldn't go running out to find that girl, if I were you. Let sleeping dogs lie. There's an expression in Ukrainian, you know the one?'

'Don't stir the shit or it'll start to stink?'

'It sounds better in Ukrainian, but of course you don't speak it. Anyway, you need a girl who is more responsible, not so hot-headed.'

'But we need someone now.'

'Well, I can't stay. Dad's still got office hours. And what's he going to eat? God knows what sort of mess he's making at home.' Claire's mother had given up her medical practice when Claire was born, preferring to look after her home and family. When Claire was a child, she'd been glad her mother stayed home, making buns stuffed with tuna salad and melted cheese, with tiny toothpick flags sticking out of them, and a nice variety of suppers: Chinese food, pyrohy, fish and chips. Claire always pitied those kids whose mothers worked. Working mothers were rare back then. If your mother worked, it meant your father couldn't make enough money; it was shameful.

'And my arthritis is very bad here, for some reason,' Elfriede continued. 'Maybe because you're so near the lake – the dampness.' She massaged her wrists and wrapped her sweater tighter around her; it was a black Tyrolean-style sweater with edelweiss embroidered on the pockets. 'Well, that sounds like Dad's car. We won't stay. Oh, I meant to tell you, there's a leak in your basement somewhere. Dad looked around but he couldn't find where the water was coming from. You'll see. The carpet's soggy under the window, at the bottom of the stairs. It smells. It gave Brita something else to complain about, let me tell you. She wanted to sleep in your bedroom but I didn't think you'd like that. I didn't know what sort of personal things you might have up there.' She got up off the chesterfield, picked up her suitcase and kissed Claire – a hearty European smack that left a cold wet patch on her cheek. 'When we agreed to stay here we didn't know we'd have a sick baby on our hands – of course, you didn't either – but you should have warned us that your Swedish nanny was crazy.' She shook her head, clucking. 'Anyway, give me a call. You can say goodbye to Ben for me. And call if I can be of any help . . .'

'Let me give Harry a quick bath,' Ben said, coming back down the stairs a few minutes after Elfriede had gone. 'I don't need to tell you what I think of this mess your mother's made. But the important thing is to get Brita back before she winds up in some kind of trouble. If it's not already too late.'

'Get her back? After what she did? Just leaving everyone in the lurch while we were out of the country? Abandoning a sick baby?'

'There's two sides to every story. Your mother can put people off sometimes, maybe without meaning to. And the language barrier couldn't have helped.'

'She called my mother some kind of shit. How do you say shit in Swedish?'

Ben sighed wearily. 'Is there any point in this, Claire?'

'I think so.'

'It's sheet. Spelled s-k-i-t.' He looked at her gloomily. 'Does it make you feel better to know that? Nobody ever claimed that Brita's a saint.'

'She sure looks it in that picture she's got – with the candles on her head and that white gown on.'

'What picture?'

'The one she has on her bureau, down in the basement.'

'That's not Brita.'

'Sure it is. What do you mean?'

Ben looked confused for a second. 'I don't know – I was thinking about something else. I don't even know what picture you're talking about. Look, my point is that Brita probably had a good reason for leaving.'

'Dirty diapers is a good reason?'

'We love Harry, and we love his shit. But we can't expect everyone else to. And like I said, there was probably more to it than that.'

'Maybe she won't want to come back. Maybe she wants to be alone, like Greta Garbo.'

'I think we should at least give her the option of returning, don't you?'

Claire shrugged. 'I'll have to think about it. Give me some time.'

'I have an idea where she might be.'

'How could you?'

'We have an old friend in common. Discovered it by accident. Remember Gosta?'

'No,' said Claire, 'I don't.'

'You will if you think about it. He's just not the kind of guy that stands out in a crowd.'

'Gosta who?'

'Lindgren. He was the micro-fellow at the General last year. He took us out for dinner. With that other couple – can't think of their name.'

'Micro-fellow. I love that term. I always picture this tiny white-coated doctor sitting in the palm of my hand. For he's a jolly good micro-fellow—'

'I could give Gosta a call. He knows Brita's family back in

Sweden. If she isn't staying with him, she probably called him
– he'll at least know where she is.'

'I really don't remember him. I remember a Vietnamese
micro-fellow, and that Swiss guy.'

'It isn't important. She may not even be there. If she isn't,
we'll have to start calling the women's hostels, the Y, places like
that. She would have had no other place to go. She's a foreigner
here, don't forget.'

'She has lots of friends.'

'I wouldn't be too sure about that, or about the quality of those
friends, if she does have them.'

'Ben, I can find someone else for Harry who's better than Brita.
There are lots of people looking for work. We could get someone
who could clean up around here, do some cooking. Someone
who's not all wrapped up in political causes.'

'You want to spend a thousand dollars on another agency
fee?'

'We could advertise in the paper. Lots of people I know have
found good nannies through the paper.'

'Well, I can't take the time off to help you interview. I warned
you about this. If you want to find someone else, you'll have to
do it on your own. Using a newspaper ad will take a week, at
least. You'll have to stay home with Harry. But you go ahead
if you want to. It's your law practice.'

He took Harry from Claire and she followed him upstairs,
then watched the muscles of his broad back moving under his
T-shirt, as he undressed and carefully lowered their son into the
bath tub. 'I bet no one's bothered to give this poor little fellow
a bath for days,' he said.

'You don't really think Brita would go to some hostel, do
you?' Claire suddenly pictured her, beaten and stuffed into some
alleyway disposal bin. Or being jostled about in a line-up of
bag-ladies and rubbies swilling after-shave, waiting for a blanket
and a bowl of soup. She was some mother's daughter, after all.
There had to be a pleasant, gentle woman back home in Sweden,
her face as puckered and lined as those apple-face dolls that
farm women make for craft fairs. She would be looking at the
Lucia picture, her eyes filling, wondering why she no longer
heard from her beautiful daughter, the daughter she'd poured

so much love and care into over the years. Claire swallowed, overcome with remorse.

On the other hand, maybe Elfriede was right. Perhaps Brita was street-wise and cunning and well able to look after herself; perhaps she was rolling her eyes and telling funny stories about the Cunninghams' small domestic traumas this very minute, sitting in a bar, surrounded by Swedish friends, drinking aquavit and *skaling*.

'I better go down and see about that leak in the basement,' she said.

'What leak?'

'My mother says there's water coming in from somewhere.'

Ben groaned. 'I don't want to know.'

At the bottom of the basement stairs, under the window on the south wall – the lake side of the house – Claire saw what Elfriede had been talking about: the dark spreading stain on the carpet. She stepped on it, testing it. It was spongy. Water squished around her foot as she leaned her weight on it. Her mother was right, it did stink – a sharp chemical smell, mingled with the odour of rotting fish, or garbage. The wall above it was cool but dry, though at the bottom of the window, the sill was wet. Probably it was a simple matter of the seal around the window not being tight enough. The Proctors had used masking tape and strips of cotton batting to seal up the basement windows, none of which adhered properly. She would have to go to Canadian Tire for some caulking or weather stripping or whatever it would take to do the job properly. She hated the prospect of wandering the aisles of that store with its stifling air smelling of rubber, paint and boredom, searching in vain for some phlegmatic teenager in a red jacket who wouldn't know much more about hardware than she did. She would have to take Harry with her as well – an impatient, easily bored Harry who wouldn't put up with the long line-up at the cash desk as customers fumbled to find their store coupons and beleaguered cashiers phoned the various departments for missing stock numbers and price codes. Why didn't she have a husband who looked after these mundane and irritating things? Ben wouldn't know a grommet from a plumber's helper. He was so busy and spent so much time at the hospital that, in the last few months, Claire was beginning to think of him as some guy who dropped in occasionally to play with Harry; who snuck in late at night, leaving only a few droppings for Claire to find in the morning – balled-up socks and underwear, a couple of turds in the toilet.

Not knowing what else to do about the wet spot for the moment, she went into Brita's bathroom to get an old towel. She had to duck to avoid hitting her head on the low overhanging heating duct, thinking guiltily about how much more awkward it had to be for Brita to use that bathroom, since she was at least three inches taller than Claire. The contractor who redid the basement had explained that it was either rip out the entire heating system or drywall around those ducts.

She searched through the bathroom cupboards, looking for a suitable towel; there was no shortage of dirty ones. She selected a grungy yellow hand-towel which she took back to the bottom of the stairs and spread out over the stain. For the time being, it would keep down the smell at least. Finally, she couldn't resist the urge to take a quick peek into Brita's bedroom. All of her clothes, jewellery and make-up were gone; so were her photographs and the red flag and – holding her breath, Claire hurried over to the bureau and pulled open the bottom drawer – so were the 'Free Skane!' pamphlets. Only the garbage and dust balls remained for Claire to clean up. Whenever she found the time.

20

Claire opened an eye to check the digital clock on her bedside table. It was almost seven-thirty – Brita would come upstairs to collect Harry any minute. It was a good thing, since she was in no shape to take him. She hugged her pillow to her chest and curled up again in the fetal position, looking forward to another half-hour of sleep after a delirious night.

But there was no Brita to come and get Harry, she remembered, her eyes fluttering open again: her mother had fired her. She should feel relief – hadn't she wanted to get rid of Brita for almost a year? – but all she felt was panic. It was Monday. She should be up, in the shower, listening as her Dresser reviewed the options for what she could wear. In the office, things would have piled up during her week in San Francisco: faxes, memos, telephone message slips from irate clients who weren't going to get any less so when they were told Claire wouldn't be in for another few days because she had to find a new nanny.

'Da da. Da! Da da . . . dada?' Harry called hopefully from the nursery. 'Day day.' Pause. 'Dee dee dee.' He was just one small baby; she could handle him without help. She'd had him to herself lots of times, on weekends and evenings. Besides, he was her son; he was part of her. He would intuitively understand her fragile state at the moment, make allowances for it; they could communicate without words. A day with Harry would be fun, even with chicken-pox.

'Eh? Eh?' he demanded, puzzled by her lack of response.

She'd taken him in a bottle less than an hour before. He should have finished it up and drifted back into a fragrant milky sleep. But some mornings the bottle had an opposite, almost tonic, effect – bracing and invigorating, especially when it prompted a big bowel movement – the gastro-colic reflex, according to Ben. There was no way of knowing in advance, which bottle on which day was going to have which effect.

'Eh?' Harry called again, louder this time.

Claire still couldn't bring herself to move. She wanted to weep with exhaustion. Her head ached from a night of interrupted half-sleep and too many sleeping pills; she felt blurred, erased. But Harry sounded so perky, rebounding quickly from his illness. He wanted to get out and get going, be entertained. He was not an introspective baby who could amuse himself for hours with a set of nesting toys: he was turbo-charged, fuel-injected, a full tank of gas that had to be used up before he would sleep again. As soon as he saw her, he would start shoving toys in her face, expecting her to force her sludgy brain and her thickened tongue to repeat rhymes for him, about bunnies, mice and chickens.

Ben had long ago left for the hospital, called in by a two-finger replant. Though semi-conscious at the time, Claire had pieced together the story from overhearing his half of the telephone conversation. The patient was being flown into Toronto, by air ambulance, from somewhere in northern Ontario. He'd been tearing down an old garage, using a chain-saw, and had tripped over the electrical cord, slicing off an index-finger and thumb. Claire also knew that the emerg doc had sealed the thumb and finger in a blown-up latex glove, then embedded the entire mess in a bowl of chipped ice. Chain-saw replants were especially difficult: the lost digits mangled and dirty; the prognosis for recovering full use of them poor. As she lay in bed, eyes closed, listening to Ben stumble around to find clean socks and shorts, she'd fantasized about putting his pager down on a smooth concrete surface, then bashing it with a sledgehammer, silencing forever its nattering beep.

'Eh? Ya?' Harry called. 'No mo yay . . .' he added, mournfully. Then he was anxious again. 'Beebee! Beebee. Bay! Ba-ay? By-eye . . .' His voice trailed off, ending with a small sob of frustration.

Get up! Claire told herself. She could tell that he was standing in his crib now, rattling the rails. He let out a series of pissed-off howls. 'Dow! Dow! Ahoo! Ahoo!' This was followed by a single loud squawk of rage, then a few fake coughs. 'Oh! Oh! Radio!'

Claire frowned. He couldn't have said *radio*. Could he? With a groan of fatigue, she flung aside the duvet and swung her legs over the side of the bed. She dug a soiled pair of sweat-pants (Ben's) out of the laundry basket beside the bed, groped through the bottom drawer of her bureau for a sweat-shirt, not caring whether what she put on top matched what was on the bottom, or even if either of them fitted.

'I'm coming, Harry,' she called, staggering into the bathroom to splash water on her face and pull a brush through her hair. If she didn't have to go to work she wouldn't have to do much else, in terms of morning grooming. How much simpler the maintenance of her body would be. She could let herself go completely to seed, become a total slob, a true Beacher. It would be expected, condoned. She could let her armpits and legs get dark and shaggy and the grey hair grow in all over her head. It would be interesting to see just how much of it there really was, since she had no idea, having coloured her hair for so many years. All the rituals of brushing, tweezing, clipping, shaving, softening and dyeing parts of her body would be reduced to two quick brush-offs. Minimalist. A hairbrush and a toothbrush. Simpler than most men, since she'd never even have to shave.

She avoided her reflection in the mirror, knowing she looked like hell – her eyes like two pee-holes in the snow – glad there was no Swedish nymphet there to make her look worse by comparison. Her mother was right to fire Brita; it was a relief, actually, that Brita was gone.

She shook a few vitamin C tablets out of a brown plastic bottle and swallowed them, along with a cupped handful of water from the bathroom tap. Lately, she'd started taking vitamins – massive doses – figuring that it wouldn't help, but it couldn't hurt. Ben disagreed. She was wasting money, overdosing her body. Besides, most of it she peed out into the toilet anyway. He seemed to be right about that: her urine was a luminous yellow colour; it hurt her eyes to look at it. She'd considered consulting a homoeopath about her lack of energy and general run-down state, but Ben had been derisive. She would only pay hundreds of dollars for a caffeine enema and a bunch of bogus injections, he said. If it was an enema she wanted, he could give her one for free. She imagined him snapping on a pair of those latex gloves, and declined his offer. Once, maybe, the thought would have been mildly arousing. It was getting harder and harder to remember that far back.

Harry, hearing her in the bathroom, was excited now, rattling his crib rails in earnest, like a convict banging his tin cup along the bars.

'So, what do we do now?' Claire asked him, standing in the doorway to his room. From behind the masses of chicken-pox, he grinned at her, so hard it seemed as though his round little face might split. 'Up. Up!' He had three and a half crenulated milk-white teeth. He was a chubby, endearing, almost totally bald baby and she should have been delighted at having an unplanned day alone with him. Any *normal* mother would have been, surely. So why couldn't she shake off this feeling of stifling boredom edged with panic? Was it just that she'd had no chance to prepare for this mentally?

'Way oh? Eh oh?' Harry grabbed hold of the crib rails, rocking back and forth, impatient with her inertia. It was going to be a long day. She lifted him up – a warm, sodden, smelly bundle – feeling a twang of lower lumbar pain, almost sublime in its intensity. She put him down on the carpet – he had already outgrown his change table – and peeled off his soggy sleeper and soaking-wet diaper. A twenty-pounder, she and Ben called these super-saturated rectangles of cloth. She lifted the top off his diaper pail to be almost bowled over by the stench. Elfriede hadn't been kidding. What if the ones at the bottom (now over a week old) were festering with furry mould? Or crawling with maggots? She stuffed the latest wet one on top and slammed the lid shut. That particular mess would have to wait for a day when she had a stronger stomach.

Harry was crawling happily out of his room, delighted to be free of his sleeper and diaper. 'Just where do you think you're going, Buster?' Claire hooked him under one arm and carried him into the bathroom – another stab of back pain – put him down on the mat beside the tub and turned on the water to run a bath.

What had happened to her creamy-skinned, silky baby, she wondered. The chicken-pox were everywhere, even on his tiny penis and in his nose. She dumped half a box of baking soda into the tub and let him splash around for a while before indulging him with an array of squeeze toys: ducks, dinosaurs and frogs; a floating marina, a flotilla of small watercraft. She tried not to get irritated by his splashing, which increased in intensity until he was sending tidal waves on to the bathroom floor. It was only water and could easily be cleaned up, she reminded herself, imagining it dripping around the fluorescent lights in the kitchen ceiling or the decorative moulding in the front hall. After ten tolerant minutes of this, she plucked Harry out of the tub, dried him, and smeared him thickly with pink calamine lotion. He didn't care for the idea of clothes: she had to wrestle with him, then distract him with a carrot squeeze toy as she struggled to get him into a playsuit. Dressing a robust and unco-operative eight-month-old baby should be a rodeo event, she thought, like steer-wrestling or hog-tying. Hogs and steer might be bigger, but they were not nearly as loud. Size had nothing to do with power.

At nine o'clock, after Harry'd thrown an Eggo, a handful of Cheerios and a training cup full of orange juice on to the floor – sticking his arm straight over the side of his high chair and fixing his eyes on Claire as he did so – she called Davina to say she wouldn't be back in the office for a couple more days, until they had a nanny again. She still hadn't decided what to do – call up this Gosta Lindgren, try to find Brita and beg her to come back, or start the round of agencies and newspaper ads. Davina made a small effort to sound sympathetic, but there was no way she could truly understand. She lived alone, had never married, had a highly organized life. She carried a smart unscarred briefcase, wore perfectly polished shoes, perky scarves, and usually looked more professional than Claire. Then there were the neatly packed, interesting lunches she always brought in to work: a Caesar salad in a Tupperware container; a Swiss cheese and roast beef on rye, saran-wrapped carrot sticks, a shiny apple and home-made chocolate chip cookies. One day, as Claire was tearing into her peanut butter on stale French stick (all she could find to bring for lunch), she'd looked at Davina's attractive meal spread out, picnic-style, on a paper napkin on her desk. She'd looked back at her own sandwich. 'What's wrong with this picture?' she'd said. Davina had only looked puzzled.

Claire told her that anything urgent could be faxed over to her, or Davina could call, anytime, if someone needed to talk to her who couldn't be put off for a few days. Potochnik hadn't called, Davina assured her. So far, there hadn't been a peep out of him, nor a sighting. For this Claire was extraordinarily grateful.

Next, she dialled Ben's pager number. A nurse called back immediately. 'Dr Cunningham is scrubbed,' she told Claire crisply, 'was it anything important?' Claire admitted it wasn't, feeling guilty and foolish for taking up the nurse's time when some patient's life was at stake, and acutely aware that the OR staff made jokes about Ben's 'domestic trauma pager'. At least the nurse was a one-pager and therefore not very attractive, Claire told herself as she hung up. It cheered her to think that, after being made to feel like an inconsiderate idiot for calling.

She let Harry empty out all of the kitchen cupboards, bang the pots and pans around, try a few on his head. Then she sat him down on the kitchen counter to let him splash around in the sink and fill up his bottles and all of the microwave dishes with water which he then dumped out on to the floor. After that, he busied himself with Mr Potato Head, spilling noses, ears, eyes and lips from the toy basket all over the living-room carpet.

Upstairs, the fax machine was churning out loops of greasy paper. Davina would be bored after a week of doing nothing but filing, and would be classifying everything on Claire's desk as Urgent and needing to be faxed. But Claire wouldn't be able to look at any of it while Harry was awake. He would plop down in the middle of the paper, crumple it in his fat little hands, stuff it into his mouth, then throw a tantrum if she tried to take him away from it. He loved the buttons and lights of the fax machine, and picking up the telephone receiver and listening for the recorded voice to tell him to please hang up and try his call again. But the things that amused him most were invariably the ones that made extra work for Claire.

She mopped up the water from the kitchen counter and floor, collected the parts of Mr Potato Head, refolded the clean laundry Harry'd tipped out of the hamper. Then she struggled to fish the pot lids out from under the chesterfield with a broom handle, swept up the Cheerios and wiped the sticky spilled juice from the floor.

It was not even ten o'clock and already she'd run out of ideas for amusing him. She called Harry's paediatrician to ask if it was okay to take him outside. It was an unseasonably mild day – bright and sunny, not at all cold. A walk would clear her head, give her a chance to consider what to do about a care-giver for Harry. The receptionist said it was all right to take him out, but to bring him back in if he seemed bothered by the sunlight. 'And keep him away from other children,' she added, 'until all of the pox are crusted over.'

'How long will that take?'

'About two weeks.'

Two weeks? Of keeping Harry in quarantine? Of avoiding public libraries, drop-in centres, the park? No wonder Brita had quit.

As Claire was gathering up the toys to put away under the bathroom sink, Ben called to tell her he'd be starting a reconstruction at four and that she shouldn't expect him home for dinner. She shouldn't bother to make him anything either, he said, since he would just grab something in the cafeteria. He hung up before she had a chance to talk to him about the nanny problem, or point out that he could hardly expect her to be thinking about dinner at ten o'clock in the morning when she had Harry to look after all day and her fax machine was on over-drive.

It took almost an hour to pack up the bottles, extra blankets, diapers, wipes and everything else she thought Harry could possibly want or need in the next little while. As she ran about the house, hunting for things, and Harry grew more and more impatient in his play-pen, she thought about a passage from *The French Lieutenant's Woman*, about how the Victorian upper class expanded every activity to fill their vast amounts of available time. They should have tried looking after their own kids, she concluded, as she struggled to push Harry in his Perego through the mess that had once been her garden. She hadn't got around to cleaning it up before winter, and it was now a mush of dried weeds, rotten vegetable matter and mud, all beginning to soften, ripening in the unusually warm weather. In a month or two, a cheerful field of dandelions would pop up there and all of their neighbours would grumble about their gardens getting cross-pollinated and infested by the Cunninghams'.

She hoisted Harry up over the retaining wall, as she'd seen Ben do, feeling another zing of pain throughout her lower back – this one much deeper and more intense than any so far. The stroller wheels jammed and balked in the damp sand, jolting Harry. She was sweating now, anxious to reach the boardwalk. A mother and daughter approached, took one look at Harry's pox-riddled face and hurried on. Harry didn't seem offended by the slight but, just the same, Claire adjusted his hat to shade his face, and tugged the ear flaps down into place on either side of his head. He pulled at the ties of the hat and whined, wanting to push it off. Then, frustrated, he tilted his head back to sniff the beach air, reaching out a chubby finger to point at a seagull swooping and diving overhead. 'Baby,' he said. He didn't seem bothered by the sunlight, though Claire had brought a pair of her sunglasses and a bigger hat for him, just in case.

At last they reached the grey wooden planks of the boardwalk, pale, weathered and gently ribbed like worn corduroy. Sand had been blown across the boards, dusting it, filling in the knot holes, like a sprinkling of cinnamon sugar. Claire's stomach rumbled, reminding her that she hadn't eaten anything yet, though it was nearly noon. She missed the café au lait and toasted bagel that she had each morning in her office. This is it, she told herself, this is what it means to be a stay-at-home mom. Wake up and imagine you'll get a chance to smell the coffee.

She dug around in the diaper bag until she found a teething biscuit – the only food she'd thought to bring. She pushed Harry along the boardwalk, feeling vaguely guilty about being there on a Monday, as if she were playing hooky and might be seen and reported. She was a nine-to-fiver. It was in her blood. The idea of being a slightly wacky, creative and indulgent stay-at-home mother had a lot of appeal, but she knew she would want it all: a six-figure salary and a socially acceptable label – LAWYER – to stick on her forehead when it was advantageous, too.

Harry seemed to enjoy the rhythm of the bumpy planks as they trundled along and was soon asleep, his head lolling over the side of the stroller, snoring with soft whistling sounds. It was amazing what contorted positions babies could fall asleep in, Claire thought. If she slept like that, she'd be seeing a chiropractor for months afterwards. She stuffed the rest of the teething biscuit into her mouth and took a clean diaper out of the bag to fold into a loose cushion which she wedged beside Harry's head to give it some support. As he slept, his lips and tongue moved rhythmically, sucking on a phantom bottle. The diaper bag clanked gently as it dangled from the back of the stroller.

As she walked, Claire's fatigue began to catch up with her. She felt dim and woozy, as she usually did, from the sleeping pills. She'd taken a double dose the night before, afraid she'd be up the whole night, worrying over what to do about Brita. She'd been awake most of the night anyway, not only worrying but being roused continuously by Harry's whimpers and sobs as he twitched with the itchy pox; getting up to pump him full of Tempra for the fever, or apply more calamine to try to soothe his itching.

The thought of interviewing another series of unsuitable nannies exhausted her even more. She had no idea where she'd filed Ben's nanny quiz, and couldn't remember which agencies she'd called before. And then there was the exorbitant fee the agencies charged – the equivalent of a month's gross pay for the nanny. They'd had to pay it for Brita, who'd come to them from an agency, even though Ben knew her family. She lifted the brim of Harry's hat and peered at his dear chicken-pocked face, smeared with bright pink calamine lotion. He adored Brita. Wasn't that all that really mattered? So what if she was a bit of a slob, and her housekeeping and cooking less than adequate? And so what if she was a Skanish separatist? She was in Canada now, not Sweden. Wasn't she entitled to hold whatever political opinions she wanted about her homeland? It wasn't as though she would be causing any trouble here, was it? Maybe they could hire a cleaning lady twice a month, to help Brita. Wouldn't it be worth it to spend a little more for Harry's happiness?

Swedes could never be said to be lazy workers, or lacking in entrepreneurial spirit, according to *Sweden For Voyagers*. *The country has*

• Sylvia Mulholland

managed to produce a large number of innovations and industrial successes out of all proportion to its small population.

'Don't be a fool,' Claire's wicked side said, 'now is your chance to hire somebody really ugly. With warts on her nose, buck teeth, less hair than you have.' She walked on, frowning, at war with herself.

All of the boardwalk's benches were occupied by Beachers or vagrants, reading, mumbling to themselves or dozing in the sun. No one was likely to move over for Claire. A group of joggers pounded past, then a woman sashayed by with a whippet on a leash – the dog so thin that, from the rear, it looked as though it had been slammed between two doors. Claire wheeled Harry over to the edge of the boardwalk, near the lifeguard station, and sat down on the edge of the planks, pulling her knees to her chin. The beach was a pale mauve colour, the pebbles and stones yellow and grey. Beyond it, the water was an undulating deep blue. Not having anything else to do, and not wanting to rouse Harry with any sudden movement, Claire scanned the ground in front of her, searching for bits of beach glass. It was one of her favourite pastimes, a totally useless addiction since there was so little that one could actually do with it, once collected. There were already three water-filled jars of it, lined up along her kitchen windowsill. She expected eventually to find the glass slimy and overgrown with moss or algae, like the coloured stones in the bottom of a dirty fish bowl, but in over a year it hadn't happened. Sometimes, she studied them, wondering why this was so and why she never needed to change the water in the jars.

There were many other mysteries of beach glass to be endlessly pondered. Why were there so few 'brownies', for example, when beer bottles were so common? Why were the red and blue pieces always so small? Possibly, they were from very old bottles – maybe hundreds of years old – so that each piece had been worn away almost to nothing by the time Claire found it. She liked to study these intensely coloured chips, imagining this one was once part of a bottle of smelling salts on some apothecary's shelf; that ruby fragment was from a set of gold-rimmed glasses in a Victorian parlour. Sometimes she found bits of china or pottery, worn smooth and dazzling white, like teeth, among the beach stones. And often there were traces of pattern in it – a fine wavy line, a diamond shape. She'd even found a few beach-glass marbles. The cat's eyes were the best, since they looked so cloudy when dry – a cat's eye with cataracts; but when wet, the iris would magically appear again, gleaming mysteriously through the glass. There was always lots of other mundane junk on the beach, of course: the usual litter of candy wrappers, bottle caps, gull feathers, twists of wire. But now and then there would be something out of place and mildly thought-provoking: a discarded sock; a condom. Seldom was there anything really unusual or valuable, though. Combing Toronto's beaches had to be a luckless and unprofitable venture.

If she were to quit practising law, Claire thought, she would have time to ponder the mysteries of beach glass, and a host of small domestic conundrums as well. Why did pairs of pantyhose always find each other in the washer? In the dryer? Was there a black hole between these two appliances into which one sock, out of each pair, always got sucked? Or would she have time for all of this refection after all? She imagined life in a bedsitter (all they could probably afford until Ben's practice got going); screaming kids, Ben bellowing, trying to write research papers to get tenure at the teaching hospital; a greasy plastic tablecloth on the kitchen table; a bare light bulb hanging beside a sticky flypaper strip.

A lifeguard climbed up into his chair to scan the shore-line from behind his mirrored sunglasses. Claire wondered why he was there in February, and why the city thought a lifeguard was necessary at all, at any time, since only the rare hardy or reckless soul ever ventured into the lake. She knew that the lifeguard wouldn't even see her, or that she would register only vaguely as a middle-aged lady with a baby: nobody worth trying to chat up. He wouldn't be able to see the varicose veins or teething biscuit from where he sat, but he would assume those. Perhaps he would think she was the baby's grandmother, if he thought about her at all. Which was unlikely. How, she wondered, had she managed to slip so suddenly from youth into middle age? Wasn't there some stage in between? Her father's parents had overcome tremendous adversity, swimming across icy rivers under Russian gunfire, finally reaching the Austrian border in a wagon full of whatever valuables they had managed to gather together, covered with an old carpet. And both Claire's parents had come to Canada, learned English and rewritten their medical exams. She could never have done it, even though Ben liked to point out that there wasn't a lot of medicine known back in those days: a few tricks with leeches; the way to pump up a blood pressure cuff. With such a sturdy, adversity-overcoming heritage, how could Claire be here now, unable to even feed herself, find her baby a nanny, report for work? Perhaps she was proof of the genetic theory that coupling geniuses would eventually produce a moron. Maybe tough and hardy peasant stock eventually produced an urban-dwelling weakling.

Harry stirred in his stroller and fussed a little, rubbing his eyes with his fists. Was he being bothered by the sunlight? Claire worried. He had 'made a poo', as Brita always put it; the odour wafted up around the sides of his stroller – Claire could almost see the radiating wavy lines that cartoonists use to depict something smelly. There was nowhere to change his diaper, she realized. She could hardly lay him down on the gritty boardwalk or the grungy sand. And if she used his blanket, what would she put over him to keep him warm? The nearest public toilet was at Kew Beach, a good ten-minute walk. She doubted it had a change table. And what would she do with the dirty cloth diaper – a couple of pounds of wet and steaming, super-saturated fabric? She'd forgotten to bring a plastic bag to put it in.

Maybe Harry could be induced back to sleep. Without much hope, Claire jiggled his stroller, trying not to seem anxious. Babies were like sharks: once they smelled your fear they'd tear you to pieces – emotionally. The jiggling seemed to irritate him. He screwed up his face and let out a shriek, his eyes glistening slits of rage. Claire hurried to push a teething biscuit at him, but that only incensed him further. He shoved it back at her and howled. The bottle she offered got the same reaction. He began struggling to get out of his stroller, straining at his seat belt, arching his back and screaming wildly. Claire stared at him in shock, aghast by the volume of sound he was able to produce. In a law firm, the noise level seldom got beyond the muted twitter of the telephone. Every now and then one of the lawyers would curse or slam a door or yell at someone. Or one of the litigators might tell some amusing story about a loopy judge and a contained measure of laughter would ripple down the halls. But it was nothing like this. Harry was so loud it made her stomach lurch and churn; it made her sweat and grind her teeth; it made her want to throw up her teething biscuit.

'Okay,' she said, 'look. Calm down. Please. Stop crying. Don't get so mad.' She tried again to give him a biscuit, then, in a panic, decided to bolt back down the boardwalk and make a run for home. She took the brake off his Perego and moved quickly, taking long strides, the diaper bag clanking as it hit the back of the stroller, enraging Harry even more. She broke into a run, wheeling her squalling son feverishly along the boardwalk, the diaper bag swinging and clattering as Harry flung himself back and forth, in a lather to get free. Everyone they passed stared, shook their heads, clucked in disapproval. Claire wanted to scream at them all to fuck off, but she hadn't time to pause and ascertain whether any of them were people she knew. It would hardly benefit her career to yell at a client to fuck off, and one never knew who might venture down to the beach, especially at lunch-time.

The stroller wheels wedged into the sand as she reached the end of the boardwalk. Ignoring her back pain, she bent over and hoisted it up in her arms, Harry and all. Her feet churned up the sand as she ploughed along, carrying the heavy load of baby, stroller and diaper bag, desperate to reach home. Then, abruptly, she was confronted by the retaining wall. She'd forgotten that she would have to climb back up over it. Harry kicked and waved his arms hysterically as she fumbled to undo his seat belt. She lifted him out of the stroller which immediately thunked over backwards, pulled down by the weight of the diaper bag. With Harry flailing like a windmill under one arm, she struggled to unhook the bag from the handles of the stroller. She would come back and retrieve the Perego later. Then she squelched over the soggy ground of the garden to reach the back door of the house, panting and exhausted.

As she charged up the stairs with Harry, he projectile-vomited his last bottle of milk. Claire would later find dribbles of milk vomit on the staircase banister, the wood moulding and the floral-patterned wallpaper of the stair well. Hurtling past her open bedroom door, she caught a glimpse of a ream of fax paper, one end of which was still hanging from the machine. It was knee-high in the room. The ADD PAPER light on the machine blinked at her expectantly.

She changed Harry's diaper and squirted two droppers of Tempra into the inside of his cheek. His fever seemed to be rising again. Then, worriedly debating whether to page Ben again, she sat in the rocker with Harry, making soothing sounds, until his thrashing and hysterics subsided and, miraculously, he fell asleep. She put him gently into his crib, got a bucket and sponge from the basement and tackled the curdled milk in the hall. When that was done, she remembered that the stroller was still outside. She grabbed the nursery monitor and hurried outside to turn it up full volume and place it on the back steps, then plunged through the garden to stand on the retaining wall to discover that, as she'd feared, the Perego was gone.

Snivelling with self-pity, she dashed back into the house and got out the Yellow Pages to begin her search under Employment Agencies – Domestics. Sobbing, she flipped through it, hating Brita for abandoning them after all her pretences of loving Harry so much – her little cucumber, her little prince. Claire would never take her back. Never. Not even if she crawled up their front walk over broken beach glass; or had to stand in soup kitchens for the rest of her life. There were some things a working mother just couldn't bring herself to forgive.

SPRING

21 ∫

(Anna) Bell

Bell, Ben observed drily, seemed to fulfil most of Claire's requirements: she was built like Mount Pinatubo and she could clean like nobody's business. She started by an attack on the kitchen cupboards, reorganizing them so efficiently that the space that had before seemed completely inadequate to house the Cunninghams' kitchen wares became almost cavernous. Claire's few battle-scarred pots and pans sat mournfully, lost in the vast amounts of available storage space. With tight-lipped determination, Bell scrubbed the cupboard shelves to a dazzling whiteness (Claire had always believed they were cream-coloured) and lined them with cheery chequered shelf paper that she shopped for in her own time. Only with a great deal of protest and obvious extreme embarrassment did she finally accept the cash Claire pressed into her hand as reimbursement. The oven and refrigerator gleamed, inside and out; she'd fished out the crud that had fallen between the stove and the kitchen counter. The burners were neatly lined with tin foil to catch any drips, and she'd even scrubbed the kitchen garbage pail, disinfecting it with Pine Sol and leaving it in the sun on the deck for an afternoon to air.

Next, Bell assailed the bathrooms. Claire came home to find their towels neatly rolled, tight as yule logs, stacked and grouped by colour in the linen closet. The face cloths were formed into miniature logs. 'Well, what the hell?' was Ben's only comment as he opened the closet door, dripping wet from his shower, in urgent need of an unpacked towel. Claire shrugged and smiled.

'I may have died and gone to heaven,' she said, unrolling a towel and handing it to him.

In Harry's room, all of his shirts and sweaters had been neatly pressed and hung up on hangers. (On hangers!) His sleepers were professionally folded (had Bell worked for a dry cleaner before? A clothing store?) and organized in the bottom drawer of his bureau. Like a bloodhound, Bell tracked down every one of Harry's tiny missing socks; neatly balled-up pairs of them were lined up in a plastic tray, tucked inside his top drawer.

She had a complicated but artful way of rolling and tucking Claire's pantyhose into tidy parcels, so that none of it became tangled in her dresser drawer, and of similarly manipulating Ben's jockey shorts and briefs.

'Why do I need some strange woman snooping through my underpants, checking out the skid marks?' Ben complained, undoing the rather complicated fold to put on a pair one morning.

'Maybe this will encourage you to wipe properly,' Claire said. 'You're getting a bit old for skid marks.' She didn't bother to comment that he never would've complained if it had been Brita who was snuffling through his underwear with such dedication.

There were tight hospital corners on their bed, made with freshly ironed (*ironed*!) sheets; their pillows were plumped, the duvets fluffed and freshened, beaten free of their winter (several winters') dust and hung to air in the spring breeze that whipped into shore from across the lake. She'd chased the dustballs out from under each piece of furniture and assaulted the cracks in the sofas and chairs with the Dustbuster, diligently sucking up ancient cookie crumbs, lint and (mostly blonde) hair. The whole house gleamed, it shone, it sparkled; it smelled of Dettol, Vanish, Fantastik and Mr Muscle. The toilets – except for perhaps the one in the basement which might never recover from Brita's neglect – flowed with efficient gurglings, the drains freed of accumulated sludge.

And Harry was miserable.

'He hates her,' Ben said to Claire under his breath, watching their son kick and flail as Bell, her face red as a tomato, struggled to wedge him into his high chair and buckle the safety belt across his writhing and arching body. In desperation, she put the empty recycling bucket on over her head and did a clumsy little dance, trying hard to amuse and distract Harry. But her performance just infuriated him more.

'She's an honest and decent person. It's just the change that's upsetting to him, that's all,' Claire said. 'Bell is someone new – he's not used to her yet. Give it time.' They were upstairs in their room, later that night, having just come home from a dinner given by Ben's faculty in honour of a visiting professor from New Zealand. Harry had cried the entire time they were out, then thrown up all his dinner; he had finally fallen asleep just minutes before they got home. Bell had struggled to tell them all of this, in her broken English, wringing her hands, goggle-eyed with anxiety.

Claire sat on the edge of the bed, pulled her sweater off over her head, and unhooked her brassiere. 'Any new nanny would be an adjustment.'

'She's been here a week already. And he's not liking her any better today than he did the first time he saw her.' Ben slid his shorts down, then kicked them up behind him with one foot, deftly catching them in mid-air before tossing them over his head into the laundry basket.'And have you ever asked yourself how she manages to get so much cleaning done? I mean, what is Harry doing while she's busy trying my underwear up in knots?'

Claire was silent for a moment, studying her chest, disconcerted by the workings of gravity on what had once been firm and perky flesh. 'I have to admit I've been wondering that myself.'

'He's so bloody active, we can't let him out of our sight for a second. So how does she do it? She could be doing anything to him – locking him in a closet or the furnace room, or tying him up outside on the deck or God knows.'

'She wouldn't do anything like that!'

'How would we ever know? It's not like the little guy can tell us.'

'I know she's not being cruel to him. She's a kind and decent person. A mother can tell these things. Look at how hard she tries – putting that bucket on her head.'

'That was one of the most disturbing things I've ever seen.'

'It's sad, really. She just doesn't seem to have much of a

way with babies. Her references were excellent, though – the children loved her where she worked before. The mother said her son was really upset when Bell left. And she didn't have to admit what happened with Harry tonight. She could have told us that everything went fine. We wouldn't have known the difference.'

'Okay, but just think what the house looks like when both of us are here with Harry. Do either of us have time to shine the bathroom faucets?'

'Maybe we're just disorganized . . . Or lazy.'

'And maybe Harry hates Bell for a reason.' He hesitated. 'I found Brita, by the way. She's staying with Gosta, as I thought.'

'That's interesting.'

'I was quite relieved to know that she's safe.'

'Me too.'

'She's looking for another job.'

'Good for her.'

A week later, Bell was gone. They didn't have to fire her: she quit, sobbing that she'd never been so hurt in her life. Never had she met a baby who wouldn't let her near him. She didn't know why he didn't trust her. She was deeply offended, disgraced, she said, her eyes full, her hand over her heart. She just couldn't take it any more.

Bing

Claire believed that Bing just got off on the wrong foot with them from the start. They'd hired her, then asked her to babysit on Saturday night, before she officially started the job. She was supposed to be there by seven: by nine she hadn't arrived. Finally, at nine-thirty, she showed up, distraught over the cab ride, claiming the driver had tried to take advantage of her, taking her miles out of her way, threatening her. She'd been terrified, she said, dabbing at her eyes with a sodden tissue. And she only took the cab because she'd fallen asleep in the afternoon and had forgotten to set her alarm, so she didn't have time to take the bus to get out to the Beach.

Ben had answered the door when she finally arrived and explained to her that if she couldn't even remember a babysitting job, they couldn't possibly trust her to look after Harry full-time. What was she liable to do? Forget him in the park some day? At that, Bing burst into tears, begging to see Claire and explain. A woman's thing, Claire sighed, coming down the stairs with Harry in her arms. Why did they always assume she would be a pushover? After a lot more talk, and stern warnings from Ben, they agreed to let Bing try the job, on probation.

She had a number of personal problems, at the root of which was her sponsorship into Canada of her entire extended family. She now felt, morally at least, responsible for their well-being. Her aged father got a job as a school-crossing guard while her mother stayed home in a bachelor apartment and looked after Bing's illegitimate niece while the baby's mother went to work in a doughnut shop. Bing's brother got in a car accident; her older sister was regularly beaten by her alcoholic husband. On Bing's third day of work, she called Claire at the office, begging her to come home. Bing's grandmother had jumped on to the subway tracks at Coxwell station. They'd pulled her up before a train came along, but she had a concussion, several broken ribs. Bing had to go right away to the hospital.

She phoned the next morning to say she needed a couple of weeks off to sit with her grandmother in the hospital, translate for her, look after the rest of the family. While she certainly didn't expect it, she wondered if Claire would mind holding the job open for her. Indefinitely.

Lavinia

Lavinia was a hairdresser by training, but she'd also been a short-order cook and had run a factory, the whereabouts of which she never revealed, that manufactured canvas tote bags. The phone number she gave Claire, to call for a reference, seemed to be permanently busy; a day later it was out of service. She had a phenomenal number of friends, acquaintances and relatives. At the end of her first day with them, Claire came home to find a dozen dirty cake plates (chocolate-smeared) in the dishwasher, that were never explained to her satisfaction. Lavinia asked for the next day off. There'd been some kind of accident in her cousin's apartment – a china cabinet had fallen over; there was a lot of broken glass to be cleaned up and her cousin was afraid of cutting herself. Also, she had to go to Immigration. Unfortunately, it was the Immigration office in one of the suburbs, since that was where she'd originally landed. There was some screw-up with her work permit documents. Also, she needed seventy-five dollars for the government fee to transfer her employment contract. And an advance of her pay. Claire refused to pay the seventy-five dollars – it wasn't her fault Lavinia was changing jobs – but gave her the advance and the day off. She never saw Lavinia again.

Lavinia's friends and relatives called for weeks after, however, wanting to know if Claire knew where she had gone, some of them complaining that Lavinia owed them money. Two of those who called were men, both of whom claimed to be her husband. Claire finally had their phone number changed. And unlisted.

Virgie

The Cunninghams agreed by now that Claire had to spend more time on the interviewing process and that Ben would have to get involved. They were getting desperate, would likely make a serious mistake if they weren't more careful. They were lucky that Harry hadn't suffered some terrible mishap already. For the next interview, Ben dug his quiz out of his filing cabinet in the basement.

'Okay, Virgie,' he said, 'that's your name? Virgie? Is that short for Virginia or what?'

Virgie beamed at him, nodding.

'Yes. You're nodding. Yes what? It's Virginia?'

A flash of dazzling white teeth was accompanied by a puzzled look in Claire's direction and another nod, this time less confident.

'Okay,' Ben raked his hands through his hair, 'so your name's Virginia.' He scribbled a note on his writing pad. 'Right. Now, what would you do if Harry – the baby – got a cut?'

'Cut?'

'Yes, a cut.' Ben made a chopping motion with his hand on his forearm. Virgie's smile faded. She looked blank, then anxious.

How can he stand it, wondered Claire, squirming inwardly at Virgie's troubled expression.

'So, what would you do?' Ben was frowning now.

'Do?'

Unable to watch the slaughter any longer, Claire hugged Harry to her and gazed out the window at the street.

'A cut,' said Ben. 'Cut. Like with a knife? Or scissors?' He made a scissoring motion with two fingers.

'Ah,' Virgie said, 'a cut.' She nodded enthusiastically and smiled broadly, clearly relieved.

'It's not a good thing to happen,' Ben said, 'so I don't know why you're smiling. Anyway, tell me what you would do.'

'I think maybe put some soo-gar,' Virgie said. 'At home we put soo-gar. To stop the blood.'

Ben was silent for a few moments. 'Well, I don't know what soo-gar is, but it's not what we use over here.'

'Sugar,' Claire said. She couldn't look at Ben.

'What?'

'Sugar. She said sugar.'

'Yes,' Virgie beamed, 'soo-gar.'

'Isn't there at least some medical basis for it?' Claire asked after Virgie had gone, very soon after.

'For what?' Ben said tightly, not even looking up from *The Unfavourable Result in Plastic Surgery*.

'For putting sugar . . . on a cut.'

Ben only sighed heavily and continued with his reading.

Edwina

Claire pressed the speed call button on her phone to dial their home number. The phone was answered on the second ring. 'Hi there, Edwina,' she said, 'it's me. I was just wondering how things were going. Since it's your first day and all.'

'Oh, no problem.' Edwina giggled.

'I mean, Harry was so upset when I left . . .'

'Sure.' Another giggle.

'Did he settle down right away?'

'Oh, sure. No problem.'

'Is there anything we need? Anything I should pick up on the way home? Milk?'

'Oh, I don't think so. Everything's okay. No problems.'

Claire nodded. 'Great,' she smiled, relieved that they finally had someone who could take control of things. An efficient, sensible girl. 'Harry certainly seems to like you.'

'Sure. Why not?'

Claire hesitated. 'I don't hear him right now . . .'

'Is that right?'

'No, I don't hear him at all. He's being pretty quiet. What's he doing? Having a nap?'

'Oh no. No nap – it's too early. He's in the bath tub. Just playing. I'm letting him put in some more water.'

By the middle of March, Ben had moved out of the bedroom. It made more sense, he told Claire. His schedule was insane – he was only keeping her awake with his pager going off every few hours and by leaving so early in the morning, coming home so late. For a few months, at least until this rotation was over, it would be better if he slept downstairs. The pull-out couch was fine. And he could study, watch some late-night TV if he couldn't sleep, without disturbing her.

One night, Claire got up to get Harry his bottle and stumbled down the stairs to stand, blinking in the blue light from the television, staring at Ben as he energetically masturbated on the pull-out couch, a girlie magazine open on the mattress beside him. 'I didn't want to bother you,' he said, his hand remaining on his penis, apparently surprised by her question. 'What did you think I've been doing all these nights? His face was ghastly in the television's light. He let go of his penis and held up his hand. 'Rosy Palm and her five sisters – the girls have been helping me out a lot down here.' He wiggled his fingers at Claire and laughed. 'I'll take the bottle up to Harry – you go back and get your sleep. You've been looking pretty wacked-out lately.'

22 ∫

The essence of skaling – whatever the occasion or setting, whether relaxed or formal – is the making of eye-contact, glass raised, with all other persons. This must be done not only before the taking of the first sip, but immediately thereafter, and before and after every subsequent sip.

Gamely, Claire fixed her eyes on her host, then on Brita, took a sip of wine and stared levelly at them again, each in turn. She'd declined the offer of coffee and cinnamon buns. Strong drink was what she needed, but watery wine would have to do. '*Skal*,' she said, making an effort to look pleasant, her eyes darting from Gosta to Brita, back to her drink, then up again. She was feeling light-headed, though she suspected it wasn't so much from the wine as from the rapid and repetitive eye-contact required by Swedish custom. Added to the humiliation of having come crawling over to Gosta's to beg Brita to come back.

Claire, Gosta Lindgren and Brita were sitting in Gosta's living-room, the atmosphere having the strained, uncomfortable air of a sixties encounter group. Claire still had no recollection of ever having met Gosta, or his wife, but it was hardly surprising. Since her pregnancy, details of just about everything, even essential information (where had she put her keys? when was Harry's last vaccination?) easily slipped her mind.

'So – *skal*.' Gosta returned her look with an expression Claire read as patronizing, and sipped his wine too. Brita, who had declined Gosta's offer of a drink, seemed engrossed by Harry's antics around the stereo: he was twiddling the buttons and dials, chortling, delighted that no one was pulling him away from it.

'Are you sure you don't mind him doing that?' Claire said. 'Fooling around with your electronic equipment like that?'

'Of course not,' Gosta said with another patronizing smile. 'In Sweden, children have an honoured place in the household – they're not pushed under the carpet as here in Canada.'

'They're hardly pushed under the carpet,' Claire smiled. An absurd image of a huge lump moving about under the area rug in the Cunninghams' living-room popped into her head. She pictured herself trying to push Harry under it. 'And our Harry is not one to be pushed. Right, Brita? Except maybe in his Perego: Which we don't have anymore.' Claire laughed lightly. Brita didn't seem to have heard.

'We don't have enough children back home,' Gosta said. 'Sweden has a declining birthrate, you know, only 1.7 children per couple. So let your son play. It's nice to have a baby in the house. What harm can he do?'

'Plenty, I would imagine.' Absurdly, Claire felt both reprimanded and ashamed on behalf of all Canadian parents who didn't truly appreciate their children. 'Our Harry can be quite creative, can't he, Brita?'

Brita avoided her eyes. It was she who'd answered the door when Claire rang the bell. '*Dra at Skogen*,' she'd said sullenly, 'what do you want?' If Claire hadn't been holding Harry in her arms, she was sure the door would have been slammed in her face. As it was, Harry went mad with joy at the sight of Brita, struggling wildly and reaching his fat sausage arms out to her, and she relented immediately, taking him from Claire, smothering him with kisses, tears in her eyes.

Gosta's wife was not home – she'd gone shopping to Ikea: she often went there to eat meatballs in the cafeteria or stock up on chocolate bars and rye crisps. 'There's no telling when she'll be back,' Gosta said, filling his pipe and settling into a tub chair, observing the women and Harry with tolerant amusement. 'I only hope she isn't doing any serious shopping.'

Looking around the cluttered living-room, Claire found it hard to imagine what more his wife could possibly need to buy, though of course, need had nothing to do with shopping. Buying things one needed was merely doing errands. *Shopping* was when you went out to buy a couple of sleepers for your baby, only because they were advertised on sale, and came home with a pair of loopy tri-coloured gold Italian earrings for five hundred bucks, as Claire had recently done. That was just before she called to ask Edwina how Harry was, and before she'd driven home in a panic, tyres squealing and foot trembling on the gas pedal, to fire her.

She fixed her eyes on Brita and Gosta again, took a drink, fixed on them again. Really, all this repetitive eye-contact could get quite tiresome, especially when one also had to watch a roving baby boy who had his personal activity dial set on 'Search and Destroy'. It would take real effort to get any serious drinking done under such adverse conditions. Maybe that was the reason Swedes stayed sober so much of the time. Maybe that was the source of the Free Skane movement. Free Skane, Free Skaling. 'Well, *skal* then,' she said again. And finished her wine. She felt a warm and pleasant sense of good will, suddenly optimistic that she and Brita would work out their differences and that Harry would soon have his beloved nanny back. She would have liked more wine, she thought, holding her glass to the light, twirling it by the stem so that Gosta couldn't help but notice it was empty.

'Well, Claire,' he said, 'it seems you know something of our Swedish customs. Where did you learn about skaling?' He sucked diligently on his pipe, working to get it going. He was the diplomatic type, the picture of patience and tact; next in line for the Nobel Peace Prize.

Swedes may occasionally appear somewhat complacent, as if they feel superior to their Scandinavian neighbours; perhaps even the rest of the world.

Claire had sat in her car, on the street in front of his house – a modest, over-landscaped bungalow – wavering over whether to go up to the door. She could already hear Christine's screams of derision. 'You did *what*? You went after her and *brought her back*? Are you insane? Do you have some kind of death wish for your marriage?' It was only Harry's incessant whining from the back seat that finally prompted Claire to get out of the car and march up the front walk, holding Harry in front of her like a talisman.

Inside, the house couldn't have been further from the pared-down, natural simplicity that was supposed to be typical of Swedish homes. The living-room was all black enamel and red and gold paint with enormous fans and ostrich feathers mounted on the wall. In one corner of the room, a sort of King of Siam figure, helmeted, curl-toed and gilded, was aiming a spear, rather threateningly, at the sofa where Claire sat. She adjusted her position, turning slightly so she wouldn't have to see it. From this new angle, she got a peek into one of the bedrooms – mauve walls, lots of ruffles, a collection of frilly-dressed period dolls. Where was the famous sauna, with its bracing birch benches? The clean lines of teak from The House of Viking? The build-it-yourself furniture from Ikea, with names like Gutvik, Gunnar and Ralf?

'Oh, one picks these things up here and there,' Claire said in answer to Gosta's question, and not feeling the need to mention *Sweden For Voyagers*. 'And Ben lived in Sweden for a couple of years, as I'm sure you know.' She looked at Brita for a reaction to this reference to Ben's time in Sweden, but her head was bent over Harry, who was now settled in her lap on the floor. 'I don't really know anything more about your customs. The drinking part is about all.'

'Some would say that's all there is,' Gosta chuckled.

Brita shook her hair out of her eyes and gazed at him with a vague, rather puzzled expression.

'Brita?' Claire was determined to get some response from her, or at least an acknowledgement that she was there in the room. 'I talked to my mother about what happened between you two – about the diapers.'

'Ah.' It was half-sigh, half-snort. 'The *satkaring*.' That word again. Claire hadn't been able to find it in *Sweden For Voyagers*.

'Yes,' she said, 'she is – she's a very caring person. And that's why she got so upset with you. She was just worried about Harry. And me.'

'*Hall flabben*,' Brita said without expression.

'Brita doesn't mean to be rude,' Gosta said, 'she's only unhappy because your mother threw her out of the house. Wouldn't you be upset? It's quite understandable.'

'*Forbannade satkaring*, said Brita, her blue eyes stony. '*Pattaglytt*.'

Frowning, Gosta shook his head and worked his pipe. On the table beside his chair, the extinguished matches had accumulated to form a small messy mountain.

'The story I heard is that Brita stomped out of the house. She quit. No one asked her to leave.' Claire's smile was brittle. 'But look, we aren't going to make any progress if Brita keeps saying things about me that I can't understand. I don't see why she doesn't speak to me in English – her English is very good – so why suddenly can't she speak it? I know she called my mother a "sheet". I know what that means. But I've come here out of good will, to see if we can reach an understanding, and put the past behind us. This isn't easy for me. It would have been much simpler to hire someone else.' Claire avoided their eyes, a relatively easy thing to do, now that she was out of wine and no more skaling was required. 'There are lots of nannies out there looking for work who would think our job is a pretty good one.'

'*Vad glytting du ar,*' Brita said, fixing Claire with her eyes. '*Jakla mog. Javla skitstovel.*'

'*Nej,* Brita.' Gosta sighed wearily and puckered his lips around the stem of his pipe. '*Var sa god.*'

'*Jag hatar—*'

'*Vad ar det for fel pa er?*'

'Now you're both doing it,' Claire said, prickling with anger.

'I'm sure Brita will come around to see your point of view,' Gosta said, 'it may take a bit of time, that's all. And she says she's sorry if she sounded rude.'

'She said no such thing,' Claire said hotly. 'I'm not a complete idiot. *Jag talar inte mycket svenska—*'

Gosta and Brita looked at her in surprise.

'I know enough to tell when I'm being insulted. To my face.'

Gosta was preoccupied again with his pipe, and Brita was watching her with a sulky expression, clutching Harry to her. Obviously, she wasn't about to make things any easier for Claire. Instead of speaking, the three of them focused on Harry, as if completely enthralled by his antics.

The Swedes are a direct people who can easily become confused or impatient with English-style circumlocution.

'I might as well get right to the point,' Claire said, after they'd watched Harry for a few more minutes, 'I'm willing to forget the insults. I – we – want you to come back, Brita. To look after Harry again.'

'*I helvete heller,*' Brita said. 'Why did not Ben come here with you?'

'Ben? He's in surgery. Besides, this is between you and me, isn't it?' Was she missing something here?

'I think, if I may help, Claire,' said Gosta, 'the problem is that Brita believes you and your mother do not like her. She does not feel comfortable in your home because she is sensitive to this dislike by the women of the house. It would have helped to have your husband here as mediator – to smooth the waters, as you say. But in his absence, I see I'll have to do.' He chuckled in a self-congratulatory way. 'A poor substitute for a handsome young hockey player, I confess.'

Claire took a deep breath. 'You remember his hockey days, obviously, though he's a surgeon now. Practically. Less than a year to go.'

'Oh yes, we remember Ben for his hockey. He was a marvel in our town of Angelholm, amazing to watch.'

'I've never seen him play.'

'Really? That's a pity. His fights were wonderful. The way he would smash other players up against the boards. Always a lot of blood when Ben was on the ice.'

Brita laughed, showing a lot of gum.

'But getting back to our problem,' Claire said, 'I know Brita thinks my mother and I don't like her. But she's wrong about that, and it wouldn't matter anyway. My mother doesn't live with us – and she doesn't even visit all that often. Besides, I think this business over the diapers was a huge misunderstanding, that's all. I don't know what you call it in Swedish.'

'*Forbannade rora*,' Gosta said. 'A bloody mess.'

'*Sluta tjafsa*,' Brita muttered.

'With Harry being so sick with those awful chicken-pox –' he was crawling energetically across the carpet now, advancing on the King of Siam – 'I think everyone was under a terrible strain while we were in San Francisco. Tell you what, Brita, you can use paper diapers from now on. How's that? And it's not true that I don't like you. It's not true, Gosta. I like Brita very much. We all do. Especially Harry.'

Brita's expression brightened. 'Ah, Harry. He is a good boy – a little prince. *Alskling.*'

Claire thought back to the thrashing, purple-faced *alskling* she'd had to deal with the day after Brita quit on the boardwalk.

'I'm glad you think so,' she said, 'that's why we want you to come back.'

Brita ran over and hugged Harry tightly, then said something to Gosta in rapid Swedish.

'Harry is the first baby she has ever looked after, since birth,' Gosta said, 'she is very attached to him, naturally.'

'Well – good,' said Claire.

Gosta hesitated. 'She is speaking in Swedish now because she is feeling very emotional. But . . .'

'But? But what?'

'There is still this troubling question about the basement.'

'What about it? What troubling question?'

Rummet ar for kallt, Brita said, *'en lacka.'*

'She doesn't like her room down there. It's too cold.' He looked at Brita who elaborated, in Swedish, with a lot of eye-rolling and gestures with her free hand. 'It's damp down there too,' Gosta said, 'and there is a smell – a bad stink?' He looked at Brita for confirmation. She nodded vigorously. 'From some leaking of water.'

'I'm going to take care of that,' Claire said. 'It isn't a leak anyway. The window just needs some proper weather stripping around it, that's all. There aren't any hardware stores downtown where I work and I haven't had a chance to go out to Canadian Tire to get what I need.' That leak had been an issue with all of the nannies they'd hired since Brita.

'And Brita's not so crazy about this waterbed you make her sleep on,' Gosta added. 'If it's so great, she says, why don't you want to sleep on it yourself?'

'It's too heavy to put upstairs,' Claire said. 'We have an old house. A waterbed would crash through the floor. Otherwise we would sleep on it ourselves.' Assuming Ben and I were sleeping in the same room, that is, she added to herself.

'It makes Brita sea-sick.' Gosta repacked his pipe with tobacco from a tassled and embroidered pouch he kept in the breast-pocket of his shirt. Claire watched him, annoyed now by the complaints Brita suddenly had about her accommodations at 67 Pine Beach Road, and wondering how anyone could put up with the nuisance and paraphernalia required of pipe-smoking. After all that filling, tamping, lighting and energetic sucking, she would have been too irritated and exhausted to bother smoking the thing. 'And there are *insekter*,' Gosta added drily.

'*Kackerlacka*!' Brita nodded, her eyes wide.

'Pardon?' said Claire.

'Bugs.'

'Bugs? We don't have bugs in our house.'

'*Ja*,' Brita nodded, 'in the basement. *Ach toiletten ar sonder.*'

'There's something wrong with the toilet,' Gosta said, 'it backs up.'

'Oh, come on,' said Claire, 'this is the first I've heard about anything being wrong with the toilet, or with the basement, for that matter. And, again, I'm wondering why I suddenly need an interpreter to talk to Brita.'

'She is uncomfortable speaking to you directly about these problems – it's easier for her to speak her mind through me. And when one is upset, one's mother tongue is best.'

'Well, I'm sorry.' Claire stood up. 'I think it's pretty clear that she's decided not to come back to us. Maybe she's already found another job. That's fine with me. There are lots of fish in the sea, as they say.' She took a step towards Brita, holding out her arms to take Harry back. Brita said something, in impassioned Swedish, to Gosta.

'Wait, Mrs Cunningham – Claire.' He shoved his pipe into his pocket. 'She says she is willing to come back if you could just improve her quarters a little.'

'We can't buy a new house, if that's what she means by improving her quarters. We spent twenty thousand dollars converting that basement, and I worked hard to make her apartment as nice as possible. I really tried. I even wallpapered it when I was eight months pregnant. It's very nice – cheerful and clean.' She thought guiltily about the low duct work in the bathroom, on which Brita had surely banged her head a dozen times, and that stain – and the smell – under the basement window. 'If the toilet is broken, we'll call a plumber and get it fixed. All she had to do was tell me.' Claire was feeling the familiar sting of self-pity. 'But other than that, I'm sorry, but there's nothing I can do to improve the accommodations, as you put it. Obviously, Brita isn't as attached to Harry as she likes to pretend.' She bent down and held out her arms for her son. As soon as she was holding him again, he started to whine, struggling to get down.

'*Och spruta mot insekter*,' Brita said, her eyes lowered.

'She just wants some bug spray,' said Gosta, 'that would do, she says.'

Claire sniffed. 'If there really are bugs, I'll get an exterminator. Bug spray isn't good for babies – or anyone – else. We'll get rid of the bugs, okay, Brita?'

'*Ja*,' she said, 'this is okay.'

'Good,' said Gosta happily, 'then all is settled.'

'I will go now and pack my things,' Brita said. 'Okay if I take Harry to my room?'

'Sure,' Claire said. It looks like he prefers you anyway, she thought.

When Brita had gone, Gosta beamed at Claire. 'I am glad this has worked out. We are very fond of Brita but it's like living with a teenager, you know.' He pulled the smoking pipe from his jacket pocket and made an elaborate show of tamping down the tobacco. 'And if I might make a suggestion, perhaps you could do something to make Brita's room a little nicer. These girls from Europe – they don't like to feel like servants. Most of them, like Brita, come from very good homes. They're not used to dampness and cockroaches.'

'Maybe if she kept her room a little tidier there wouldn't be any cockroaches, if there really are.' Claire tried to sound as though she was working hard to come up with an amicable solution. 'There were bags of stale nachos in her room when she left. Not that I was snooping, of course.'

Gosta smiled indulgently around the stem of his pipe. 'We could go on and on, hearing your grievances about each other. But what's the point? When the time is right, I will mention to her that she could be more tidy. But I think you will agree this is not the best time for more complaints. She only wants to feel part of your family. Try to make her feel as though she belongs.'

'I wouldn't mind another drink.' Claire picked up her wine glass from the floor and held it out to Gosta, 'while we wait for Brita to get her things. Why don't we do a little more of that skaling?'

Gosta shook his head. 'You must be more responsible, Claire. You have to drive home – and with a baby in the car. In Sweden we don't dare take alcohol before we drive. Even a chocolate with liqueur filling is too much. They take away your licence – the fines are steep. Canada is much too lenient.'

'I had no intention of drinking beyond the legal limit,' Claire said, flushing.

'No, of course not. But think how I would feel if something happened. How could I explain it to Ben?'

They looked at each other in silence. 'Well then,' said Claire, putting her wine glass down on an end table, hot with humiliation, 'I suppose I'd better go and see if I can give Brita a hand with her packing.'

'That would be a nice gesture.' Gosta nodded.

'Just one thing, Gosta, I meant to ask you. It's about Skane.'

'Sure, Skane. Shoot, as they say in America.'

'There's some kind of movement going on there, is that right? To become Danish?'

'Well,' he chuckled, 'not quite. It's a bit more complicated than that. But things are becoming a little uncomfortable there some say – I don't know that it is true. But that is why Brita left. She is a peace-loving person, as are most Swedes.'

'Really? I somehow got the impression that she was very involved in some sort of free-Skane separatist movement.'

'Oj! Brita?' Gosta laughed, showing all of his teeth, rather menacingly, Claire thought. 'You must be mistaken. Not Brita. And the whole thing is preposterous, this movement. Imagine how surprised I was to come to Canada to find the same thing going on here.'

'Yes.'

'But then – perhaps there is some justification for it here. The French against the English. The Danish against the Swedes. I don't know. Everybody seems to enjoy disliking someone. It's human nature, isn't it?' He turned away from her. 'Brita?' he called sharply over his shoulder. 'Skynda pa!' He turned back to Claire. 'She should hurry up. There's no need for her to take all day. All day is what it will take us to clean up after her.'

Was there something malicious about his smile as he said that, Claire wondered. As if he knew she was wading deeper into troubled waters and would quite enjoy watching her drown? Behind Gosta, the gaudy golden paint on the King of Siam gleamed in the afternoon sun, the end of the spear glinting aggressively, and pointing directly at Claire's head.

23

By the time they finally left Gosta's house, the sky was a dense, bruised purple, deepening to black along the horizon. Claire had just enough time to pack Harry and Brita into the car before the first raindrops were squeezed from the constipated sky. As she pulled the car away from Gosta's house, they started falling faster, plunking onto the windshield and bonking on to the roof of the car, heavy as condom water bombs.

Claire was glad she had to concentrate on navigating through a noisy storm: it gave her an excuse for not talking to Brita. She needed some time to sulk over the litany of complaints she'd had to absorb about the basement apartment, and to contemplate the number of aggravating phone calls, estimates, and troops of trades people she would have to deal with (and pay) to fix the toilet, track down the bugs and dry out the basement carpet. Then there was Ben's mother and all that Claire would have to hear about paper diapers and the havoc they were wreaking on the environment.

Brita, who'd insisted on sitting in the back with Harry, seemed already to have forgotten the entire discussion at Gosta's, or that she'd ever walked out on the Cunninghams in the first place. She was babbling cheerfully to Harry, alternating between Swedish and English, calling him *snutiks* and *askling* and other terms of what Claire supposed was endearment, and generally acting as though Claire was not even there with them in the car.

'So, what have you been doing for the past two weeks?' Claire finally asked, over the slap and thunk of the windshield wipers. The rain was so heavy she couldn't see the road, so she'd given up on driving for the moment and pulled over to the side to wait until the storm let up a bit.

'Oh, just on holidays,' Brita said, 'I needed to rest. *Jag kanner mig frisk.*' She kissed Harry with a loud smacking sound. 'I am okay now.'

So much for Brita getting snapped up by another family, Claire thought: she hadn't even been looking for a job. 'Holidays,' she said, 'that must have been nice.'

'*Ja.* Very nice.'

'So – I'm just curious – you asked about Ben. You know what long hours he works. Why did you think he should have come to Gosta's? In the middle of the afternoon?'

Brita didn't answer immediately. The rain pounded down on the roof, the heavy drops as big and white as ping-pong balls. It looked like hail. Claire frowned. It was. 'Ben is my friend,' Brita said finally. 'I know him for a long time.'

'But I'm your friend too, Brita. I hope you believe that.'

'That is nice. But Ben – he is very good to me.'

'Oh?' Claire turned off the wipers and glanced at Brita in the rearview. Again, that shag of hair obscured her face. 'In what way is he so good to you?' she asked. Just then, the rain began to pound so hard on the roof of the car that it drowned out Brita's reply, if she'd given one. 'It's hard to imagine Ben having the time to be good to anyone, since he's away so much,' Claire said, raising her voice to be heard over the racket of the rain.

In the mirror, she could see Brita slide lower into her seat and bend her head down over Harry. 'Harry must be changed soon,' she said.

'What? I can't hear you.'

'Harry must be changed soon! He is very wet!'

As if on cue, he began to fuss, apparently just noticing the hail raining down on top of them, and not liking it. Claire started the car and turned the wipers on again. They flew back and forth across the windshield as she drove, cautiously, glad she hadn't had anything more to drink at Gosta's. The water churned up under the car's fenders with scraping and rasping sounds that made her tense and edgy.

As they neared the Beach, the sky took on a luminous quality, like a scrim in a theatrical set, lit from behind. Shards of lightning sliced through it, cutting into the choppy swells of the lake. In the back seat, Harry started to scream – the way he did when they drove through an automatic car wash – in sheer terror. The air inside the car was oppressive and humid. Brita shushed and cooed, holding Harry's hands and tickling him under the chin, trying her best to calm him.

Once, Claire had considered storms nothing more than romantic backdrops for passion: fine things to be going on outside while she was snuggled under a down duvet with a warm man. Now, they unnerved her. They were a threat to life, limb and property; another source of stress. And living on the edge of the lake exposed one to the elements in a way she'd never experienced in a high-rise apartment. Howling storms, fierce winds and crashing waves made her crave the security of a tight-packed cosy mid-town street, where she could look out any window and right into a neighbour's cheery kitchen, maybe even see what they were having for dinner or watching on TV.

As she turned the car into their driveway, the black oaks in front of the house raked their Rackhamesque branches, clawlike, against the hallucinogenic sky. They were ancient trees that showered twigs over the yard during every storm, clogged the eavestroughs with leaves, dropped acorns that pinged dents in the hoods of parked cars, and entwined their roots through and around the drains under the Cunninghams' lawn. Though they were a nuisance, Claire usually thought of them as benign homes for squirrels and birds and, because of their advanced age, better entitled to remain on the property than the Cunninghams. Now they looked sinister, plotting; or else destined to be split by lightning or torn up by the wind to come crashing down on to the Cunninghams' roof. One of them, Claire calculated now, in alarm, could easily fall right through the ceiling of Harry's room.

She parked the car in the garage, hoping that the ancient structure wouldn't be blown down or swept away by the wind, and told Brita to take Harry down to her room in the basement, where the noise of the storm would be less frightening. Then she ran around outside, battening down the hatches – latching the garage door, struggling to secure the gate to the deck steps.

• Sylvia Mulholland

By the time she was finished, her clothes were clinging to her and her hair was streaming. Too bad Ben wasn't around, she thought, glancing down at her chest: he always claimed to be turned on by that mud wrestler look. As she pulled shut the back door, the house seemed to shudder, creaking like an old wooden ship. The thunder and lightning were coming quickly now, close together. The lawn and lake flashed, strobe-like, with a lurid greenish hue.

The level of the lake had risen and the waves were crashing against the retaining wall at the foot of their property. She'd never seen waves that high, wouldn't have believed they could ever reach that wall, though it must have happened before, she realized, thinking about the water marks on it. When big storms hit Toronto, the sewers overflowed and backed up into the lake, adding tons of human waste to the already polluted waters. If waves were coming up over the retaining wall, it meant that human excrement could be tossed up into their backyard, along with whatever else was out there.

Brita had the television on loud in the basement – the theme song for *Polka Dot Door* – and Harry was still howling, though less hysterically. Claire filled a kettle with water, put it on the stove to make tea, and sat down at the kitchen table, worrying about the garage, remembering photographs of the last hurricane in Florida, of homes smashed into piles, looking like the old game of pick-up-sticks she and Christine used to play as children. She wondered whether a tidal wave was possible, rising up out of Lake Ontario. Outside the kitchen window, the hydro and telephone wires were swinging crazily, whipped sideways by the wind, like children's skipping ropes whirling 'double Dutch'.

Suddenly, there was a tremendous crash, followed by the sound of breaking glass. Seconds later, a hysterical Brita burst into the kitchen, carrying Harry, his face an open square of howling terror. *'Mein gott! En flud!* In the basement! The lake is coming into the house!'

Claire hurried down the stairs to stand, in shock, on the bottom step. The basement – their cheery little nanny apartment, their twenty-thousand-dollar renovation – had been turned into a lake itself, or a swamp. The back window, the one she'd never got around to sealing up, had been shattered, burst open by a torrent of water. Shards and splinters of glass littered the soaked carpet. The laundry room drain had also backed up; rank sewage bubbled and gurgled around it. The stench was overpowering.

'My things!' Brita wailed from behind Claire's shoulder. 'You made me take them down there. I must get my things. I put them there, on the waterbed.'

'I'll get your things.' Claire pushed her back up the stairs. 'You take Harry up to the kitchen and stay with him.'

More water poured in between the jagged glass of the shattered window. Claire pulled off her shoes and socks then, holding her nose and gagging, hopped through the icy mud of the laundry and sitting-room to reach Brita's bedroom, yanking electrical plugs out of the wall as she went. Harry's toys – a rubber Big Bird, his Roly Poly Chime Ball, a string of multi-coloured play-pen animals – sat forlornly on top of the muck.

In the bedroom, she pulled out the plug for the waterbed heater and grabbed Brita's heavy bag. Her feet aching from the cold, she hopped back towards the stairs, past the bathroom. The mess was even worse in there. The toilet had backed up and squatted, like a gleaming porcelain Buddha, in the middle of a sea of sludge, and – what were those things? She picked up a floating gelatinous object, like a tiny jellyfish, then threw it down in disgust. Condoms! As she looked around, she noticed dozens of them, some of them ribbed, others coloured. The water-filtration plant! Their house was under siege, deluged with gunk from the plant!

Gasping for air and wanting to vomit, she struggled back through the stew of sewage to reach the stairs, lugging Brita's bag, trying to hold it up out of the sludge to keep it dry. There was nothing she could do about the basement now. Once the storm was over, she would call the City. They had to be responsible; someone had to be to blame for this disaster – some city engineer, some cost-cutting trustee.

'Here's your suitcase,' she panted, pulling shut the basement door behind her. Brita had put Harry down in his play-pen and given him a biscuit and a bottle of juice. He seemed to be settling down as the storm outside subsided. The rolls of thunder were fading, the lightning flashes less frequent.

'I am making some tea,' Brita said.

'Good idea.' As Claire put Brita's bag down on the floor, something fell out of the side pocket. It was a picture, the framed photo of Brita in her St Lucia outfit with the wreath of candles on her head. Claire picked up the picture but it had fallen apart – a sheaf of cardboard sheets and other photos slid out of the back of it and on to the floor.

'*Jiddra inte!*' Quick as a cat, Brita leaped for it, deftly scooping up the cards and photos, glaring at Claire, her eyes dark.

Claire drew back in surprise. 'Brita, really – I was only trying to help.'

'No – this is okay. I can fix it.' She turned her back to Claire, hastily stuffing all of the pieces back into the side pocket of the suitcase.

Claire didn't have time to try to interpret this bizarre reaction. That was all she needed now – a psychotic nanny back in their home. She grabbed a tea-towel and dried off her feet, noting with distaste the mucky footprints she'd tracked over the tiled floor. She would have to wash them in disinfectant; God only knew what sort of bacteria were being carried into their house with all that sewage. 'You'll have to sleep upstairs, in the study,' she said, 'until we figure out what to do about the basement.' Brita nodded, without expression, then disappeared up the stairs, lugging her bag.

If the City wasn't responsible – if they wouldn't pay for the damage – what could it possibly cost to have a basement sucked dry, cleaned out, recarpeted? Morosely, Claire stared out of the window at the storm, as if expecting to find some answer up there in the sky. Huge dollar signs, flapping away on wings, was all she could see. Her shoulders sagged as she stood watching the rain, looking at their yard through the rivers of water streaming down the window glass.

She frowned, staring hard at the scene outside for a few moments, in total stock. Then, with a strangled cry, she fell back into a kitchen chair. The retaining wall had collapsed! Most of their yard was sliding into the lake! It was a muddy, soupy landslide, carrying the remains of Claire's wretched garden out to join the rise and swell of industrial pollutants and human excrement pouring into the lake from the sewers. She jumped up again to watch, in horrified fascination, as a wire tomato trellis, bearing the remnants of last summer's vines, shuddered, teetered, then tipped over and disappeared beyond the bottom edge of the yard. She pulled the blinds down over the window, unable to watch any longer, then slumped again into her chair.

'Baby?' Harry said from his play-pen. 'Mama?'

A staccato of rain, hard as bullets, drilled against the window as the tea kettle blasted out its cheery whistle.

24

Loudly clearing her throat, Claire waited her turn at the dry cleaner's counter. Throat-clearing was a newly acquired nervous habit that would probably, some day, turn into laryngeal cancer or, at least, inflamed tonsils. These sorts of fears, and being able to put neat labels on them, were a part of the package deal you got when you married a doctor.

'So, do you know what these stains are?' the cleaner asked, pulling the rumpled pile of clothes across the counter towards him. 'Here. On this skirt.'

Claire looked at him dimly. 'Shit,' she said.

'Pardon me?'

'You know – excrement. Dung? Baby doo-doo? My son pooped on me, well, not actually on me. He did it in his diaper. But cloth diapers aren't leak-proof. They don't tell you that, those enviornmental types. I guess you're supposed to figure that out for yourself.' She sighed. 'I promised our nanny we'd switch to paper, but I spent so much on the cloth ones, fancy covers for them, all that. Anyway – do what you can to get them out, the stains. It's a very good skirt, part of a suit.' And not yet even paid for, she thought. 'And this stuff, on the jacket here,' she pointed to a vivid green smear, 'that's Play Doh. Don't ask me why his nanny is giving him Play Doh . . . maybe "play doh" means something else in Swedish – maybe she's confused. Who knows? The Swedes are a baffling and unpredictable people. It maybe doesn't say that in *Sweden For Voyeurs*,' she laughed artificially, 'but that's my personal opinion.'

'Voyeurs?'

'Did I say that?' She laughed again. 'Voya*gers* I meant. I don't know what I'm talking about these days. It's the drugs.' Her eyes met his. 'Sleeping pills – not what you're thinking.' Her smile faded. 'Play Doh is that stuff kids play with. That coloured doughy stuff. Everybody knows what Play Doh is.'

'Well, I'm sorry I don't. What's it made of? Is it an oil-based substance?'

'How should I know? Do I look like a chemist?' Who *was* this person anyway? Cleaner to the Queen? Cleaner of the Gods? Used to removing Pol Roger stains or caviar smears but nothing . . . dirty? 'Look, just write "Play Doh stain" on your tag there – somebody will know what to do with it.'

She took the cleaning tickets and made her way unsteadily through the maze of corridors towards the tower where Bragg, Banks and Biltmore had its offices. Why in hell was she bothering with dry cleaning, when her backyard had disappeared into the lake, her basement had become a primordial oozing swamp full of condoms, and Ingrid Bergman was lounging around, nude, on the other side of her bedroom wall every night? Oh, and Potochnik. While she was making a list of all the things that were terrorizing her lately, she'd better add his name. After letting her twist in the wind for four months, clinging to a faint hope that he wouldn't, he'd finally filed his complaint with the Law Society. The cream-coloured, deckle-edged letter of inquiry, with the no-nonsense black seal and the words 'Private & Confidential' on the front, was on her desk, hidden under the desk blotter. She'd had it for a week, but still couldn't face opening it. She had a pretty good idea what it said.

Feeling very much the pathetic stereotype – the working mother who just couldn't cope – she tick-ticked down the marbled corridor in her high-heeled pumps, swaying slightly, trying her best not to stumble or turn an ankle on the smooth glazed floor. The floors weren't designed for high heels; they were made for the broad flat feet of the business suits, hustling on to make their luncheon meetings at the Board of Trade. Once, Claire had turned her ankle and fallen face down on that floor, at high noon. She'd lain there in shock as the crowds rushed past, more astounded that no one stopped to help her up than that she'd fallen in the first place. All she got was one, token 'Are you okay?' from a passing suit who barely paused long enough to hear her muffled reply. Even the women didn't stop – too afraid of breaking an acrylic nail probably, if they tried to help her to her feet. If she fell down now, she just wouldn't bother getting up, she decided. She would just lie there, her nose, breasts and hip bones pressed against the cold marble. The struggle of getting on with life was becoming too great.

Pills. She had to get more of those sleeping pills. She was forgetting everything lately. Just that morning she'd got into the shower, then climbed out again, to stand naked, shivering and dripping on to the bath mat, wondering why. It was a common enough occurrence, going momentarily blank, but people usually remembered why they were standing in front of the open refrigerator, say, or what they'd gone upstairs to get. But Claire hadn't remembered. She was dressed and half-way to work before she remembered that she'd got out of the shower to get her razor, meaning to shave away the shag of her underarms.

Once she'd prided herself on her amazing memory; now she made lists. And how well she got through a day depended on whether or not she'd made an accurate list, then whether or not she'd remembered to take it with her when she left home in the morning. Question: how to drive a working mother off the deep end? Answer: steal her list. She started off each day as if blasted from a cannon, clutching her crinkle of lists and reminder notes: pick up cleaning; get Ben's shoes fixed; get formula!!! buy guilt toy for Harry; fix marriage. Her life was hurtling on without her, leaving her behind as she dashed around in circles, going nowhere, afraid she would rip off her fingers, break an ankle or get strangled with her own fashion jewellery as she flew through revolving doors and careened around corners. She had no time, and even less patience, for the simplest of necessary activities. Any box, package or container she savagely attacked, to open as fast as possible with her teeth and nails; instruction booklets were left unread, warranties tossed out with the packaging, clothing ruined. Who had time for fine print? For filling in warranty cards or driving broken junk around for repairs? For hand-washing those idiotic appliquéd T-shirts she'd bought on sale? Who had time for niceties? For chat? Niceties and chat were the exclusive domain of the nannies now.

She had reached the end of the corridor and was standing,

dumbly, in front of Pharma-Plus, wondering why. She reached into her handbag, impatient to find her list. She squinted down at the rumpled piece of note paper. Sleeping pills. Of course. It was right there at the top, just above a scribbled jumble of hieroglyphics about calling someone (who?) to rebuild their retaining wall, pull the backyard back up (who??) and suck out the sludge from the basement (who???) (how much?!) and just after the reminder to call her bank to see if she could get their line of credit extended by several thousand.

The pharmacist was a pleasant enough fellow, but Claire knew he disapproved of her pill-popping. Ben had told her that they kept computerized lists of who was taking what – nosy buggers – mostly to track down narcotics addicts and other abusers of the public health care system. They probably chatted about their customers over lunch. 'That Mrs Cunningham's been in for Canesten ovules again,' one of them would say, biting into a cheese sandwich.

'She gets around, eh?' another would comment.

'Yeah? Since when did *she* get a sex life?' a third would ask. 'I hear her husband sleeps in another room.'

No topic would be too unappetizing for pharmacists.

When Claire had time, she walked over to a different drugstore in one of the adjoining underground malls to find a pharmacist who didn't recognize her. Today she didn't have that kind of time. She put the prescription on the counter and tried to look perky and pleasant instead of drugged-out and wired. The pharmacist picked it up, gave her a quick appraising glance and nodded, lips pressed together. Damn. He'd recognized her. 'It'll be a few minutes,' he said. Studying the prescription, he strolled towards his dispensary, frowning.

As Claire waited under the fluorescent hum of the drugstore lights, her mind chugged along in low gear, trying to recall what had actually gone on over the past twelve hours. She'd had a ghastly night, seemed to have woken up every half-hour, imagining she heard voices whispering until dawn. The tone of the voices rose and fell, sometimes heated, sometimes conversational. The funny thing was, the discussions were in Swedish. At one point, she'd reached out her hand to touch Ben. Had he been there? Or gone back down to the pull-out couch in the living-room? Was he on call or off? She couldn't remember now.

She'd dreamed that she was setting out for a sail on an artificial lake, navigating a raft, which turned out to be Harry's stolen Perego. It wasn't watertight and there was a strong undertow. As she was about to be sucked down, a noisy party boat cruised by, with her first husband, Simon, standing on the deck, leaning forlornly over the siderail. He saw her floundering, sinking fast, on her stroller-raft, dove in and rescued her. He wanted her back, he told her, as they thrashed in the water, struggling to reach the party boat; they never should have divorced; they should have tried harder to make it work. Later, he took her to a drugstore for a blood test and they discovered she was pregnant. His handsome brow, so often likened to that of Michelangelo's *David*, creased in tidy parallel lines of consternation. This was going to be a problem, he said: he didn't want any children; never had, actually. Then they were back on the love-boat cruise, surrounded by boozy revellers. Claire wondered how she was going to tell him about Harry, then, vaguely, what had happened to Ben.

Other than that, her dreams were jumbled and fragmented, lost in a fog of floods, wreckage, people screaming and swearing in Swedish. But it must have been only what she thought was Swedish, since she couldn't have been dreaming in a language she couldn't speak. Could she? Or was it like speaking in tongues? Your mind reeling off some unknown language, spewing out accumulated garbage, as though it were doing a huge computer dump?

'Mrs Cunningham?' The pharmacist had returned, still holding her prescription, still frowning. 'What is the doctor's name on here?'

'Cunningham, same as mine. He's my husband.'

'How many of these have you been taking?'

'One a night – sometimes two. And it's not every night,' she lied.

'Two! These are ten-milligram tablets. Two would be enough to fell a horse.'

'That right?' She gave a short laugh, almost a whinny. 'Well, I've been having a lot of trouble sleeping lately. You see, we seem to have misplaced our back yard. And we've got other problems, but I won't bore you with details. I'm not feeling all that well. Could you just fill the prescription and let me get out of here? Please?'

The pharmacist studied her, the picture of avuncular concern.

'I'm not surprised you don't feel well. And you say your husband's been prescribing these for you routinely?'

'In exchange for sexual favours,' Claire laughed, 'which are never delivered of course. Not my idea – I'd be happy to. Anywhere, any place, any time.' She cleared her throat. Coughed.

'Well, actually, Mrs Cunningham, he's not supposed to be prescribing drugs to his family. Especially tranquillizers, narcotics, hypnotics. The College of Physicians and Surgeons has strict new guidelines on this issue. He'd better be careful. The optics, as they say, are not good.'

What the hell was he talking about? She wasn't there for reading glasses. 'It was a bit of an emergency,' Claire said, 'when he prescribed these.'

'But this prescription says "Repeat three times". Look, right here.' He pointed to the paper, pushing it under Claire's nose, as if she were myopic. He shook his head. 'And you normally take two, you say?'

'No, not normally. There is no normally. I hardly ever take them.' Claire cleared her throat again. What if someone she knew was standing behind her? A client, say, or one of the firm's partners? Overhearing her desperate pleading with the pharmacist, like a junkie, trying to wheedle a fix?

'But your last refill was only three weeks ago. I looked it up on the computer.'

Claire smiled thinly. 'Are you going to fill this prescription or not?'

'Not without calling your husband.'

'Okay, forget it. I'll pass along your concerns.'

'I could call him right now, if you don't mind waiting.'

'You'd have to page him and he never answers his page unless he's with an ugly nurse.'

'Excuse me? I'm not sure what you mean—'

'Never mind. I don't really need this prescription anyway. They were prophylactic, the pills. A condom for the brain. Half of the time they don't even work.' Claire snatched the prescription from him, stuffed it back into her handbag, then headed up the aisle towards the front of the drugstore. 'Condoms,' she muttered, passing by a rack of them, 'I've got a basement full. And what would I do with one anyway?' She laughed. Then she stopped, turned around and marched back to the prescription counter, scowling. 'And by the way,' she said to pharmacist, 'I already have a mother. And a mother-in-law. So why don't you butt out of my business?'

Congratulating herself on having put him in his place – who did he think he was? – she made her way back out of the drug-store. She'd be obliged to wander the underground malls for the rest of the morning if she wanted to find a druggist who would hand over the pills without a lecture. She was sure it was Ben's idea to take a double dose. It was even typed on to the label: 'Take 1–2 tablets at bedtime,' it said. At least, she thought it said that. She would have to check when she got home – the empty bottle would still be in the bathroom garbage pail. Her eyes burned and her head felt pressurized and achy, as if it were stuck inside a bell-jar. She looked at her watch, wondering what she was supposed to be doing that morning. She had to put in an appearance at the office, answer calls, check her mail, attend to any due dates. And Davina – she had to find some busy work for her. She'd been off for three days, getting Brita back, dealing with the wreckage left by the storm. Maybe Davina'd already quit. Or maybe Claire had been fired herself. It would be there on her e-mail: 'Claire Cunningham is no longer with the firm. Please join us in wishing her well in her new endeavours.' And she had to make more calls about their house and yard, before the remains of both floated out into Lake Ontario to join the rest.

Incredibly, there was a Yellow Pages listing under FLOOD. It was FLOOD DAMAGE RESTORATION, to be exact. Under it was a Subheading: 'See Carpet and Rug Cleaners'. Their basement was too far gone for carpet cleaners, but the second sub-heading was more promising: 'See also Water Damage Restoration'. Claire flipped to the end of the book, under the Ws, encouraged to see an entire column listing of people who were apparently ready, willing and able to suck dry their basement, who did things like that every day. Mahmood's Moisture Control didn't sound serious enough – they weren't talking mere *moisture* here, they were talking *deluge*. 'Moisture Control' suggested a group of elderly ladies dabbing at their basement floors with hankies. Then there was 'With Discretion Home Inspectors'. What was the implication there? That all of the others would kiss and tell? While these guys would pull up in an unmarked truck, collars upturned on their trench-coats, so as not to let on to the neighbours that you had – well – shall we say, a dampness issue? The Cunninghams didn't need a cloak-and-dagger service; the whole Beach was talking about their basement and backyard already. It was roped off with yellow police emergency tape, as if a murder had been committed there. She continued to scan the listings until she found one that had the right tone. She wrote down the phone number for 'Home-Buddy's 24-hour Water Extraction and Deodorizing'. They sounded friendly but no-nonsense, as if their sleeves were already rolled up and they were eager to tackle the wetness; the kind of guys, too, who could put up with a little stink.

Feeling more optimistic about the basement, Claire focused her mind on the backyard dilemma. There was no heading for LANDSLIDES, unfortunately, though there was one for LAND CLEARING AND LEVELLING. 'See Excavating Contractors – Residential', it said. She was about to flip to the Es when Davina rapped officiously on her door, then pushed it open without waiting for Claire's response.

'The tomato king's on my line,' she said, her striped bow-tie aggressively jaunty. 'He needs a brand-name for his tomatoes. He has to order a thousand crates tomorrow. He's got twenty different names and he's called a hundred times since yesterday. He wants to know why you're avoiding him.'

'Tell him it's nothing personal – I'm avoiding everybody.' Claire continued flipping through the telephone book. 'I'm kind of busy right now – I've got to find someone to catch a runaway backyard.'

'I went through the names with him. He really wants to go with Vine-Ripe or Sun-Ripened but I told him to forget it – they're too descriptive. Also too common.'

'So you're giving out legal advice now?' Claire said, peevishly.

'Somebody around here's got to.'

'Meaning what, exactly?'

'Meaning I can't afford to lose my job. And if you get canned, I go with you – secretaries aren't being reallocated any more.'

'They're not going to can me, like I'm some kind of tomato.'

'Well, you're making me nervous. I don't want to be redundant here. I don't even have anything left to file. You were away for two weeks in February and March, then you were in only part-time. Then these last three days.'

'We had nanny problems. Can't you understand that?'

'Well, the world goes on, Claire. Business is business.'

'Harry has to come first.' Claire looked up at her secretary, nostrils flaring, her eyes beginning to sting. In a second, she would be bawling. 'If you'd seen some of the nut-cases we had looking after him . . . I've done what I can to put out fires here. There haven't been any disasters. You're making it sound as though I've been off in cloud cuckoo-land or someplace.' Her eyes were filling now. She didn't feel like telling Davina about her trip to the library with Harry on one of her many days off – where she'd taken him, not only for picture books, but to see if she could dig up more information about Skane, or at least Sweden's political situation (she couldn't). What she had discovered, in the children's book section, was the frightening progression of titles, of self-help books for young children: *My Mom and Dad Are Fighting*, *When A Family Comes Apart*, *Staying At Dad's*, *Mommies Alone*.

'But Claire, you haven't put in any dockets for almost a month. We're supposed to be billing this week. What am I supposed to bill? You haven't *done* anything that can be billed.'

'Bill? I don't know what you can bill. Bill Mike Potochnik. Who cares? Just bill. That's the attitude around here, isn't it? Nothing else matters.' She pulled the pile of messages towards her. 'Tell me what's important in this mess, will you? Nothing is making any sense today.'

'I can't answer that – you have to make the calls yourself.' Davina looked frightened now.

Claire had turned her attention back to the telephone book and was running a broken fingernail down the column under Excavating Contractors. 'These guys all say they do bobcat and backhoe excavating. I wonder what that is. They also do demolition, but that we don't need. Demolition we've got already.'

But her secretary wasn't about to let her off the hook so easily. 'I've been trying to hold down the fort here, manning the phones, putting your clients off with excuses, but you've stopped responding to the faxes I send you.'

'It's under water – the fax machine.'

'And your phone mail – you never clear that out. You're way behind on your fee budget for the year too. How long do you think we can go on like this?'

Claire looked up and was shocked to see Davina's face. If Davina were about to lose it, things had to be getting pretty serious. 'I don't know how long we can go on, Davina, but I've got some real problems right now, with the house, my marriage too if you must know. You'll have to do the best you can. Just give me a day or so to get things straightened out. And I haven't slept – not since Monday. I'm sorry about all of this. You're doing great and you're saving my ass. No one's going to fire you. You can probably have my job, if you want to wait a while.'

'How about "The User-Friendly Tomato"?'

'What?'

'It was my idea. For Mr Pennacchio's tomatoes.'

'Sure,' Claire said, 'why not? If he likes it, go for it.'

'And you've got a new client waiting in Meeting Room B.'

'I do?'

'He's been there since nine. A referral from Mr Spears.'

'He has? He is?'

'It's in your diary.'

'What does he want?' Claire knew that she sounded absurdly paranoid.

'He's an inventor – a referral from Gillian. He makes bags to catch mobile homes when there's a hurricane. The Wind Bag, he wants to call them. I think it's kind of cute, don't you?'

Claire rubbed her face with her hands. This type of project had once excited her. 'I don't suppose you could meet with him? Give him a coffee? Tell him we'll search the name and send him an opinion.'

'You don't think it's too descriptive?'

'Tell him I'll think about it. Say I wasn't feeling well. Give him my apologies. Say I had to go home. A family crisis.'

'Well, I hope you're planning to come in on Friday. Exec wants
you for a meeting. It's on your e-mail.'

'About what?'

'I don't know. The Ukrainian Situation – that's all it said.'

Brita and Harry were sitting on the living-room floor, watching
Reading Rainbow when Claire got home. Beside them, in a laundry
basket, was a neatly folded pile of clean clothes. 'Your mother
came and took the washing,' Brita said, 'then she brought it back
all done.'

'So she saw the basement?'

Brita nodded.

'The backyard too?'

'*Ja.* She started to cry.'

'But you two didn't have a fight again—'

'Oh no, no fight. She was very nice, your mother.'

Claire put down her load of parcels and hung up her coat. She'd
bought a new toy for Harry after leaving the office: a huge plush
English Sheepdog. It was a soft, comforting sort of toy with a
joyous lolling pink felt tongue. She'd bought two of them, actually, since they were on sale and she thought a second one
might come in handy. There was someone she knew, she seemed
to recollect, who was due to have a baby in the near future.

After the toy store, she'd stopped at a candy kiosk in the mall
where she bought herself a bag of gummy bears. Then she bought
the kiosk display. It was a three-foot-high Mickey Mouse, dressed
as the Sorcerer's Apprentice from *Fantasia*: red cloak, a pointy
hat with stars. It was made out of plaster; she thought it would
look good in Harry's room, maybe when he was a bit older. The
salesgirl didn't really want to sell it; Claire had had to negotiate
with the owner of the kiosk, by telephone. Probably she'd paid
too much. She wasn't thinking all that clearly. Her head still
had that pressurized feeling, as though her cortex was swollen
– something, at any rate, was pressing up against her skull from
the inside. Likely, it had nothing to do with her cortex. She wasn't
really sure what her cortex was, or where it was located.

'I may have to go out again,' she said to Brita, taking one of the
toy dogs out of the store bag and presenting it to Harry. 'I forgot
to get something from the drugstore.' Then she remembered that

she'd meant to check the label on the sleeping pill bottle. But she couldn't go out now: the Home-Buddy guy and the bobcat and backhoe boys were coming over to assess the damage and give her an estimate. No one would even discuss the cost over the phone. They wanted to get a look at where she lived first, see what kind of car she drove. Harry grinned at the sheepdog, gave it a quick squeeze, then threw it aside and went crawling over to the television set.

Discouraged, Claire left them and went upstairs, carrying the other dog and the cumbersome Mickey Mouse. She would probably have to hide both for a while: Ben had really stepped up his anti-shopping campaign since San Francisco. She packed the dog and mouse away in the back of the linen closet along with all of the things she'd bought for Harry that turned out to be too advanced for his age: the watercolour set, finger-paints, puzzles, the My First Recorder and sheet music, the plasticine moulds, the china tea-set.

Then she went into the bathroom to find the pill bottle. She'd finished the prescription the night before – the empty bottle should still be there, in the garbage pail. But the pail was empty.

'Brita?' she called down the stairs. 'Did you empty the garbage pails today?'

'They took it – the garbage – this morning.' She stood at the bottom of the stairs, looking up at Claire, holding Harry on her hip. 'Did you lose something?'

'No, it's okay.' Funny. She didn't think Wednesday was garbage day. Had the City changed the schedule? Well, she would just have to remember to ask Ben about those pills, when he got home. She changed her clothes, then decided to take a quick peek into the den where Brita was now encamped. There was nothing particular she wanted to see, she just felt a prickling curiosity mingled with a vague sense of dread. The den was a bedroom, actually, and had been done over as a child's room by the Proctors, or someone before them. The wallpaper was pastel polka dots, with a border of blocks and teddy bears. She and Ben had wedged an old sofa in there, and all the books they'd accumulated over the years. A series of mismatched and unstable book-cases lined the walls. Though it wasn't much of a room, Claire liked to read in there occasionally, and often thought that she would some day turn it into a proper library – her own personal quiet space.

Although Brita had only spent two nights in the room, it was already a disaster – strewn with fashion magazines and underwear, a pair of jeans that she'd slid down, stepped out of and walked away from, the usual litter of empty pop cans and chocolate wrappers, the stumps of melted candles on the book-cases. If she didn't know better, Claire would have thought Brita'd thrown an all-night party in there. If she didn't know better.

She stood leaning against the doorjamb, musing. Did she really know better? Or did she just think she did? Or did someone else want her to think she did? Someone who was in cahoots with her husband, double-dosing her with powerful sleeping pills to make sure she never did know any better? Whoa there, she told herself, trying to rein in her thoughts which were galloping in several paranoid directions at once. What if, she thought, her heart thudding unpleasantly, I suddenly pull back that blanket on the sofa, and find a used condom? Or maybe several? What if I find a whole mess of them, just like in the basement? And whose condoms were those down there, anyway?

She approached the sofa cautiously, lifted one corner of the blanket and thoughtfully ran it through her fingers. Then, with a swift motion, she yanked it back. Nothing. A rumpled sheet, a few crumbs. That was all. She swallowed, her heart still pounding, not much reassured. That irritating St Lucia photo of Brita was on the book-case, behind the cluster of candles. Feeling bold, Claire picked it up and turned it over. From downstairs she could hear the theme song from *Reading Rainbow*. The program was ending. Now was the time to look. If she was going to.

She slid the glass and the mounting out of the frame, and the sheaf of cardboard and other papers with it. Her hands shaking, she turned over each piece. More pictures of Brita, in various stages of dress and undress: shyly holding up a dead trout, a fishing rod at her side; in a red ski-suit and helmet; in a string bikini. Then there was a picture Claire wasn't quite ready for, though she'd somehow known she would find: Ben and Brita, sitting together on a bench in a European cobblestone square;

ancient red brick buildings and planter boxes of geraniums in the background. Their arms were around each other. Brita was wearing a sky-blue dress, hiked up a little at one side to show off her long, sun-browned legs. She was holding a loose bunch of wild flowers that cascaded prettily across her skirt. Ben looked remote, a slightly dazed smile on his lips, one hand resting on Brita's thigh.

Claire was suddenly on a roller-coaster, the floor dropping away from under her, then rolling back up, sweeping her high on the crest of a sickening wave. Her hair was blown back from her head, yanked away from her scalp. The wind screamed in her ears, the short hairs on her neck prickled. Stunned, she turned the picture over. 'Brollopsdag – Angelholm' was written on the back, in a typically European, cramped scrawl.

Brollopsdag, brollopsdag. Dag was day, she knew that much. '*En san underbar dag*', wasn't that what Brita often said? It's a beautiful day. Well, it would be no beautiful day for Brita today, that was for sure. The jig was up, oh yes it was.

Claire stuffed everything back into the photo frame, keeping out the photo of Ben and Brita which she squirrelled away at the back of the underwear drawer of her bedroom bureau. Then she hurried down the stairs to retrieve her briefcase from where she'd left it in the hall.

'Claire?' Brita had turned off the television. 'I will make dinner now? *Fiskpinne*?'

'Huh?' Claire stared at her blankly.

'Fish sticks? I should make them now?'

'Sure, go ahead.' She narrowed her eyes at Brita. I'm on to you now, she thought. All I need is a few more minutes, just one more tiny piece of evidence. Her head pounding and the blood singing in her ears, she grabbed her briefcase and ran back up the stairs with it. She stopped half-way up. 'Where's Harry?' she demanded.

'In his play-pen – in the kitchen.'

Claire clumped back down the stairs and into the kitchen, hoisted Harry up under her arm and carted him upstairs with her. She wasn't going to leave her son with some nutso psycho pamphlet-distributing Swedish babe who was helping to drug her, maybe conspiring with Ben to poison her. Not for one more second. Let her stew over her *fiskpinne*, wonder what was going on, worry that she was about to be unmasked!

Claire plonked Harry and her briefcase down on her bed, snapped open her briefcase and took out *Sweden For Voyagers*. She flipped anxiously through its various sections, trying to find '*brollopsdag*', or just *brollops*, since she knew that *dag* was 'day'. The book was organized into what the authors must have thought were handy reference sections: At the Doctor; The Beauty Parlour; Shopping; Making Friends. She looked through the Bs in each section, finding only *bockling* (pickled herring), *blomkal* (cauliflower), *busshallplats* (bus stop) and *brost* (breast). She tossed it back into her briefcase and snapped the lock shut. Intrigued, Harry started tugging on the handle of the case, trying to open it again. Claire chewed on her lower lip, watching him, her muddled brain trying to process what she'd discovered so far. She needed that word . . . Gosta! She could call Gosta for a quick translation. She'd pencilled his number in the address book she kept in her bedside table.

'Gosta, hi. It's Claire Cunningham.' She tried to sound natural and pleasant. 'I'm here with some friends and we're arguing about the meaning of a Swedish word. It's a silly debate, really, but I was wondering if you could help. Brita's gone out for a while, so we can't ask her.'

'And how is she getting along? Happy to be back with you? Settling in again?' Claire could hear him sucking on his pipe, anticipating a gossipy chat. It was unusual for doctors to smoke, she suddenly thought. Come to think of it, it was unusual for doctors to be home in the middle of the afternoon, and unheard of for surgeons. He'd been home the day she went to get Brita, too, a Monday.

'I'm surprised to find you at home,' she said casually.

'Sorry?'

'Why aren't you in the OR? In surgery?'

'Why?' Gosta chuckled. 'Is there some part of me you think requires cutting out?'

'I mean – you were home the day I came over to get Brita – you're home now. Why aren't you in the OR?' Her voice was shrill.

'Because I work at home.'

'What? On your kitchen table? With bread knives? Nobody does surgery at home!'

'Surgery? My dear girl, I'm not a surgeon.'

'You're not a micro-surgeon?'

'I work with micro-computers. That's about as close as I get to micro-surgery. I'm a consultant.' He paused. 'That's why I work at home.'

Claire nodded, not even surprised any more. 'Had you ever met me before that day I came to get Brita?'

'No . . . that is, I don't think so. More's the pity, as they say.'

'And *brollopsdag*. What does that mean, in English?'

'I'm sorry? Your accent – I don't mean to be critical – it's nice to hear someone try to speak our language—'

'Cut the crap, Gosta. What does it mean? *Brollopsdag*?'

There was a pause, a click as he tapped the receiver with the stem of his pipe. Claire could tell he was squirming, not wanting to answer, but she already knew the answer. She felt hot acid saliva, slightly sweetish, collecting in the corners of her mouth – that telltale sign that she was about to vomit.

'Wedding day,' he said, finally. '*Brollopsdag* is the wedding day.'

Claire put down the receiver. Through the bedroom window, she could see the Home-Buddy truck pulling up to the house. Then, incredibly, Ben's car turned into the driveway. She took a deep breath, fighting back the nausea, picked Harry up and hugged him to her. It was time to start kicking butt at 67 Pine Beach Road.

25

In Sweden, spring begins on 30 April, celebrated by the Feast of Valborg, known in English as Walpurgis Night. This occasion is often marked by large community bonfires and what is generally known as hell-raising.

So when did Ben have the time to carry on this affair? That was the most intriguing question. Did he squeeze it in after rounds, between his call schedule, his ORs, seminars and Brita's duties with Harry? It didn't seem possible: he couldn't even get time off for a haircut. Or so he told Claire. She pictured Harry dropping off to sleep for his afternoon nap – then Brita paging Ben, using some secret code they'd agreed upon to signal that the coast was clear: the baby asleep; the old *satkaring* gone, back behind her desk, safely stranded in her office tower, pushing papers around. Ben would then spring into action, yank off his surgical mask, hustle out of the operating theatre, leaving his patient anaesthetized, partially sutured, while he, with his hands of the gods, dashed home for a quickie with his son's nanny. Maybe they wouldn't even wait for Harry to fall asleep. Maybe they would let him watch!

'Claire! Come back here!' Ben burst through the front door as she struggled to release the safety brake on Harry's stroller. She'd never got around to replacing the Perego, so she was now obliged to try to manoeuvre the heavy upholstered one, 'the Cadillac of strollers', according to Storkland – with its complicated series of levers, clamps and release buttons that always confounded her. It was a gift from Christine – a showy, demonstrative outpouring of affection for new baby Harry. Claire hated the stroller. Not only was it almost impossible to open up, fold down and get going, but it had a twisted, sadistic mind of its own once it was going: each wheel rolling along independently of the others, wobbling and wavering in all directions, a nightmare to steer and control. If anyone had stopped her and asked why she didn't just load Harry into her car and drive away, it might have saved her a lot of aggravation at that moment. But nobody did. Brita stood in the front window watching, twisting a lock of blonde hair between her fingers. In fact, everyone on Pine Beach Road was probably watching, but Claire didn't care.

'Just give me a chance to explain!' Ben pleaded, bounding down the porch steps.

'There's no possible explanation that won't make me *sick*! So save your breath. My lawyer will be in touch with your lawyer.' She continued to struggle with the brake, panicky and perspiring, finally giving up on it and half pushing, half dragging the stroller down the driveway. Harry was bundled up in a jacket, his hat with the ear-flaps, several blankets. The day was fresh and windy, but not actually cold. 'Leave me alone!' She shook Ben's hand off her arm. 'You hideous bigamist! I might even call the police.'

'I am not a bigamist.'

'You got some other word for a guy who's married to two women?'

'I'm not married to two women.'

'Oh? Then you're divorced. That's a relief. I feel so much better knowing that you hired your ex-wife to look after my baby!'

'Our baby.'

'Get out of my way.'

'Where do you think you're going?'

'I don't know – away from you is all I care about right now.' She'd thrown a few of Harry's clothes, dramatically, into his diaper bag, before picking him up and struggling out the door with him, as Ben and Brita watched in shocked silence.

'I never married Brita,' he protested.

Claire laughed shrilly. 'Okay, I get it now. She just thinks you married her, is that it? You went through some phoney form of marriage with her – some *brollops* – to make her believe you had married her. Well, that makes it all better. Now shove off.' She gave the brake a hearty kick which somehow, surprisingly, released it, then started wheeling Harry quickly up the steep and hilly Pine Beach Road, her thighs protesting vehemently, heading towards Queen. She would have preferred an escape to the beach to clear her head and try to think about what to do next, but remembered, as she was trying to yank the heavy stroller out the back door and on to the deck, that they no longer had a backyard and there was no access to the beach or boardwalk. The Home-Buddy man – a pleasant fellow named Eb or Zeb – was still squelching around in their basement, and the excavators were due to arrive any minute. Claire no longer cared about any of it. All she wanted was to take Harry and run away, turn her back on the whole mess, leave it for Ben and his real wife to deal with.

'I never married her and I never pretended to marry her,' Ben panted, puffing along beside her.

'Then why does it say *wedding day* on the back of that damn picture?' Claire's voice was rising towards hysteria. 'You and her on a bench – all kissy-faced and pie-eyed. And she's holding a goddamn bridal bouquet! You expect me to believe you weren't married? How stupid do you think I am? You thought I'd never find that picture – but I did, right behind that innocent St Lucia photo she's always dragging around. *Brollopsdag!* It says that right on the back! Angelholm! Hello. Does that ring a bell?'

'Can't we stop for a minute and talk?'

'No!'

'At least slow down then, just so you can hear what I have to say. That isn't Brita, in that picture – that isn't her in any of them. If you weren't working so hard to find a reason to break up our marriage, you'd realize it couldn't be her. The girl in that wedding picture is twenty-four. I was in Angelholm in 1985 and 1986, Claire. Brita was only seventeen.' Claire stopped abruptly, her quadriceps screaming with pain. 'It's her sister,' Ben said, shamefaced, 'in those photos.'

'Her *twin* sister?'

'Her older sister, actually. But they look a lot alike. Looked, I should say.'

'You married Brita's *sister*?' Claire shrieked.

Ben puffed out his cheeks, then let his breath go with an exasperated sigh. 'It actually gets a bit more complicated than that – if you want to hear it.'

'I'll bet. I'll just bet it does. I bet it's a doozy. A dilly.' Claire started pushing the stroller again, then, as they crossed Queen Street, struggled to jerk and pull it over the bumps of the street-car tracks.

'Let me help you with that thing.'

'Get lost.'

'Harry's getting whiplash. Look at the way his head's hanging over the side.'

'He loves it. He loves a rough ride. And that's what he's had since the day he was born, thanks to you and your philandering. Don't you touch him! And I don't want to hear any more, you lunatic! You must be out of your mind. You think I should be relieved because you married some Swedish nymphet – some underwear model – and then hired her *clone* to look after our baby? And what happened to this wife of yours? Did you kill her with a drug overdose too? Or did she get a lethal injection? You were the silver medallist in med school – a scientist – you should be able to figure out what to inject that wouldn't leave any traces. What was wrong with her anyway that you had to get rid of her? Did she just get too *old* for you?'

'What are you talking about?' Ben was running his hands through his hair. 'What drugs?'

'Those sleeping pills – you prescribed a double dose. Two tablets. It's enough to fell a horse. That's what the pharmacist said. *Fell a horse.* Those were his exact words. How handy for you. Keeping the old nag knocked out so you could frolic around in bed with your ex-wife's clone. In the next goddamn room! In the house that I'm paying for! I'm the bread-winner here!' Her voice resonated unpleasantly in her head. She could feel the big artery popping out in her temple. Her vision was blurring. Maybe she was going to 'stroke out', as Ben would say, right there in the middle of the sidewalk. Would he even try to resuscitate her? He would probably just grab Harry and make a run for it, leaving her sputtering and spinning spastically on the ground as the life ebbed out of her. She took a deep breath. She couldn't let that happen; she owed it to Harry to protect him from this monster in surgical greens who was his father.

'Would you please stop calling her that? My *ex-wife's clone*? There is no ex-wife.'

'So how did you pop her off?' Despite her sneering, swaggering bravado, Claire felt a tingle of fear. What if he really was a killer? She thought she knew Ben, but she obviously didn't. He hadn't even told her he'd been married before. What else hadn't he told her? 'Never mind. I don't want to know.'

'She drowned – but I had nothing to do with it – not directly. I mean, I didn't conk her over the head with an oar or toss her overboard or anything.'

'Oh God! This keeps getting worse. You're screwing your dead wife's clone. How sick!'

'I'm not screwing anyone!'

'I don't want to hear it. Spare me your confession, if I hear it then you'll have to kill me too. Bigamy is one thing, but you're a murderer. And I'm not going to sit back and let Harry be deprived of his mother!' With a sob, she started to run, legs churning, pounding along Queen Street with Harry, stroller wheels clattering and wobbling madly. She looked wildly around for the police, a telephone. But she couldn't stop to use a telephone. Ben would kidnap Harry if she let go of the stroller for even a second. Maybe she could flag down a passing motorist. Harry was leaning his head back against the plush upholstery, clearly enjoying the pace, oblivious to what was happening behind him.

'I didn't murder Kersti!' Ben shouted, then looked around quickly, afraid someone might have overheard. 'It was an accident. Maybe a suicide. But I wasn't even there. Please stop and listen to me. I may be a fool – an asshole – but I'm not a killer.' Suddenly, he slowed down his pace, no longer running after her. 'Okay, forget it then,' he called after her, 'you don't want to try and understand. So go ahead. Break up our family. But you don't even know why you're doing it.'

Claire walked on for a few yards, then turned to see him standing dejectedly on the sidewalk in front of the Beach Grocery, his hands in his pockets, surgical greens flapping disconsolately around his legs, his dark hair whipped against his forehead by the wind. He had to be very upset. Normally, such a wind would drive him wild – he hated having his hair messed. She slowed down, still looking back at him over her shoulder. She stopped. She was, after all, married to the guy. And it was still daylight – he was unlikely to kill her right there on Queen Street with all the traffic bustling by. And though she was appalled by what she'd heard so far, there was a part of her brain, the salacious, soap-opera-watching, *Cosmopolitan*-reading part, that was dying to hear the rest of his twisted story. She turned the stroller around, took a few steps back. 'I'm not making any promises,' she said, 'about anything. But I suppose I owe it to Harry to at least hear what you've got to say.'

'Can we go inside somewhere? I'm freezing. I didn't have a chance to get a jacket, the way you bolted out the door like that.'

'Only if it's someplace public. A restaurant.'

'You have to promise not to make a scene.'

'I make a scene every time we're in a restaurant. You can't ask me to promise that.'

'Okay. How about Loons?'

'Loons? We had a huge fight in there. On our anniversary. Don't you remember? You had too much wine and started saying that I should take Harry, how he didn't even look like you, and your life would be over if you didn't leave me right then—'

'Okay, you don't have to go on about it, All I remember is that I'd had way too much to drink.'

'So you claim.'

'I'd just come from a stag. It was bad timing.'

'So, where are we going to go?'

'Ap. Appie,' said Harry, pointing joyously at a basket of apples outside the grocer's.

'Did you hear that?' Ben looked down at him in amazement. 'He said apple.'

'Don't change the subject.'

'What about Swiss Chalet?'

Claire turned the stroller around again. 'It's a bit of a hike, but okay.'

'Can I push Harry for a while?'

'No.'

Ben walked along beside her, hands still in the pockets of his greens as they headed west towards Kew Beach. 'You begged me for those sleeping pills. I didn't want to prescribe them for you – I could get in serious trouble with the College. I kept telling you that – you seem to have a selective memory. But it was still better than listening to you clomp up and down the stairs, complaining that you can't sleep, or thrashing around in bed, trying to find those yellow earplugs you're always losing.'

'How would you know what I do in bed? You haven't been there lately.'

'Only because of you. Out of consideration for you.'

'Ha!'

'As for the dosage – I prescribed one half a tablet per night. I don't know where you got the idea you should take two. Look on the bottle. I'm sure it says one half.'

'I can't find the bottle – of course – Brita threw it out.' Was it possible that she'd read ½ as 1–2, Claire wondered.

'And you should never have asked me for sleeping pills anyway. I'm not in psychiatry.'

'This is not a psychiatric problem,' Claire said hotly.

Ben didn't say anything – he just kept walking, looking away down the street, apparently lost in thought.

Claire watched him narrowly. Probably, he was trying to figure out how to weasel out of the mess he was in. She could practically hear the wheels and gears clunking along in his brain, his ready lines for dealing with women who had backed him into a corner spinning like bullets in a pistol chamber, as he tried to decide which to fire first. 'And the only one who would ever describe you as a nag is you,' he added.

'Don't tell me you wouldn't rather have some nubile young woman in your bed. Someone your own age, even.'

'If that's what I wanted, I could pick one up in any bar any night of the week.'

Claire snorted.

'You don't think so? You don't think a thirty-two-year-old guy who walks into a bar and tells the girls he's a year away from becoming a plastic surgeon could get laid? It wouldn't take more than thirty seconds.'

'Oh yeah?' Claire couldn't think of anything more clever to retort, especially as they both knew he was right.

'But where am I going to find a quirky, crusty old grimalkin like you?'

'Don't try and flatter me. I'm immune to you, Doctor.'

Swiss Chalet had three red clay-tile steps leading up to a front door under a perky red and white awning. Lined up along the side street, the delivery cars sat waiting, with their fez-like red signs on their roofs.

'You're not going to insist on carrying the stroller up these steps by yourself?' Ben said. 'With your back?'

Claire hesitated for a moment, then stepped aside, allowing him to lift the stroller up into the restaurant, but keeping one hand on it. As soon as they were inside, she busied herself with unpacking Harry – pulling off his hat, fluffing up the bit of blond fuzz on top of his head, taking off his blankets, unzipping his snow-suit. Ben, meanwhile, was already standing at the counter, placing his order. 'I'll have the quarter-chicken dinner,' he told the girl behind the counter, 'no, wait – better make that the half. And can I get extra sauce with that? And a double order of fries? Oh – and a slab of pie and a Diet Coke.' He grinned disarmingly at the girl. 'Got to watch my figure.' Then he struggled to fill both hands with miniature pouches of ketchup while Claire ordered a Diet Coke, not because she wanted one, but because Harry liked to play with the straws and plastic lid, and because she wanted to have it ready in case she had to satisfy the urge to dump something cold and wet all over Ben.

'How can you eat at a time like this?' she demanded, as Ben followed her to a table, balancing the heavy tray. She pulled a high chair for Harry out from the wall, and manoeuvred him into it.

'Time like what?' Ben looked genuinely baffled. 'I'm starving – I haven't eaten a thing all day. We had one case that started at eight this morning and didn't finish till four-thirty.'

'But your family is falling apart, Ben, right under your nose. I will probably leave you – or kick you out – after I hear whatever gruesome confession you have to make. And your stomach is your main concern?' How could he be so thick? How could she impress upon him the enormity of his offence?

'You're kidding, of course.'

Claire stared at him in disgust. Men were incredible. What power they had to just get on with things: essential, basic things like sex, food and sleep, and usually in that order. It was women who became the bulimics, the anorexics, who lay awake all night crying or playing 'I should have said' after a fight. 'Let's just get on with this story of yours,' she sighed.

Ben tore open one of the ketchup pouches with his teeth, stabbed a few french fries with his fork. 'You probably aren't going to like me any better after you hear it. Except that it shows how much I've changed. Matured.' He squeezed a line of ketchup across the fries, then stuffed the whole mess into his mouth. 'Why don't I give Harry a fry? See what he does with it?'

'He's doing fine with those straws, and babies don't need fried food. Come on, talk. I'm waiting.'

'Okay.' More ketchup, more fries. 'As I think I've told you, I had a bit of a drinking problem when I lived in Sweden. No – it was more than that, I have to be honest.' He tore the leg off his half-chicken. 'I got shit-faced almost every night. I was always getting into fights, getting laid.'

'Basically having a great time.'

'Basically. Though you've got to understand how much of it was peer group pressure. Though I know I have to take full responsibility for my actions. I do know that. But you have to imagine the circumstances, put all of this into the proper context. Okay?' He raised an eyebrow, waiting for Claire's grudging nod before continuing. He smeared some sauce over the chicken leg and bit into it. 'Anyway, there were a couple of times I know I went too far. I remember waking up one morning in a ditch in Germany, covered with mud, with the autobahn whizzing over my head. Maybe that was a pretty standard type of event, come to think of it. But the day I got married – that's another story. I didn't want to get married – I don't even remember doing it. I didn't even want to stay in Sweden. Who wants to work their whole life for a little apartment, a colour TV, maybe a cottage somewhere, and pay seventy-five per cent income tax? I told Kersti I didn't want to get married. I told her I couldn't stay there. But she was never going to leave Sweden – she had no interest in Canada or the States. Unlike her baby sister.'

'So this Kersti person got you drunk and took advantage of you, is that it? Slapped a marriage licence on you when you weren't looking?'

'Sounds stupid but that's basically it. They make this home-brew over there – it's kind of like a gut-rot vodka. Called *hembrant*. She couldn't have afforded to get me drunk in a bar. It took a lot of booze back in those days, and drinking in Sweden is very expensive, as I've told you. And then her kid sister – Brita – who was always coming on to me and who really wanted to get out of Sweden, away from her parents—' He shook his head, sighing. His appetite, however, soldiered on. He stripped the rest of the meat from the drumstick, then hunkered down to attack the breast with the plastic knife and fork. 'I don't think you want to hear this, come to think of it.'

'Oh, that's where you're wrong. I'm completely intrigued.'

'She – Brita – who was only seventeen at the time . . .' He hesitated. 'Well, basically, I was drunk, as usual. It was after a good game. I was feeling no pain. Kersti had to go out somewhere, to see some friend of hers who'd just broken up with her boyfriend. Anyway, one thing led to another, as they say.'

'Doesn't it always?'

'And the next thing I knew, Brita and I were in the sack.'

Claire nodded. 'I see. Well, that makes everything all right then, doesn't it? You actually hired your Swedish lover – mistress – who happens to look exactly like your ex-wife, but is actually a lot younger – to come over here and be our *nanny*.' Her voice was on the rise again. 'And you made me pay a thousand-dollar agency fee for the privilege!'

'You said you wouldn't make a scene.'

'I said no such thing!'

'Scoring was all that mattered over there, both on and off the ice. But I never really wanted anything to do with Brita.'

'Until you married me and I had Harry.'

'Can I finish telling you what happened?' He gave her a hurt look. 'I'm getting to the really sickening part of the story.'

'Do you expect me to feel *sorry* for you?'

'As it turned out, Brita got pregnant. Though I still don't think it was mine – the baby. And, this is the worst part—'

'How could it possibly get worse?'

'Brita got an abortion. They're easy enough to get in Sweden. But for some reason, she had to tell Kersti what happened. They never really got along, those two – they were always at each other. It used to drive me nuts. Anyway, they had a huge fight one day, I can't remember about what, Brita wearing Kersti's clothes or something. And Brita told her. About the baby.' He looked up at Claire mournfully. 'Kersti got on a boat going over to Denmark, got loaded over there, and either fell or jumped overboard on the way back over to Helsingborg.' He sighed. He'd stopped eating finally, either because he was too upset or full. 'Anyway, Kersti drowned that night. That's about all there is to tell.' He leaned his head back against the red plastic banquette, pressing his lips together, eyes closed, waiting for her verdict. There was a smear of Chalet sauce on his chin.

'This is so ghastly, so horrible—' Claire said.

'You can imagine how Brita and I felt – still feel – about what happened. It was our fault – both of our faults – that Kersti died. It's why I almost never drink any more. I can't remember the last time I got really drunk.'

'I do. It was our anniversary.'

'That stag. I don't really know what happened there. But I don't remember saying those things I'm supposed to have said.'

'Well, before I take Harry and walk out of your life for ever, perhaps you could explain to me what exactly you thought you were doing by bringing Brita over here.'

'I didn't bring her over. She got here on her own. I hadn't heard from her for five years but she called the med school and found out what hospital I was at. She knew I'd gone into medicine – I got accepted while I was over there in Sweden.'

'So you two decided to get together again and work through your grief, is that it?'

'Actually, I didn't want to see her – she was the last person I ever wanted to see again. In fact, I didn't like Brita much. I never liked her in Sweden and I liked her a lot less when I heard her voice on the phone, that day she had me paged.'

'So why didn't you tell her to get lost?'

Harry was kicking fitfully in the high chair, bored with his bent straws. Claire went over to the counter to get him some plastic spoons, then sat him down on the banquette beside her.

'She wanted a job. She had to get one before her visa ran out. They were going to kick her out of the country. She didn't say so exactly, but I got the impression she was in a mood to tell you all about my sordid past if I didn't do something to help her out.'

'So you hired an extortionist to look after Harry?'

'She never threatened me. She never went that far.'

'Sounds like she didn't have to.'

• Sylvia Mulholland

'And for all her faults, I knew she'd be good with Harry. If I seriously thought she was a psycho, I wouldn't have let her anywhere near him. And she has been good with him – we have to give her that. She only wanted to stay for a year, she had all sorts of plans for going to the States. She'd been getting too involved in that separatist movement – her parents thought she should get away from certain influences over there. She had a letter to me from them. They're good people. I thought I was helping them too. After the way I wrecked their family, it sort of eased my own guilt about Kersti. I thought she'd be out of our hair soon and you'd never need to know about what happened in Sweden. And we'd have a good nanny for Harry for a while.'

'Did you have to make me pay an agency for her?'

'If she'd just shown up on our doorstep, out of the blue, I knew you'd be suspicious. But she was signed up with an agency – it seemed legitimate that way.'

'What a fool you are.'

'Fool, yes. But I have no attraction to her, believe me, and I never did. I admit I kind of liked having her around here at first. She always flattered me, and it was good to talk about old times a bit, catch up on what everyone I knew back in Sweden was doing. But I was getting nervous, especially when she started coming on to me again, around Christmas. But then she had that big fight with your mother and left on her own.'

'And you told me to get her back!'

'At first I thought we'd have to. I was worried that she'd be mad enough to call you up and tell you the whole story, just out of spite. I didn't want to risk it. Look at the stakes. I could have lost you, lost Harry. Still could, I guess.' He looked down at their son, babbling happily on the banquette. 'But then time went on, we hired other nannies and we didn't hear from Brita. I thought maybe she'd gone back to Sweden. I didn't really care where she went – I just hoped she was out of my life for good. But then you had to go and get her back. I couldn't believe it. But we had such bad luck with those others, I didn't see how I could convince you not to. It would have looked too suspicious. But then the basement flooded and there she was upstairs, suddenly, right next to our room. We had a big fight that night. I told her to back off. She was going to be trouble. I would have had to tell you all of this anyway, even if you hadn't found that picture. All you can really fault me for is my past – that I didn't tell you I was married before. Other than that, I'm clean. Lots of people have things in their past they don't necessarily want anyone to know about.'

'How about the fact that you and Brita were lovers? Doesn't that count in your book?'

'No. Not really. Maybe to you, but it doesn't to me. It didn't mean anything. It was a stupid thing I did when I was too drunk to think about what I was doing. You don't understand the hockey-player mentality. Back in those days anyway.'

'I see. It would have been a loss of face, would it, to pass on such an opportunity? Of making it with your sister-in-law.'

'Except that I never wanted to get married. You're forgetting that.'

'Is that supposed to make a difference?' She glared at him.

'I'm a desperate man – grasping at straws, just like Harry here. What can I say? I'm sinking fast.'

'And what about your other lies? Your pal, Gosta. He's no micro-surgeon, is he? He's not even a doctor. And I never met him before.'

'He's just a guy Brita and I knew, back in Sweden. He's an old friend of Brita's family.'

Claire looked helplessly out through the plate-glass window of the restaurant. Was this the way to end a marriage? In the hot, close atmosphere of Swiss Chalet, the air thick with the smell of fried chicken? Harry was struggling to get down from the banquette now, his overalls bunching up around his knees. He had spied the large potted plant beside their booth. 'We left her alone in the house – Brita.' Claire put a restraining arm around Harry.

'I have a feeling she won't be there when we get back.'

'And the Home-Buddy man – we left him there in the basement.'

'Maybe they'll run off together.'

'I guess I'll have to count the silver.'

'She wouldn't steal anything. Her parents are very well off. She didn't even need a job. Not for the money. She just wanted to get her landed immigrant status. Look, I don't want you to leave –

or throw me out. But I guess, seeing all this from your point of view . . .'

'It's pretty hard to want to have you around.'

'Although I am a good dad.'

'When you show up.'

'I've almost finished this residency. Things'll get better.'

'You've been telling me that for years.'

'They will. I'll have more regular hours. I think I might even have a job already, at St Mike's.'

St Mike's? Claire thought about its dim narrow corridors, flaking paint, the row of pawn shops across the street. It was the grand old dame of hospitals, lately victimized by a number of hasty additions, quick and thoughtless renovations. 'Is that really where you see yourself?'

'Well, it's not the States. We can stay in Canada. You can keep working, if you want to. I thought you'd be pleased.' He hesitated. 'I just hope you aren't going to do anything hasty.'

'I don't know what I'm going to do. If it wasn't for Harry . . .'

'I admit I made a mistake.'

'A mistake? One?'

'Okay, a number of mistakes. But I'm not a lost cause. I've learned a lot since then. I've learned how important my family is to me.'

Claire got up to catch Harry, who had already thrown two fistfuls of soil from the plant over the quarry tile floor, and was digging in for more. As she pulled him away from it, freeing the soil from his hands, he began to howl, thrashing furiously, wanting to get back into the dirt. With a lot of effort, she managed to carry him back to the table, thinking about life as a single mother. Where no one would be coming home, ever, to help her with Harry, play with him, or talk to her, about anything. Ben would have his visitation rights, of course. She pictured him pulling up in the driveway (she would still be in 67 Pine Beach Road) in his Lamborghini, some good-looking babe in the front seat beside him, to whisk Harry away for the weekend to God only knew where. That is, if Ben stayed in Canada. If he moved to the States, she would have to let him have Harry for summer vacations, alternate Christmases. Thousands of miles away.

'So, what was it you got Brita for Christmas?' Claire suddenly asked.

Ben seemed to perk up. 'It was a bottle of hair dye. Brown. I told her it was to dye her roots. To look more North American.' He chuckled. 'I don't expect you can see the humour in it, but then, you never lived in Sweden. Some of those girls would kill to be American.'

Claire busied herself by struggling with a squirming Harry, getting him back into his jacket, straightening out the blankets in his stroller, at the same time contemplating various acts of revenge she could take against Ben. She could cut up his suits, she supposed, though he only had one – the one she'd bought him for their wedding, but it would be months before he noticed it was missing, and he likely wouldn't care even when he did. That was the type of vengeful act more appropriate for the wife of a well-dressed businessman like Rick Durham. It would be better to get Ben where it really hurt: slice up his medical texts with a razor-blade, neatly removing essential paragraphs and illustrations, or reorganize his slides. Maybe she could pull the drawstrings out of all of his surgical greens so that the pants fell down when he wore them. No, she decided, he would probably like that. And so would the nurses. Better to knot up the fingers of his latex gloves; smear petroleum jelly all over his precious loops – those expensive magnifying eyeglasses he used for microsurgery. She zipped up Harry's jacket, tugged his hat down into place, feeling better for her childish fantasies. 'Are you going to eat your pie?' she said to Ben.

'You can have it.'

'I don't want it.'

'Well . . .' He looked at her, his brown eyes questioning. 'Maybe I should take it home with us then.'

'Well, maybe you should. For the time being, anyway.'

26 ∫

Claire was sitting at her desk, feet up on the cardboard box of dead files under it. Her credit cards were spread out in front of her, fan-shaped, like a losing hand that she – always a lousy gambler – had just slapped down in defeat. She took a pair of scissors from the top drawer of her desk. The Canadian Tire card would be the easiest; she would start with it. The scissors flashed in the sun that streamed through her windows, from between the office towers that blocked her view of the lake. The red and white halves of the plastic card landed in the garbage pail, clattering on to the cover of *Sweden For Voyagers*.

She scanned the remaining cards. Royal flush? Full house? She was trying to decide which should be the next to go. Sears. She hardly ever shopped at Sears. She hesitated. Except sometimes for kids' stuff – diaper pails and what-not. Maybe Sears would be the one to keep, out of all of them. She put the blue and white card to one side and picked up Victoria's Secret. She positioned her scissors across it, closed her eyes and snipped straight through the fine gold line that separated its black top half from its deep coral bottom. Somewhere inside her head, her Dresser gasped.

Snipping up credit cards was quite the satisfying experience. Claire could get addicted to the practice, she thought. She almost wished she had a few more.

She spread out the remaining cards, rearranged them. Mastercard was next; then American Express. A pair. She didn't even have to think about those two. Amex had always irritated her. What good was a credit card that you had to pay off every month? You might as well not have one at all. And Mastercard didn't give out any special bonuses, perks or presents to thank a person for using it. Claire liked to see some tangible reward for over-spending. The four gold pieces of plastic card landed in the garbage pail on top of the others.

'Now, just wait a minute here!' her Dresser cried, dry-mouthed with panic. 'Have you lost your mind? That Mastercard had a twelve-thousand-dollar limit!'

Pushing her aside, Claire picked up Neiman Marcus.

'Not Neiman Marcus! They'll stop sending you those fabulous catalogues! Stop! Don't do it.'

Claire tipped the card this way and that, studying its seductive glint. It was silver, with the store name in its distinctive white cursive. They'd insulted her by not giving her a gold card – it was a rush issue, on the spot, while she was in the Washington Galleria store. But still, they should have coughed up a gold. She turned the card over. 'Welcome to the world of Neiman Marcus', it said on the back. 'This card is your passport to a unique and memorable shopping experience.'

'Passport,' Claire snorted. 'Well then, *bon voyage*.' She took up her scissors again. 'Or should I say, *farval*?'

Her Dresser let out a strangled sob. 'Please, this is a knife in my heart.'

That left only Sears, the gold Aeroplan Visa that gave an air-mile point for each dollar spent. And Holt Renfrew. High card.

'No, not Holt Renfrew!' her Dresser shrieked. 'Are you insane? Stop and think about what you're doing! Do I have to get down on my knees?

'Holt Renfrew.' Claire tried saying it in a number of different ways, trying out a few accents, rolling her r's, flexing her scissors.

'But think of all the sales on right now. Think what you might be able to pick up for summer!' her Dresser cried. 'At least wait for the fall merchandise to come in.'

Claire hesitated, flicked a bit of lint from the blade of the scissors, sighed. 'Nice try,' she said. 'I always admired your chutzpah.' She snipped through the card, then decided to finish off the Sears card while she was at it. Put it out of its misery. Slow lingering deaths were unpleasant for everyone.

Inside her head, her Dresser keeled over: tits up, toes curled, like the Wicked Witch of the West. Black wisps of smoke rose from the frazzled tips of her Enzo Angiolini leather basket-weave flats.

That left only the Visa, widely recognized, universally accepted. Wild card. What if she had an emergency? A car accident, running out of gas, getting stuck on the expressway in a blinding snowstorm? How would she pay the towing service? The emergency repair? Her Journey's End motel bill? She held up the card. It was becoming an uncomfortable exercise, now that she was down to the short strokes. 'It is essential to amputate the diseased limbs to ensure the survival and health of the entire body,' she finally said.

'Cure the disease and kill the patient.' It was a faint cry, barely audible. Her Dresser was struggling, valiantly, to rise again from the ashes, like the only-pretend-dead villain near the end of a bad movie.

'What did you say?' Claire frowned.

'I said your meeting starts in five minutes. They're all up there waiting for you.' Davina was standing in the doorway of her office, polished heels together, diary and pen poised. 'May I cross it off your calendar? I assume you'll be attending.'

'Right.' Claire slid the gold Visa back into her wallet and sighed. 'The Ukrainian situation. God. Why do they have to keep using that ghastly euphemism? The man has a name, for Christ's sake.'

'Maybe it's too politically hot.'

'Yes. That makes me feel a lot better.'

'Look on the bright side – it's the end of the day, end of the week.'

'End of my career.' Claire dug her leather-bound folio out from under a teetering pile of papers. The folio was a gift from Simon, who'd once believed in her future as a (highly paid) advocate. She pulled the Law Society's letter out from under her desk blotter. 'They'll be wanting to discuss this too, no doubt,' she said, shoving it into her folio. 'So where's this meeting?'

'Main boardroom.'

'That's the biggest boardroom we've got. Why is it in there?'

'Search me,' Davina shrugged.

Claire gave her a peeved look as she headed out of her office and proceeded down the corridor. The main boardroom could seat twenty-four people; if the walls were moved back, forty. She'd expected Potochnik, Rick Durham, a couple of the boys from Exec. But there was no way they needed a boardroom that big. Unless the whole Convocation of the Law Society was planning on attending. Or the Discipline Committee. Or maybe Exec was just hoping to intimidate Potochnik by the scale of the firm, the grandeur of the boardroom. If that's what they had in mind, they were dreaming. Scale and grandeur would only piss him off more.

Shelagh was suddenly behind her, catching up with long strides, her arms full of files, a pen stuck horizontally, like a Spanish dancer's rose, between her teeth. 'Hear you fired your gorgeous Swedish nanny,' she said around her pen.

'Bad news travels fast,' Claire said. 'It only happened yesterday.'

'Yeah, well, that's life in the collector lanes.' She let the pen drop on to her pile of files.

'We would have fired her, but she was already gone.'

'So who've you got now? Who's home with the kid?'

'Ben, for a few days at least. We were hoping to start interviewing tonight. But I've called three agencies and they don't seem to have anyone right now for us to see. The nanny bank seems to have dried up since Immigration tightened the requirements for domestics.'

'You had a bad run last month, didn't you? And all those problems with your house too. Is the City paying for any of that?'

'Some, but not enough,' Claire sighed. 'They'll clear out the condoms, at least.'

'What condoms?'

'From the water filtration plant.'

Shelagh nodded. 'That's the Beach for you. And to think they wanted to turn that plant into some kind of tourist attraction. Do they know what made the sewers back up into your house?'

'They're not sure, but cloth diapers probably had something to do with it. The washing-machine was full of lint, and the crap wasn't draining out properly. I guess Brita never bothered to rinse the diapers before she washed them. So the City doesn't want to pay for that part of the damage. And the retaining wall collapsed because it wasn't put in properly. Basically, it just slid away into the sand. Ben wants to sue the Proctors – the people who owned the house before us – but we'll never find them. They've moved several times apparently. Probably skipped the country.'

'Bummer.' Shelagh looked thoughtful, snapping her gum. She had recently had a tiny device surgically implanted behind her ear to help her quit smoking. But she claimed it made her hallucinate, mostly at night, giving her out-of-body experiences that she really didn't need. 'Listen, I don't want to butt in, but I might know someone who's looking for a nanny job. Local girl. She's a niece of my brother, but it's not like we're really related. I mean, I wouldn't be pissed if you fired her – if she turned out to be a dud.'

'Sure,' Claire said hopelessly, 'give her my number. We'll talk to her.'

'Might save you another agency fee.'

Claire stopped in front of the main boardroom door and turned to Shelagh. 'Well,' she sighed, 'this is my stop.'

'You're in the big meeting?' Shelagh was obviously surprised.

'In it? I'm the star attraction.'

'Really? So what did you do to deserve that?'

'It's a long story. You don't want to know.'

'That's where you're wrong,' Shelagh called over her shoulder. 'Talk to me when you get out.'

Incredibly, as she stood outside the double oak-panelled doors of the boardroom, Claire thought she could hear music. A tinkly, spunky little tune. Played on – a bandura? She pushed open the door and the music swelled. She wasn't prepared for it, or for the carnival atmosphere in the room. On the long granite table was a *smorgasbord* of cold foods: ham, tongue, stuffed eggs, pickled mushrooms, sauerkraut, sardines and caviar. A huge wall map of Eastern Europe had been put up, and Ukrainian knick-knacks were everywhere: embroidered pillows, decorated Easter eggs, carved wooden boxes. Two women dressed in Ukrainian national costume – embroidered blouses, flowers wreathed around their heads, coloured ribbons streaming down their backs, with dazzling white aprons over their flowered skirts – were circulating around the room, pushing food on everyone, urging them to eat, saying '*Proshu*,' and '*Na zdorovya*.' The firm's cleaning lady and coffee hostess. Everyone else in the room Claire also recognized – at least Rick had had the good sense not to invite the Law Society to witness this madness. They were all lawyers of Bragg, Banks and Biltmore – about a dozen altogether. The only outsider was Mike Potochnik. Had they all gone bonkers? Is this what it took to sweeten client relations that had soured? Was Potochnik such a threat? Had she screwed up that badly?

'Claire!' Rick bounded over to greet her. '*Khrystos rodyvsa!*' He held out a broad warm palm, took her hand in both of his, pumped it.

'Pardon?' Claire said.

'He's a little confused with the greetings – my friend Roman,' Potochnik called over from where he was standing by the buffet, loading his plate with pyrizhky. 'His Ukrainian is a bit rusty. But we'll fix that.'

'Rick,' Claire said, dazed, 'not Roman.' She smiled slightly so that Mike wouldn't think he was being criticized.

Rick was giving her one of his earnest looks, still gripping her hand. 'No, Mike's right. It is actually Roman – Roman Durko. I changed it early in my career – during law school – I'm ashamed to admit. Look around, Claire,' he said. 'There's Alexander Spears.'

'Anton Stachiw,' said Alexander.

'And Dan Evans,' Rick pointed, 'really Demyd Ewasiuk. All of us in this room – look around – Ukrainians all.'

'This is a joke, right?'

'No joke.'

'You're all changing your names back?'

'Not officially, no. It would be a massive amount of paperwork. The Rolls of the Law Society would have to be changed and all that bureaucratic stuff. It's like going to Rome for a Papal decree. Come on over here, have some zakuska.' He took her elbow and steered her towards the buffet. 'We're just letting it be known, generally, that we have roots in the Old Country.'

'Have some of the pickled herring,' Potochnik said, 'they're not half bad.'

Claire looked at him suspiciously. 'So why are you here?

Suddenly so buddy-buddy with all of these Bay Street law-yers?'

'Why?' he said, flushing, the scar on his cheek glowing. 'Because I've offered your firm an incredible deal, that's why.'

'Mike has decided to open a chicken franchise in Kiev,' Rick said excitedly. 'Eastern Europe – the final frontier. We're going to do the master franchise agreement, the property leasing, register his trade-mark.' He looked pointedly at Claire.

'Chicken Kiev. Am I right? It's too descriptive.'

'So, you'll help him find another name. Some of the work will be *pro bono*, of course, given what Mike's been through with our firm recently.'

'And don't look so shocked, Claire Wolaniuk. You tried to buy me off with a janitorial job. Now here I am, a major client of the firm. A big boy.'

'I told you that we might be able to use you in information systems. Nobody said anything about janitorial.' She turned to Rick. 'It's a great idea, this chicken chain,' she said care-fully.

'And Mike will function as a bridge between two cultures – east and west. He was born over there. They actually had storks nesting on their roof – a thatched roof. Can you believe it?' Rick laughed with delight. 'He'll be doing all the hiring, the property scouting, get everything computerized. He's a computer genius, did he tell you?'

'Basically,' Claire nodded. 'He mentioned that.' She studied Rick, then Mike. 'So, apart from getting Mike a trade-mark—'

'In English *and* Cyrillic. In all fifteen republics—'

'That's right,' Rick added. 'He isn't going to limit his chain to the Ukraine. He wants to expand into Khazakistan, Uzbekistan . . . The Baltics. And Mike's going to be our man in Moscow, too. We might even open an office over there.'

'So, what does all this have to do with me?'

'Nothing directly, but you might read your mail occasion-ally. The Law Society gave you ten days to respond to their letter. Fortunately, Mike had copied Exec on his complaint, and we approached him on an informal basis, to see if we could work something out, settle this grievance against you. We were surprised – and pleased – when he told us about his plans, and that he was willing to use our firm. And he agreed to withdraw his complaint, which he certainly was not obliged to do.'

'It's only temporarily withdrawn,' Potochnik said, 'I reserve my right to re-activate the letter.' The room rippled with congenial courtesy laughter.

'Mike represents our foothold in Eastern Europe,' Rick said, 'and Ukraine is perfect – the heart, the bread basket. He's giving us a pile of work. Every firm on Bay Street is trying to get in on the act. What do you think the hottest-selling Berlitz language course is these days?'

'And I guess every firm has its full complement of newly revealed Ukrainians,' Claire said.

'Not just Ukrainians. Estonians, Azerbaijanis. You name it.'

Claire picked up a plate, selected a stuffed egg, a couple of pickled herring, spooned on some cold beet salad. 'Well, well,' she said.

'We would actually like you to think about going over there with Mike. Just to help him set things up. You two go back a long way, I understand.'

'Pardon? I'm not sure I heard what you said.'

'We want you to think about going over there. Temporarily, of course. It would only be for a few months – a year at most.'

'You want to ship me off to Siberia?'

'Who said anything about Siberia?'

'You know what I mean.'

'Kiev is a very westernized city, Claire.'

'Since when?'

'It would be a fantastic opportunity for you, and the firm would remunerate you very well.'

'But I don't even speak Ukrainian.'

'None of us do. But you, like us, have a natural advantage.'

'Look, Rick—'

'Roman.'

'I can't go over there. I have a baby. My husband's still in training.'

'Yes,' said Potochnik, 'there is the husband to consider. He's a very persuasive man, your Ben.' He smiled thinly. 'Like a Treblinka guard.'

'How do you know Ben?'

'Let's just say we've had words.'

'When? When did you have words?'

'Not important for purposes of this discussion.'

Claire looked at him with distaste. A year abroad with Mike Potochnik? In a cramped and dingy office with no telephone? She and Mike lining up together, every morning, in the grey Kiev dawn, to buy toilet paper? Knowing him, he'd make her do it for both of them. And where would Harry be while she was trudging the streets of Kiev? Who did they suppose would look after him? She looked anxiously around the room at the Bragg and Banks partners.

'I know it's a big step, with many arrangements to be made. Just say you'll think about it,' Rick said.

'Somebody's got to do it,' Alexander looked critically over the jellied veal tongue, then dug into the holubtsi.

Claire smiled weakly and nodded as she stabbed a piece of herring with her fork.

Half an hour later, she closed the boardroom doors behind her, over boisterous shouts of *Na zdorovya!* as the others cracked open the Ukrainian vodka and began enthusiastically toasting each other, at the same time arguing energetically about whether Moscow or Kiev would be their best bet for setting up a law office. At least they hadn't called her *comrade*, she thought.

Rose-marie Schmertz was the name of Shelagh's brother's niece. She had to be overweight, or at least, cheerfully plump, Claire decided, as she went to answer the front door later that night. It just wasn't possible for someone named Rose-marie Schmertz to be gaunt, pale and pinched-looking. But it wasn't Rose-marie who stood on their front porch, holding the collar of her Burberry closed to keep out the evening air, and looking around her with mild disapproval. It was Christine.

'What are you doing here?' Claire said.

'Don't act so glad to see me.'

'Of course I'm glad.' Claire held the door open for her. 'I'm just surprised.'

'What's that ghastly noise?' Christine stepped gingerly into the hallway.

'It's the excavators, in the yard. A backhoe loader, to be exact. Lately I've been picking up all sorts of useless information like that.'

'Right, Mother told me – something about a flood in your cellar.'

'Basement.'

Christine made her way into the living-room, took off her coat and draped it over the arm of the chesterfield. She looked around edgily. 'Where's the little doc?'

'Out on the deck with Harry. Watching the digging. Harry loves heavy machinery.'

'Don't talk to me about digging – that's what got me into the mess I'm in.'

'Why? What's going on?'

'Mother hasn't told you? They found a *toe* in the backyard of our place, that's what's going on. A human toe.' She shuddered. 'Actually, the workmen didn't find it, the dog did. And Nita brought it into the house, poor thing. She and the dog.'

'I didn't know you had a dog.'

'A Great Pyrenees – near the top of the doggie-dumbness scale. Of course, no breeder will tell you that. But Nita kept bugging me for a pet, so I gave in. They looked good in the dog book she had.'

'Oh, Christine, that's awful.'

'We gave him away – back to the breeder. Let him rip up their lawn. We're not dog people.'

'I meant about the toe. What did the police say?'

'Police? I didn't call the police. I paid off the workmen to bury it, fill in the backyard again and keep their mouths shut. Then I listed the property for sale. Who do you think would buy it after the whole place was dug up, while the police looked for other body parts? Have you got any cigarettes?'

'I haven't smoked in over five years, Christine.'

'Too bad. I just can't bring myself to actually go out and buy a pack.'

'Nobody but you would think it was too bad that I had quit smoking.'

'You know what I mean.' Christine pinched the skin above her eyebrows, grimacing. 'Shiatsu massage,' she said, 'don't mind me. Could you go out and tell them to stop that noise? It's too late in the day to be pushing dirt around.'

'I like the noise – it's the sound of progress. So what kind of toe was it?'

'Kind? What do you mean what kind?'

'I mean black or white? Male? Female? A big toe?'

'How should I know what kind? I'm no anthropologist. And it's not like I sat around looking at it all day. Really, Claire, I can see I'm going to get about as much sympathy from you as I did from Mother. You know what she said? Why were you excavating to make a bigger swimming-pool? You're not going to need a pool at all. Don't you know there's a new ice age starting? Within one generation the ice will reach as far south as Mexico.' She flopped down on to the chesterfield, exasperated.

'What happened to global warming?'

'I can't believe we're having this conversation,' Christine said.

Claire perched on the edge of the wing-chair, her arms folded. 'I can't believe it either, to tell you the truth. And I can't believe the way you just blow in here, without even a word to me about how I am, or how Harry is or what's going on in my life.'

Christine looked at her in surprise. 'All right. I was getting to all of that. Christ. Give a person a chance.'

'I'm tired of giving you chances. I know I'm never going to hear from you unless you've got some problem or unless you want to show off some new purchase – real estate or a fancy car. You never call because you want to find out anything about me.'

'Not true. I called several times asking what was happening with your Swedish nanny. Didn't I?'

'Just to find out if you were right, just to gloat.'

'And wasn't I right?'

'There. You're doing it again.'

'If you want to characterize it as gloating instead of sisterly concern, that's your problem. And you should talk – how often do you call me?'

'More than you call me.' They looked at each other in hurt silence. 'Look,' Claire said finally, 'I don't want this – I can't fight with you. I have enough aggravation in my life without having to remember that we're not speaking. Besides, it's too hard on Mom.'

'Fine. I didn't come here to fight.'

'So what did you come here for?'

'Well, I could hardly stay down there, could I? Thinking about God-knows-what being buried around my house. It was that old couple – the pack-rats – for sure. I bet they had bodies everywhere. They'll probably find some mass graveyard.' Christine sighed, leaned her head back against the upholstered back of the chesterfield. 'Maybe we can turn it into a tourist attraction, if the house doesn't sell before one of those workmen blabs. But who'd want to buy it? It's a white elephant, let's face it.'

'I hate to sound like a lawyer, but you can't just leave body parts buried around your house. You're concealing evidence of a crime.'

'Not necessarily.' Christine raised her head slightly. 'Maybe some worker person had an accident on the property – maybe it was years ago even. Ben's always getting stray fingers and toes in for stitching back on, isn't he? Well, this is maybe one of the ones that got away. And whoever it was didn't want it reattached.'

'Get serious, Christine.'

'They can't get me anyway,' she sulked, 'I'm a Canadian citizen. I'll just sit up here, claim I didn't know anything about it. And I don't.'

'What does Bernardo think?'

'Who knows? He's left us, me and Nita.' She closed her eyes, looking pained.

'Nobody told me.'

'Left me for that leech-farm woman. Maybe you noticed her in the exhibitors' hall at the convention?'

'I remember the leech-farm exhibit, but not who was running it.'

'Well, she was the dame with the sequined cat glasses. She's a gorgeous woman, actually – French, I think. I don't know why she wears those unattractive glasses.' How like her sister to express admiration for the appearance of the woman who had just walked off with her husband, Claire thought. 'So what can you expect from a Mediterranean? I don't know why I should be surprised.' She pinched the back of her neck. 'They've got olive oil for blood, makes it easier for them to slide in and out of tight spots. Things weren't going well for me and Bernardo anyway – not for a long time. I'm sure you noticed. I'm sure the whole family's been gossiping about us for years.'

'Not me.'

'That's right. You never notice anything, do you? Anyway, the cat lady was just an excuse. A catalyst, I guess you could call her. You should appreciate that – you always liked word games.' There were dark crescents of perspiration under Christine's arms, staining the silk of her shirt.

'And your business – Canuck-talk? Who'll be looking after that?'

'No one. It was a total failure. Worse – a disaster. Canadians don't know a good opportunity when it hits them right between the eyes. They all deserve to sit up here in the cold and rot.'

'You don't rot in the cold – you freeze. Cold is a preservative.'

'Whatever.' Christine rubbed her eyes. 'Lord, what a mess. I'm so tired. Nita's staying with Mother and Dad for the night. I need a break.'

'Stay here if you want.'

'Thanks, but I think I'll check into a nice hotel, maybe the King Eddy.'

'I guess if you want chocolates left on your pillow, this isn't the place for you.'

Christine smiled weakly. Outside, the backhoe grader stopped abruptly. 'Thank God,' she sighed. There were a couple of thumps on the deck outside, the sound of the screen door being opened, closed and latched. Then the refrigerator was opened and the microwave beeped as Ben set the timer to warm a bottle for Harry.

'Let me get you a drink,' Claire said, going into the kitchen to head Ben off. 'My sister's here,' she whispered, 'Bernardo's left her and they found some body parts in her backyard.'

'That's interesting.' He put Harry down on the floor, handed him a plastic mixing bowl and a wooden spoon to play with. 'Which parts?'

'A toe.'

'Really? Distal phalanx? Articular amputation?'

'She wouldn't talk about it much. She's really upset, so try and be nice to her.'

'We can't compete with body parts – all we've got are some-body's used condoms.' The microwave beeped its ready signal. 'Are we going to start interviewing nannies sometime soon? There is a really interesting neck dissection and free flap on tomorrow that I'm going to have to miss. I'm only off this week – I couldn't get any more time.'

Down on the floor, Harry put the mixing bowl on over his head. 'Hat?' he said.

Claire and Ben looked at him. 'I could have sworn he said hat,' Claire said.

'He did say hat.'

At that moment, someone rapped on the front door, banging the brass knocker with more vigour than was necessary. 'You've got company,' Christine called wearily from the living-room.

'Rose-marie Schmertz,' Claire said. 'I almost forgot she was coming.'

'Who is Rose-marie Schmertz?'

'Harry's new nanny – maybe. If we're lucky.' She hurried to the front door, noting, as she passed, that Christine was reclining on the chesterfield, her fingers pressed to her sinus region, as if she had a nose-bleed.

27

Rose-marie Schmertz was indeed plump – though not unattractively so – and very pink. Her hair was a dazzling bright copper, and there was masses of it, framing her face, tumbling down over her shoulders. She looked like a giant kewpie doll with her head on fire, standing there, brightly illuminated by the porch light. Another hairball, was Claire's first, uncharitable, thought.

'Hi!' Rose-marie smiled, dimpling deeply. 'You guys are looking for a nanny, right?'

'Right, right. Come on in.' Claire followed her into the kitchen; Rose-marie seemed to know the way. 'So,' Claire said, 'Shelagh tells me you're a local girl.'

'Grew up right here in the Beach. You're not going to believe this, but right on this very street. Is that Harry?'

'Good guess,' Ben said, putting his son into the high chair and handing him a bottle of milk.

'Hiya, Harry! Would you like me to be your new nanny?'

Harry grinned at her, put the bottle into his mouth and started to suck on it diligently.

'I have two kittens, Harry. Schnitzel and Noodle. Schnitzel's the girl.'

'Schnitzel? You're not of Scandinavian background, by any chance, are you?' Claire said.

'Heavens no,' Rose-marie laughed. 'It's from *The Sound of Music*. You know? Two of my favourite things? Schnitzel and noodles? Corny, eh? I never saw it, actually, the movie – it was before my time. Anyway, my Dad's Jewish but my Mom's Irish. That's where I get this hair from.' She grabbed a clump of it, holding it out from her head, as if Claire could somehow have missed it. 'My friends call me Big Red,' she added, as Claire wondered how much of that red hair she would have to vacuum out of the carpet, from in between the sofa cushions.

'Would you like to see my kitties, Harry?' Rose-marie asked, chucking him under the chin. 'I've got pictures of them.' Harry regarded her soberly, sucking hard on his bottle. 'What a great kid,' she beamed. 'He looks like a good eater. I love to cook. I hope cooking's part of the job.'

For the first time, Ben seemed to take an interest in her. 'What kind of stuff can you make?'

'Well, baking is my absolute passion. I've won prizes for my cake decorating. Last year I did a baby shower cake, all iced to look like a pile of ABC blocks. But I can make just about anything.'

'Chili? Can you make chili?'

'I could make chili in my sleep. Harry here could make chili.'

'What about prime rib? Meat loaf? Pot roast?' Ben looked at her hungrily.

'You name it, I can make it. If you've got a piece of paper, I could jot down all the things I can make, right off the top of my head. I went to cooking school for two years. I almost got my professional chef's papers. I also took bartending. And a beautician's course. I could do your nails,' she said, turning to Claire, 'facials, leg waxing. And I do horoscopes.'

'But the job is looking after Harry,' Claire said nervously. 'That's the main thing. Even the cleaning isn't important. As long as Harry's happy. And safe.'

'Of course. But he's only one baby. I'll have lots of time to do other things. And he can help. Kids love mixing things up, cake batter, cookie dough. It helps them learn, develops their fine motor skills.'

Ben looked at her curiously. 'So why do you want to be a nanny,' he said, 'with all this great expertise you've got?' He and Claire looked expectantly at Rose-marie. It was the obvious question.

'Because I love kids, basically. And I want to be a really good housewife some day,' she said, without missing a beat. 'I don't like working outside of the home. I hate getting dressed up every day, taking the bus, the subway. I want to have six kids of my own. I figure you need to go into training for that.'

Was she lying, Claire worried. Had Shelagh helped her rehearse that too-good-to-be-true answer? That answer that every working mother longed so desperately to hear? Christine had appeared in the doorway to dig Claire in the ribs. 'If you don't grab her right now, I'm going to,' she hissed. Her breath was hot, tinged with alcohol.

'And being a nanny isn't such a bad job these days,' Rose-marie continued, dimpling again, 'compared to a lot that's out there. You wouldn't believe what you have to put up with if you work in a commercial kitchen. From the men, I mean.' She rolled her eyes dramatically. 'I could tell you some stories. Okay if I look through your kitchen cupboards? I'd like to check out the site. See what kind of equipment you've got here.' She bustled around, all businesslike and efficient, opening cupboard doors, peering inside. 'Wow,' she said, her head inside one of the cupboards, 'I haven't seen a blender like this since I was a little kid. Does it still work? They called them Osterizers, didn't they?' She surfaced again to pull open the kitchen drawers, one by one. 'I can see I'm going to have to bring some of my own equipment over. Knives, anyway. But that's not surprising. Nobody has decent knives. Most people think a knife is just a knife, but there's a lot more to it than that.'

Claire, Ben and Christine looked at each other, bulldozed into silence.

'So which way's your spice cupboard?' Rose-marie demanded, tossing her flame-coloured hair over her shoulders. 'You can tell an awful lot about a person by the kind of seasonings they keep. Some people read tea leaves – I read spice cupboards.'

Apprehensively, Claire opened the door of a narrow cupboard over the stove.

'That's your first mistake right there – you should never keep spices near the stove. The heat kills the flavour, dries it right out. But don't feel bad – everyone does it.'

Claire wondered what Rose-marie's psychological assessment of them would be, after she saw what was in there: fusty bay leaves, dusty cinnamon sticks, a jar of cloves enfeebled by advanced age; a pile of yellowed Cellophane packages of dull dried leaves.

Rose-marie sniffed a couple of the bags, frowning. 'I think you'd better trash all of this and start over. I can make you a list. And you'll need some good olive oil, balsamic vinegar. But don't worry, it takes time to build up your seasonings. And we've got time. I'll do a necessary list for you and a wish list, okay?' She closed the door, washed her hands at the sink, then charged over to Harry. 'Are you going to help Rose-marie make beautiful food?' she demanded.

He took the bottle out of his mouth, grinned, and held the bottle out to her.

'Hey, look at that – he wants to share his milk with me. Okay if I take him out of his chair?' Without waiting for an answer, Rose-marie undid Harry's seat belt, popped back the high chair tray and hoisted him out. 'You really should think about getting him off the bottle,' she said, 'it's terrible for his teeth.'

'That's exactly what I've been saying,' Ben said.

Rose-marie peered into Harry's face. 'Maybe a couple of more months, but that's it, Big Guy. Deal?'

Harry laughed joyously, let his bottle thunk to the floor, grabbed a fistful of Rose-marie's hair. Pulled.

'Doesn't that hurt?' Claire said.

'I've got tons. I can afford to lose a little. Besides, I have a high pain threshold. I've actually been tested for it.'

'What would you do if Harry got a cut?' Ben said suddenly.

'Cut? What kind of cut? Laceration? Incision? Or do you really mean a contusion?'

'I mean a cut. A simple laceration.'

'How deep?' She gave him a challenging look.

'One centimetre.'

'I'd do my best to clean it out, then put on a bandage and hold pressure on it until the bleeding stopped. I'd probably call you or your wife, too, if it looked like it might need a stitch – or if it was anything more than a very minor cut. If it was really serious, I'd call 911. Though I do have my CPR, and my Bronze Medallion.'

'You're insane if you don't grab her,' Christine whispered, poking Claire again.

Ben looked at Claire. 'Well,' he said, 'I'd be glad to let Rose-marie give the job a try. What do you think?'

Claire nodded. 'Sure, great. She can start tomorrow.'

'Cool,' said Rose-marie.

'You'll have to sleep on a waterbed,' Claire said, 'once we get the basement fixed up.'

'No problem-o. I can conk out anywhere. And I think waterbeds are cool. They're so seventies.'

'Say, have you got any girlfriends?' Christine said. 'A sister? What about your mother? Do you think she might be interested in a part-time job?'

Later that night, after Rose-marie and Christine had gone, and Harry was sound asleep in his crib, Claire and Ben sat against opposite walls of their living-room, sharing the footstool in the middle.

'I'm not sure I'm all that thrilled about having our home described as "a site",' Claire said.

'And we'll probably get as fat as pigs,' Ben said. He was pretending to be interested in what she was saying, but his eyes kept darting towards the flickering TV screen.

'But I think we've finally found the person we really need around here,' Claire sighed. 'I was afraid not to hire her. I got the feeling she wouldn't have taken no for an answer.'

'Just like you wouldn't have taken no for an answer.'

'What are you talking about?'

'You wouldn't take no for an answer when you asked me to marry you.'

'I did not ask you to marry me!'

'Of course you did.'

'I did not.' She pushed the footstool out from under his feet. 'And I better not find out that you and Rose-marie Schmertz were high-school sweethearts.'

Ben laughed shortly: an all-purpose response he used when he wasn't really listening. His eyes had returned to the television screen – the new Frozen Bitch music video. If Claire wasn't there in the room, he would have cranked up the volume to a teeth-grinding level.

'So when did you have this mysterious talk with Mike Potochnik?' Claire said.

'You know about that?'

'I just heard today.'

'It was last week. I got his number from Davina. Then I called him up and asked him out for a beer.'

'You had a beer with Mike Potochnik?'

'And I just reasoned with the guy. Convinced him to drop his complaint, give up on the idea of suing you. After I volunteered to punch his lights out, that is.'

'You threatened my client?'

'No, it wasn't a threat. Just a man-to-man talk. He understands. He's not pissed off.'

'I could've handled him myself. I'm a professional. He was not a major problem.'

'Sure.'

'He was a minor irritant.'

'But you were losing it – I could tell. You were on the edge.'

Claire sighed. 'I suppose I should thank you—'

'No problem. I enjoyed doing it.'

'But it's backfired. The firm now wants to send me over to Kiev with Potochnik. I'm not going, of course. I couldn't leave Harry. Or you. Hopefully, my job doesn't depend on me going. And it looks like I'm going to be working for a long time, with all these debts. Repairing half the Beach, my credit cards. I've cut them all up, by the way, except for one. But I'll only use it in an emergency.'

'Like when you need a new pair of shoes?' Ben's eyes were back on the television screen as a series of violent and disturbing images flashed across it: writhing contorted couples locked in some form of embrace; a man with a shaved head, screaming from his straitjacket. Then the camera zoomed in on an anaemic youth, poised over a yawning abyss, tweaking the strings of an electric guitar. Great cumulus nimbus clouds rolled around him in time-lapse photography speed.

'How stupid,' Claire said after watching for a moment, 'there's no amplifier there – his guitar's not even plugged in to anything. Do you know what an electric guitar sounds like without an amp? It sounds like snapping rubber bands.'

Ben pushed the mute button on the remote control. 'Okay, so let's watch something else.' His practised finger flickered over the buttons. Like all men, he was a channel surfer, flipping through three or four programs during any commercial break. It always frustrated Claire who got interested by advertisements and always wanted to see how they ended. They were short stories that unfolded and were wrapped up in thirty seconds or less. How *did* that frazzled mother get those stains out of the carpet? What *was* it the world-famous paediatrician had to say about cloth diapers versus paper? 'So what do you want to watch?' Ben asked. 'The weather channel? Home shopping?'

'News would be good. It's about that time.'

He flipped through a number of channels at a speed that made Claire dizzy, finally parking at the CBC and turning the sound back on. There was a panel discussion going on: four concerned scientific types, on a split screen, were discussing the coming ice age. Claire watched in silence, aghast at what they were saying. 'I don't get it,' she said. 'I thought we were supposed to be worried about global warming, the greenhouse effect. Maybe the ice age will cancel out the greenhouse effect and everything will just stay the same.' The idea might not be very plausible, but at least it offered some hope. 'What do you think?' She looked over at Ben. His head had dropped down on to his chest, his hand limp on the remote control. He began to snore. Sleeping man. Sleeping baby. My two kids. Claire yawned, content to be the only one left awake, the one back in control.

In the kitchen, the cat-clock rolled its eyes, swinging out the seconds with its long black tail, while outside, one of the wooden planks of the porch floor, eaten away by termites, finally dropped through, on to the sand below.